FORGE OF

THE UNDEAD

R.M.HAMANN

FORGE OF THE UNDEAD

R.M.HAMANN

Published by Blue dragoon Books

Art Cover by Freddy Flores

Copyright 2020 R.M.HAMANN

Local authorities in Cape May County New Jersey are "disturbed" after discovering what some people are calling a ZOMBIE BABY. The gruesome remains were found in an old farmhouse in the Dias Creek area of Middle Township. Authorities stress there is no cause for alarm and that further information will be released as it becomes available.

UPS NEWS SERVICE UPDATE RE: ZOMBIE BABY 7/11/2012

6:29 PM

Federal authorities have been called in to assist various local law enforcement departments in the investigation of a dead child found in an abandoned farmhouse. An unnamed source who was present when the body was found said the "child" appeared to be twelve to eighteen months old. He further added that said child possessed a mouthful of sharp teeth, not unlike a shark, and one eye that seemed to stare at everyone at the same time.

Another witness told me the body showed signs of decay in spots, but otherwise was in remarkably good condition.

Its skin had a yellow tint and the fingernails had continued to grow, forming spirals that resembled claws. The toenail had curled under, then grown upward thru the hairy feet. When I asked if he thought it was a Zombie, he simply answered, "Yes."

Nobody seems to know who first reported the body to authorities, or how long the Zombie has been buried, hidden, waiting? The feds have yet to release any information on the investigation. As further information is received (or at 9:00 PM tomorrow) we will update our news flash service to keep you informed on the latest developments to this baffling mystery.

Government investigation answers few questions. By James "Jimbo" Zackman

At 9:00 this morning, John Greenburg, senior FBI agent in charge of the Phil.-S. Jersey region, released this statement. After a brief but intense investigation of the so-called "Zombie baby, the FBI, in conjunction with other federal agencies, have determined the entire matter is a hoax, perpetrated by person/persons unknown. Everyone can relax. There is not, nor ever was a "Zombie baby". The appropriate authorities will continue to investigate this case but limited in scope to finding the author of the hoax. Now, let me make something perfectly clear. The child was a man-made doll. During testing, the doll was severely damaged, and the remains were incinerated. The FBI will issue no additional statements regarding this incident.

The above statement from the FBI is the total report generated by this investigation. Not one word about why anyone would hide a creepy looking doll in a farmhouse. Why was the doll incinerated so quickly? Was it in discomfort after its test? Why the hurry? Did the Feds think the doll was going to run away? Seriously, of the six people who saw the "doll", three can no longer be found. The other three, all in law enforcement, have "no comment". These things do not pass the sniff test, nor does this. The county fire marshal, acting on the advice of the FBI, ordered the old farmhouse burnt to the ground.

I understand from talking to colleges that very few people know about this incident. It seems mainstream media has no clue that the government may be telling the public less than the full truth. I will make every effort to keep those of you reding my reports informed. Hopefully, more will follow when I have new information, and perhaps some answers to this incident.

He knew the next time he left his bed it would be for a trip to the morgue. Since his wife had left, he and his valet de chamber had lived a quiet life in a small village in southern New Jersey. He had not left the house in years, which was ironic, because his wife had left him after many sudden, and usually long disappearances. He often thought of telling her about his activities, but she would have either not believed him, or thought he had lost his mind.

His valet, Fredrick, had read him the reports about a "Zombie baby" being discovered. The old man's blood ran cold. "Fredrick, call my son!" but before the call was made, he changed his mind. "Please call my Grandson instead. Tell him to get his ass here post-haste!" The old man settled back into his bed, praying he had not waited too long.

A knock on the bedroom door roused Roland from a restless slumber. As he said "Enter," the door opened and his Grandson Maxlyn appeared in the threshold. The young man was tall and powerfully built. The old man waved him to his side. "There is something of great importance that I need to tell you. I should have told your father about years ago, but I did not think it was necessary. I now fear I have made a grave mistake that could cause untold pain and suffering!" Maxlyn felt a chill run down his spine, but knew he could not tell his Grandfather he did not want to listen. "Grandson," the old man said, "go fetch yourself a comfortable chair and something to drink. Tell Fredrick to bring us more drinks and food later. This story will not be told in a few hours!" Ten minutes later, with Maxlyn seated next to the bed, Roland Dralonson began a tale of wonder and terror so strange that Maxlyn had to rethink his Grandfathers sanity.

Untold ages before Mankind first appeared on earth

Demigods, Elves, Trolls, and other entities fought for domination. The Demigods had held rein for eons, but with the dawning of the "Age of Mankind" the "Lesser Races" mistakenly thought there would be a decline in their power. They hoped an alliance with Man, who according to the Gods, would process great strength and valor, would help them break the bonds that were holding them vassal to the Demigods. They failed to understand to true intent of the Major Gods.

The Gods had been creating life forms since time immortal. Most of the time things went well, Pixies, Fairies, Elves and the first crude humanoid like creatures. Others not so well. The Troll Race were most numerous of the second group. There also existed a few members of two species that were so vile, they were not spoken of, not even by the Gods themselves. The safety valve in the Gods plan was that with the coming of Man, the Elder races would slowly die off, on their own. Mankind would not necessarily have to eradicate them to correct the misadventures of the Gods.

Lord Odyden, the Evil One, was the most powerful of

the Lesser Gods. He was also by far the vilest. He held a dark secret that would visit terror and bloodshed upon humans. For Odyden, in defiance of the Gods, had studied at length from the forbidden "Scroll of Life". Using his gleamed knowledge, he desired to birth a new life form, totally dependent and obedient to himself only.

Hidden deep underground, away from the prying eyes of his fellow Demigods, Odyden threw himself fully into his task. Many years he toiled in secrecy, attempting to bring animation to various foul creatures. Failure after failure was the only fruit of his endeavors.

Hoyden's body was paying a price for living without any sunlight. His once sun-bleached hair was now listless and dirt encrusted, hanging gray below his bony shoulders.

His skin that had lost most of its color and seemed almost translucent. The pupils of his eyes had enlarged to the point that they looked like the glowing orbs of an owl or perhaps a lizard.

Frustrated and furious, Odyden was considering ravishing his workshop hewed from stone and returning to the surface to dwell, when a wee bit of movement caught his eye.

Fearful of missing further motion Odyden slowly crossed to the other side of the lab and gazed down at the small rat like creature lying on a stone slab. Bending over to get even nearer Odyden watched the rhythmic rise and fall of the small animal's ribcage. Standing erect he let loose a victory cry so loud he was afraid the Demigods on the surface of the earth would hear. As he thought about it for a moment, he realized he did not care. He had just created life! He was a Demigod no longer; he had just ascended into the ranks of the Major Gods.

Odyden was now as powerful as most Gods, but unlike the others, who wished for Man's success, he wished only to spew terror and evil upon them for the pure joy of watching them suffer. Knowing the other Gods would have a difficult time stopping him, even if they knew of his plans, he set himself back to his work with renewed vigor. Venturing above ground for a prolonged period for the first time in years, Odyden sets traps baited with lures to capture Trolls. The Ogres, although ugly and extremely violent, are intelligent and more importantly, physically strong. He planned to use the captured Trolls to greatly enlarge to size of his underground fortress. Within a week's time he has ensnared a dozen Trolls, including to his delight and utter amazement, the Troll Lord, Zomba. After being enslaved to Odyden's will, the powerful Trolls, led by Zomba, quickly enlarged the size of the hidden stone fortress. He then sent slaves to capture and bring back Pixies and Fairies. After being completely enthralled to his will they are released, ready to return to do his bidding when summoned.

Being in the sun again temporarily helped his appearance but was short lived when he again vanished into the bowels of the earth. He had no intention of returning to the sunshine anytime soon, for he had his own method of illuminating his underground fortress. Choosing rocks the size of his fist he caused them to emit an eerie blue light with just the touch of his hand. Among the Gods this was considered child play, among the Elder Races, evil dark magic.

Now alone in his stone lair, with the ability to create live, Odyden devised a plan to lay waste to the minds and bodies of the newborn Humans. The Evil Lord, by virtue of his secret studies, knew not only when Man would first appear on earth, but also the nature of his conception. Using his somewhat limited knowledge of creation, but trusting in his mastery of black magic, the Master of Evil attempted to preempt the Gods with his own perverted version of Mankind.

His first attempt did not turn out well. The slightly human looking body was missing vital parts, such as a second arm, leg, and ear. A thinking brain was not a huge consideration currently, animation of the flesh, ergo life, was. There was neither.

Odyden walked to the far end of his redoubt, across from the Troll hewed stone stairway that led to the earth's surface. Here the Trolls had been forced to chip away at the living rock with primitive tools, constructing their own prison. Standing outside the cell the Evil One caused his dilated eyes to glow. An eerie yellow light enveloped their cell, awakening the always hungry Trolls. After forcing them to the back of the cell with a deadly stare, Odyden motioned for one of the Trolls to follow him. He did not bother to lock the cell, hungry or not, they would dare not leave.

He had found by trial and failure that a starving Troll would eat nearly anything including another Troll. Pixies and Fairies were difficult to catch but once in hand, with wings removed, a delicacy. Elves were tough and stringy but edible if bleed out and roasted on a bed of hot rocks. Odyden would now determine whether the Troll wished to expand their diets. Approaching the semi-human form lying on a waist high flat stone slab, Odyden bid the Troll with him to eat. Reaching the body, the Troll gripped the right arm with a huge clawed hand, and with a vicious twist was rewarded with the severed forearm. Gingerly sampling a mouthful of flesh secured by sharp yellowing fangs, the Troll moaned, as if in ecstasy. Never in the Trolls life had he ever experienced anything that had given him more pleasure than gnawing on the flesh of the Human.

Odyden saw the glow of terrifying hunger in the eyes of the Trolls remaining in their cell and knew that even he might not be able to control them. He bid them come forward and feed.

He stood off to the side, quiet and spellbound by the morbid sight unfolding before his eyes. Zomba, the alpha male and Lord of the Trolls was huge, towering nearly a foot above most of the others. He had come and laid claim to the humanoids head for his own. A clawed hand, infused with the strength of his race, closed around the cadaver's neck. A moment later the severed head was his. Using both hands the head was brought to his lips where a little suction around the eye socket rewarded the Troll with a tasty treat. A bite or nip here and there rewarded Zomba with a nose, lips, and ears. Zomba knew that the internal organs of living things were, by far, the favorite treat of Trolls. Looking down to find some tender part to ingest, Zomba roared with such intensity and rage that it reached earth's sun-drenched surface. Gazing about at the few scraps of uneaten humanoid flesh that remained left, those meager pieces of meat hanging from talon or fang of his fellow Trolls, Zomba viciously slammed the head in his hand onto the raised stone slab that had held their morbid entree. Zomba, glancing up from the shattered skull observed that the other Trolls had sated their appetites to the point where they would not contest him for a taste of brain, the only thing remaining of the once human form. Picking up a shard of bone with gray matter still attached Zomba crunched the bone as would a wolf with a deer bone. The instant gratification nearly staggered him. Unable to trust his senses he picked up a larger piece of skull and cleaned it of brain matter with an oversized, wart covered tongue. This time the results are even more overwhelming. Zomba was the Troll Lord and had existed for untold years. He had experienced all the joys and pleasures available to the powerful, but he had never, ever experienced the ecstasy he felt while feeding on the flesh and brains of the Humanoid.

Odyden's surge of joy from his accomplishment soon changed to concern, for he now realized that the Gods plan to eradicate the Elder Races would affect his own. Not willing to lose what he had labored so hard for he hurriedly began the next phase of his terrifying plan. He was still unable to create a living humanoid, but he had come to realize it really did not matter. He would start a breeding program, designed to isolate the Trolls with the most robust appetite for human flesh and brains. Luckily for Odyden, trolls were both lusty and quick to mature.

During the breeding phase of his program Odyden continued to create human forms to feed his Trolls. The Trolls who gave up the teat and began feeding on Human parts at the earliest age were the ones he sought. Odyden came to accept the fact that until The Gods conferred life to Mankind, his vile creations would remain inanimate, for even the Master of Evil was not mighty enough to trump the collective will of the Major Gods. Odyden would wait, for he had learned well the use of time.

Odyden's young Trolls, which he called Feeders, grew

strong as they neared the age when they could reproduce. He knew that with the "Awakening of Man" the Elder Races would start to disappear from the earth. Odyden knew that this would include his newly breed flesh eating

Trolls, and this he could not allow to happen.

Not having seen sunlight since he had formulated his plan, Odyden had dire need of current events on the surface above. Summoning his enthralled Pixies and Fairies, he sent them forth to gather news of the realm and to spy on the Gods. Petite to begin with, the Master of

Evil had used black magic to render the wee fluttering entities virtually invisible. Gaining access to the Hall of the Gods was accomplished with little effort by the diminutive spies. The gathering of information requested by Odyden was swiftly obtained, as the Gods hid nothing amongst themselves in their own hall. Leaving as quietly as they had come, the miniature spies reported back to Odyden. They informed him that there was great excitement but also concern among the Gods, for the awaited time was nigh. With the ascension of the next new moon, Human life would be established on earth, and the "Age of Man" would begin.

Odyden listened to the report with growing unease. He

knew what needed to be done, but

he did not know if he could do it. The Gods planned to populate various areas of the earth with humans. Minor variations in color and appearance would help the First-born adapt to their environment. They would be free, and even encouraged, to sexually mingle with the members of other groups of humans. Men would outnumber women out of necessity. By virtue of the strength and sense of self bestowed upon them by the Gods, they would fight. They will battle over land, possessions, women, and they would die. Had the Gods fully realized the great price the Humans would pay in their epic struggle against the Trolls, the Gods would have isolated Mankind in areas far from the influence of Trolls, for the future of the First-born would be in serious doubt.

Odyden knew the Troll species would soon begin to

die off, as planned by the Gods. He needed to transform the Trolls hunger for Human brain to the one species not scheduled to disappear, the First-born! But there he had major problems, the first being to secure Humans to be used in his morbid plan. Using his slave labor force, he had sturdy traps erected. Odyden would bait his snares with fluttering Pixies and Fairies, while the curiosity of the newly awakened humans would do the rest.

The Evil Lord began to dream of things to come. Knowing the First-born were to be created in the image of the Gods, Odyden realized the men would be handsome, the women a joy to behold. If perchance he captured a female of exceptional beauty, he would enslave her to his will, both mentally and physically. Hiding from his own kind and unwilling to have sex with the Lesser Races, the act of fortification was a fond but distant memory. With luck and the rising new moon Odyden hoped to end both his loneliness and self-imposed sexual fast.

Odyden felt a shutter run through his body as another thought crossed his mind. Although he had studied the "Scroll of Life" from front to back, he had no idea as to the fate of the Gods.

He knew more of the destiny of Man than his own. He was uneasy with his lack of knowledge of the Gods future, but that problem would have to wait, for he had more pressing issues at hand.

The Master prepared for the arrival of his "guests". Separate male and female cells were chipped out from the bowels of the mountain he called home. A nursery area was created to aid in the maturing of his "feeders". Vast quantities of water and provisions were laid in. His slave

Trolls, taught to create the humanoid forms used as food, were working in shifts around the clock. Odyden wished to breed Human eating Trolls and that required large amounts of flesh. If the slaves did not supply enough humanoids, Odyden informed them they would be used as food.

Odyden had observed the mating rituals of the Trolls on numerous occasions. He knew beyond a doubt that a female Human could not survive a mating session with an adult Troll. The large penis of a Troll was a minor source of concern to Odyden but nothing in comparison to the sheer violence inflicted upon the female as the male Troll neared climax. He had been working on a fornication cage, designed to protect the woman's body from the claw and fangs of the Troll, but her vagina would have to endure the encounter. The Evil One would attempt to mate the smallest sexually mature male in his stable of Trolls with a fully mature woman who had many sexual experiences.

Odyden guessed that if she was lucky and strong, she might endure the sex and hopefully conceive. He doubted she would survive childbirth. The average Troll could weigh twenty pounds at birth.

His idea to impregnate a She-Troll was much more basic. With her legs spread wide and ankles shackled to stakes, she would be bent over a large log and chained into position, her vagina readily available for penetration from behind. Odyden planned on covering her hairy body with a tarp, leaving only her smoothly shaved ass exposed. Knowing a vigorous penis would be required for the undertaking, Odyden would introduce a captured Human female into the Men's cell. With his prior knowledge about Man, Odyden was aware that the Gods would create the First-born with a heightened sense of sexuality. He planned on personally teaching his new Human sex toy, whom he would call Adelia, the finer points of preforming oral sex on a male. Needing to ascertain the size of the male's penises and the quantity of sperm ejected, and hence the chance of siring a Troll, Odyden would teach her how to give facials. He would not abide the sex slave hiding a penis in her vagina or up her ass, hidden from his view. He could enjoy some erotica and also gain the information he needed. A rare smile crossed his face, for his tenure as teacher was about to begin.

Returning his thoughts to the present problem, Odyden knew it was a large one. Troll females, like many of the other Elder Races, would only copulate when in heat and Odyden knew he could not torture or threaten Man into mating with the She-Trolls. Fear and an erection were not compatible. Odyden pondered his problem long before the obvious solution dawned on him. He did not need the sex slave. The First-born males would be vain and proud. Put into captivity, they would view amongst themselves for supremacy. Odyden felt that if challenged, the

Humans would rise to the occasion. First dare them, then promise reward.

The Human males, plucked from cages after the night of the new moon, would sample sex for the first time with comely Elf females supplied by him. Odyden would personally check the vaginal depth of all his captive Elves, selecting only those who were truly small. Odyden would count on the frustration Men would feel when finding out the sexual organ of the Elves could not fully accommodate their erections. Odyden hoped that Man, after spurting his seed into shallow containers, would dare hope for a deeper receptacle. With nothing but their hairless butt exposed, the First-born would have little reason to hesitate. He wanted them to bury their penises deep into the She-Trolls.

Odyden, now confident with his plan, would order Zomba, his enslaved Lord of Trolls, to prepare three young virgin She-Trolls for the carnal attention of Man. Although not needing

Adelia to orally stimulate Man, Odyden still had dire need of her. Above the chain bound

She-Trolls, he would hang a flat wooden platform, suspended by chain from the overhead rock.

Out of the reach of Man but within easy view, a naked Adelia, sitting on a plain three-legged stool with knees spread wide, would attempt to bring the First-born males to full arousal. Odyden. physically tired and mentally drained, retired to his private quarters.

Reviewing his plans yet again he knew there was little more he could do until the "Coming of Man". He had the motivation and wherewithal to deal with the New Race, what he sorely lacked was the proper respect for the intellect of the Gods.

Thoridon, Lord of the Gods, had long monitored the movements of Odyden. Studying forbidden text tended to draw attention to the reader, regardless of how secretive they be

Thoridon long had his own spies, drawn from members of the Elder species. After all, the Gods were responsible for their existence. Odyden accomplished little that the Gods were unaware of. His plans were of another matter, for he confided in no one.

The Gods, knowing the privacy of their hall had been compromised, sought, and found the intruders. Ordering them to speak true, the Gods were able to deduce most of Odyden's evil plan. Erasing the last hour of questioning from the wee spy's mind, the Gods openly discussed the approaching "Coming of Man". They decided the next full moon would herald in the "Age of Man". The Fairies and Pixies, heads full of disinformation, fled back to Odyden's fortress to give him the good tidings.

Thoridon, now aware of Odyden's vile plan, delayed the emergence of humans.

He also altered the makeup of Man; insuring Mankind would rather die than sexually touch or be touched by a

Troll. If raped, a woman would commit suicide at the first opportunity.

Odyden arose early the morn of the eve of the new moon. Sleep had eluded him, so great was his excitement. Summoning the Troll Lord, he ordered Zomba to place the traps for ensnaring Man into their predetermined positions. He wanted the cages baited with captive Pixies and Fairies by noon. Emotions that threated to overwhelm him arose. Within the day he would begin the education of Adelia, his personal sex slave. After her training was complete, he would be able to begin breeding Trolls and Humans. Odyden realized that although he had Trolls with a desire for Human flesh and brains, Mankind, after discovering that Trolls wished to eat them, would most likely resist. He reasoned that Man would flee or fight when encountering Trolls. If a Man could be bred with a Trolls hunger for flesh, Odyden would continue to mate his monsters with Human females, hence ridding them of major Troll features. He did not need perfection; unattractive Humans would serve his plans. He was not sure how many generations it might take to evolve into the desired results, but with an endless supply of Human females to choose from he planned to enjoy the wait.

Odyden would teach his creatures to seek out small groups of Humans to befriend. After gaining their trust, the monsters would visit violence upon them during the long hours of darkness, partaking in an orgy of vile gluttony. They would vanish before the sun rose. With no survivors to spread the tale of terror, the creatures would seek out their next meal of living flesh. Being Human looking, albeit on the ugly side, they would need to find the correct size group of Humans ere their hunger for flesh took control of them. For if that were to occur, they would attack the first Human they saw, regardless of the chance of success or ensuing consequences.

Odyden realized none of this mattered until he had Humans to experiment on. The Master, calling once again for Zomba, was assured by the Troll Lord that indeed the traps were in place and properly baited. Odyden, confident that all was for the First-born, retreated to his quarters to eagerly await the Coming of Man. Wait he would. First thru the night, then into the day. Anxious days turned into weeks and still no sign of Mankind. Odyden seethed with rage, but another new moon would rise tomorrow, surely

Man would follow. When dawn illuminated naught but empty cages, no one, except for Zomba, was safe from Odyden's ire. The Pixie and Fairy spies paid a horrible price. Odyden clipped one wing then threw them into the Trolls cell to be used as finger food. High pitched screams filled the underground as the Trolls caught and devoured them. In rage, he ordered the wings cut off the Fairies and Pixies which served as bait in his cages. Free of bars they will serve as food for birds of prey and wolves, which had never tasted their flesh. The Trolls who had tended the cages did not escape the carnage. When the last disemboweled and headless Troll was hauled from their cell, Zomba knew he had the daunting task of restocking the slave labor force. Odyden, fearful of an attack by the Gods, barricaded himself in his quarters to lick his wounds. Zomba out of necessity, ran the rest of the underground compound.

The Gods, quickly learning of Odyden's unbated snares and lack of spies, decided to bring forth Man. Thoridon, the Creator, modified his original plan. He would now concentrate

Mankind in one place, far from Odyden's influence or cages. Odyden, hiding angry and frustrated in his fortress, missed the next new moon, and with it the far away appearance of Man.

Thoridon's Humans were of prime breeding age. The Gods, with a limited number of

Humans available, had little use for the very young or old, for they wished the First-born to go forth and populate the earth. Food was not a problem, fruit and vegetables were to be had for the picking. A warm climate eliminated the need for clothing. The Gods, who had created Man in their own image, knew what the sight of the naked form of the opposite sex tended to do. They very much wanted to encourage this behavior.

Newborn Man, curious and sensual, explored their environment to a limited extent before deciding they would rather explore each other's bodies. Using various body parts, lubricants, and positions, they swiftly became addicted to the ecstasy of sexual release. Many females became pregnant, but their sexual appetite was barely diminished. A horny male could usually talk a female into a sex act, especially one of short duration.

The Gods were well pleased, having bestowed on

Mankind the gift of recreational sex,

They were gratified to see it being used. Thoridon had given females the ability to conceive at any time, not just a few times a year as with the Elder Races. The Human male had the ability to rise to the occasion at any time. The Gods now had no doubt that Mankind would not merely survive but would densely populate the earth.

Babaduk, Shaman of the Free Elves, peered deeply

into the eyes of the young brought before him. He knew if he made a mistake the cost would be the Elf's life. The Shaman was looking for the telltale tint of a speck of yellowish-green mucus in the white of their eye. This would signify the presence of a deadly virus. The virus took many years to develop and Babaduk knew not how the disease was acquired. He did know the first symptoms appeared as the Elves reached adulthood. He also knew that once this occurred, in a short period of time, all bodily fluids of the infected Elves would become highly contagious. Sending a misdiagnosed Elf into isolation with the infected amounted to a sentence of death

Babaduk knew all this and more as he culled the Elves

before him. Those not passing his inspection were immediately separated from the other Elves. All Elves suffered from an absolute obedience to authority. The unfortunate ones were herded into a group and isolated from the general population of Elves. Told to stay and await the coming of their guide, they did,

Unlike the older Elves, who had witnessed the "Judgment" on a yearly basis, these young

Elves has no inkling as to their fate. This would change when older friends and family began showing up with provisions, as for a long journey. The visitors, knowing relocation awaited those chosen, wished them goodbye and luck at arm's length, before hurriedly departing.

With darkness approaching and without further instruction, the young Elves settled down for the night, fearful of what dawn may bring. But daylight brought only sunlight and Alfred, an aged Elf they had never saw before. He asked, in a kindly voice, if the Elves would be so kind as to gather around him so he would not need to shout. Bidding them to make themselves as comfortable as possible, he preceded to tell them of their doom.

"You are afflicted with a disease that has no cure. The first signs you will notice will be small sores or boils that will manifest your bodies. Your condition will slowly worsen, the minor lesions will become areas of corrupted flesh, secreting a sickening stench. Your fingers and toes will darken and rot. Hands, feet, aye even the flesh of entire limbs, will become putrid before falling from your bodies." A comely Elf maiden, with a look of horror on her face asks, "Why would a virus attack our bodies and not the rest of the Elves"? Babaduk told her honestly, "I do not know, but I must tell you this." Taking a couple of deep breaths, he continued, "It is not only your body that will suffer. Your nose, lips and ears will evolve into a rotted glob of slime before oozing off your face." Hearing the horrified murmur around him, Babaduk told them that he will now explain the true horror of this disease and sadly noted the totally shocked look on the Elves faces. Raising his voice so that all could easily hear, he continued once again. "You are thinking that you could never endure such pain and torment, that you would kill yourself or beg someone else to do the killing out of mercy." Babaduk looked at the young Elves then demanded, "Am I, not right?" Seeing several nodding heads, he goes on. "This I will tell you and hear well, you will feel no pain, not even discomfort! For while the virus is eating away your flesh, it has already attacked your brain. The virus first ravishes the pain center, thus eliminating any pain to your body. Then, with pain under control, the virus is free to leisurely devour the remainder of your brain and as much of your body as possible, while keeping it mobile.

Alfred explained that the disease would affect each Elf differently. Some would not notice the first red and painless sores until years had passed, others would be infected relatively swiftly. Regardless of the onset, the results were the same. The virus, having eaten the Elves brain, would become dormant, leaving behind a decaying mindless shell of a body, wandering as if in search of something.

Elves, other than those chosen at "Judgment", knew little of the doom awaiting the Elves with the infection. The general population of Elves were led to believe that the virus laden youths were being relocated to a much warmer climate. There, with their disease in remission, the Elves would happily live out their lives.

Babaduk, the Shaman, passed among the doomed Elves, stopping at the side of

Alfred. Solemnly addressing the assembled Elves, he offered them two options. Travel to the South Lands and live out their doom or stay here in total isolation until the first red sores appeared. When this occurred, the Elf was deemed too infectious to tolerate and was disposed of.

Alfred and Babaduk were the only Elves, other than the warriors to ever see or witness, the result of the virus. They were in total agreement as to what their choice would be.

Alfred explained to Babaduk that the current holding area used to hold infected Elves was dangerously overpopulated. Elfin warriors patrolled the perimeter of the enclave. Inside the

Elves lived as best they could. The yearly arrivals often created friendships and babies. The offspring, although doomed from the start, would still live a relatively long and totally pain free life.

Elves, at the end stage of their infection, were the concern the warriors charged with keeping them within the compound. The newly arriving Elves, who followed their guide Alfred to the new lands, were told to stay, and they did. Infected Elves, brains eaten away by the insidious virus, were the wards of the warriors. With no mind left, the command to stay was lost to them. Left to wander on their own the Elves would spread terror and deadly infection amongst any Elf or other being encountered.

The Elfin people were by nature loving and gentle, but after untold generations of their kind being hunted for food, sport, or sexual gratification they, began to breed their own warrior caste. Long years of selecting strong and aggressive Elves resulted in an Elfin cadre feared even by the violent Trolls. The warrior caste, while not wildly popular with the Elf population in general, managed to produce enough offspring to replace the old or lame among their ranks, but no extras. This group of Elfin warriors guarded the Elf reservation. Wielding both sword and bow, knife strapped to their calf, no mindless Elf had ever wandered away. Nor had any entity ever ventured within, save Alfred and his charges.

The problem, as understood by Alfred, was numbers. Elves had been placed here for ages.

Add in the children produced and the problem became apparent. The large amount of mindless

Ghouls, needing to be destroyed, was taxing the Elfin warriors. Not only was their destruction required, they were also charged with removing and cremating the putrid remains. Dirthlyn,

Commander of the warriors told Alfred truthfully that the cadre was hard pressed to preserve the integrity of the borders. The placement of more infected Elves into the enclave would surely result in escapes. This must not happen.

Dirthlyn, walking with the Elfin Shaman, and the guide, told them of his idea. The next group of diseased Elves must be taken further south. When Dirthlyn mentioned the slow pace of the virus both the other Elves understood at once. For many years, if not a decade, the Elves would need no guards, for with intact minds they would stay where told. The warriors, without a steady influx of bodies would slowly find a measure of relief from a gruesome workload. The Elves, after addressing other concerns, agreed to the plan. Alfred would leave at once, leading the condemned Elves south to their new home, Babaduk and his old friend Dirthlyn would hurry ahead of them to find it.

Odyden was weary of hiding underground. Correctly assuming that the Gods were not planning an attack, he ventured into the light of day. Summoning Zomba, the Troll Lord, he bid him gain knowledge of the current conditions in the Realm of the Gods. He was ordered to follow any news concerning Man. Zomba secured secondhand information from the third Pixie he captured. After tearing off its wings he learned the Pixie had heard of a new life form far to the south. The wee informants reward was not hearing the small burp emulating from the Troll's lips. Moving ever southward the rumors evolved into truth, Mankind was on earth and multiplying rapidly.

Zomba knew he faced prolonged questioning upon return, so he preferred to have answers. Lord Zomba studied newborn Man for some time. He noted the availability of food for the taking, and the balmy weather which made clothing an uncomfortable burden. He was in awe of the sexual appetite of the Humans. Trolls could breed three times a year. Human females were copulating that many times a day, sometimes more, for they were the First-born, lusty and proud.

While fascinated by the beauty and sensuality of the New Race, Zomba knew the information he harbored was of dire importance to Odyden. Departing the Land of Men, Zomba headed north. He slept the heat of day away, traveling during the cooler hours. Late in the afternoon of the third day of his trip home, he viewed a strange sight. A group of Elves, perhaps fifty or so, seemed to be encamped for the night. Zomba searched with care but found no sign of Elfin warriors guarding them. He had heard the warriors guarded lands the living could not enter. He did not know the only ones to exit were the dead.

Sensing something amiss, Zomba shadowed the Elves southeast for the next four days.

He was now torn with indecision, continue his observation, or retreat north with all due haste. Then his dilemma solved itself. The Elves, now in the middle of a broad grassy slope leading to the Great Southern Sea, stopped in masse. The older Elf, whom Zomba assumed was their leader, bid them gather around and be at ease. He explained to the Elves that this place was to be their new home. Food in abundance grew nearby. The shore of the sea lies within easy walking distance, the waters filled with numerous edible delights. Shelters could be erected, if desired. The climate did not warrant them. Alfred, even after untold years of leading the "chosen" to their doom, still felt pain in his heart for these innocent young Elves.

Hiding in deep grass on a gentle rise above the Elves, Zomba heard none of the conversation. He was fairly sure they had reached their destination for the only thing before them was the sea. He also did not hear Alfred wishing them well or strictly ordering them not to venture more than a day's walk from where they now stood. Walking away northward, Alfred glanced back once more toward his forsaken charges and noted the position of the huge

Troll that he had first spotted following them five days ago. Feeling there was little more to gain by further spying on the youthful Elves. Zomba also turned north, being careful to avoid detection by the old Elf.

The Gods were not pleased, seeking to thwart their

plans did that to them. Odyden's plan they found especially odorous. Having Mankind used as food for the Troll Race was not the future they had envisioned for Man; it simply would not be permitted. A plan would be devised to foil Odyden's evil dream. Areius, God of War, championed the immediate death of Odyden, for he foresaw naught but treason ahead. Voices of many Gods echoed the same opinion. Great was the ire of the Gods, the thought of revenge sweet. Thoridon sensed the rising blood lust of the Gods, so he stood and called for silence. He then reminded them of their complete domination over all living things, but not each other. He told them the creator surely had plans unknown to them. Slaying a being, especially a Demigod Lord made by him, could have dire unintended consequences. Thoridon informed the other Gods that he was not willing to take that chance. He bid them recall their own plans for the Elder Races, that, with the Dawning of Man, the Sub-Human Races would face their twilight.

Thoridon then asked them to consider another option. The Gods would speed up the demise of the Trolls. They could not rid the earth of them in one fell swoop, but they could vastly speed the process. Debating hard and long, the Gods agreed to accept his plan. The Gods were pleased when, within a short period of time, results were seen.

The Gods, with cooperation not usually shown, worked together to hasten the Trolls demise. They caused the She-Trolls to become barren, the Gods would suffer no further Troll offspring. Minor youthful diseases, part of the normal Troll aging process, brought an early and pain laden death. Small wounds and cuts grew red and angry looking as infection set in, fever and death shortly ensued. The Gods thought, that with luck, most of the Trolls would be extinct ere Odyden learned of Mankind's existence.

The Gods joy was somewhat muted when they discovered that the sanctions imposed upon the Trolls also affected, to some extent, all the Elder Races. While regretful, the Gods realized that it was necessary.

Zomba, Lord of Trolls, felt unease. Holding a northward bearing toward home he had expected to meet some of his free roaming kin by now, hence his concern. Cresting a low rise in the land, he saw the first corpse. Three young Trolls lie face down in the grass. A huge clawed foot rolled the Trolls face up, revealing no fatal wounds. Zomba, learned in such matters, knew from the flush of their skin that they had died from a simple disease, usually contacted in early adulthood and seldom if ever fatal. Unable to fathom why they died, Zomba ventured back to his northern trek.

The Gods were feeling confident in their plan. Trolls were dying off at a faster than anticipated pace. The other Elder Races, while affected, fared much better. Elves, the heartiest of the Elders and most attuned to the land, sensed the upcoming end of their age. Having been preceded by Pixies, Fairies, Trolls and some things not spoken of, the Elves were the newcomers to the Land of the Gods. They now suffered much less from the ailments that were besetting the earlier Races.

The Elfin guide Alfred, returning from the southern enclave of infected Elves, was among those not readily affected by the Gods sanctions. On in years but agile and strong, he would not be susceptible to childhood disease, self-inflicted injury, nor a barren womb. Using the Traveler's

Star as a beacon, Alfred moved by night, resting during the day. He took note of the decaying bodies of Trolls, and even an Elf. He also noted with disappointment the absence of the Troll he had espied at the southern compound. Perhaps he should have left an easier trail to follow, a small conversation with him would have been enlightening.

Moving ever northward, Zomba continued to come across more dead Trolls, and an occasional Elf. The Troll Lord now realized what was bothering him. The carcasses of the dead were untouched by wolves or cats. Not even carrion eating vultures would venture a taste. He knew something was terribly wrong and knew he could do nothing to stop it. Forgetting decaying Trolls and the Elfin guide, he fled northward, for the first time in his life experiencing fear. Zomba traveled fast and hard, stopping briefly for rest or nutrients. A full night of sleep was not an option. Nearing the limit of his physical endurance, struggling to remain erect, Zomba espied the formidable mountain that Odyden called home. He would, out of necessity, now sleep for the duration of the day, and the night too, for he would get none when Odyden's questioning began.

Arising before the sun, Zomba crawled from the small grotto where he had spent the night. Somewhat refreshed, he steeled himself as he approached Odyden's lair. Nor had he forgotten that Odyden's fortress also served as prison to many enslaved Trolls. Odyden, hearing that Zomba had returned, met him at the top of the stairway. Leading him to a private room within the holding cell area of the compound, Odyden bid Zomba to sit. Forthright he asked, "Did you gather the information I requested?" Zomba quickly replied, "Aye, my Lord, and more." First and foremost, Odyden wished to know of Mankind. "Where are the First-born located?" What is their condition?" Odyden asked firmly. "They are many days travel to the south, near the sea. They appear to lack nothing necessary to their wellbeing," Zomba replied. This information came as little surprise to Odyden, but Zomba's next statement shocked him. "The Humans are not truly New-born, for I observed women with child and male and female living as couples." Odyden roared, "That is not possible, I would have heard." Zomba reminded him, as tactfully as he could, that he had killed all his flying spies.

The Troll Lord then told him of the strange sight he had beheld. "To the north and east of the Humans new home there is an Elf enclave. I have no thoughts as to why it is there. I saw one older Elf who appeared to be a leader or guide." Continuing he said, "I believe the guide was an Elfin warrior, as he was able to avoid being tracked by me." Odyden then inquired, "Why did you wish to follow an old Elf?" Zomba, not knowing if Odyden knew the facts told him, "I have heard of only one Elfin enclave, guarded at all times by warriors for unknown reasons.

\I simple wished to follow and perhaps have words with the Elf." Odyden sighed and told the Troll, "I too believe a talk would have been informative, but that is the past and we must now deal with the present."

Odyden ordered his Troll Lord to capture a new hoard of Pixies and Fairies. The Evil Lord would then enslave them to his will, for he was in dire need of news from the Realm of the Gods. Odyden ordered them to venture nowhere near the Hall of the Gods. In due course the tiny spies returned with the information he requested. The news did not make Odyden very happy. Men in the south were already growing bold, and rapidly multiplying, thanks to comely escorts supplied by Thoridon, Man's creator. They told him members of the Elder Races were dying at an alarming rate, as if possessed with a deadly malady. The Troll Race was being decimated to the point that Odyden worried over his future slave supply if the mysterious pox also spread to his beloved breeders and "feeders". The Pixies and Fairies were also hard hit by death. Only the Elves were not in danger of eminent extinction.

Odyden now sensed that Man would never mate with Trolls. First, they had coupled with and enjoyed the females of their own race. Secondly, by the time he captured enough Humans there may not be any Trolls left alive to breed them with. Accepting the failure of his original plans he schemed anew, ruing the lost time and planning, but mostly the lost chance to mold a part of the New-born Race to his base desires.

Recognizing that the union of Trolls and Mankind

would not happen, Odyden turned to Elves and Humans. To this end he was pleased to recall that Zomba had reported a group of Elves living near the new Race of Men. He could secure both Elf and Man during a single hunting trip. The Evil Lord smiled at this development but knew he needed to send Zomba south again at once. He summoned the Troll Lord once more, although he knew his body had not yet fully recovered from his last trip. Using occult powers stolen from the Gods, Odyden erased all weariness from Zomba's already hard body, increased his strength and endurance, and finally his mental ability. If a body dared challenge him, they would probably be in dire straits.

Odyden studied the Troll and felt he was up to the task before him. The Master of Evil bid him south, with slave Trolls, and all equipment he deemed necessary, to secure a goodly supply of Humans and Elves. He would of course remain behind, to finalize plans and prepare for the arrival of his breeding stock. Odyden felt deep worry over his lack of concrete plans for his new program. Should the Troll Race become extinct, his human flesh eaters along with his dream, would die. This he would not allow to happen.

The Evil Lord, sitting alone as always in his cold private quarters, awash in self-pity by the dismantling of his plans by the Gods, almost let the thought pass. Odyden now knew the answer to his dilemma was simple, yet so vile, that it sent a cold tingle down his spine. Odyden summoned Yanto, warden of the cells, to his quarters. "You will prepare comfortable lodging for about forty bodies, half being female. I do not wish the captives to mingle, so make ready two holding areas," Odyden ordered. "I also want you to send someone you fully trust to the petroleum springs in the Agali Valley. He is to return to me one gallon of the finest oil available." He then abruptly added, "He will leave for the valley today." Dismissing Yanto with a curt nod, he allowed himself a faint smile, for the pieces were once again falling into place. He could see himself standing, a nimble young naked woman at his side, watching his creations mature.

Alfred the guide was also a skilled Elfin warrior, trained since youth to fight. None save perhaps a well-armed Troll would survive battle against him. For this reason, he had felt no unease that the Troll that had followed him. In fact, he was now really peeved that he had not let the Troll attempt to capture him. After finding more and more dead Trolls, he knew a talk would have been interesting.

Upon leaving the northern Elfin compound Dirthlyn and Babaduk had quickly ventured to the shores of the Great Southern Sea. Without the building of boats, they had reached the limit of the Realm of the Gods. They had heard tales that Elves and Gnomes that lived underground inhabited the far side of the sea. But here, well east of the Lands of Man, the Elves would establish their second enclave for the infected. The proximity to Man was a concern, but not as much as permitting the Elves to live free and roam as they desired. Their futile hope was that some warriors would be available before Man discovered and tried to mingle with them.

With the location chosen, Dirthlyn and Babaduk turned back northward to intersect

Alfred and his southbound troupe of Elves. Four day later they met the Elfin guide and his charges, still heading southward. They informed Alfred of their choice of lands near the sea for the new compound. The two would travel together back to the northern enclave. Alfred, after leading the Elves to their new home, would trail after them, for he had no need for want of a companion.

After receiving final orders from Lord Odyden, Zomba lead his hunting party of Trolls out of Lord Odyden's stone fortress. The group numbered less than he wanted but Odyden had changed his mind, telling him there were no more Trolls to spare. They had also abandoned the idea of using traps with live bait. First, they would need to haul the cages untold miles. Second, there was already a good chance that Mankind had observed Pixies and Fairies. Third and most important, if Man detected the traps without being ensnared, it might not be possible to capture them without doing them harm. Nay, Zomba planned on doing it the tried and proven way. Needing only ten Elves and Humans of each sex, Zomba would come at night. The Humans, having never faced danger, would be sleeping, safe and secure. The enslaved Trolls that Zomba commanded would soon change that. The docile Elves would pose little or no problem.

Setting a course for the area between the Lands of Man and the new Elf compound Odyden's hinting party, led by the Troll Lord Zomba, departed for the south. Ignoring their request for rest and food, Zomba drove the Trolls ever southward toward the Lands of Man and Elves. Finally, after repeated pleas and begging that did not work, the death of a Troll from hunger and exhaustion caused him to relent. He granted his party a full day of rest and food as desired, the rest continuing unabated thru the night. The next morning, to the utter amazement of the Trolls, he ordered two scouts afield with instructions to return at dusk, granting the rest of the party another day of rest. Zomba knew but withheld from the others the fact that they were close to their quarry. He wanted his hunting party well rested before attempting the capture of Man or Elf.

That night, sitting beside a small cooking fire Zomba talked with his scouts. "Did you go in different directions as I suggested?" One of the scouts instantly answered, "Yes My Lord."

"Did either of you see any sign of Man or Elf", he asked with a bit of edge to his voice. "No", they responded, almost in union. He thought this odd, for with the days traveled he knew they must be near their destination. Zomba tried again, "Did you view anything at all that you found interesting?" The taller scout replied respectfully, "Yes Zomba, I did." He explained to Zomba that he had espied a vast body of water, larger than anything he had ever seen.

His shorter fellow scout chimed in that indeed he had also viewed it.

Zomba was secretly pleased, he was where he wished to be. He would set up his base camp here, far away from the eyes of Elf or Man. He was unconcerned with his scout's inability to locate Man or Elf, for on the morn they would be found by him. The next day, with little difficulty, Zomba located Man. The southern Elfin enclave location easily followed the following day. Studying the habits of Man and Elf he found, as he surmised, no great surprises. Lacking danger, neither Race had need for security, so his original plan for night raids would be used. Zomba chose the Elves as his first target, reasoning that being smaller and docile, they would be easier to keep under control then the powerful Humans.

Sitting with his two Troll commanders, Zomba chose the night of the next full moon for the capture of the Humans, preceded by one night the raid on the Elves. He was assured by his commanders that all would be readied. Dismissing them with a slight wave of his hand, Zomba rested.

The First-born, warmed by the sun rays, slowly stirred to life. Rising on unsteady legs, they stared in utter amazement at their surroundings. Everywhere Man gazed wonderment appeared before his eyes. He would need to examine all he saw, but first he needed to satisfy a more basic want. Feeling pangs of hunger, Dralon, as he would come to be known, walked to a tree laden with ripe fruit. Instinctively he plucked an apple from the tree and bit. His handsome face broke into a smile, the apple was delicious. Sampling other fruits and vegetables at his disposal only deepened his smile. Dralon noticed the rest of the First-born watching him feed. Man had been bestowed with the gift of speech from the Gods. Using voice for the first time Dralon urged the others to join him. Long the First-born ate, and well. Discovering a small stream, flowing sweet and cool on its way to merge with the sea, they drank. In time the First-born Men would explore the limits of their land and more, but for now, fed and content, they were more interested in exploring the lush bodies of the women.

The Elves watched the form of the guide until it merged into the horizon. Now, for the first time since their ordeal began, the youthful Elves felt truly alone. The Elves had no friends or family, just each other, with a terrible fate awaiting them all.

Joeluk, who by default was leader of the doomed Elves, summoned them to gather around. "Stop your despair," he implored. "Your fate was sealed when you chose to move south," he reminded them. "All of you have many years, some decades, yet to live. You may dismay and suffer a miserable existence, or live each day full of gusto, enjoying each day you have left." Taking a deep breath, Joeluk then tells them," I will opt for the later."

The Elves knew they had heard the truth and went about establishing some normalcy to their lives. Wanting shelter, but enjoying companionship, they decided on a communal hall.

Using basic tools supplied by Alfred, they erected a wooden sided building, and after thatching a roof, they created a comfortable home. Suffering no signs of virus, the Elves began to pair up and do what young couples tend to do. They could forget, at least for a while, their impending doom.

Unknown to the Elves, almost half of them would suffer great torment, perhaps even death, much sooner than expected. For as the Elves settled into a routine, the Trolls made ready their hunting party. The time had come.

Zomba arose ere the sun the day of the Elfin raid.

Fearful of Odyden's wraith should he fail, he left nothing to chance. Uncounted times he studied and reviewed his plans, each time coming to the same conclusion. If the Troll hunters followed his orders, they would succeed. If not, great woe would befall them. The Trolls were aware of this for Zomba had explained the punishment for failure in gruesome detail. Zomba grew weary of contemplating failure and went in search of the camp cook. The Troll Lord found him in a cave dug by the Trolls to keep the provisions somewhat cool and safe. Zomba ordered the cook to serve up a double ration of semi fresh raw meat, a rare treat indeed. He wished his Troll guards to know that if they took care of his needs, he would see to theirs. Then, in an action overboard for him, he granted The Trolls three hours of free time after they had eaten, to rest or sleep as they saw fit. Tonight, he would abide no Troll with sleep or food on his mind, only the directions given by him. Sure, of the readiness of his troops, he retired with them.

"That hurts", Arena cried out, pushing Domigo's hand from her breast. "I'm sorry", answered the First-born, "You said play with my nipple, so I did." "I know," she replied, "But in the future try not to pull it from by body." Domigo promised to remember. He had first been drawn to Arena when he saw a hunger in her eyes that food nor drink had sated. Taking her aside from the rest of the First-born, he simply wished to touch her. Domigo had gazed upon all the New-born Women. Being created in the image of the Gods all were beautiful, Arena was stunning. Peering at her naked body brought a physical pain to his loins he longed to be rid of. He hoped, correctly, that Arena could make it go away.

Domigo stood chest to breast with her, hands rubbing her lower back and massaging the cheeks of her comely ass. Feeling the surge of blood into his penis for the first time, he bent to the ear of Arena. She listened well and to herself smiled, for unbeknown to Domigo or any other First-born, she had been cloned by Thoridon from Ambrosa, the Goddess of sexual lust and desire. Upon her awakening, Arena would possess all the carnal skills and wonton physical desires of the Goddess.

Looking up at the face of Domigo, she could feel the head of his penis probing her lower belly. Wetting her lips with her tongue, she dropped to her knees before him. Moving moist lips toward him she abruptly stopped, much to the dismay of Domigo. He quickly smiled again when she shifted onto her hands and knees before fully engulfing his huge cock with a superbly talented mouth. She had wantonly stuck her delectable ass in the air, hoping to attract additional attention. Sensing her proffered charms would not be taken advantage of she resumed her attention to Domigo's penis and soon had him experiencing Mankind's first ever orgasm.

Arena lie next to Domigo, her saliva moistened fingers penetrating her already well lubricated vagina, before retreating to massage her erect clitoris. Unfulfilled, she glanced over at the prone body of Domigo, noting his flaccid penis and wished that one of the First-born had taken advantage of her upturned assets. Bored with playing with herself, she gently caressed

Domigo's cock. As she expected, his now semi hard penis surged to life. Domigo started to rise but was restrained by Arena. She sat up and motioned for Domigo to kneel between her widely spread legs. Being horny, she had no time for instructions. Grabbing his head by his ears she led his tongue to where she needed it to be. Instinct and the unrelenting lust bestowed by the Gods took over as his tongue brought her to climax. Arena, at least for a while, was satisfied. She would now begin to teach Domigo the finer points of making love.

Zomba, roused from his brief nap by a sentry, ordered all troops be awakened and sent to him. Gathered around him they received final instructions for the hunt. All would carry a short sword and small lightweight leather shield. The two commanders also carried a small dagger on their belt, signaling them out as leaders. Selected others would tote ropes, chains, and shackles for use on the Elves. Once caught, Zomba planned on them staying caught. Knowing many miles of march lie before them before reaching the Elfin compound Zomba ordered them into traveling formation. Taking the lead, he quickly led them off in the direction of the Elves. Mile after mile he held true to the same course. Then just before sundown he signaled his Trolls to halt. Having been here before he knew the Elfin communal house lie a short distance ahead, beyond a slightly rising knoll. Zomba would use the last rays of day to position his hunters in the places he had previously selected. There they would wait, quietly, until the full moon showed its face.

The Troll Lord, feeling the time was nigh, removed a small woolen pouch from inside his leather tunic. Opening the bag, he withdrew a small glowing stone. A gift from Odyden, he planned on using it as a signal to begin the attack. Zomba looked skyward into the cloud covered night when, as if ordered to depart, a large windblown cloud moved downwind, revealing the face of the nearly full moon. Lifting the glowing stone high above his head, he slowly moved his hand in a circular motion. The attack had begun!

The Trolls streamed from their hiding places and soon surrounded the common house of the Elves. Quietly entering the home of the Elves, they quickly trussed and shackled many half-asleep Elves. Some who were indulging in sex or otherwise awake, managed to escape. Joeluk, their leader was not among this number. Zomba cared but little, for he had captured the requested number of Elves. The First-born of Man were next.

The surviving Elves, now without a leader, were in total shock. They had not been told but assumed that the Elf leaders would have made known to the other species, the formation of a new viral colony for infected Elves. This in itself should have kept them safe from intruders.

The Elves could not fathom why any being would want to capture an infected Elf.

Zomba saw no need for himself and most of the other Trolls to waste time escorting the

Elves to the base camp. After naming the guard Tonego leader, he chose five other Trolls to accompany him, charging Tonego with the safe delivery of the captives. Zomba gathered his remaining troops and set a hard pace back toward camp. The Trolls now acting as wardens were well pleased and full of themselves as they drove the docile Elves northeast toward their base camp. The newly named sadistic leader of the Trolls, Tonego, took great delight in tormenting the placid Elves. Using hand, threats and even the point of his sword, he granted little peace to the Elves on their forced march.

Knowing the shackled Elves posed no danger to them, Joeluk hailed Tonego, the Troll most responsible for their discomfort. "Troll, we are but few and harmless to you," he declared in a low voice meant to be heard by his adversary only. Then with a daring that surprised himself, he asked, "Why seek meek and diseased Elves, have you not the fortitude to attempt domination over those who would resist?" Hearing the diminutive Elf demean him meant nothing, the excuse to visit violence upon him did. Approaching Joeluk, the Troll delivered a backhand blow to his head. Tonego knew that a forehand, which would involve talons, would also involve death. Looking down at the prone body at his feet he kicked it lightly and detected no response. Now concerned for his own safety, he glanced down again and saw movement. He was both relieved and pleased, for he was not yet finished with this arrogant Elf.

Tonego ordered one Troll to stay with the Elf until he regained his feet. At such time they would run, catching up with the others. An hour later the Troll watching Joeluk grew uneasy, for the Elf, while seemingly conscious, had not risen. Fearing punishment if he did not regain the main group in a timely manner, he slung the much smaller Elf over his shoulder, turned and followed the path the others had taken. Moving with haste, little bothered by the burden on his back, he soon espied the main party of captive Elves and slowed to a fast walk. Feeling the Elf begin to struggle he lowered him to the ground, halting long enough to tell the Elf, "Run forward and join your kin or die here." Joeluk quickly reunited with the captive Elves. Tonego, seeing the return of the taunting Elf, dropped back from the lead. He simply stood and stared at the Elf, and then departed, a cruel smile forming on his sadistic face.

Retaking the lead Tonego, increased the pace, the base camp now but an hour's hard march away. The Trolls are tired and hungry. The only thing that remained of their last meal, the one of raw meat, was its memory. In due course the encampment was reached, and the Elves handed over to awaiting Trolls.

Tonego, proud of his accomplishment, planned to build a victory fire, sit around it, and secretly sip a little bukka, a highly intoxicating herbal/narcotic brew. He thought he should invite his five fellow Elf herders.

The night brought more than vile darkness. It also spawned fire, drunkenness, and madness beyond belief, for Tonego had a foul plan and the besotted Trolls were more than willing to help. Warning two of them to be quiet, he sent them to the Elfin holding compound with orders to return with Joeluk the Elf. While waiting their return, Tonego and the other three Trolls busied themselves with fueling and then placing a layer of rocks on the fire Tonego had started.

Soon after the two Trolls returned with their hapless captive Elf. Tonego wasted no time, ordering the Elf's ankles to be tied to stakes he had previously driven into the ground about three feet apart. Drunkenly pointing at the two largest Trolls he told them to stretch the Elf's arms tight and not to let go until told. Withdrawing his dagger from his belt, he sneered at the Elf as he cut his clothes away. With the smallish Elf pleading for his life, Tonego inserted his knife into the Elf's torso just above his penis and slowly opened up his belly to his navel. The Elf looked down at his steaming intestines oozing from his body in shock induced disbelief. Tonego and his drunken companions roared with laughter at the disemboweled Elf, finding it terribly amusing. Tonego, in a moment of sanity, realized the noise they were making had a chance of reaching Zomba. Moving his blade to the throat of the softly moaning Elf, he ended his nightmare. After taking another sip of bukka, the fields dressed the body, making it ready for the fire with a few quick slices of his knife.

Two of the Trolls placed the Elf's body carefully onto the prepared bed of hot rocks.

Others covered it with sweet, new cut grass. Come morn the Trolls had plans to eat well, Tonego more so, for he solely claimed the roasted head of the arrogant Elf for his own. As he drifted off to sleep, he remembered that he had something of extreme importance to tell Zomba concerning the Elves, but in a drug induced stupor he could not recall what it was.

Sitting with his two commanders, Zomba noticed the two Trolls heading in the direction of the captured Elves but paid them no mind, continuing to talk of plans to harvest Humans.

The Troll Lord believed he had heard a muffled cry in the quiet night air, and raised his hand, signaling his commanders for silence. Listening intently, Zomba knew whence the sound had originated. Ordering the Trolls to follow, Zomba rushed to the Elfin holding pen. The already terrified Elves, upon seeing the Troll Lord approach, retreated to the far reaches of their cage, afraid they could be the next to be taken away. Zomba did a fast head count, his face gaining color. By the end of the third count he was in a rage. An Elf had escaped, surely some Troll would pay a dear price. Walking back to camp while discussing plans to search for the missing Elf, Zomba detected a familiar odor in the air. Although cooking fires were long cold and fresh meat had not been on the menu, Zomba could easily identify the aroma of roasting flesh. Following his nose westward, Zomba came to the top of a shallow ravine. Gazing down, he viewed six Trolls lying about a fire. Nothing was unusual there, but the strong smell of cooking meat emanating from the smoldering fire was. The Troll Lord used his sword to fashion a long sturdy staff from the limb of a nearby tree, then descended into the ring of Trolls. Ignoring the listless sleepers, the Troll Lord proceeded to the smoking fire pit. Using the long wood staff, he peeled back the heavy blanket of wet grass covering the simmering mass, revealing the semi- cooked body of the missing Elf.

Zomba was Lord of the Trolls for good reason. He bested any Troll who would dare challenge him. He also had powers bestowed on him by Odyden, his Lord. The Troll now felt a towering rage engulfing him. The drunken

Trolls lolling about the fire would die, but not in their sleep. Uttering a primal scream, he woke the startled Trolls. Discarding the wood staff, he replaced it with a finely-honed dagger, while his other hand wielded his sword.

The first Troll, just awakened, gasped in surprise at the appearance of Zomba. He barely had time to widen his eyes before the Troll Lord's sword separated his head from his body. The other Trolls, fully awake by now, sensed their coming fate. Jumping to his feet, Tonego called out for the others to join him, believing in strength of numbers. Zomba thought this was a fine idea also. Striding into the now amassed Trolls with unbridled fury, he delivered his first sword thrust deep into the chest of the nearest Troll. Spinning around as he pulled his sword from the Trolls body, he landed a vicious blow that crushed the head of another hapless Troll. The stricken Ogre stood for a moment, his mouth literately agape, before collapsing into a heap at Zomba's feet. Tonego positioned himself between and slightly behind the two other remaining herders. He counted on being able to flee while Zomba fought the other Trolls. He had neither the desire nor intention of battling the Troll Lord. Zomba, with blood lust raging unabated, eyed the three remaining Trolls. Two were familiar faces, but nameless. The third brought a new surge of ire, for Zomba saw it was Tonego, the Troll he had just made a leader. Trembling with rage, the Troll Lord bent low and closed slowly in on the foe to his left, seemingly paying no mind to the others. Clenno, the Troll to his right, knew he now had a chance. Raising his sword above his head he charged Zomba from behind, knowing Zomba could not turn around in time to block his sword. The first Troll, seeing Clenno rushing Zomba from the rear, quickly came up with a plan of action. If Zomba turned to confront Clenno, the killing blow was his. If not Clenno would strike the fatal blow from behind. Either way the Troll Lord's long life was over. As if being stupid, Zomba continued forward, his weapon still at his side, a look of utter confusion on his face. The Trolls could not believe their good fate, for Zomba was now within reach of both their swords. The Trolls struck a pair of powerful downward blows a second after Zomba collapsed to the ground. Rolling to the side he kicked the ankle of the nearest Troll and was rewarded when he heard the distinctive sound of metal tasting bone. Looking up he saw one Troll already dead, his head cleaved in two. The other Troll well on his to way to bleeding to death compliment of a deep wound to the side of his neck. He gave them no further thought.

Zomba heard footfalls retreating into the distance and assumed it was the Troll Tonego, attempting to escape. Confirming his target, the Troll Lord flung his dagger at the fleeing figure.

With barely a sound, other than the sharp intake of breath from Tonego, the blade of Zomba's knife found a warm home deep within the hamstring of the Troll. Zomba approached the crippled traitor and with great malice told him. "Pull the knife from your leg, for in your haste to avoid me, you shunned your own weapon." Giving the Troll an evil grin, he added, "You now have one of mine to use." Tonego begged, "Lord, it is but a small dagger, still embedded in my flesh, how am I to deal with sword?" Suddenly tiring of the violence, and wishing the night to end, he told

Tonego, "Troll, pull it and fight me to a slow and painful death on your part, or use it otherwise."

Mere seconds later, Zomba watched Tonego gingerly ease the blade from his thigh. Piercing his arm at the wrist, he raised the blade to his elbow, opening his forearm wide. The doomed Troll then repeated the same procedure on his other arm. Suddenly feeling weak, the Troll slumped to the ground and silently watched as his life ran from his body.

Spent from the sickening ordeal of slaying his own, Zomba retreated to his quarters, but not before ordering his commanders to burn the Elf's body to ash. Morning would not bring roasted Elf as a victory repast.

Zomba was ill pleased with himself, killing one of his Trolls, forgivable, but slaying six of his hunting party, incredibly stupid.

The first-born Dralon wished to explore the area surrounding them. Talking

Domigo into accompanying him, they traveled far to the east. After days of travel seeing nothing but the lush flora of the coastal plain, they suddenly viewed a large building in the far distance. While still far from the structure, they were hailed by a being they had never viewed before. Other than being a bit shorter and having slightly pointed ears, he could have passed for one of the First-born at the age of puberty. The Elf, as they would learn this Race was named, told them to stay where they were. "Come no closer", he ordered. "I know not what or who you are, but you need realize this is a place of doom." Dralon, wishing to learn more about these beings called Elves, asked them if they would tell him why they were damned. The Elf asked them to wait while he talked with the other Elves. Dralon and Domigo waited a surprisingly short time ere the Elf returned and agreed to relate his tale of woe.

The Elves, he told them, had always suffered from a deadly incurable malady. Not all, but enough Elves caught the infection, that joy of life was impossible before the "culling." He explained to them that this was a rite of passage for the young. Any youth who did not pass muster ended up here, slowly awaiting their death.

The Elf told further of the attack by the Trolls. "What is a Troll?' interrupted Dralon.

Studying the First-born carefully, the Elf replied, "Taller than I, less than you. Heavy with muscle, hands and feet both adorned with viciously sharp talons. They are hairy, ill tempered, and grossly ugly. Aye, if you venture upon one you will surely know. But do not make the mistake of thinking them dumb or stupid."

The Humans, totally fascinated with this information, urged the Elf to tell them more. They heard much more, some of it good, some not. They learned of Pixies, Fairies, and the Elves. Also told of was wild animals, such as the snow cat, living in the far reaches of the north. They heard of bears, wolves and snakes that lived in trees and could swallow an Elf whole. More importantly, they learned of tools, clothing, fire, and weapons. Also etched into their minds from the talk with the Elves, was the idea of hate and dominance over other Races. Mankind, although young, would never be the same.

Wento was not happy being sent alone to the Algali Valley, for it was wrought with grave dangers. His chief concern was reports of snow cats leaving the higher elevations of the mountains to traverse south. These large vicious felines had no natural enemies, save Trolls.

Odyden had told him that he believed the demise of Trolls was causing the mushrooming population of the cats. Wento feverishly hoped to be back in the underground fortress before a hungry cat mistook him for a meal. Wento traveled by day, staying on the ancient foot path that led westward. Before dark, he sought out caves or shallow grottoes in which to spend the night. A snow cat, even famished, would be leery of sticking its head into a recess with the scent of a Troll within.

As the days and nights began to merge together without excitement, he finally felt he could relax a bit. Wento was now moving to the west quickly, the path he had been following gradually dropping toward the mouth of the Algali. Odyden had told him that halfway thru the valley lie the petroleum pools, his goal.

The attack came at night, as expected, but unexpectedly by a pack of wolves, not a snow cat. Led by a huge male, long of fang, with glowing yellow eyes, the pack quickly surrounded Wento's small cave. He knew the wolves were suffering terrible hunger, for attacking an adult Troll, even in large numbers, would result in many canine casualties. Wento, while concerned, did not overly fear for his safety, for Odyden had given him special provisions for his journey

The first snarling face appeared in the mouth of the cave and was swiftly silenced by a short sword thrush to its throat. Wento kicked aside the dying body of the wolf blocking the entrance to the cave and awaited the second charge. There was none. After carefully shifting his body position to better swing his sword, the Troll peered out of the cave. The wolves were gone.

This did not sit well, for he knew they would return, but not when. Awaiting daylight with an uneasy sleep, Wento arose with the sun. Reassuring himself that no wolves lurked nearby he exited the cave.

Moving fast, always alert, Wento continued his decent into the valley. The oil deposits lie at the bottom of the valley in small pools, just before the Agali began its upward climb. He reckoned one more day would see him there, and he could begin gathering the oil. But for now, with the setting of the sun, he needed to find safe shelter for the night. Long hours before dawn, he was awakened by the howling of wolves from afar. Wento rolled over and went safely back to sleep. The wolves had found food.

Rising early, as normal, Wento was exiting his cave when he happened to duck his head back inside to make sure he had left nothing behind. This saved his life as the powerful, clawed paw of the snow cat whistled over his head. With a roar of rage, the feline launched itself from the stone ledge above the cave. Wento had his sword drawn and high overhead when the supple cat impaled itself on its honed length. Wento finished the job by opening the cat's torso to the neck before withdrawing his bloody sword. Panting, more from fear and excitement than exercise, he sat and rested. While sitting idle he had a stroke of insight. There should be no other cats nearby in the valley, for they would fight for possession of territory in an area of this size.

Wento knew the wolf pack would be back when hunger struck again. Searching him out, the large body of the gutted snow cat, still fresh, would serve as an admirable substitute. If he hurried in his chore, he should be well on his way out of the Agali Valley ere the pack needed to hunt again.

Feeling renewed, Wento set off for the petroleum springs, arriving just before sundown.

Sensing no danger nearby and desiring a break from sleeping in dank caves, he spent a refreshing dreamless night by the edge of the warm oils. The morning sun found him gathering oil samples from all the various ponds in the area. Upon being filtered, the oil with the best lubricating properties would be selected for bottling.

While his samples were being filtered Wento fetched a large flat rock from a nearby pile.

He carefully wiped it free of all sand and dirt. Placed at a convenient height, the stone would serve as his test lab. Retrieving the samples, Wento dipped his index finger into a vial of oil up to his first knuckle and let to soak for a moment. Withdrawing his digit, he slowly traced a line across the flat stone until his finger ran dry. Carefully cleaning his finger, he repeated the test with each sample of oil, tying hard to exert the same amount of pressure to his finger each time.

When he was done, he simply determined the longest line of oil on the stone. This was the finest quality lubricating oil to be found on earth. He knew Odyden will be well pleased.

Working without food of rest, Wento soon had the chosen oil in a hastily constructed filtering vat before noon. Midafternoon found him and his precious cargo traversing the now acceding and seldom used path leading out of the Algali Valley.

Odyden's unease grew along with the length of day, as spring was now upon the Northern Mountain Lands. The Elder Races, with the exception of the Elves, were vanishing quickly, the remaining Free Trolls especially so. Odyden had believed his captive Trolls, held underground, were immune from the malady laying waste to the Elders. This thought proved untrue, when within the last week, one of his slave Trolls had sickened and died after sustaining a minor wound. The Evil Lord now knew it was just a matter of time before he was left with no

Trolls as slaves. He now needed Elves and Humans more than ever, and he needed them now.

With the report from an enthralled Pixie, Odyden learned of the capture of southern

Elves. This news brought him hope. If Zomba had also acquired the necessary, compliment of

Humans, he may well be on the return.

Zomba knew his problem was mostly of his own

making. He had let his emotions take charge, now he would pay the price for slaughtering his Troll guards. One third of the hunting party's sleep time now became sentry duty, and the Trolls received precious little sleep to begin with. The loss of sleep for the foreseeable future was nearly intolerable. He also guessed, correctly, that having witnessed him slay the Trolls without a hint of mercy, he would hear no complaints from his hunting party, at least not to his face. Nor had he told the Trolls that Odyden himself had told him the New-born would be proud and strong. They would not accept captivity and if captured would strenuously resist. Odyden knew they would require constant watching, lest they escape. With the acquisition of Humans, the Trolls would quickly realize how easy they had it now.

Summoning his two commanders, he revised his plan for an attack on the First-born. Men, unlike the Elves in their communal home, were spread about the land. Attacking in masse would accomplish little, for seldom would more than a few Humans be found close together. On numerous occasions, a dozen men and an equal number of women could be found together, to the utter delight of the participants, but the Trolls had no knowledge of this.

Zomba decided to use a hunting party of ten. While seeking out couples, they would still be capable of dealing with a larger group of Humans. Upon capture, and after being shackled, they would be escorted back to the Troll's base camp. It was agreed that one armed Troll should be able to handle two bound Humans. After delivering his charges to the guards remaining in camp, the Troll was to rejoin the hunting party. In this manner, Zomba hoped to maintain the hunting party's numbers. His fear was that the harvesting of the First-born would take a long time. Out of necessity, the Humans had to be held together, but he did not want them to have time to plan or scheme. They were powerful beings and born free of yoke.

The Troll Lord would order his guards to quickly gather the First-born. Catch, truss, shackle, and deliver them to the awaiting guards. Repeat as quickly as possible. Zomba then surprised his strangely silent commanders by asking, "Will this work?"

Returning to the Land of Men, Domigo and Dralon quickly held council with the other

First-born. Recounting the plight and despair of the Elves, they asked for their guidance. But having no clue why Elves infected with a deadly virus would be taken captive, no guidance was forthcoming. The good thing was that having been alerted to the Elves disease, there would be no chance contact with them.

Sensing there was no more to be gained from this conversation, Dralon signaled Domigo to draw near. At his side he is asked by Dralon, "Did you not observe the walls of the Elves lodging? They are erected from hewed logs, ergo sturdy tools, with sharp edges." Domigo considered this before replying, "I did, but infected Elves process them, not I. In fact, they told us about tools that could be used by warriors as weapons." Dralon countered, "True, but with their shelter built, perhaps they will share." Domigo was uneasy at this prospect, "What of the virus? Can it survive on the surfaces of tools?" Dralon sought to reassure him, "We will take no chances, the metal will go into a fire. We will replace their brunt wood with our own." He then explained that he planned to ask the Elves to place the axes, hatchets and assorted other metal tools that had a sharp edge into the fire. He and Domigo would build a fire pit at the limit of the Elves travel range. Once well-lit, the Elves would stoke the fire with the wooden handles of their tools, the Men departing to avoid even the smoke from the pyre. The following day they would return to gather up the now cold, virus free weapons.

Both First-born agreed to this plan but knew the Elves held the final say. They would wait to tell the others of their plan. They first needed the cooperation of the Elves. With this in mind they made preparations for another trip to the enclave of the doomed.

Hanto, senior of the Troll Lord commanders, did not always tell Zomba what he wanted to hear. This was one of those times. "Lord, we departed with eighteen Trolls, a small number to begin with. One was lost on the forced march south, six others by your own hand." Hanto felt Zomba glaring at him but went on unabated. "You wish to use a hunting party of ten and deliver the prisoners to the guards waiting at the base camp. Have I recapped the plan correctly?"

"Aye Troll," Zomba gruffly replied," that is my plan. What fault do you find with it?"

"One of numbers Lord Zomba, for with a ten Troll hunting party, there is but one guard left to watch over captive Elves and receive captured Humans." This would not work, explained Hanto. The Troll Lord had no choice but to agree.

Plotting yet again, they determined that a minimum of five Trolls must remain as guards.

They would also play a vital role in the capturing of the First-born. In the new scheme, Zomba himself would lead the remaining Trolls south, deep into the Lands of Man. They would travel by the dark of night, avoiding detection. Upon gaining their desired position, they would turn their sights to the Troll encampment in the north, driving the horrified Humans before them. Zomba would place Hanto and Tyreno, his Troll commanders, with one other Troll each, on the flanks of his position. He thus hoped to drive the First-born into the embrace of his waiting hunters.

Zomba knew he would miss capturing many Humans by using this plan, but as with the

Elves, he did not care as long as he caught the required amount. He also had a huge plus on his side, for Trolls could see at night much better than Humans. He knew of this from a conversation with Odyden, who thought the information could be of use in the future. Zomba would wait for a totally dark night to attack the First-born. The Humans, having never seen or heard a Troll before, would go fleeing before the howling dark figures, into the waiting arms of the Troll guards. Envisioning this scene in his mind, the ugly Troll Lord almost soiled himself from laughing so hard.

Dirthlyn and Babaduk took leave of the Southern

Elves and departed for the Northland and home. Many days into their journey they were startled to see an Elf warrior coming their way. Even stranger was the fact that he was astride a horse. Although plentiful on the grassy steppes below the Northern Mountains, the wild mounts were rarely broken to saddle. Dismounting from the heavily muscled steed, he approached the two Elves. "I am Moluk, of the Free Elves and once a warrior, in search of Babaduk and his companion Dirthlyn," he informed them. "Then your search is over," responded Babaduk, "you have found us."

Dirthlyn, himself a warrior, had a burning question that he needed answered. "The horse

I can understand, you obviously have the talent and brawn to break one, what I cannot fathom is how you can be both warrior and Free-Elf." Seeing the determined look on Dirthlyn's face, he told them of dire happenings in the Northern Realms. "The Elder Races are beset by a deadly malady. Trolls, Pixies, Fairies, and aye, even us hardy Elves, are dying at an alarming rate, although Elves at a much slower pace than the others. The leader of the Free-Elves sent me to find Babaduk the Shaman, for they sorely need both his insight and guidance."

Dirthlyn then told Moluk, with a hint of irritation in his voice, "I understand what you have told me, but what I still wish to know is why you are not at the northern Elfin compound with the rest of the warriors?" Moluk, sensed the growing frustration of Dirthlyn and told him,

"The commander of the Elves, after long conversation with the Free-Elf leader, released me from my oath of service." Continuing, he explained, "I was then asked by the same leader to travel southward in search of Babaduk and yourself. I believe the Free-Elf leader was told I processed a horse and could travel vast distances in but a short period of time. Regardless I agreed, the rest you know."

Babaduk, after consulting with Dirthlyn, agreed he must return north to the Lands of the

Free-Elves with all due hast. Dirthlyn is torn between loyalties. He knew he should rejoin his fellow Elves at the northern enclave, but his heart was telling him the Elves in the south deserved knowledge of the demise of all the Elder Races.

Having quickly made up his mind Dirthlyn turned and

asked Moluk, "Will not your sturdy steed bare two smallish Elves?" Moluk's response was positive, his question expected, "Where are we going?"

Wento and his precious gallon of lubricant were making good time leaving the Algali.

Valley. He reckoned one more day of hard travel would bring him to the steppes surrounding the foothills of the Northern Mountains. He noted that with the longer days of spring, his daily hours of walking also increased. Although there was still some time before dark Wento was tired.

Wanting a good march, the next day, he sought out and found his nightly cave. The Troll ate some dried meat, had a few sips of water from his flask, and quickly fell into a deep sleep.

With the rising of the moon, the wolf pack silently gathered near Wento's grotto. Normally unwilling to take on a Troll, they now had little choice. The snow cat population, usually kept somewhat in check by Trolls, had rapidly increased. The large vicious felines ate anything they could catch, and the wolves were famished.

Converging before the cave, the alpha male snarled loud enough to awaken Wento. Glancing out, he saw the moon reflecting off a dozen sets of glowing yellow eyes. His quick look also revealed a grave error on his part. The mouth of his cave was too wide to defend. Plus, two, perhaps even three wolves would come for him at the same time. Wento had feared little before slaying the snow cat. Now with the gifts Odyden had given him for the trip, the wolf pack was not a great concern. Wento reached into his leather tote and withdrew a small pouch containing a glowing stone, given to him by Odyden. Wento counted on the eerie glow, emitting from the cave, to hold the wolves momentarily at bay. Again, dipping into his bag, he removed two egg shaped objects wrapped carefully with oiled parchment. He unwrapped the orbs, holding them in his huge left hand. Moving quickly, he checked the dagger on his hip, then tucked his sword under his left armpit. Knowing he could not fully swing his sword in the confines of the cave if the wolves advanced, he tossed Odyden's glowing stone into the center of the ring of wolves. Gripping his sword with his now free right hand, he exited the cave, following the eerie light radiating from Odyden's stone.

Wento was enjoying a slight advantage. The glowing

stone in the midst of the wolf pack had temporarily disoriented them. This edge abruptly disappeared when a famished wolf, lurking in the shadows by the mouth of the cave, darted forward and sank his glistening canines into the back of the Trolls thigh. Roaring more in rage than pain, Wento swung his sword backward and down, cleanly separating the head, holding the offending teeth, from the rest of the wolf's body.

The second wolf came at him while he was still shaking the head of the first from his leg. This wolf gained his lower leg until a mighty sword stroke destroyed its spinal cord.

Wento was now concerned, for he knew that if the wolves attacked in masse he would be in serious trouble, but instead of fear he felt only disdain for the wolves. Ignoring the snarling canines surrounding him, Wento calmly placed his sword at his feet. He would trust his life to the second gift given to him by the Dark Lord.

Dralon and Domigo, having been this way before, made excellent time on their trip back to the Elfin enclave. Halting in the same area as before, they soon saw the approaching figure of the Elf they had previous conversed with. This time he identified himself as Mikali, newly chosen leader of the Elves. Knowing he had warned them to stay away, he now wanted to know why they had returned. Asking leave to sit, Dralon explained their need for weapons to the Elf leader. Listening carefully. Mikali heard little gain for his people, save the loss of currently unused tools.

Dralon, sensing the forthcoming lack of assistance from Mikali, told him. "The Trolls did not take your kin away alive, only to be killed later. They were captured for a reason!" "Aye," responded the Elf, "but even if we knew where they were, we are not permitted to leave, nor are we warriors." Dralon of the First-born replied, "I understand this. Now hear me out and well." Taking a deep breath, he began. "Give us now, in our need, your axes, hatchets, and other tools with blades or sharp edge. In return, I will pledge the help and friendship of the Human Race." Mikali debated this, but shortly the alliance of Man and Elf was formed.

Dralon beckoned Domigo near and told him he was unwilling to wait for a conference with the other First-born before securing weapons from the Elves. Domigo disagreed, causing the first serious argument between

Men. Mikali, now serving as mediator, solved the problem. The Men, when ready to depart, would build the fire pit as planned, then immediately leave for their homeland. The Elves would transport and sterilize the arms of the Men. Should for some reason the Humans reject the alliance and arms of the Elves, it would cost them naught but the time and effort of replacing the wood handles. If the First-born agreed, as Mikali thought they would, the sharp bladed tools, now free of virus, would await their return.

After gaining permission to ride with the Elf warrior Moluk, Dirthlyn told him of his desire to inform the Southern Elves of the impending doom overtaking the Elder Races. Having never ridden a horse, he had no idea of how long it would take to return to the Elfin enclave. Moluk, who was totally unaware of its existence, was of no help, but suggested they depart immediately.

The Elves helped each other mount the horse and were soon southbound at a speed which astonished Dirthlyn. He watched as objects appeared on the far horizon, only to fade into the distance mere hours later. As darkness neared. Moluk located a small rill, the water flowing cold.

Ensuring there was plentiful grass for the horse, they stopped for the night. Moluk hobbled his horse, then retrieved the tote lashed to the saddle. Removing a pack of dried food, he bid Dirthlyn eat his fill. Appetites sated, the warm breezes of the mild southern climate caressing their tired bodies, the two Elves were soon fast asleep.

The Elf warriors, having refreshed themselves in the cold stream and taken nourishment ere the sun rose, gained the broad back of Moluk's steed and continued on their journey. They had stopped twice to eat and rest the horse when Dirthlyn stared in wide eyed disbelief as the silhouette of the Elfin communal hall came into view. The horse, carrying two Elves, had traveled the same distance in less than two days that Dirthlyn had traveled in ten. He now knew an Elfin warrior, mounted on such a steed, would be a formidable adversary indeed.

Domigo and Dralon wasted but wee time on eat or drink and slept precious little. They wanted to get back to their lands so they could confer with the other First-born. But as much or even more so, they wanted to sample anew the carnal lust of the New-born Women. Domigo would search out Arena, and her charms, Dralon would content himself with the multiple orifices and opportunities that would surely present themselves. Being both young and proud, he believed he would rise to the occasion.

Domigo and Dralon, out of necessity, dealt with the serious matter first. Meeting with all the First-born that wished to attend, Dralon told them of his discovery and conversation with the stricken Elves. He told long and well, trying to withhold nothing. When his lengthy discourse was over, all knew as much as he.

The First-born, as one, urged Domigo and Dralon to return for the arms at once, taking others to help transport them. Dralon responded that the amount being given is limited, and he and Domigo could well manage. He told the assembled First-born, not totally truthfully, that he and Domigo would leave for the Elf compound as soon as possible. Having dealt with the needs of Mankind, they would now deal with their own.

Wandering off by themselves, they soon came upon two of the First-born. Briarean, a statuesque, dark skinned beauty, lie on her back with her muscular thighs well spread, the tongue of Erigon buried deep within her vagina. Arena lie beside them, gently massaging Britrena's erect nipples with saliva moistened fingers, while playing with her pussy with her other hand. Glancing up from her manipulations, she saw Domigo standing there, watching her, his erection already growing. With an unbridled glow of lust in her eyes, she looked around and decided the involvement of the obviously aroused First-born would be enjoyable.

After rising unto her hands and knees and wantonly licking her lips, she beckoned Domigo to her side. Before engulfing his erect cock, she requested that Dralon stand behind her, to do as he saw fit. She was determined that this time her up-turned assets would be put to good use. Arena wiggled her ass enticingly, then turned her head back Domigo's now throbbing cock. Knowing her partners had been without sex for a while, she quickly wet the head of his cock, then took half of its length into her mouth. Before she had the chance to move her head, she felt Dralon's penis fully penetrate her willing, and wet vagina. With one First-born's cock deeply buried in her pussy, she moved her lips forward, until the other penis was deep in her throat. Scant minutes later, on the verge of orgasm, her body stiffened as both the First-born ejaculated. After a short rest, the First-born spent a pleasant afternoon, experimenting with different sex positions and techniques. Arena was very happy. The Men, while slow, were willing learners. Shortly she would stop teaching and simply enjoy the attention they would give to her ripe body.

Their needs abated, Domigo and Dralon gathered supplies for the trip. They headed east,

moving quickly, hoping to make up some of the time lost to their afternoon of recreation. The First-born found a suitable spot to spend the night just as darkness overtook them. With plentiful fruit and water available nearby, the Men had a satisfying meal. Reliving the day's activities in their minds, they quickly were asleep.

Alone and sad of heart Babaduk slowly made his way

back toward the Realm of the Elves. He had sprung from an ancient line of Shamans, dating from the time of the first Elves.

Normally he was attuned to the earth, often sensing changes in nature before they occurred. Of the doom overtaking the Elder Races he knew, nor felt a thing, having only the dispiriting words of Moluk the warrior to go on. This troubled the Shaman deeply.

Clearing the South lands, Babaduk saw the first dead

Trolls, their bodies strangely unmolested by carnivores. He examined the cadavers but found no sign of violent death. He swiftly came to realize that this must be the doom of the Elders. After leaving the rotting Trolls and returning to his trek, Babaduk now had his first insight into the mysterious malady lying waste to the Elder Races.

Babaduk was aware of a way to gain the information he searched, but it was wrought with grave danger to himself. The Shaman, if he dared, could attempt to gain cosmic consciousness, hoping his released spirit would return to his physical body. The soul, once freed from the limits of the flesh, and not limited in years to a single life span, would have little desire to return to its physical home, preferring to romp with mystical being, thru the endless esoteric universe, for all of time.

The existence of the hallucinogenic drug, that would enable this knowledge to be gained, was not a closely guarded secret. But only the strongest willed, mostly Shamans, attempted its use in other but minute quantities. Babaduk would now try.

Gathering wood of various size, he soon had a small fire burning. Unwilling to wait any longer, lest he change his mind, he knelt by the edge of the fire and sprinkled a handful of the dried herbal drug on it, creating a dense cloud of smoke. Leaning forward on his knees, Babaduk inhaled deeply, totally filling his lungs with the arid smoke. Retreating a safe distance from the fire, Babaduk reclined on his back, his lungs still smoke filled. Holding in the smoke as long as he could, he slowly exhaled, then watched in utter amazement as his spirit seemingly turned into a vapor and drifted upward, to mingle with the smoke rising from his lungs.

Babaduk's spirit reformed from the mist and soared to the outer reaches of the universe in a single beat of his heart. All of Earth's Knowledge was his for the taking, but he wished only to know the cause, and hopefully the cure for the malady decimating the Elder Races. Merging his spirit with the cosmos, Babaduk sensed a shudder ripple throughout the universe, as his will united with the consciousness of all living things. Now the battle for his soul would begin.

Babaduk lie still on his back, but his body trembled and

grew sweaty with his attempt at retrieving his spirit. All thru the long night and then into the light of day, the war between mind and soul raged. Babaduk's body had rid itself of the psychic drug but would remain in a trance like state until mind and spirit could reunite. The now odorous body of Babaduk, lying immobile on the ground, would soon be visited by wolves, or a displaced snow cat.

Wento did a quick count on the remaining wolves, finding seven left of the pack. Filled with ire at being bit, he did not want the wolves simply gone, he wanted them dead. Transferring an orb to his right hand, Wento coldly stared at the hungry pack. Seeing three wolves in the center of the semi-circle crouch to begin their charge, Wento threw the orb he was holding at the fore paws of the center wolf. A brilliant flash of light, nearly blinding Wento, seared the eyes of the wolves. More importantly, the front legs and muzzles of three wolves erupted into flames. Placing the other orb safely behind a nearby rock, Wento retrieved his sword. Striding into the midst of the disoriented wolves he methodically butchered them, save the flaming ones. These he joyfully watched as they burned to death.

Wento looked with pleasure at the carnage around him. No wolf would torment him the rest of this night. And perchance a cat was around, a ready supply of fresh meat outside his cave would surely keep the feline satisfied. He would indeed sleep well the rest of this night.

Sulking in his stone vault, Odyden envisioned his dream falling apart. He had not one Elf or New-born at his disposal. He also needed the oil from the Agali Valley. But above all, he needed Zomba as never before. Odyden wondered how, with all the time and effort he had invested in his scheme, things could go so awry. Then, grasping the fact that brooding about these things will not change them, he swiftly dismissed his doubts.

Sending for Glento and Sutata, two of his dwindling supplies of Trolls, he ordered them to make ready to travel to the south and west. Odyden sent the slave troll Glento into the west, to look for Wento. Odyden cautioned him, "Do not enter the Algali Valley. If you have not found him ere reaching its border, return, for Wento will be within, dead."

Odyden then told Sutata, the mouthy and sometimes irritating Troll, "You will traverse to the south and attempt to locate Zomba. If you find him with both Elf and First-born captives, you will order him, with my authority, to return to me at once." Giving further thought, he continued. "If he does not possess Human captives, order him to attack them at once." Odyden's voice rose with frustration as he further told him, "I will book no excuse or delay. Secure the Humans I desire and bring them to me, or suffer dire consequences!" The two Trolls were dismissed with a gruff, "Now go!"

Dralon and Domigo, miffed at being awakened by the blazing sun, opted to forego their morning repast. Packing up provisions from the night before, they were soon heading eastward. The First-born soon fell into a routine, eating when hungry, sleeping when tired. Using long strong limbs supplied by Thoridon the Creator, they loped nearly effortlessly for hours at a time. The Men covered distances in a day that Elves or Trolls could only dream of. Ergo the Humans were back at the Elfin compound long before the Elves deemed possible.

Dirthlyn and Moluk had arrived at the northern border of the Elf compound shortly after mid-day. Finding suitable grass for the horse, with a dense stand of towering trees nearby, Moluk hobbled his horse. Dirthlyn joined him and together they planned to walk to within hailing distance of the Elves. Having traveled but a short distance, they were spotted by a wandering Elf who duly noted their presence. Cognizant of the fact there was nothing else they could do; they would rest and wait.

Makali, the new Elfin leader, hailed them just before dark. "Dirthlyn, why have you come back? Are you going to take us home?" Implored Mikali. The warrior shook his head, "No, I have dire news which concerns us all," Dirthlyn responded. "Would you rather I tell you privately or address the Elves as a whole?" Giving the matter thought, he replied, "The Elves will assemble here, two hours after the rising of the sun, to hear your message." Dirthlyn, knowing conversation had ended for the night, bid Mikali, "Sleep well."

The morning rays did not find Domigo and Dralon abed. In truth, both had awakened well before daybreak. Having refreshed themselves and taken food, they sat silently in the predawn darkness, awaiting the sun before they hailed the stricken Elves. In due time, the light revealed figures of Elves moving about the compound. Dralon, with a hearty shout and wave of his hand, gained the attention of one. When the Elf came within speaking distance Dralon bid him seek out Makali and inform him that they had returned. Promising to do so, the Elf departed to locate the Elf leader.

Makali had delayed telling the other Elves of his meeting with Dirthlyn and his warrior companion, mostly because he had nothing to tell them. Now, with the rising sun, he gathered the nearest six Elves he could find. "Go and inform all Elves of a meeting of great importance to all. Tell them to amass at the northern border of the compound in one hour," then added, "Nay, I have no inkling as to what will be told for, I am not the speaker."

The Elf sent by Dralon to find the Elf leader quickly located him. "Makali, the visitors on our border wish conversation with you.'" Sounding slightly on edge, the leader of the Elves responded, "I know, we meet in less than an hour." The Elf, sensing he was dismissed, left.

Babaduk had now approached the limit of his physical endurance. He had the energy, perhaps, to attempt one last time the reunion of his mind and spirit. If he failed, his body would become nourishment for roving beasts of prey, his spirit flitting unbridled about the cosmos for all of time. Summoning the last of his mental strength, he willed the wayward soul back, with no apparent success. Babaduk, near to being comatose, was shocked back to alertness as he sensed the nearness of his spirit. Using a surge of renewed hope and the last of his mental determination,

Babaduk managed to unite his mind and soul once again.

While desperately needing sleep, he knew a safe place to sleep was mandatory. Gingerly rising to his feet, he collected his meager belongings lying to the side of last night's burnt out fire. Using a snapped off tree limb, in lieu of a walking staff, Babaduk continued his trek north, physically spent, heavy of heart.

Domigo and Dralon waited, with growing impatience, for the return of the Elf sent as messenger. Noticing mass travel within the compound, Dralon hailed a group of Elves and asked their destination. "We are strongly urged to attend a meeting of Elves, things of great importance will be revealed," he hesitantly told them, having never before viewed the proud First-born.

Dralon's cold hazel eyes followed the Elf to ensure he did not disappear. Then he asked, "Where is this gathering to be held, for Elves and Man are now allies and we wish to attend." The Elf, knowing the Humans could not enter the infected enclave to take a shorter route, respectfully responded with a simple, "The northern border."

Two hours after the sun rose, most of the stricken Elves had gathered just inside the northern border of the compound. A few minutes later, Makali, still looking for stragglers and waiting for Dirthlyn, joined them late. As he started to address the assembled Elves, he noticed that many of them were looking north, in rapt attention. Lifting his eyes, he followed their gaze across the unmarked border. He was stunned at what he saw. A short distance north of the border of the enclave stood Dirthlyn the Elf, along with Domigo and Dralon of the First-born, and an unknown Elfin warrior. Seeing the question on Makali's face, Dirthlyn told him. "His name is Moluk, once a member of the Northern Guards, now a Free-Elf. Perceiving more questions from Makali, Dirthlyn asked him, "Should I not now address the assembled Elves? Afterward, when the other Elves have departed, we may converse at our leisure." Agreeing whole heartily, Makali bid him to proceed.

Dirthlyn gave out a yell, while waving his hands in the air, gaining the attention of most of the Elves. "My name is Dirthlyn and I bear naught but disastrous news," he solemnly began.

"I have no way of easing the pain of what I am to tell you, so I will simply begin. All of the Elder

Races, aye the Elves included, are dying off." Taking a deep breath, he continued. "Pixies, Fairies, and Trolls are disappearing at an accelerated pace but we Elves will still vanish." He then informed them, "Babaduk, the Shaman who traveled with you here, has gone back to the Land of

Elves to help as he may. I am sorry I cannot give you more information or insight, for this is all

I know."

Dirthlyn turned his head slightly to listen to the

question he knew would be asked.

"Cannot Babaduk the Shaman, with his great powers, find a cure?" Before he could respond another youthful Elf chimed in, "I know we are the forsaken, but many of us have long years yet ahead." Dirthlyn thought long before replying, "I have nothing but great esteem for Babaduk, but I also grasp the magnitude of the tragedy that is overwhelming us." He then concluded, with brutal honesty, "I have but scant expectation that one Elf, however learned in the ways of nature, can spare us from the calamity that is threatening to eradicate entire species. Long that I am wrong."

Wento arose early, not from benefit of a peaceful night's sleep, as his aching leg had allowed but little rest. Gaining his feet, he felt his right leg, the one bitten by the wolf, tremble when he put his weight on it. This was not good. Wento knew he had a day of hard travel ere clearing the Agali Valley. This was important to him. Once clear of the valley, the way home was well known, and with free roaming Trolls about, relatively safe.

He set out, ignoring the burning pain in his thigh, but

soon realized there was more to the pain than the minor bite from the wolf. He also understood the need to continue. Leaving the traveled way, he located a small tree with correct limb spacing. Using his sword, he quickly fashioned a crude homemade crutch.

Again, he set off, stumbling forward a step with his healthy leg, then dragging his suddenly infected leg, dripping foul smelling pus, forward to rejoin the other. Wento knows this could not last long.

The First-born Women were a little bit irritated with their male counterparts. With Domigo and Dralon off to the Elfin compound, the Men wished only to discuss the weapons they would return with, neglecting the physical desires of the females. Emelia, Patrena, Celena and Angelena lie in a rough circle, gently touching any egregious zone within reach, even if it was their own. It seemed no one wanted to exert the energy required to reach orgasm. Klitrena stood off to the side, watching, as her desire and nipples both hardened. She was beautiful, as were all the First-born Women, just a little slim. Men found her large breasts firm and tasty, her hips a source of dual delights. They simply did not pay her as much attention as some of the other Women. This bothered her not at all after she found that by using the phallic shaped man-fruit on herself while watching others have sex, she could join them in simultaneous orgasmic release.

Klitrena walked off a way to a stand of trees the First-born Men referred to as man-fruits. The Women called them dilnos. Picking among the fruits, she chose five which were semi ripe and one that was still green and hard. All were large.

She returned to the circle of Women, her eyes now lust filled, and knelt in the center of the four females. Selecting one of the slightly unripe dilnos from the pile by her side, she made a show of slowly peeling back the yellow skin covering the fruit, revealing the moist penis shaped fruit inside. Placing the large dilno at her side, she moved on hands and knees toward Celena.

Reaching her goal, which was between the silky-smooth thighs of Celena, she relaxed and spread out on her stomach. Her hands sought out the tender flesh of Celena's inner thighs. A combination of mild pressure, urging the legs to part, along with a slippery wet tongue trying to gain entrance, soon yielded a wide-open invitation, followed by a low moan from deep in the throat of Celena.

Reaching back, Klitrena picked up the peeled dilno. Placing the first couple of inches of fruit into her mouth, she bit down lightly and withdrew the fruit with a circular motion. Looking at the end of the fruit, she smiled lasciviously as she saw it was ripe enough to seep its sweet nectar. Returning to the spread legs of Celena, she easily separated her vaginal lips with her left hand. Dipping her head again, she assured herself that the first of the four Women was indeed well lubricated. Raising her head, she used her other hand to guide the large dilno toward Celena's eagerly awaiting vagina. Changing her mind as she began to make her first stroke up the lips of Celena's pussy, she returned the fruit to her own mouth. Extending her tongue to run circles around its end, she looked at the frustrated face of Celena and saw the unbridled lust in her eyes.

Not wanting to make her beg, Klitrena lubricated the dilno's tip with a goodly amount of saliva and watched it glisten in the sun, as it slowly ran down the sides of the large penis-like fruit.

Sitting up, she pushed her legs under Celena, so that her ass lies in her lap. Using her hands, she raised Celena's legs high into the air and spread her knees, leaving her wide open and breathing in short gasps. The dilno, slick with saliva from Klitrena's mouth and wielded by her experienced hand, soon breached Celena's vaginal lips. as it began its travel inward. With the

First-born now impaled and softly whimpering for more, Klitrena decided to tease her a bit.

She spent many minutes inserting another inch or so of the dilno into Celena, only to abruptly withdraw all that she had pushed in, plus a little more. After wiggling and spinning the dilno around in place, the leisurely insertion would begin anew, slightly exceeding the depth of the prior probe. Enjoying herself immensely, Klitrena slowly continued her violation of the

First-born's body until Celena, now moaning constantly, had almost nine inches of dilno buried in her trembling body.

Klitrena had to stop. Her own body was on fire, nipples and clitoris erect, crying out for attention. Pulling the dilno halfway out of Celena's vagina, she released it and pushed herself out from under Celena's ass. Looking up, she saw that her hand had already been replaced by Celena's on the dilno, the rhythm fast, and the penetration deep. Glancing about, she noticed the other Women were now highly aroused, nipples standing proud and tall, numerous fingers hidden from view. One First-born, Patrena, had given her a wanton look, and sensually licked her lips when Klitrena had looked her way. Fetching three fruits from the nearby stash, she stood and moved to Patrina's side. Giving one dilno to Patrina, she placed the second fruit by her hip and reserved the last for herself. Peering down at the face of Patrena, she peeled the skin from her dilno and smiled with anticipation as she watched the First-born woman duplicate her actions.

Klitrena's body was flushed, almost shaking with desire, as she lifted her leg to straddle

Patrena. Before having the chance to squat or kneel, Klitrena felt a wet finger easily slip into her well lubricated vagina, stopping at the second knuckle. Klitrena, afraid the sudden contact would end, stood as still as her trembling body would allow, as a second finger joined the first. Moving her hips back slightly awarded her with fingers buried in her pussy up to the palm, but she craved more. Dropping to her knees and elbows she lifted Patrena's legs and locked them behind her arms. With the sound of her own pulse pounding in her ears, she pushed her tongue into the wetness below. After slipping her tongue deep into Patrena's pussy she relaxed a bit, greedily sucking on the erect clit between her lips. Suddenly, she felt an unusually large and juicy tongue penetrate her vagina. Forgetting her own endeavors with Patrena, she pushed her hips back against the hot probing tongue, hoping to gain an extra inch of fulfillment. The oversized tongue, seemingly with a mind of its own, did its best to accommodate her.

Klitrena so enjoyed the private sensations that the wet tongue was causing deep within her loins, that she temporarily ignored the tasty treat lying right beneath her chin. However, that did not last long before she wanted to increase the lust Patrina was feeling. She removed her arms from in front of Patrena's legs and repositioned her hands under the backs of her thighs. Reaching up with moistened fingers, she spread the lips of Patrena's vagina wide, exposing a reddened erect clitoris, engorged with blood. Bending her head down, Klitrena placed her wet lips around the swollen base of the fiery protrusion. Sucking gently to draw the full length into her mouth, she rapidly flicked her tongue across the tip of her clit, stopping on occasion to suck the full length of it into her mouth.

Klitrena knew that Patrena would not last much longer before reaching orgasm and she still had other plans for her. Withdrawing her head slightly, she let saliva run off her tongue onto

Patrena's already wet pussy. The slowly seeping downward stream was halted part way down the crease of Patrena's luscious ass by a slightly embedded finger. Hearing the soft moans of Patrena,

Katrina was well satisfied; she had worked another First-born Woman into a state of carnal lust nearly as great as her own. With this thought in mind, Klitrena decided it was time for some serious sex, enough of this foreplay!

The captive Elves, after the death of Joeluk, had not been overly mistreated. The females suffered still the vulgar comments and gestures of the Trolls. The male Elves were frequently on the receiving end of a blow from the flat of a sword. But the guards, after viewing the terrible violence visited upon the Trolls responsible for the gutting and roasting of the Elf Joeluk, would no longer dare to do them serious physical harm.

Not wishing to use the provisions they had transported

from the north on Elves, the

Trolls permitted a few Elfin Women at a time to forage for food. They were not overly concerned with them running off, as they were unlikely to leave their fellow Elves. They also had nowhere else to go.

The Elfin Women were adept at locating food. Nuts, fruits and edible roots made up the majority of their finds, along with an occasional treat of ripe berries. Bethlyn, while foraging the day before, had come upon a sizable patch of berries. After eating her fill, she quickly filled her container with the ripe fruit and returned to camp to share her wealth with the others. Today, with the help of two other women, she returned, laden with containers, to the berry patch. Picking hastily, they soon filled their bowls with sweet berries from the thorny canes. The Elfin Women were well pleased, their overflowing containers would supply a feast for the Elves, for if not eaten soon, the delicate fruit would be lost to spoilage. When they arrived back at the Troll's camp Bethlyn placed her bowls of berries on the ground. Glancing down at her forearm, she noticed a smallish red spot. Feeling no pain or discomfort, she assumed she had scratched herself on a thorn and gave the matter no further thought.

When Dirthlyn finished telling the Elves of their doom, Mikali, the Elf leader, listened to the Elves talk amongst themselves. Perceiving that the mood is one of dejected acceptance, he sent them back to the communal house. With the Elves departed, Makali hailed the Men and remaining Elf, asking for council. "If you will gather near Dirthlyn, at the border, I will join you, although no closer than loud talking distance." With the council assembled, Makali wasted no time before he asked, "Dirthlyn, who is the mounted Elf traveling with you?" Dirthlyn responded, "As I told you, his name is Moluk, and you met him yesterday, but he was afoot." "Yes, now I recall," remarked Makali, "but I saw no horse." Answering for himself, Moluk told him, "The horse I left behind, in the area where we spent the night." Dirthlyn then added, "I met Moluk many days travel north of here. By horse we returned in less than two." Dralon listened to the conversation fascinated, before asking, "Elf, are you saying that your horse will gladly bear Elves upon its back?" Moluk, a bit perturbed by the question, answered with a terse, "Aye Human, that is what I said." Dralon, irked by the attitude of the Elf, took two steps toward him before he found himself flat on his back, staring up at the blazing mid-morning sun, along with the stern face of Moluk peering down at him. Now, more impressed with the prowess of the Elf than he is miffed, Dralon looked up at his smaller adversary and asked, "Elf, can you teach me how you did that?" Moluk answered, "Aye Human, I could, that and much more." A smile formed on his classic Elfin features as he reached down and helped Dralon to his feet. Reuniting with the others, they made themselves comfortable, for the questions were both varied and many.

Toward twilight, Men and Elves, still deep in conversation, took a break to build a small fire and partake of a hot repast. Refreshed, Dralon continued his questioning of the Elves. "Do you think you can teach us to ride?" Then, before Moluk could respond, he heard. "How can we capture horses of our own?" Dirthlyn, himself a warrior, raised his voice to gain the rapt attention of the First-born. "Moluk shall teach you in the way of horses. You will be told how to capture, break, and ride a horse." Knowing he now had the rapt attention of the First-born, he told them what he wished from them, if they were willing. "I shall teach you how to strengthen both your body and spirit. You will seldom experience hunger. If something moves, you will kill and eat it. But mostly, I will teach you how to visit devastating violence upon your enemies."

Domigo and Dralon looked at one another, neither sure the other was up to this commitment. The Elves, aware of the desire of the Men to discuss matters, and needing to attend to the horse, invited the First-born to spend the night at their camp site. The early departure of

Makali, with a look of abject despair on his face, was not mentioned.

The two Men walked slowly toward the camp of the Elves, talking as they went. "Dralon, should not we gather the edged tools as planned and return to the Land of the First-born?" asked

Domigo. "We could, replied Dralon, but we have little, if any, knowledge of their use." Thinking a chilling thought, he added. "The Trolls came and harvested Elves for unknown reasons. What is keeping them from paying us a visit?" Domigo had to think, but shortly later he agreed that Mankind needed to know how to use weapons.

A moment later, a worried Domigo wanted to know something. "If we stay here and learn from the Elves, the other First-born will lose all contact with us. I do not wish for that to happen." Dralon understood his concern, for he did not wish this either. He needed a plan, and quickly.

Glento and Sutata were not happy. They were aware of the untimely deaths of Trolls, especially following minor mishap or wound. Traveling vast distances west, and south, seemed an unwise idea to them. Regardless, the two Trolls departed the underground lair together, climbing stone steps to the surface. Reaching the top, Glento wished Sutata well before turning to the east where the Algali Valley lie. Although he did not want this task, he knew it was much easier than the one assigned to Sutata. His trip was along a fairly well-defined traveled way with no rivers or gorges to hinder his progress. Things could be worse.

Sutata acknowledged Glento's departure with a nod and a slight wave of his hand. Trolls were not dumb. A bit ungainly, smelly, and ugly yes, but not stupid. Sutata regarded his mission as nearly impossible. He was one lone Troll, being sent to find Zomba and his hunting party, roaming somewhere deep in the south. But Sutata, who knew he had no choice in the matter, turned, like Glento, toward his destination.

Wento was in agony, his infected leg now leaking a putrid smelling yellowish liquid.

Refusing to stop stumbling forward, he could now view thinning trees. The scrub pines and oaks, giving way to the grasses of the steppe. Realizing the end of the valley lie just ahead, Wento took heart. Perhaps Odyden had sent someone to look for and help him. Those thoughts in his head were abruptly replaced by the roar of a snow cat. Wento could not understand this, the meat of the dead wolves should have satisfied the cat. A moment later, his question was answered, when he heard two felines roar in unison.

Domigo and Dralon rejoined the Elves at their camp site, partially obscured by a dense stand of trees. Dirthlyn bid them to make themselves comfortable. Having done so, Dralon asked the Elves, "How long would it require to teach us to ride your horse?" Moluk answered the question. "My mount has never encountered a Human, if he accepts you on his back, the learning will go swiftly." Upon hearing this a plan began to form in Dralon's mind. "Dirthlyn, I gathered from our conversation that it takes long years of training to become a warrior. I question how long it might take us to defend ourselves against an equally armed foe." Dirthlyn gave the matter grave thought before responding. "Dralon, hear well, for I will speak the truth. Never has the earth seen a physical presence such as Mankind." Staring at the First-born hard he continued. "Equally armed and with a minimum of training, none of the Elder Races will be able to stand before you. May you show mercy to the Elves." Stunned, Dralon turned toward Domigo to ensure he had heard correctly. The shocked look on his companion's face confirmed he had.

Returning his gaze to the small fire his hosts had kindled, Dralon sensed another piece of his plan fall into place

Wento realized he was in dire straits, male cats did hunt prey, female cats did. After the dual roar of the cats had died out, Wento heard the imitating lesser roars of the young cats. The offspring of the powerful snow cats were being taught to hunt, with a deathly ill Troll serving as prey.

Glento was aware the grottos of the valley were behind him, the best he could find was a large flat isolated boulder, to shield his back. Setting the container of oil slightly behind the rock, he collapsed with his back to the stone. Lying his sword at his side he opened his tote, and removed the second orb given to him by Odyden. Carefully unwrapping the globe, Wento looked for signs of the felines. Accepting his swiftly approaching death, he was determined to take the snow cats with him.

Glento made good time on his jaunt to the west.

Being springtime, the days were long, and he took advantage, stopping seldom to eat, traveling until near darkness forced him to find shelter for the night. The mountain he called home, to the northeast, soon grew small, then disappeared beyond the horizon. Arising on a typical morning, Glento exited the shallow depression in the ground, where he had spent the night. After relieving himself and drinking from a small stream, he plopped a hunk of dried meat into his gaping mouth and set out again. He had traveled not long before he noted a stench in the air. Following his nose, he left the path he had been on and came upon the body of a dead Troll, which was in an advanced state of decay. Glento knew this was highly unusual. Wolves, a misplaced cat, and numerous smaller carnivores were native to this area. With the odor emulating from the dead Troll, the flesh should have been devoured long ago.

Sutata was also experiencing the doom of the Elder races, but to a greater extent as he journeyed in the more populated lands to the south. He had come across not only dead Trolls but also uneaten Pixies and Fairies. Then this very morn the first dead Elf, with not one bite of a carnivore upon the body. Sutata feared something dreadfully wrong. For the first time since his capture and enslavement, he wished he was back in the bowels of the mountain, locked safety away in a cell made from stone.

Dralon continued staring at the fire, giving himself time to organize his thoughts. Getting to his feet, he peered into the face of Moluk and in a soft voice told him. "The Elder Races days are numbered, your fate sealed. Your fellow Elves have been taken away for reasons unknown, but the same doom is upon them. The age of the Elders is ending, the age of Mankind just beginning, but we are in desperate need of your help." "How so?" asked Moluk. Dralon, his voice rising with hope, explained. "In the morning introduce your steed to us. See if he will abide us astride him." "And if he does?" asks Moluk. "Then I ask that you travel with Domigo, back to the land of the first born. Take what tools you can bear that will most serve our purpose. Most of all, meet the new-born Humans. They and their children are the future of earth. If the Trolls come to capture us, as they did you, and if we lose many defending ourselves, we humans, as a race, may not survive." Dralon motioned Moluk to his side. Long they sat in conversation, glancing up from the fire from time to time to emphasize a point with a finger pointed in the other's direction.

Finally, Dralon stood, towering over Moluk. Looking down upon the shorter Elf, he quietly asked of him "And your decision?" Moluk eyed the taller man, and told him he first had another question. "What do you wish to know?" Dralon asked. Moluk responded, "If Domigo and I travel back to your homeland, what do you and Dirthlyn plan to do. I have no desire to leave him here alone, with none but infected Elves for companionship." Dralon had a ready reply. "I have accepted the promise of Dirthlyn to teach me the ways of a warrior, limited in scope to the time we will have together. While you are gone, I shall eat, sleep and train as a warrior would. Dirthlyn promised me no mercy during my training and I will ask for none. During rare periods of rest and while we eat, he will tell of the forging of weapons, the breaking of horses, and all other things he deems necessary to the survival of humans." Dralon now hoped he had not presumed too much. Moluk took a moment to grasp what had just been told and informed Dralon of his decision, sort of. "We can do little more tonight and we are all growing weary. Tomorrow man and his horse shall meet, and we will go from there." Biding the humans and Dirthlyn peaceful sleep, Moluk retired to his bedroll beside the now dead fire and was soon fast asleep.

Domigo and Dralon talked softly back and forth while lying on the soft soil still holding heat from the fire. Domigo whispered to Dralon that he had one last question. Dralon, sounding tired, simply said, "Ask it." Domigo said he was wondering why they had not discussed who would go back and who would stay here" Dralon, rolling off his back onto an elbow, looked deeply at Domigo and asked him a question. "What would you had said if I suggested you stay here, while I took a trip home, ergo enjoying the erotic delights of Arena and the other First-born women?" "I think there might have been a problem," Domigo answered honestly. "Well Domigo, I did not and there is not, now go to sleep".

Men and Elves, both having conversed long into the night, allowed the morning sun to awaken them. Dralon, arising first, roused the others from their slumber. He then strolled off into the trees to relieve himself. Returning to the camp with an arm load of dried limbs, he quickly lit a fire atop the ashes from last night. Dralon realized he was but a visitor at this camp, he also knew they may never partake of a hot meal together again. Moluk helped with the preparations, and soon both Man and Elf burped with the satisfaction of a hot, hearty breakfast. Moluk, cognizant that the delay had gone on long enough, went to retrieve his horse. He shortly returned, leading the horse by its halter.

Dralon and Domigo stared in abject awe at the noble

animal before them. Towering over the Elf, the horse stood proud, mane flowing long and wild, its color was that of the starless night sky. Dralon noticed the horse's blazing eyes, flared nostrils and heavily muscled flanks and had no greater desire at the moment than to be upon its back. Moluk also saw the horse's flared nostrils, but knew it was because the animal had never before encountered a human. Moluk heard the gentle snort from the horse and let him move forward to stand eye to eye with Dralon. The First- born slowly raised his right hand to stroke the neck of the horse. Sensing no resistance, he gave the horse a healthy slap before reaching up with both hands to scratch the noble steed behind the ears. The horse responded with a questioning look before trying to bury its nose under his armpit.

Viewing the scene from the end of the horse's rein, Moluk knew that the biggest question had been answered. Dralon, unable to wait longer turned, and using Moluk's left shoulder under his left hand, vaulted onto the back of the horse. The mount, to everyone's surprise, simply looked back as Dralon's substantial weight landed on its back. Given the reins and a few basic instructions, Dralon was soon experiencing pleasure he deemed second only to that provided by the First-born Women. Dralon reluctantly returned to Moluk and handed him the reins. Domigo had more need of learning to ride, for he had the horse, Dralon had but his feet. The rest of the morning was spent on riding lessons and finalizing their plans. The four agree that no purpose would be served by Dirthlyn and Dralon staying at the Elfin compound. They will trek to the north, Dralon under the unrelenting tutelage of the Elf warrior, toward the land of the wild horses. Domigo and Moluk will travel as planned to the Land of the Firstborn. When done they will travel northeast and meet up with Dralon.

Dralon, now the acknowledged leader, told them, "You will have but two days with the Humans. You shall teach them what you can during this time of weapons and defense. Inform them I am in need of men to the number of six, if they will volunteer." He then continued, "Either way, tell them we will return for them as soon as we can. This I promise." Not wanting a drawn-out farewell, Dralon busied himself packing the provisions he will take with him. Glancing up from his chore a while later, he saw that the horse had been loaded with the makeshift weapons and provisions, with the Elf Moluk astride its back. With a barely audible good luck and wave of the hand, he watched his fellow First-Born and friend Domigo head to the west, running swiftly to stay astride the horse.

The snow cats, crouching in scrub pines fifty yards

away from Wento, sensed something was wrong. Instead of the bouquet of fresh bleeding meat, the stench of fetid corruption hung in the air. This being a training hunt for the young cats, the Troll would be stalked and slain, but the rancid flesh would be left to putrefy in the summer sun. Using whatever cover availed itself, the cats crept forward.

Wento sat perfectly still, his back against the rock, the only motion coming from his swiveling eyes peering down the path ahead, then off to the sides, watching for any hint of movement. His sword lies across his lap, his right hand lightly held the incendiary device given to him by Odyden. Ignoring, for a brief moment, the agonizing pain racking his body, Wento recalled the burning and butchering of the wolves. The scene, relived in his mind, brought him satisfaction and pleasure, the last of either that he would ever experience.

The snow cats were now neatly within charging distance. Staying side by side, the two deadly felines kept the younger cats behind them, forcing them to observe the strategy of the unfolding hunt. A few more silent paces brought to cats to the edge of the scrawny bushes and trees. Exploding without sound from the underbrush, the snow cats charged directly at Wento. Seeing the blazing eyes of the ferocious cats bearing down upon him, Wento shifted slightly to his right, his back just clearing the rock behind him. This would enable him to throw across his body, at the rapidly closing cats, if he chooses. The lead carnivores, seeing they have been spotted, let loose blood curdling roars, designed by nature to instill motion stopping terror upon its prey. Wento looked at the cats, unimpressed. He had determined that it would be vastly more to his advantage to be eaten by the snow cats than suffer longer with his unbearable pain.

On came the cats, the two young felines snarling, not yet capable of a full-throated roar. As the razor-sharp fangs of the lead cat closed around his windpipe, Wento gave one final smile as he felt more teeth at his legs and groin. Using all of his remaining strength, Wento lifted the orb high above his head, then flung his hand backward into the rock behind him, instantly turning four snow cats, and himself, into a huge ball of fire.

Hours later, all that remains is smothering shards of bone, the melted metal from the Troll's weapons, and an undamaged gallon of lubricating oil.

By noon, Dralon had completed his preparations for the journey, but Dirthlyn informed him there were still things to be done. The Elf told him of the colder climate they were headed toward, also he had grown tired of viewing the naked Man, especially when he awoke in a state of excitement. Previously, he had the Elves of the compound gather a hemp-like plant that could be woven into cloth. He had them fashion a crude set of clothes, including a sturdy leather jacket. For now, and in this heat, he would happily settle for seeing him in the loin cloth they had provided. He had those items boiled in water then heated, nearly to the burning point, above an open fire to sterilize them. Besides, Babaduk had told him that at this time, there was little chance of the infection being spread. Getting Dralon to wear the loin cloth was surprisingly easy. Dirthlyn simply retrieved a sword he had found and hid during his first trip to the compound. Given a sword to wear, Dralon quickly realized the need to have something to hang it on.

Dirthlyn signaled for Dralon to follow and traveled to the stand of trees where they had spent their first night. Selecting a large sapling that he deemed suitable, he bid Dralon try his sword. A light swipe at the base of the tree separated it from its roots with ease. Returning to their camp, Dirthlyn picked up a draw knife not taken by Moluk. Deftly wielding the knife, he expertly fashioned the young tree into the shape of a long bow, sized to height of the Human. Asking supplies of the Elves, Dirthlyn bound the bow in strips of animal hide and glue. Biding Dralon follow he moved south, toward the shores of the southern sea, talking as he went. "Dralon." he started, "we will travel north many weeks. I will impart to you what I know of weapons and fighting. If you but put half your desire and energy into what I teach you, by the time this trek ends, you will be my better on the field of battle. Dirthlyn, bear in mind that none, save perhaps a superbly armed Troll, can survive combat with me. My wish is to instill in you more, mostly loyalty and mercy. For once mounted on a horse, you will become the most dangerous person on earth." Dralon digested this information with a sense of disbelief before he told Dirthlyn, "My friend, I will do my best to earn your pride." Continuing to the shore of the sea, Dirthlyn led him to an area covered with reeds. He bent and snapped off an arm's length of reed. Dirthlyn explained that the stems were perfectly straight and not effected by heat or moisture. Dirthlyn ordered him to collect a large armload of reeds, for he knew of nowhere else to gather them, other than by the shores of a small lake well to the north. Dirthlyn had not known the reeds grew here but his hunch had been correct. Walking along the shore of the sea, Dirthlyn shortly came upon an area where many shore birds had amassed to breed and rear their young. With the feathers deep underfoot, Dirthlyn quickly filled a virus free bag supplied by the Elves. Carrying their booty, the two made their way back to camp, conversing as they went. Dralon knew there would be no departure today. Man and Elf spent the afternoon in camp, Dralon learning to feather and mold points from metal, or by necessity, sharply chipped stone. He learned of the vine that would be used to string his mighty bow, also how it keeps it silent. A sheath was made to hold the blade of a small knife given by the Elves. Dralon, proudly strapped it to the outside of his thigh, just above his knee, within easy reach. He had no plan to remove it anytime soon. Breaking for the last hot meal they will enjoy for a while, Dirthlyn informed Dralon that he must still make a quiver to hold his arrows. Nodding his head in accent, Dralon finished his repast. He then followed the instructions from Dirthlyn and completed his arrow holder by the light of the fire he built. Dirthlyn looked at Dralon and then the weapons. He realized that all arrows are not feathered and armed. The bow still needs time to cure before it is flexed, but he also knows there is little more to be accomplished by remaining here. Striding to stand beside the kneeling Dralon, still intent on fetching more arrows, he told him simply, "Make ready, for on the morrow we depart for the north." Dralon, full of excitement, cannot sleep and prepares arrows long into the night.

Domigo and Moluk moved eastward throughout the afternoon, Moluk talking, the First-born listening. The Elf spoke of many things but mostly of weapons and self-defense, as Dralon wanted. Moluk explained that the axes, hatches and other sharp-edged tools that they had were serious arms, but with minor modifications, they could become deadly weapons. The Elf had much information to give the Human, he hoped he would remember some of it.

The Man and Elf fell into a routine, rise early and eat, travel hard for about five hours, then start looking for suitable grazing and water for the horse. Taking their midday meal, they rested while the horse fed. Then they would locomote eastward till the falling sun forced them to encamp for the night. Domingo chose not to ride the horse. He knew the horse could not bear both Man and Elf and still carry the arms. If he rode the Elf walked, and Domingo knew the shorter stride of the Elf would add time to their excursion. He would walk.

Sutata felt lost, adrift in a dream in which he had no control. Go south, he was ordered, and locate Zomba. The south lands were a vast area and he had never traversed them. Sutata had little expectations of finding the Troll hunting party but he also knew that he could not return without them. He was truly lost Sutata, thinking of his best chance to succeed, decided to head due south for at least a week. He would then travel southwest for one day, then turn to a southeast heading the following day. He would travel only during sunlit hours. If he missed espying

Zomba, passing him while en route the south, he would be doomed. Proceeding south, Sutata wishes he had another Troll or two accompanying him. With the start of the demise of the Elder races, the numbers of carnivores had dramatically increased. An extra sword or two would have been comforting.

Sutata held true to his plan. Meeting no difficulties worse than boredom and biting summer insects, he lodged his first week of his jaunt to the south. The next morning, he bore to the south by west and soon thereafter found the malodorous body of a decaying Troll. Staring down at the Troll's body, a realization comes to him. Something so foul is killing off the Elder Races that even beasts of prey refuse to eat the corrupt flesh. Yearning deeply to be almost anywhere else but here, Sutata continued on to the southwest.

Sutata completed the first day on his southwest heading. He had increased his attention, scanning the lands to the east and west of his travel for movement but saw nothing moving on the now hill less terrain, Troll or otherwise. Late one afternoon Sutata was going about setting up camp for the night when he happened to jump a rabbit. Envisioning fresh meat, he began to salivate as he hurled his knife at the nearby rabbit. Plopping a hunk of dried meat into his mouth, he finished setting camp for the night. Sutata arose and broke camp before daybreak. He would depart southeast come dawn, allowing him the longest possible time to travel in the light of day, while constantly scanning the landscape for any sign of Zomba.

Sutata became locked into a rut. Rise early, rest briefly at mid-day, continue until dusk, all the while searching for Lord Zomba and his elusive hunting party. The next day he would vary the routine by moving southeast instead of southwest. Quickly the days merged into weeks and still he could find no sign of Zomba.

Following the discovery of the foul carcass of the Troll, Glento traveled fast, wanting distance between himself and the unknown malady that was eating away members of the Elder-Races. Not willing to slow and look for shelter in the late afternoon, as was his want, he had to settle for a small grotto, formed beneath the roots of a huge tree, partially felled by heavy wind. With full darkness near upon him, exhausted and hungry, Glento crawled into the small cave. Loosening his leather jacket, he abruptly fell into a troubled sleep.

Glento awoke with a start, sensing something was wrong, then froze still as death as he recognized the sound that had awaked him. It was the high-pitched hiss of a day viper, a venomous, heat loving snake that hunted only during the warmth of day. He also knew he had felt motion about his ankles. There was more than one snake sharing the makeshift grotto with him. Daring no movement, other than shallow breaths, Glento lie perfectly still as damp slithering forms began to converge atop his body. A small involuntary shiver convulsed his body as he took in the fact that he had chosen to spend the night in a den of snakes.

Babaduk, in dire need of rest, finally came upon a site that looked safe. A huge treat was the nearby small stream, flowing gently, and deep enough to bathe in. Babaduk soaked long, trying to refresh his body. When hunger urged him from the water, he dressed and went in search of food. Again, being lucky, he found, not far away, berries and a nut tree, both yielding tasty ripe fruit. Babaduk returned to the small outcrop of rock he had first noticed, with three small boulders in front. Drawing his sword, he eased himself between the sun-warmed boulders and the rock face. Placing his weapon by his side, he fell asleep while pondering how much to tell the First-born, providing he lived long enough to meet them.

Glento experienced a fear greater than he had ever known, as he felt the vipers wriggling upon and around his body, seeking an opening or looseness in his clothing, to gain the warm flesh beneath. He felt his upper arms slowly being inched away from his body, as the snakes, fighting and hissing each other, struggled for prime position in his armpits. Glento ordered himself to remain calm, thinking this nightmare could not get worse, then gave a silent scream as he felt the futile attempt of a snake attempting to worm its way into the heat of his body.

Still they came, covering his torso, then his legs, until the vipers had engulfed his body. Two snakes fought for the prime locale just beneath his nose, where his exhaled breath would gently caress them. Finally, the den of snakes quieted down, seemingly content on enjoying their unexpected source of warmth. Glento, although terrified, is cognizant of one simple truth; if he moves, he dies.

Hours later Glento still lie as if dead, but his body was racked with pain. Some parts were totally numb, waiting to explode in excruciating agony with the return of blood circulation. His back, having been held rigid since his ordeal began, felt like someone had inserted a molten metal rod into the length of his spine.

Glento had but one hope now. He simply wished to view the rising sun and perhaps with its accompanying warmth the departure of the vipers engulfing his tormented body.

Before dawn Sutata woke to the slight odor of smoke in the air. The approaching dawn gave no hint as to its source. Setting out again, Sutata now forgot about east and west, driving himself due south. After two days, he realized that unless he missed seeing Zomba on his way south, he must be close, for he could now see the gleaming surface of the Great Southern Sea, reflected off low hanging clouds. Sutata knew his trek was at its turning point, find Zomba and deliver Odyden's orders, or fail and await abhorrent punishment.

Sutata's search came to an abrupt halt around midday.

Seeking a place to rest, he espied motion to the south. Forgoing food or rest he hurriedly made for the area where he had detected movement. As he grew nearer, he could make out bunched forms which soon became the outline of individual Elves. Shortly later, he saw his first live Troll since heading south. He had found Zomba's hunting party.

Sutata warily approached the Troll camp, noticing the apparent Elf captives, guarded by two bored looking Trolls. Startled by Sutata's sudden appearance, the Trolls leapt to their feet, drawing swords, before recognizing him as a fellow slave of Odyden. Dropping their swords, one of the Trolls went to locate Zomba and inform him of the new arrival. In a short time, Zomba appeared in the distance and walked to the side of Sutata. Wasting no time on pleasantries, he abruptly asked, "Troll, where is the rest of your party and why are you here?" Sutata, a little put off by his tone of voice, replied, "My name is Sutata, sent by our Master Odyden, with orders for

Zomba, slave of the Evil Lord, to be obeyed without question." Cognizant that this was not the proper way to treat an emissary of Odyden, he tried anew. "Sutata, how many Trolls are in your party," he calmly asked? "I came alone," was the simple response. Unsuccessfully attempting to hide his disappointment, Zomba continued, "And what is your message from Odyden?" Sutata, not having food nor rest since before sunup, asked Zomba if they could sit, perhaps with a\ bit of food and drink before them, while he relayed Odyden's orders. Zomba readily agreed to this, sending two guards back to the main Troll camp to make the preparations.

Dirthlyn woke before the sun had risen, walked to where Dralon lie and nudged him awake with his foot. After a hasty breakfast, the two set off for the north. Dralon was heavily loaded with provisions for the trip, plus clothes he needed not yet wear and arrows not yet ready to fire. Stopping briefly for a swallow of water, Dirthlyn demonstrated a sword sweep he wished Dralon to learn. The remainder of the day, baring only a short break at midday, Dralon practiced, ten sweeps with the right hand, ten with the left. This continued until they stopped for the night. Dralon, his overused arm muscles aching with pain, dropped his sword heavily to the ground and gained a sharp reprimand from Dirthlyn, "In times of trouble that sword is your best friend. Do not treat it so lightly." Dralon, tired to the bone, hoped his nod of agreement was sufficient.

The ensuing days brought pain to new areas of Dralon's body as the Elf warrior worked on both his muscles and endurance. One day leg work, the next arms, all the while learning various sword fighting techniques. Other days were spent just running, ahead, to the side, to the rear, Dirthlyn did not care, as long as he kept Dralon moving.

Dralon was beginning to feel the results of his training. The burn in his muscles were slowly giving way to a pleasant feeling of tautness and unused power. The Elf warrior was amazed at the progress shown by the First-born. Things that had taken him months to master, Dralon had learned in a day or two. His body, already in prime condition, now gently rippled with muscle when he moved. Dirthlyn was growing proud of Dralon, but also fearful, for he realized that with a bit more training, should they ever fight, he would come up second best.

Having traveled this way before, Domigo knew he and Moluk were making good time.

By his reckoning, they should arrive back at the Land of

Men by tomorrow afternoon. Moluk was preaching to him about something, probably weapons or such, but his mind was far away, buried deep between the lascivious thighs of Arena and the other libidinous First-born Women. In truth, Domigo was hoping to get the Elf out of his clothes and into a woman or two. Domigo figured that if he was enjoying the delights of the female's bodies, perhaps their trek to the lands where horses roamed could be delayed by a day or two.

By the time they stopped for the night, Domigo realized he had been overly optimistic about their time of arrival. They would not reach the outer reaches of Man's realm until almost dark. He and Moluk agreed they would decide by noon tomorrow whether they wished to arrive well after the sun had set. For now, they would eat and sleep.

Zomba and Sutata walked slowly to the main camp, where food and drink awaited. The

Troll Lord bid Sutata sit and partake of anything before him. Giving him some time to eat, he could wait no longer and asked, "What, exactly are my orders?" Sutata swallowed his mouthful of food and answered, "If I found you with both Elf and Human captives, I was to order your immediate return. Unless you have Human prisoners elsewhere, you are ordered to capture them now, today." Zomba was distressed by this, for he was still waiting for a completely dark night to implement his plan for capturing the First-born. Sutata then concluded by ordering, "Harvest the Humans tonight, for come dawn we depart for the north. Odyden said he would accept no excuse or delay, and I have no desire to experience the wrath of the Master of Evil."

Zomba began to argue with Sutata, telling him briefly of his plan, inching closer to poke him in the chest while making a point. Sutata had half expected something like this to happen. Brushing Zomba's hand away, Sutata rose and stared into the eyes of the taller Troll.

With his voice growing ominously low, he growled at the Troll Lord, "Zomba, hear this and well,

I did not come this far to consult with you. I speak with the authority and full backing of our Lord Odyden. Do not make me inform him that you would not follow his orders. Make your raiding party ready, for tonight we hunt!"

Dirthlyn awoke before dawn and made ready a hearty breakfast for Dralon and himself.

He was of high spirit today, for he planned on letting Dralon draw back his great bow for the first time. With their meal over Dirthlyn took the First-born in search of tree limbs. "But I thought the arrows were ready," protested Dralon. "Not so," replied the Elf, "you must still supply a notch for the string." After gathering a dozen or so tree limbs of the correct diameter, they returned to camp. Dirthlyn then showed Dralon how to cut the limbs into proper lengths. A notch was cut in one end, the other tapered with the edge of a well whetted knife, then was inserted and glued into the arrow shaft. With a good number of arrows ready Dirthlyn departed, returning shortly with Dralon's bow. Using his own bow in demonstration, he showed Dralon how to string the weapon. Taking the bow from him he attempted, and failed, to draw it more than halfway. Returning it to Dralon he watched in amazement as the mighty First-Born easily drew the great bow full.

Dirthlyn sent Dralon to fetch the hide of the rabbit they had eaten for breakfast. He had him hang it from a branch of a nearby tree. Using his bow, he showed Dralon how to notch his arrow, draw, and aim at the skin being used as the target. Dirthlyn stared incredulity as Dralon's second arrow cleanly passed thru the animal skin, quickly followed by a third and fourth. Calling a halt, he moved Dralon further away from the target, but the results were the same.

Feeling a wave of astonishment overtaking him, Dirthlyn had one more thing he needed to know. Walking with Dralon, he located a large, old, gnarly oak tree, well out of the range of the Elfin bow he carried. Pointing at the tree, he bid Dralon launch an arrow at its center. Seeing the shaft hit home, Dirthlyn headed for the oak tree, followed closely by Dralon. The Elf warrior looked keenly at the arrow, its metal point totally embedded in the trunk of the tough oak tree, then up at Dralon, who did not grasp the implications.

Still looking at Dralon, now in bewilderment, he solemnly told him, "You are in possession of the most powerful weapon on earth. At a distance, none may stand before you. May you use your bow well." Shocked into silence, Dralon gathered his spent arrows and returned to camp. He knew the rest of the day would be long, his sleep troubled.

Glento was nearing the end of his physical endurance. If he did not soon move his body, it would begin to tremble in pain. The body parts previously numb were now burning in agony.

The Troll, knowing he could not endure any more pain, was deciding whether to sit up or simply roll to his side, when he noticed the first faint rays of dawn piercing the eastern sky. Glento knew that full sun was still hours away, but having endured this long, he would attempt to wait further.

His greatest hope was a bright, sunny day, with not a cloud in the sky.

Glento started by trying to last one more minute before moving. It painfully evolved into the first hour. The second hour brought almost unbearable pain before it delivered a slim bit of hope, for the sun, now well above the horizon, began to spread its warmth. Peering cautiously about, Glento saw movement from the snakes furthest away from him. Understanding engulfed him like a tidal wave. The heat from his body was less than the sun's rays. The snakes were following the heat and leaving his body. He believed, for the first time since awakened in this miserable grotto, that he might live to leave it.

Zomba, comprehending the consequences of disobeying an order from Odyden, mumbled his assent to Sutata. Then in a louder voice, he ordered his aide to locate Tyreno and Hanto, his commanders, and bring them to him. They must finalize their plans for capturing Humans because, as Sutata had said, "tonight we hunt."

Zomba, conferring with his two commanders, decided to stick with their prior plan, but with one minor exception. Sutata seemed to want to hunt Humans. Zomba would ensure that he got his wish. The plan called for Zomba to man the center of the hunting party with a commander on each flank. Each of the commanders would have one guard with them, Zomba two, since Sutata would be joining him in the middle of the action.

Tyreno had an idea for the attack on the Humans. He suggested the three Trolls assigned to the commanders and Zomba gather up their stiff leather bedding hides before the attack. When the Humans were sighted, the

Trolls would hold the hides high over their heads, hopefully giving the appearance of a large winged beast. Zomba and the commanders would run, screaming in fright, in front of the howling monsters, as if being pursued. Tyreno explained that Man had never viewed a Troll. What he would see was a large beast fleeing in terror from an even larger winged monster. Mankind, if possessed of any intelligence, would head the other way, being driven by the Trolls into the waiting arms of the guards. Zomba looked questioningly at Hanto and received a hardy nod of approval to Tyreno's plan.

Looking back at Tyreno he said, "Commander, your plan has many merits and merges well with mine, we will use it." He then continued, "The moon tonight will rise well before midnight. We must attack shortly after full darkness. Commanders, make your guards ready, for the time to hunt Humans is upon us."

Domigo and Moluk thought they had a minor decision to make. Travel hard and still arrive at the First-born's compound well after dark, or lay up late in the afternoon as usual and greet the humans in the morning.

The good-natured bickering began shortly after the morning repast. Domigo urged them to push forward with all due haste. Moluk countered with, "The horse has had a hard trip and needs frequent rest." By the time the midday meal was over Elf and Man were in agreement. They would not stop in the late afternoon as they normally would but precede on toward the area that the First-born frequented. If perchance a Human was spotted before dark, they would send the messenger ahead with news of their arrival.

Moluk, although heavily armed, did not wish to come unexpectedly into the midst of Humans in the dark of night, mounted on a creature they had never seen before. Nay, for he had viewed both their strength and temperament. If Man is not found ere dark, the reunion will await the dawn.

They traveled throughout the afternoon, Moluk speaking still of manly things, Domigo still thinking of women's parts. Their usual stopping time came and went, Man and Elf continuing to move east. Domigo knew they were within the Lands of Man, but they saw no signs of Human life. Moluk, mounted on the horse, looked over at Domigo and informed him, "We need to quickly find a grazing area for the horse before total darkness sets in."

Domigo, trying not to show the disappointment he felt, tersely agreed.

Domigo had approached to help with the unburdening of the horse, when Moluk though he heard distant sound. Ordering silence from the Human, Moluk cupped a hand around his ear to listen. Gazing at Domigo he knew the First-born had also heard the sound, but by the questioning look on his face, did not recognize it. Moluk felt the hairs on his neck stand on end and his blood chill, for he did know the source of the terrifying howls being carried on the gentle southern winds.

Zomba realized that he had no time to waste. For the plan to work, the Trolls need to be south of the Humans before sunset. They will have to travel well east or west to avoid detection and it now being midafternoon, the Troll Lord was not sure if he had the time. Yelling for his aide, he ordered him to tell the commanders to gather the guards and meet back here. He also told the

Trolls staying behind to break out the clothing that the Elves had made for the First-born. Zomba had a hard-enough time keeping the Troll's hands off the Elves. He was not looking forward to the upcoming grope fest that was bound to occur when the Trolls captured the wanton Human females. Zomba's commanders arrived shortly, followed closely by the remainder of the Troll hunting party.

With his party amassed, Zomba gave his final instructions. The two commanders, along with three guard bearing animal hides, would travel south along the eastern edge of the Human's range. The Troll Lord would move down the western side with the rest of the Trolls. One hour\ before sunset both groups would turn toward the other. "We must rejoin and be ready to start our plan when full darkness comes," Zomba told them, "now go, and good hunting."

Glento's hopes were rising nearly as quickly as the

morning sun. He stared in disbelief as the vipers slithered off his body, following the warmer rays of the sun. Relief washed over him when he saw the snakes crawling out from within his clothing. Seeing no snakes about his feet, he allowed himself a slight wiggle of the toes, then permitted a huge smile to crease the course features of his ugly face. Checking his hands, he repeated the procedure, relishing the burning tingle of returning blood flow. Glento next gingerly flexed his elbows, gaining sensation to his arms. About to lift his knees, he once more froze, as he sensed, rather than felt, movement between his legs. With no feeling below the waist, except for his feet, he gently raised his head and peered down at his groin area. At first, he saw nothing, but looking intently, he noticed slight movement under his clothing.

Glento cursed his luck, for he knew that if this one viper bit him, he would be just as dead as if bitten by fifty. Unable to turn away from the morbid sight, he watched in horror as the snake moved about under his clothing, searching for a way out. Glento was forced to put his head back down as a new wave of pain radiated outward from his spine. Mouthing a silent moan, he again lifted his head and gazed downward. The sight brought a surge of immeasurable relief, for a snake's head, then its lengthy body, was slowly emerging from the clothing at the Troll's waist.

Waiting until the snake had cleared his body and fully departed the grotto, he let out an audible moan and rolled onto his side. Rising to one elbow, he let the pain flow from his body. A few minutes later he managed to sit up, then finally gain his feet. The Troll gathered up his few processions and left the accursed cave. He walked to the west but stopped before going very far.

Placing his gear on the ground, he began collecting small twigs and limbs, suitably for kindling.

Arms full, he returned to the snake's den.

Glento quickly had a small fire burning in the small cave. He now gathered larger limbs and small logs to feed the blaze. When the tree root itself burst into flames, he added a few more\ large logs to the inferno. Glento did not know where the den of snakes would spend the night, but it would not be here.

Zomba pushed his Trolls hard to the south. He remained in sight but well east of the other group, alert for any signs of the First-born. He knew there was no need to go further west than necessary. Hanto, on the eastern flank, is doing the same. With any luck, the Trolls would have the Humans encircled to the south ere the sun set.

The Troll Lord finally saw the form of a Human, far to the east, but it soon passed from sight. Checking the sun, he knew it was time to turn and meet up with the others.

Signaling to his guards, he waited for them to join him before they all headed due east. Zomba's good fortune continued, for within twenty minutes of walking he saw his two commanders and the other Trolls moving toward him thru the lush grasses and trees of the Land of Man. The Troll Lord and his hunting party now moved to the north, closing in on the defenseless First-born.

Glento walked away from the blazing grotto, thinking that perhaps the tunnels of the snake den led to a grotesque nursery. This possibility momentarily brightened his mood. He had not slept since the night before and hunger was gnawing at his belly. He needed to eat and sleep.

Collecting his gear, he once again headed west, simply seeking a safe place to rest.

Having traveled for less than an hour, he found his spot of safety. The swift running stream ran just yards from the entrance to the solid rock cave. A flat slab of rock stretched between the mouth of the cave and edge of water. Glento, after ensuring there was no hidden entry to his lair, left his gear and again went to gather kindling. He returned, stacked his tinder into a cone shape, then went to collect three larger arm loads of wood.

Glento was growing weary but was determined to rest easy. He made one last short trip, coming back with a tree limb with leaves still attached. Lying the branch aside, Glento struck his fire. Now, with the fire well established, he went fishing. After finding the narrowest part of the stream Glento dropped his hand into the water, palm up. He had learned, long ago, that it was a simple matter to raise his hand quickly and flip a fish onto rocks or sand. In a short time, he had more than he could eat in one sitting. Not wanting to gut the fish here, he picked up his catch and retreated to the edge of his fire. The Troll added more wood to the fire, then cleaned his fish, throwing the offal into the blaze. He then picked up the forked tree limb he had cut and stripped it of leaves. He used the knife he had gutted the fish with to sharpen the ends of the forks. After cutting the other end to length, he impaled the fish on the wooden prongs. The Troll arranged the shaft of the fork across a log, holding it in place with another, so the fish would slowly roast over the fire. Glento sat back against the warm rock face of the cave. He could have eaten the fish raw and whole, but he was treating himself. He had earned it.

Zomba led the hunting party northward, toward the First-born. The closer he could get without the lumbering Trolls having to run the better, for the beasts had neither great speed nor endurance when running flat out. The Troll Lord espied the Humans just before the sun set into the west and signaled his party to stop. Although too far to determine for sure, Zomba assumed by the figure's fluid motion that he was viewing one of the First-born Woman.

Crouching low in the grass as he moved forward, Zomba waved for the other Trolls to follow him. With no hint of interest from the Humans, the Troll Lord drew ever nearer, fervently hoping to locate more than a single New-born wench before total darkness set in.

Marena tired of Redali's halfhearted attention to her body, had gotten up and gone for a walk. Strolling south, she stopped at a fruit tree and ate her fill. Refreshed, she planned on returning to Redali and demanding his uninterrupted carnal prowess, unaware that Zomba and his Troll hunting party followed close behind.

Zomba did not believe his good fortune. Trailing but one Human, he had located their current encampment. As he peered carefully about Zomba quickly realized that the Humans had neither guards nor sentries. He saw them lolling about, in small groups, talking, eating fruit, and to his utter amazement, seemingly each other, though he saw no sign of blood. Zomba dropped back to talk to his commanders. He ordered them to deploy a bit east and west of him and howl in a subdued voice, as if still far away. Zomba knew that if the First-born fled to the four points of the compass upon hearing the howling of Trolls, he would not have a chance of capturing the required number. The Troll Lord needed the Humans to gather together in fear, then flee away from the wailing beast into the Troll's trap.

Zomba looked on in dismay as the faint howls carried across the coastal plains. The

Humans were not acting as expected, some paused in their eating, others not stopping whatever they were doing to one another. Zomba dropped back and ordered his Trolls to howl louder. This got the attention of the First-born, for all activities instantly came to a halt. The Humans had no idea of what was coming, but they knew it was growing nearer. The Troll Lord knew he could ill afford to give the First-born time to devise a plan. He ordered his "monsters" to begin pursuing the "beasts", baying and screaming as loud as possible.

The Humans did not know what bore down on them, nor did they have the desire to wait and greet it. After seeing something large and ugly, fleeing in fear from a howling creature, the

First-born ran pell-mell, spreading across the dark landscape.

"Moluk, what was that?" demanded Domigo. The

Elf, still astride his horse, told him, "That is the sound of Trolls openly hunting their prey. I think your fellow First-Born are their target." "Then we must rush to aid them," urged Domigo. "No," answered Moluk, half in anger. "You listened to nary a word I said concerning arms and fighting. You would only be a hindrance to me. Stay, if I live, I will return for you." With that, the Elfin warrior thundered off, leaving Domigo dumbfounded. He had no idea of the real speed the mighty steed was capable of.

Moluk rode hard, simply heading toward the sound of the nearest howls. The Trolls were helping him immensely. Had they remained silent and stalked the Humans, he would be hard pressed to locate them in the dark. Moluk had closed to within fifty yards of the Trolls before he saw their silhouette in the night sky. Peering into the darkness ahead of the hunters, he saw the outline of six or so Humans, fleeing mindlessly from the shrieking Trolls.

Moluk stopped his horse about fifty feet from where the engrossed Trolls, pursuing the

First-Born should cross in front of him. The Elf warrior notched an arrow and sat motionless in the night, waiting for the Trolls to appear. Within moments, the screaming lead Troll lie quietly in the grass, the shaft of an Elfin arrow protruding from his neck. The following Troll, seeing his companion die in front of him, ceased howling and dropped the thick leather hide, looking for the archer. This action saved his life, as Moluk's second arrow embedded itself deeply into the thick animal skin. After the third shot Moluk decided he would waste no more arrows on an animal hide.

Hanto, the Troll commander, searched the direction whence the arrows had come and saw Moluk astride his horse, his bow undrawn. Roaring in rage, the Troll hurled his knife at the

Elf, then ducked back behind his hide, using it as a shield. Moluk looked down, more in annoyance than pain at the dagger lying below his feet. In the dark he had not seen the Troll launch his knife. Luckily the blade had only nicked his forearm, causing no real harm. Changing his mind, he wasted two more arrows before turning his horse toward the sound of another howling Troll. Hanto, realizing he had little chance of capturing Humans by himself and unsure if the Elf warrior had companions, rose and followed the mounted Elf as best he could. Perhaps he could gain a measure of revenge.

Domigo could not stay and wait. Running after the horse, he was within sight of the Elf when Moluk broke off his attack and headed west. Domigo was standing still, deciding what to do next, when he got his first distinct look at a Troll. The First-born slowly crouched down in the tall grass. He had no desire to be seen by the heinous form quickly emerging from the vegetation.

He watched as the Troll gathered something under his arm, turned, and ran in the direction the

Elf had taken. Domigo took a deep breath, belatedly wishing he had paid more attention to

Moluk's talks concerning arms, for there was a large supply of sharp tools nearby which could be used as weapons.

Moluk had told him he believed the Trolls were hunting Humans. So, Domigo reasoned, the First-Born had to be somewhere ahead, hiding in the darkness, for they made no sound.

Gaining his feet, he headed in the direction he hoped the Humans had taken. At a full run his long legs almost carried him past the group of First-Born who were only a hundred yards or so in front of the hunters. Umiki, the elder male in group, had ordered the others to stay close together and remain silent when the howling of the Trolls had stopped. He did not know what had happened to quiet the Trolls, but he sensed that their lot had changed. Domigo would have bypassed them if not for the faint reflections of a dim star off their amassed naked bodies, gleaming with sweat.

Umiki recognized Domigo and called out softly to him. Walking over to the Humans.

Domigo urged them to their feet. "What were those things pursuing us?" one of the Men blurted out.

"I was told, by Moluk the Elf warrior, that they are called Trolls. He believes they wish to capture us, he knows not why," answered Domigo. "But why was one of the Trolls so much larger than the other?" another wanted to know. Domigo glared at him and demanded, "What other Troll? I saw but one and he followed the Elf to the west." The First-Born again explained that they had been chased by the things called Trolls. They had seen two, but there well could have been more hiding in the night. Domigo, beginning to fathom the situation, called Umiki to his side and together they walked toward the spot where the Troll was last seen. Reaching their goal, both stared at the ferocious looking form lying in the tall grass, a feathered shaft protruding from its throat. The two First-Born looked at one another, thinking the same thought. If this was the smaller beast, they were indeed in dire straits.

Moluk closed in on the second group of hunters, but changed his mind before firing an arrow. He would attack the last hunters in the west, while his steed still had stamina. Glancing over his shoulder, he saw a familiar glow emulating from just below the horizon. The moon was ready to rise. This put the Elf warrior at a disadvantage. Before, he could locate the Trolls by their howling, now a surprise attack was unlikely.

The Elf warrior's luck held, for within minutes, with little light yet in the night sky, he located the Trolls. They were behind the Humans, baying and screaming, but it seemed that they were not really trying to catch them. It looked as if they were attempting to turn them to the northeast. Moluk did not know why, but if he survived the battle he intended to find out.

Moluk edged forward a bit, trusting the night would hide him for a few more minutes. He could now clearly see the Trolls, howling and screaming, but there were only two. The baying of Tyreno, the Troll commander, turned into a roar of pain as he glared at the feathered shaft embedded in his thigh. Before the Troll could drop the leather hide, he held above his head, a second arrow found space between his ribs. Tyreno roared as he felt the arrow penetrate deep into his chest. Unwilling to give the second beast a chance to pick up the animal skin to use as a shield,

Moluk launched three arrows in quick succession, then smiled briefly when he saw the feather of three shafts protruding from the torso of the Troll. The hunting party for these two was over. The Elfin warrior had turned them into the hunted.

Moluk was feeling good about things. He had faced four Trolls and three now lie dead or dying. More importantly, not one First-born had been captured. Moluk greatly desired to investigate the north, but realized there were Humans who needed his help. Gathering up the Trolls weapons, he turned his horse to the east and went after the remaining Trolls, unaware of the additional guards waiting to receive the captured Humans.

Domigo was at a loss until he remembered Moluk telling him to stay put. He also realized that weapons awaited them. Between them, the First-born should be able to figure out how to inflict damage on a foe. Domigo reasoned that any plan of action is preferable to standing here looking at one another.

Domigo led the other First-born back to where he and Moluk had unloaded the horse. Umiki and the other males examined the tools Domigo had returned with, some asking questions as to their use. Domigo had actually retained some of what Moluk had told him about arms, so the Humans listened to what he said.

Domigo had no idea if or when the Elf might return, but he recalled Moluk telling him of guarding the Northern Elfin Enclave. The Elves had guards patrolling the perimeter of the compound, not only to keep the diseased Elves in, but also to prevent anyone or thing from approaching undetected. Domigo reasoned this would be a good time for sentries and asked for two volunteers. Umiki left the group immediately and stepped forward. No one else moved. Finally, Marena, her short blond hair and voluptuous breast both slicked with sweat, moved to stand beside Umiki. She asked Domigo, sexily, in a voice he well remembered, "Can I not be a guard? You yourself have told me that I have great eyes." Domigo could find no reason to deny her request, so he readily agreed.

Domigo, now feeling just a little full of himself, assigned a tool to each of the First-born, male and female alike. Continuing in his role as commander, he ordered the Humans to carry their tool with them at all times. If they must flee in haste, there would be no time to search out the makeshift weapons in the tall grass. He and Umiki would bear the responsibility of toting the balance of the tools until more of the First-born were located. Domigo then called Umiki and Marena aside and explained to them their duties as sentries. He stationed one to the southwest, the other northwest of the main group of Humans. He was relatively sure that if another attack came, it would be from the western side of their camp. If Trolls were spotted the guards were to alert the others. The Humans planned on staying low in the grass, hopefully hidden from the Trolls view. Domigo did not think they would announce their coming with howls and screams. Nay, this time the Trolls would come in silence, seeking both revenge and captives. Domigo told the First-born that if they were found, they must stand and fight. Fleeing would ensure the capture of the slowest Humans, most likely the women. Domingo found that possibility totally unacceptable.

Hanto, running after the Elf, realized he need not follow Elf or howling Troll, he knew where they are heading. Breaking off his pursuit, he angled to the northeast, hoping to intersect Zomba traveling from the south. Hanto ran on, hearing faint baying in the distance. He was beginning to tire slightly when the howling grew louder. Hanto stopped for a moment to survey his surroundings. His good night vision, aided by the rising moon, allowed him to locate the Humans moving ahead of Zomba's hunting party. Hanto now knew why he had caught up to the Troll Lord so quickly. The Trolls were herding the Humans northward, rather than attempting to capture them. Hanto did a quick head count and came up with only a dozen, far less than the number requested by Odyden, the Master of Evil. He profoundly hoped Tyreno, on the western flank, had captured more than his fair-share of First-born. Moments later, Zomba, along with Sutata and another Troll, came within hailing distance. Gaining the Troll Lords attention, Hanto hurried to his side. "Zomba", he asked breathlessly," have you seen the mounted Elf?" Sneering at him, the Troll Lord demanded, "What are you rambling about, what Elf?" Hanto stared intently at Zomba for an uncomfortable moment before he told him, "The one who placed an arrow in my guard's throat and used me for target practice. The one who is probably responsible for the lack of howling and screaming in the west. That Elf my Lord!" Zomba appeared stunned by this news. What was an Elfin warrior doing this far from the enclave of the infected Elves? Why was he aiding the First-born? Most importantly, where was he now?

Zomba realized that he might have lost Tyreno and his guard to the Elf's arrows, leaving him with just the three Trolls with him. Knowing there was little time left before the mounted Elf returned, Zomba ordered his Trolls to quickly attack the Humans. The Trolls, being surprising fast runners, captured three unsuspecting women from the rear of the group. Screaming as they felt a claw tipped arm encircle their naked flesh, they were soon subdued. Four of the First-born Men turned to attempt the rescue of the wailing women. The men scooped up broken tree limbs on the run to use as weapons. The men, with no training in the use of arms, soon found that tree limbs were not of much use against swords. Although inflicting minor wounds on three Trolls, two of the men were captured. One of the Men, Maregon, knowing they would not escape the bonds of the Trolls holding them, yelled to the other two men to flee. Maregon realized that the Trolls could not travel faster than the slowest First-born. He guessed they must be under orders to keep the Humans alive.

Maregon, to slow the pursuit of the Humans, planned

to fake a limp. He shortly found out that was not really necessary. Zomba was now more concerned with a mounted warrior loosing deadly shafts at them than in capturing more Humans. Besides, the First-born were still traveling toward his encampment and awaiting Troll guards. Zomba ordered the hands of the men to be tied behind their backs. He deemed this not necessary for the women. The Troll Lord now instructed the three guards to each lash a naked female to their hip. The women would serve as living shields. Zomba would walk between the two men, a noose around each of their necks. He did not think the Elf warrior would attack under these circumstances, but only time would tell.

The odor of cooked fish aroused Glento from his slumber. He would have gladly eaten the fish raw. Cooking them was his treat and reward for enduring the night in the snake den. Removing the fish to let them cool a bit, Glento threw the rest of the wood onto the fire. Picking up his fish, he moved into his cave to enjoy his repast. Once sated, he fell into a deep trouble-free sleep, unconcerned about slithering things by virtue of the flames on his doorstep.

Glento slept thru the day and deep into the night, awakened only by the need to relieve himself. Avoiding the still warm embers from the prior day's fire, he went in search of a suitable fallen tree, then returned to yesterday's fishing spot. A fifteen-minute wait brought enough light for him to see the glimmer of passing fish. Half a dozen flicks of his wrist delivered a raw fish breakfast. Glento collected his few belongings from the cave, reluctant to leave the sanctuary the stone grotto provided.

The Troll knew his trek was nearly half over. The Algali Valley should lie within a day's travel. Thinking this over, he decided the return trip should be much shorter, since he would not be seeking the body of Wento.

Umiki and Marena were both in the general area assigned to them by Domigo, guarding the western perimeter of their hiding place, for it could not be called a camp. Domigo had promised to send replacements to take over sentry duty, but he had not said when. Umiki was doing a fine job of looking into the night, straining his eyes to see nothing but darkness. After three hours or so, he finally saw something reflecting light in the distance. As he stared intently, Marena's form appeared, the moonlight softly reflecting off her short blond hair. As she approached, he could see her erect nipples leading the way and he heard her breathing in short, quiet gasps.

M arena was also bored at searching for nothing in the night and thought she might find something of interest protruding from below Umiki's belly. She knew that with her vagina already well lubricated, and her breasts begging for attention, this was not the time to be coy. Coming to a stop in front of Umiki, she placed her left hand behind his head, pulling it down to her opened lips, as her right hand reached down and began to fondle his hardening penis. Umiki raised his hands and encircled a firm breast in each. Using his thumb and forefinger, he gently massaged one of her hardened nipples. This evoked a low moan from Marena, along with a tightening of her fingers. Umiki dropped his right hand to her ribcage and slowly let his fingers travel down her body. He ran a fingertip leisurely around the perimeter of her belly button before lowering his right hand further. The soft roundness of her lower belly soon gave way to the soft golden hairs covering her sex. Umiki, running his long middle finger down the length of Marena's inflamed vaginal lips, became totally aroused when his fingertip slipped easily within. Marena, feeling her body being penetrated, held her breath as she inched her shapely hips forward onto his probing finger.

Domigo was mad. He and Alalyn had come to the spot where Marena was to stand guard and she was nowhere to be found. He was planning to leave Alalyn here as a replacement sentry for her. In truth, using one pretext or another, he was going to ask Marena to walk with him for a while in the direction of Umiki, whom he was to relieve of duty. Well out of sight of Alalyn, he would attempt to take full advantage of Marena's wanton nature and lascivious body. The prospect of not having sex with Marena was the real reason for him being mad, not the lack of a sentry.

Umiki moved back from Marena slightly. Moving his hand from her breast he replaced it with hers. Kneeling before her, he urged her knees further apart and inserted his finger fully into her wet vagina. Looking up from the erotic view between her thighs, he saw her lick her fingers before forming little circles on her erect nipples. Withdrawing his middle finger to a squeal of protest, he moistened his index finger, then slowly reinserted both of them, one inch at a time. With Marena's pulse pounding in his ears, her hips began the same beat, thrusting forward to accommodate more of Umiki's large fingers. Umiki, having noted her high state of sexual arousal when she had arrived, sensed she was close to achieving organism and this was much too soon. Pulling his fingers from her body he cupped her ass cheeks in his palms and buried his tongue deep in her vagina. Moving slowly up her lips, with little flicks of his wet tongue, he eventually reached the base of her swollen clitoris. The tip of Umiki's tongue and Marena's clit made love until he placed his lips around the base of her clitoris, and with mild suction, drew its full length into his mouth while still licking the tip. Marena, moaning softly and often, let her trembling legs relax, knowing strong arms held her. Umiki gently lowered her quivering hips to the ground and after teasing the tender flesh of her inner thighs, placed her knees over his broad shoulders. Rolling her head from side to side, her knees in the air and spread wide, she had thought he was going to pull her hips forward, impaling her on his fully erect penis. Unwilling to wait any longer, she guided his lips to her wet, open vagina.

Domigo, knowing he would not find Marena in the area, told Alalyn. "Stay here as planned, your replacement will come at dawn. I am going to Umiki's location, for something could be amiss." Domigo asked Alalyn to watch the spare arms, and gaining his assent, turned and disappeared into the night. Domigo moved south at a brisk pace. He quickly learned the way was easy, with the ground being somewhat lit by moonlight. Domigo broke into an easy trot, and before long, neared the perimeter of Umiki's watch. Domigo could discover no sign of movement. The First-born moved ahead cautiously, looking and listening for anything out of the ordinary, when he heard a faint sound that sent a chill rippling down his spine. Domingo could not be sure, but the feeble cry sounded like a woman whimpering in abject pain, and he was aware of but one woman who was not in their makeshift camp.

Zomba ordered his three remaining Trolls forward,

each with a Human female tied to their hip. He needed to get back to his compound as fast as possible and learn if any additional First-born had been ensnared. Zomba had little expectation for detainees from Tyreno in the west. He now realized that the abrupt ending to the Troll's howling did not bode well. He had much greater hope for his own group, for they were successfully herding the First-born toward the Troll guards when Hanto had appeared. Zomba had secured five Humans with just three Trolls. With luck, his guards may have ten or more waiting for him. Remembering Odyden's orders, he desperately hoped this was the case.

Moluk, heading eastward, had his mighty steed at a

distance eating gallop when he heard the first far off screams. Halting his horse, he sat motionless and listened to the sounds being carried on the night wind. The shrieking was from terrified Human females, followed shortly by loud howls and enraged bellowing. Moluk leaned forward and silently stroked the neck of his horse, for he perceived that Mankind and Troll had irrevocable met.

Moluk continued to sit quietly astride his horse, gathering his thoughts. He decided to get as close as possible without being seen, for he knew nothing concerning this group of Trolls. He urged his mount into a trot and rode perhaps five minutes before slowing to a walk. Spotting no trees nearby, he dismounted and hobbled his horse. He now proceeded on foot, for in the tall grass the Elf would be almost undetectable. Listening keenly, once again he could clearly hear gruff voices and grunts a short distance away. Getting even closer, he could see the Human prisoners, the women literally an extension of the Trolls' gross bodies. The Men were being led by ropes tied about their necks, their handler a huge, scarred Troll. Moluk understood that for these unfortunate First-born, there would be no escape. Moluk ran to the northeast, well wide of the group of Humans and Trolls. Wishing to learn more, he hid in the tall grass, waiting for them to pass. As the Humans neared, he saw that they were battered. The men suffered from numerous bloody cuts. They had not been captured without difficulty. The women's chief complaints were bruises, especially on their breasts and about their hips. What surprised him the most were the jagged cuts and swollen welts he observed on the bodies of the Trolls. Moluk sensed that the Trolls knew, had the Humans weapons, there would now be four dead Trolls lying in the moonlight.

Sutata had stared in fascination at the bare breasts of the Human female since he had joined her to himself. Unlike the breasts of She-Trolls, the bosoms of Women were hair free and bounced with enticement as they moved about. Sutata glanced at the other Trolls, and detecting no interest in his action, reached out with a foul paw and attempted to fondle her breasts. He was readily rewarded with a viciously thrown elbow to the side of his ugly head. He reeled back a step, almost falling and dragging her down with him. The other Trolls, hearing the woman screech, halted and viewed Sutata being hit by a female. Upon seeing this, the Trolls roared with laughter, nearly doubled over in glee. Zomba, eyes blazing with rage, strolled over and laid the flat of his sword hard across the back of the nearest Troll's thigh, bringing an abrupt halt to the merriment.

The Troll Lord ordered the women's hands to be

securely bound behind their backs, like the men. This brought an evil smile to the face of Sutata. He realized that with one hand across her mouth to stifle any whimper, he could now lean over while walking and suckle on the nipple of the horrified woman. He thought of further exploration with his other hand, but knew the possible harm he might inflict on the woman with his talon finger would pale in comparison to the violence Zomba would visit upon him. While binding her hands behind her back he had a thought that has never crossed his mind before. His tongue, although large and decorated with warts, was never less well lubricated. It should cause no detectable physical damage. Sutata's prior evil smile returned to crease the features of his cruel face.

Sutata had just finished securing the females hands when he heard Zomba roar for them to get moving. Giving the female a slap on the butt to urge her forward, he let his hand linger on her ass cheek and was shaken by the look of pure hatred flashing across her face. He instantly understood. If given even half a chance, she would attempt to kill him. Right now, he had another thought on his mind. He needed an excuse to be moved to the rear position of the guards, away from the forward-looking eyes of the other Trolls.

Sutata was daydreaming of ways he could molest his combative female captive without leaving evidence, when Zomba suddenly signaled for a stop. Peering in the direction the Troll pointed out with a claw tipped finger, Zomba felt a sudden chill. For studying them from a mere fifty yards away, a look of bemused boredom on his face, sat the mounted Elfin warrior.

Zomba, growing increasingly uneasy under the stare of the Elf, raised his arms, sword in hand, and roared a challenge to the mounted warrior. The Elf responded with a look of total indifference as he wheeled his steed and galloped hard to the north.

Umiki had a different sex act in mind, but readily allowed his head to be moved into position. However, after she reached climax, he expected her to respond in kind. Extending his tongue, he buried it deep within her vagina, slowly forming little circles. He used his left hand to fully expose Marena's aroused clit. His right hand found her ass and massaged her cheeks. Umiki now began a rhythm. After withdrawing his tongue from her vagina, he would slowly lick upward, until tongue met clitoris. Engulfing the protrusion, he slowly ran his lips up and down its length several times before nibbling on the tip and then retuning his tongue to its starting spot, deep within her vagina.

Marena stopped her moaning long enough to breathlessly demand more. Umiki was totally at sea until he recalled a conversation with Trylon, a dark skinned First-born and frequent sex partner of Marena. Moving his lips away from hers he directed a stream of saliva to a point just below her vagina. Feeling the warm flow inching toward the center of her ass, she took in a gasping breath and held it as she felt Umiki's middle finger trying to gain entrance. Lowing his head once again he licked her, timing the flick of his tongue on her clitoris to the gentle probing of his fingertip, patiently waiting to slide into her delectable ass. As he maintained his duel assault on her body, he felt her ass begin to nip at the tip of his finger. Umiki raised his hand slightly and eased his middle finger deep into her vagina, thoroughly wetting it. Looking up and seeing the hunger in her eyes, he pushed in his index finger to merge with the first. Withdrawing his hand, the First-born brought his fingers to his mouth, ensuring his fingers would enjoy easy passage. Moving his left hand up her body he encountered a nipple harder than he thought possible. His right hand returned to the valley between Marena's ass cheeks. With her ass well lubed, the prior little nips to his fingertip became an aggressive attack, attempting to ensnare the entire length of his finger within the clinging grasp of her body.

Umiki gladly let her capture the end of his middle finger, inching more of it into her ass. Marena whined in pleasure at his finger's inward travel until it was stopped by his palm, then moaned softly as she felt another finger gingerly sliding into her body to join the first. Umiki, feeling the quivering of her hips, knew it was too late to change positions, for Marena was close to reaching orgasm.

Moving his hand from her breast back to her vagina, he spread the flesh surrounding her clitoris out of the way, exposing a target for his tongue every bit as hard as the nipple his hand has just left. Marena, with two fingers in her ass and lips surrounding her clit, began to have second thoughts, for she longed for a penis buried deep inside her. Her idea quickly dissipated when she felt Umali's thumb enter her vagina and a third finger rest at the entrance to her ass. Marena's body could take no more. With her clitoris being sucked on like a miniature penis and fingers pumping erotically in both her ass and vagina, her breath was gained by short ragged gasps. Umiki raised his left hand to again toy with her nipples, but had his hand brushed away, for she was too sensitive to touch. Taking the hint, Umiki removed his other hand from her body and laid down beside her, simply holding her close. He felt her trembling subside to quivers as her breathing slowly returned to normal. A smile formed on Umiki's face as erotic thoughts formed in his mind. He looked at the short blond hair of Marena, the curves of her soft body, both bathed in moonlight, and knew that after a brief rest, it would be his turn.

Domigo froze at the sound of the woman's cry.

Listening intently, he heard nothing more and grew increasingly worried, for if Marena had been captured, what had become of Umiki? Domigo had no idea what was happening but needing answers, he crouched low in the tall grass and moved forward, as silently as possible. He had no way of knowing, but he would not be moving far.

Marena lie quietly in the soft grass. As her breathing

returned to normal, so did her wanton nature. Glancing down, she saw Umiki's penis throbbing with a life of its own. Leaning up on an elbow, she hungrily kissed him, her tongue joining his in an erotic dance. Marena's other hand traveled to his knee and began a leisurely trip up his inner thigh. Pausing for a moment to gently massage his balls, she ran her fingers up the length of his penis. Umiki moved his lips from hers and drew a sharp breath as he felt her fingers encircle, then gently squeeze, the swollen head of his penis. Knowing foreplay was long over, Marena rolled onto her knees and knelt between Umiki's spread legs. Reaching down with both hands, she spread her fingers along the base of his penis and pressed down imperceptibly, watching with growing lust as the already large shaft grew longer and the reddened head swelled even more.

Domigo again stopped to listen, this time thinking he had heard another sound, possibly made by a male. He now grew greatly troubled. If Trolls held Umiki and Marena, he needed a plan to free them. The First-born now rued not having paid attention to Moluk's lectures concerning fighting and arms. Moving ahead yet again, Domigo gained only a few yards before he halted in wide eyed amazement.

This time relief, not fear, flooded his body. Umiki lie supine on the grass, propped up on both of his elbows, Marena kneeling between his legs. Studying the scene before him carefully, especially Marena's form with her ass pointed at him, he could discern no physical harm to either. A huge smile formed on his face, for he now knew the moans in the night were cries of passion, not wails of pain.

Having retrieved his horse, Moluk sat in the moonlight, watching the Trolls move northward, along with their Human captives. He had already determined he could not help this group of First-born, but he needed to know where they were heading, for he had made a grave mistake. After slaying the Trolls in the west, he had rushed back here, neglecting to advise the terrified Humans as to where they needed to go. He should have had them take a circular route to the west, where Domigo and weapons waited. Now he believed his best option was to ride ahead of the Trolls and hopefully locate the rest of the First-born before the hunting party did.

Riding hard for a quarter of an hour, he slowed his steed to a walk, the Troll hunting party well behind. Moluk's current run of good fortune continued when he spotted motion ahead and to the right of his position. Urging his horse forward, Human forms evolved out of the darkness. Grasping the fact that the First-born had never seen a horse before and were fleeing from other creatures, Moluk dismounted and ran towards them. Closing to within easy sight of the Humans, Moluk stopped and hailed them. Startled by his sudden appearance, they nearly turned back and fled. Moluk hastily explained that he was a friend and companion of Domigo, and he would try to help, however he could. Sensing no threat from the Elf, the questions exploded from the newborn lips. The warrior could spare but little time on answers. The Trolls were just behind, and he knew not what lie ahead. Moluk gestured to the Humans to gather about him, but before he could speak, he heard his horse snorting in the distance. Ordering the First-born to stay where they were, he removed his bow from his shoulder and went to see what was disturbing his horse. Moluk could hear excited talking in the distant gloom, but to his utter relief it is the sound of the Humans, not Trolls. Hanging his bow over his shoulder, he hurried to meet the First-born. This encounter went eerily like the first, but once again his help was gladly accepted. Urging haste, Moluk guided the group to reunite with the first, permitting no time for a homecoming. He knew he must move the Humans quickly, for the Trolls had to be near. He was not sure where.

The Troll Lord knew he had no choice. He must follow in the wake of the Elf, for his encampment lie north. Shouting at his Trolls, he ordered them forward at a fast pace, telling them to drag the females if they could not keep up. Sutata was totally unhappy with this development. Faced with a forced march, he would not be able to molest the arrogant woman tied to his hip. As he and his captive moved forward as ordered, the Troll immediately began to dream up a reason to get her alone once their encampment was reached.

Moluk decided to send both groups of Humans to the east where they could join Domigo. The Elf had noticed that Trylon, dark skinned, and Naydor, one of the most powerful of the First-born, have the respect of the other Humans. Moluk had no time for group discussion, so he called the two aside. He hastily explained that they must leave at once, and asked them to lead the rest. When Trylon and Naydor agreed, he pointed out a star, telling them to keep it off their left shoulder. He further instructed the Men to tell Domigo to stay in his present location. Moluk planned one more trip to the north, still not knowing where the Trolls were heading. He would then rejoin the First-born in the east to rest and plan their next move. Moluk watched as the two Men rejoined the other Humans and talked rapidly in hushed voices, before setting out in the direction of Domigo. Moluk ran back to his horse, remembering something on the way. Mounting his horse, he quickly rode to the front of the Humans, enjoying the look of awe on the faces of the First-born when they saw his mighty steed pass by, with him sitting high upon its broad back. Hailing Trylon and Naydor he passed each a sword he had collected from the dead Trolls. He looked in amazement at the size and apparent strength of Naydor's hand and forearm when he grasped the sword. He quickly understood that with little training, sorry would be the Troll that had the misfortune of crossing his path. Giving a last bit of advice, he suggested that Trylon move to the rear of the group to defend the First-born from behind. He realized the Men had no experience with arms, but he also saw the battering the Trolls took in capturing but two of them. He felt this group would not be attacked tonight and he planned on being back before dawn. Turning his horse to the north, he was once more swallowed up by the night.

Moluk reckoned he had about three hours before dawn. If he found nothing in the next hour, he would retreat to join the First-born in the east. He was afraid that if he did not show up in a timely manner, the Humans would come searching for him. The Elf rode hard for perhaps five minutes before seeing what appeared to be structures rising above the tall grass. Moluk rode well to his right before dismounting and hobbling the horse, wishing to keep himself between the Trolls and the Humans, for he now realized that what he was viewing was the tents of a large Troll encampment.

Dralon and Dirthlyn were making good progress on their trek to the Land of the Horses. Dralon, now as fit as his Elfin mentor, pushed his shorter legged companion to the limit of his physical endurance almost every day. The Elf had not told Dralon this, but he is leading them to his homeland, for it was not far out of the way.

He and Dralon had come across the corrupt body of a Troll about a week ago.

At Dralon's insistence, Dirthlyn took up the Troll's sword. The Elf had told Dralon that he could fight equally well with either hand. Now, with two swords, he was forced to defend himself both day and night from mock sword attacks from the newly trained Human warrior.

Dirthlyn got little sleep, the increasingly hard human little cared. The Elf was hoping that once among his kinfolk Dralon might relax a bit, perhaps seeking carnal pleasure with one or more of the lovely Elfin women who would surely be attracted to him.

Days turned into another week, the daily routine becoming a mirror image of the day before. Dralon would rise well before dawn and run a wide circle around the perimeter of their camp. Arousing Dirthlyn from his slumber, he allowed the Elf a short time to relieve himself and have a brief breakfast. He then fell in step with the Elf on their northern trek, picking the warrior's brain of knowledge, while urging the Elf to move his feet faster.

Dirthlyn knew they must past the northern enclave of infected Elves but realized he had misjudged his present, location when an Elfin fletched arrow embedded itself in a nearby tree. Dirthlyn knew the shot was a warning, for he spotted a warrior standing on a limb of a huge oak tree not twenty yards away. He instantly wrapped his arms around Dralon to prevent any stupidity on his part. He knew the First-born would now be dead if he were traveling alone, with no questions asked. He also sensed there was at least one more warrior with drawn bow. A hidden Elfin warrior, seeing no obvious threat, stepped out of concealment, his bow string taut. Dirthlyn whispered to Dralon to relax, and after receiving a nod in agreement, released his grip on him. The first Elf descended silently from the tree and grinned at Dirthlyn whom he knew well. The second Elf also lowered his weapon, and both hurried to greet the long-gone warrior. The three Elves hugged each other, two of them acutely aware of the tall Human staring down upon them. Stepping away from the other Elves, Dirthlyn suddenly realized that the Elves had never seen a Human before and knew Dralon was truly lucky to still be alive.

Dirthlyn asked the Elves to draw near and attempted to tell them everything that had occurred since he left. Mostly, he stressed the fact that Elves and Mankind had formed an alliance, for the Trolls no longer want to kill them. They want to capture them alive. He illuminated that while non-warrior Elves were timid and obedient, the First-born were proud and physical. All of Mankind, including the women, would violently resist captivity. He further informed them that more Men would soon join them. The two Elf warriors nodded respectfully toward Dralon, gladly accepting him as an ally, silently thankful that the tall, stern Human carrying a great bow, was not an enemy.

Jeflyn, one of the sentries, led them to the crude shelter that served as both guardhouse and quarters, leaving the other sentinel to continue his patrol. Entering the dingy structure, Dirthlyn spied a crude bed, with a mattress stuffed with grass. Unable to help himself, he stretched out on the bed, emitting a soft sigh. This was the first time in months his back has reclined on anything other than earth. Dralon started at him, a questioning looks on his face. Why would anyone wish to rest indoors, in the middle of the day?

Zomba was dissatisfied with the progress of his

hunting party. Pulling on the ropes binding the necks of his two male captives, he moved to his left, letting the three Trolls with female prisoners pass him. Now at the rear of the group, Zomba set a much faster pace, knowing the Trolls in front of him dare not let him climb up their ass. A half hour of hard running has the Trolls breathing heavily, their muscles burning and threatening to cramp. The long-limbed First-born, although tired, refused to show anything but scorn for the short-legged Trolls. Sutata, somehow stuck at the head of the pack, saw the encampment in the distance and signaled for a halt. Zomba came forward, his two Human males in tow. He handed the rope attached to the necks of the First-born to Sutata, instructing him to hold the restrains in one hand, his sword in the other. Unlike the other Trolls, Zomba still had an abundance of energy and used it to swiftly close the distance to the encampment. Crouched low in the grass, the waiting guards did not see him. They were expecting to hear howls and screaming before seeing movement. The Troll Lord could find no fault with the five guards he had left behind to capture the Humans. They were in correct position, there simply was nothing to catch. Zomba stood and roared for the others to join him. With the group together, Zomba lead them to his camp. He called for the nearest guard to join him. "Troll, how many Humans have you captured while I was gone?" he asked hopefully. "Lord, the only Humans we have ever seen are the ones with you." he replied truthfully. Seeing a look of total bewilderment on Zomba's face, he added, "Earlier, we could hear unfamiliar screams, mingled with the howl of Trolls, but of late only silence." Zomba dismissed the guard with an icy glare and slight wave of his hand and called for Hanto, his remaining commander. When he arrived, Zomba asked him in a slightly dejected tone, "What would you propose I do next?" Hanto thought for a while before answering, "I would secure the prisoners, post sentries, and give all others a few hours of rest. With the light of day, send out a five Troll hunting party. The First-born are taller than us, we should see them before they can detect us." The Troll Lord nodded his head in agreement to this, so Hanto continued. "If we have any luck, we should be able to harvest at least five more Humans, doubling our total." Zomba thought for but a moment before accepting Hanto's plan. The Troll Lord ordered the Humans to remain bound, an armed guard watching over them. Two sentries would patrol the perimeter of the compound while the rest of the Trolls slept. One hour after sunrise, the Trolls would meet and go in search of Humans. Zomba strolled toward his private tent and a few hours of sleep, unaware that the Elf warrior, lying motionless in the night, had been watching his every move.

Moluk waited until the camp had settled in for the rest of the night before moving. He had seen two Trolls leave the center of the camp, probably to act as sentinels. Two other Trolls had taken the captive Humans to the north, one returning after a short period of time. Moluk perceived the answers he sought lie just to the north, in the wake of the returning Troll.

Breathing as quietly as possible, Domigo watched the lewd scene unfold before his eyes. Marena licked her lips then bent her neck down, the head of Umiki's throbbing penis disappearing into her mouth. She paused a moment before inching her lips downward, slowly wetting and then sucking in more of Umiki's erect shaft. Domingo stared at the erotic sight before him, his lust and erection both growing, as Marena's lips stop their travel down his shaft, only to return to suck on his blood engorged head of his penis. Domingo felt his breathing becoming heavier as he watched Marena lower her head again and in due time take a half inch more penis into her wet mouth than she had before. Domigo, now fully erect, doubted that Umiki could last until Marena's lips encircled the base of his penis. He never had.

Marena, still kneeling, removed her right hand from the base of Umiki's penis and softly pinched her hardened nipples before dropping her hand to her vagina. Emitting a low moan, she pushed two fingers deep into her still wet vagina then lowered her head, taking another full inch of penis into her wet and willing mouth. Umiki was looking at Marena's beautiful face, her full sensual lips lovingly wrapped around his twitching shaft, when he suddenly sensed movement behind her. In the instant it would have taken him to remove her mouth from around his penis, he saw that it was Domigo, approaching them. Marena, glancing at Umiki's face, saw that he was peering intently into the predawn darkness and disengaged her mouth anyway. Gazing over her shoulder she saw Domigo. She quickly noted that he was sexually aroused, his swaying penis preceding his belly by a good eight or nine inches. Marena said not a word. She simply gave Domigo a lustful smile.

She withdrew her fingers from her vagina and used them to pinch the bass of Umiki's penis, causing the head to swell even larger and twitch with every beat of his heart. Marena raised her ass up to what she hoped would be the correct height and spread her knees wide before lowering her head and taking a solid six inches of erect cock into her mouth. Domigo usually wished to engage in prolonged foreplay, but now, after having thought of Marena's naked body most of the day and viewing the current ongoing sex act, he was not sure how long he would last before ejaculating. Marena's twitching muscles were causing her ass to wink at him, begging for attention, while below, the lips of her vagina lie open, gleaning with moisture, her clitoris exposed and hard. Putting a hand on each cheek, Domigo spread her ass wide then pushed her cheeks tightly together. After doing this a few times, he watched as her mouth accepted another inch of Umiki's cock. Domigo ran his penis up and down the span of Marena's vagina, moistening the head. He then positioned his cock at the portal of her ass but made no attempt at penetrating her.

He simply squeezed her ass together again, lifting one check while pushing down on the other, massaging his cock with an erotic rocking motion. Domigo felt her ass muscles gripping his swollen head, urging the rest of its great length to burrow itself deep within her body. Looking at Umiki, he noted that only an inch or so of his penis was visible below Marena's full, wet lips. She lifted her head so her mouth could encircle the head of Umiki's cock. Domingo could tell by her hollowed cheeks that she was now applying a great deal of suction. He guessed that Umiki could not last much longer and he wished to anoint her libidinous body with simultaneous ejaculations.

Opening her cheeks to release himself from her ass, he repositioned her hips slightly, aligning the greatly swelled head of his penis with the portal to her still wet pussy. Domingo's balls were beginning to ache as he worked his cock into Marena's body. Once the head of his cock was well entrenched, he moved his hips forward with short powerful thrusts, driving his penis ever deeper into her now quivering vagina.

Marena knew her body would soon be racked by another intense orgasm, after which her body would abide no further touching. Judging from the movement of the throbbing cock in her mouth, she could make him come at any time. She pushed her hips back with force, then gasped in ecstasy, as nine inches of hard cock stretched her vagina to the limit. Rocking forward on her knees, she totally engulfed Umiki's penis with her mouth while allowing Domigo's cock, except for the huge swollen head, to slip out of her body. Marena now began an erotic rocking motion. Moving back, she was rewarded with the full length of Domigo's penis tightly filling her vagina and the blood engorged head of Umiki's cock twitching between her lips. Rocking forward, she again buries her lips in Umiki's pubic hair, the head of his penis deep in her throat, her pussy muscles gripping the huge head of Domigo's cock, preventing its escape. She knew from prior trysts with him that he loved to bend her over and watch as his huge cock penetrated her from behind. Marena continued rocking for another minute or so before she felt the onset of her orgasm. With her body beginning to tremble, she pushed her ass back against Domigo's cock, taking in all its rigid length, at the same time relaxing her muscles and allowing Umiki's cock to snake deeper into her throat. She was rewarded when she felt both penises swell even larger, ready to ejaculate. Unable to delay her own orgasm, she continued to milk the twin cocks embedded in her body until she felt the heads of their cocks growing yet again as they spurt hot jets of sperm deep into her. Marena's quivering body and moist lips drained the last of the lust from the spent bodies of the Men. Disengaging herself from her lovers, she laid down between them and soon fell into a deep sleep.

Domigo lie quietly on his side, staring at the still flushed body of Marena, waiting for his breathing to return to normal. Noticing Umiki was awake, he told him they needed to make plans but quickly realized they could well wait until the morn. Within minutes, all three sated Humans were fast asleep in the warm predawn night.

Moluk crept silently north, approximating the route the Troll had taken, then understood, by the lack of grass underfoot, that he was on a frequently used path. Peering to either side of the traveled way, he spotted numerous large mounts, covered by animal hides. Suspecting they may be provisions, Moluk knew that they needed to be destroyed. Staying low, Moluk moved forward and presently saw the silhouette of a Troll in the distance.

Skirting the guard by moving in a wide circle to his right, he stopped and stared in utter amusement, for before him, sleeping in the open, were the captured Elves from the southern enclave.

With this development, Moluk has a dilemma. He knew he had no hope of rescuing twenty Elves, but knew he could not depart without telling them that he was aware of their plight. Moluk studied the guard for a while and realized he had no set area to patrol other than keeping tabs on the docile, sleeping Elves. The Elf warrior waited for the guard to turn away from where he lies quietly in the grass, then crawled his way dangerously close to the nearest infected Elf. Hoping the Elf would not cry out, Moluk prodded him gently with his sword. A young Elfin woman sat up with a start, but made no sound. Moluk whispered for her to remain silent, he had things to tell her. Since the Troll was still walking away from him, Moluk felt safe talking to the Elf in a subdued voice. He explained that at this time there was no chance of him freeing the captives. He promised to monitor their movement for as long as possible, and if receiving aid from Elves or First-born, attempting to free them from the Trolls. Moluk then asked her if she knew what was stored in piles under the animal hides he had seen. She told of viewing Trolls retrieving food and other supplies from the mounds. She also told him one pile was clothing woven by the Elves, to cover the naked bodies of the First-born. Moluk, seeing the guard turn back toward them, raised a finger to his lips to end conversation and backed into the darkness whence he came. The Elf now realized he could not destroy the Trolls provisions, for depending on where the Elves were being taken, they may well need them to survive. Moluk stayed low in the grass until out of sight of the sentry, then stood and hurried back to his horse, suddenly aware of the dull ache in his arm from the minor knife wound. He needed to rejoin Domigo before sunrise, the cut would have to wait until then. Un-hobbling and mounting his horse, he headed in the direction of the soon to rise sun, sensing that Domigo would see the glowing face of that orb, ere his own.

Zomba was roused from his brief sleep by a Troll incessantly calling his name. Emerging from his tent, eyes blazing in anger, he confronted Sutata standing before him in the first light of day. Zomba glared down at the shorter Troll, his voice hoarse and trembling with ire, as he demanded, "Why have you awakened me from my slumber?" Sutata stared back at him hard for a moment before answering. "Have you forgotten your new orders already? We should be marching to the north now, not setting out on a futile hunting trip." Hearing the insolence of the annoying Troll, Zomba sorely wished to relieve the Troll's body from the weight of its mouthy head. But being dangerously short of guards, he dropped his hand from his sword. "Sutata, you well know I have orders to bring back twenty Humans. I have but five," he quietly explained. "No" injected Sutata, "you have new orders to return at once, with the captives you do have." "If I deliver a mere five First-born to Odyden, he is likely to severely punish me," argued Zomba. "This is true," agreed Sutata, "but if you fail to return as ordered, he will surely kill you." Zomba accepted the fact that he had but two choices, kill Sutata, then hunt Humans, or follow his orders. Calling Hanto, his commander, to his side, he instructed him to prepare to break camp. The Troll Lord shook with rage as he swore to himself that Sutata would not live to see the stark mountain fortress they call home.

Hanto roused the remaining Trolls and had them draw near. He informed them of Zomba's decision to leave for the northern reaches and home. The Troll Lord, still filled with ire, strolled over to the group and ordered Hanto to make sure the Humans were clothed. He was tired of the distraction the naked female bodies were causing to the libido of the Trolls, himself included. He told Hanto to have provisions tied into bundles. If the Humans wished to eat, they could tote their own food. Zomba planned on a forced march to the north. With the possibility of Elf warriors to contend with, there would be no time for foraging or other excursions.

Zomba was aware that he could not make good time with hostages lashed to guards, so he again called Hanto to join him. "I see a problem Hanto. With Humans tied to our guards, our progress will be greatly slowed. Do you have any ideas?" After giving the matter some thought, he told Zomba, "We will tie the First-born together by their ankles, intermixing them with the Elf captives. Leaving walking space between each hostage, we should be able to form a large elongated circle of captives, with us Trolls safely tucked away in its center. Zomba actually smiled at his commander, for there was nothing in the plan not to like.

The Troll Lord then ordered two guards to fetch clothing for the Humans. Noticing Sutata jump at the chance to help the females dress, Zomba ordered him to retrieve the large coil of rope from storage. Sutata was tersely told to begin binding the ankles of the captives after waiting for the Human females to don clothing. Sutata went about his task in a foul mood, knowing his tongue will have to wait to sample the ripe body of the Human female. Other guards packed satchels and provisions, while others stowed their crude traveling tents and other supplies in preparation for moving north.

The Trolls soon had Elves and Humans formed into a large loop of captives. Zomba and his Trolls were safely enclosed within. Hanto was concerned over such a large amount of provisions being left behind, but the Troll Lord was unwilling to spend the time to destroy it. Once he had made his mind up to move north, he would allow nothing to slow his progress. Using threats and flat of sword once more, the Trolls finally manage to get the slave caravan slowly moving north, toward the Dark Lord and his awaiting chamber of horror.

Babaduk became aware of his new power one incident

at a time. Awakened from his slumber by the snarls of wolves, he abruptly sat up. Staring at the animals, he wished they would just go away, avoiding being slaughtered. To his utter amazement they did just that, vanishing back into the darkness whence they came. At the time he thanked his good fortune, threw more wood on the fire, and restlessly awaited the coming of dawn. Two days later, while seeking a place to spend the night, a snow cat attacked just before sunset, roaring its terrifying hunting cry, designed to paralyze its prey in fear. The huge feline exploded from the thick brush on the side of the seldom trod path. Babaduk heard the chilling roar before he saw the animal, his sword already drawn. He thought his best option would be to wait for the cat to leave its feet. He would step back far enough to avoid the cat's claws, then slash at the animal's neck as it passed him by. Then the thought crossed his mind that this cat would be elsewhere if it had chosen other prey. As if reading his thoughts, the huge cat pivoted not ten feet from him, its paws kicking up tufts of grass and soil as it sped directly away from him. Following the form of the disappearing snow cat into the brush, Babaduk sensed that something had happened to him and he believed he knew the cause.

Babaduk found a comfortable place to spend the night, then went about the chore of gathering firewood. He would once again set his mind free, but this time on a much lesser scale. He built the fire, and as it burned down a bit he partook of a light meal, then walked off to relieve himself. Returning to the fire, he made a comfortable place to sit. Babaduk removed a small bag of herb from his tote, but this time put only a small pinch on the fire. Waiting for a dense cloud of smoke to rise, he leaned his head over the fire and deeply inhaled the arid smoke. This time, with his spirit under control, the merging with the cosmos was nearly instantaneous. What he had thought was true. During his prolonged battle for his soul, his mind had learned far more than he had ever wished to know.

Having already gained the information he sought, Babaduk, with but little effort, reunited his body and mind. He sat in the glow of the dying fire and shivered, for he had learned, although in reality he already knew, that other than Demigods and possibly a few other Shamans, he was mentally as powerful as any entity on earth. He no longer needs fear wolf or snow cat, for if he wished them gone, they would go. Babaduk was a wee bit leery, but decided he would try his power on a Troll. Perhaps, when given the proper chance, he would try it on his frequently nagging woman. A small smile came to his face at this thought. Maybe this was not such a bad thing after all.

Babaduk added more wood to his fire before moving upwind and stretching out on his bedroll. He could sleep easy tonight and all nights to come, for nothing could come upon him unaware in the night. Not having to be concerned with attacks against his person, his northward progress to his homeland would only be limited by his physical endurance, and the way was not far or overly difficult.

Moluk had been ridding hard to the east for hour or so when the rising sun greeted him. Shortly thereafter he located the First-born, milling around as if lost. The sight of an armed Elfin warrior, sitting astride a huge beast they had never viewed before, only added to their confusion and anxiety. "Where is Domigo?" he demanded of the nearest Human. "He went to check on, wait, maybe he said relieve, the two sentinels," the First-born informed him. Seeing he would learn nothing of use from the Human, he tersely asked, "Could you possibly tell me the way he went?" Turning his mount in the direction of the pointed finger, the Elf warrior went in search of Domigo. While riding, he realized there was still a group of Humans wandering on the coastal plains. Hopefully, he would locate them before the Trolls did.

The hot morning sun woke Domigo from his sleep.

Rubbing his eyes, he saw Marena's head still lying on Umiki, using his belly as a pillow. Prone on her side with her voluptuous ass tempting him, and her lips tantalizingly near to Umiki's penis, he considered a repeat performance of last night before banishing the thought from his mind. Bending down, he gently shook his two companions awake. Glancing up at Domigo standing over them, they half expected to be censured for not attending to their duties before remembering that Domingo had not been totally vigilant either. Now fully awake, the three Humans began the walk to rejoin the rest of the First-born.

Traveling in the general direction indicated by the First-born, Moluk quickly found the Human called Alalyn. The Elf could see the wonderment and awe on his face as he gazed upon the mounted Elfin warrior. Noting the alertness in this Human's eyes, Moluk asked the same question, "Where is Domigo?" Without hesitation Alalyn responded, "He went south, seeking Marena, the sentry who was assigned to the area, who is now missing." Taking an instant liking to this outgoing Human, Moluk reached out a hand to Alalyn, inviting him to enjoy the scenery from the back of his mighty steed.

Elf and Man had not journeyed far before they espied Domigo and the two other First-born making their way back to the main group of Humans. Sitting astride Moluk's horse, Alalyn said naught, but disappointment was written all over his face. He realized his ride was too soon at an end. Sliding off the horse to land lightly on his feet, Alalyn swore to himself that one day he would process such a noble animal.

The Elf warrior also dismounted, and seeing his horse nosing the Human, left to engage Domingo. The First-born, catching the look on Moluk's face, innocently asked,

"Have you been waiting here long? I did not expect you back quite so soon." The Elf eyed him coldly before telling him that was evident. Domigo, with no knowledge of deceit or deception simply informed him, "I sent out sentinels last night and Alalyn and I went to relieve them. When we reached Marena's station she was nowhere to be found. I left Alalyn there and went south searching for her." Seeing the look of concern on the Elf's face he continued, "Upon reaching the area of Umiki's watch, I found him and Marena engaged in a sex act." Looking at Moluk sheepishly, he added, "I joined in."

The warriors of the northern enclave for infected Elves treated Dralon and Dirthlyn to a hot repast, a truly rare event. They even managed to come up with metal mugs full of a cool brewed beverage. Dirthlyn did not ask how it was obtained. Finished with their meal, the warriors who had been able to join them, returned to their duties. The Elf and Man sat long and conversed. "Dralon, we really should depart for my homeland before attempting the capture of horses, Dirthlyn insisted. "Nay, we are wasting valuable time, even as we speak," Dralon argued. The Elf, seeing he was not getting his point across, harshly responded, "No, you do not understand. Two people, even warriors, would be hard put to capture a single horse." Then looking pointedly at Dralon, reminded him, "You want many more." Beginning to come around to Dirthlyn's point of view, Dralon asked, "And if we go to your homeland?" Sensing the change of tide, the Elf informed him, "We will recruit Elves, some of which have been on previous hunts."

Dralon, while not totally happy, recognized the truth of Dirthlyn's words and reluctantly agreed to the Elf's plan. Another hour of discussion wrapped up the rest of the details. Tomorrow, with the rising of the sun, Elf and Man would depart for the homeland of the warrior.

Arising well before dawn and downing a light breakfast, the travelers were on their way before the sun's rays illuminated the ground beneath their feet. Dirthlyn had never felt more comfortable on the trail. With his training, he feared but little to begin with. Now with a mighty Human warrior and his great bow at his side, he feared nothing. His only regret with having the First-born at his side. was attempting to keep up with him, for Dralon well-remembered the grueling training forced on him by the Elf warrior. His shorter Elfin legs were now paying the piper.

The mindless days of travel, with little threat of danger, was eroding Dralon's physical and mental skills. Determined to fight off boredom, Dralon unshouldered his bow and notched an arrow. Not wanting to waste his arrows shooting at trees, he aimed at the earth many yards ahead. Dralon noted the angle he held the bow at and then released the shaft. Walking to retrieve his arrow he counted his paces. Re-notching the arrow, he changed the angle he was holding the bow at and fired. Again, he counted his paces as he walked. By late in the day and no longer bored, he knew exactly at what angle to hold his bow for the longest shot possible. As a bonus, he had not damaged even one arrow. Tomorrow he would work on his long-distance accuracy.

Enduring another uneventful night, Dralon was glad to be back at archery practice. He located a fir tree about six feet tall, and using his sword, trimmed off all the lower branches, and sharpened the trunk, while leaving the top of the tree uncut. With the pointed trunk of the tree pushed into the ground, the top branches were approximately the size and height of a Trolls head. This, he thought, would serve as a fitting target. Dralon had the Elf take the target about fifty yards away, and get out of the line of fire. Launching his first missile, Dralon asked, "Where did I hit?" Dirthlyn started to explain that he thought the wind had pushed the arrow wide to the right, when Dralon waved for him to come back. The First-born knew only experience would permit him to adjust his shot to allow for the wind. "Dirthlyn," he explained when the Elf rejoined him, "you need use but four words. They are high, low, left or right, and never more than two on one shot." The First-born thought about this for a moment, then added, "I said you needed but four words so I guess a hit will be announced by silence." The Elf, having now grasped what the Human was trying to tell him, walked back to the tree and yelled out to him, "Low right." Dralon nodded, then smiled at his companion before shouting at him to move the target farther and farther away. Then he added that he wanted to lose many more arrows.

Days of constant practice transformed the First-born into a deadly archer at nearly any range, the Elf warrior, into a bored lackey. This abruptly ceased when Dirthlyn began seeing vaguely familiar sights. Telling Dralon he must now concentrate on locating landmarks, the First-born collected his spent shafts and followed the Elf into the outer limits of his native land.

The Troll Lord was in a rage. At the rate of progress, he was making. it would take months, if not longer, to reach the Northern Mountains and the underground fortress of Odyden. Zomba knew he had neither the provisions nor the patience to endure that long. The captured Elves, while much more numerous than that of the Humans, were not a problem. Told to walk, they readily responded. Ordered to stop, they would do so in mid-stride. Nay, the docile Elves caused him no worry, but the powerful and proud First-born were another story entirely. Ordered to their feet, they stared with open contempt at the ugly Trolls until forced to stand by vicious kicks. Zomba feared a broken leg or ankle would bring forward travel to a virtual stop.

Zomba is at sea. He can think of no way to force the Humans to move faster without inflicting great physical harm. Recalling that his commander, Hanto, had given him sound advice in the past, he walked to join him. Noticing the arrogant Troll Sutata hovering nearby, Zomba lowered his voice. "Commander, we have a grave problem. If we cannot make better time, Humans and Elves will both starve to death, for I have intention of stopping to allow the captives to forage. When I meet Odyden, he will hear early and often of the incompetence of the Trolls he sent with me. Perhaps he will allow me to live." Hanto also realized the consequence of failure but is forced to tell Zomba, "Lord, I can think of no good answer right now, but I will give it much thought." Zomba, feeling his ire building, snarled at his loyal commander, "Aye Troll, you do that."

Inching innocently closer to the Troll leaders, Sutata had caught the gist of the conversation. Walking nonchalantly away, an idle thought quickly transformed itself into a vile scheme. One which would permit him to grossly molest his First-born tormentor. This time he would do it with Zomba's thanks and gratitude!

Going back to the spot where he had stashed his bedroll and supplies, Sutata removed a well-honed knife from his tote. Sitting down to help steady himself, he carefully cut away the claw on his right index and middle finger, leaving barely a stump. His hand felt naked with the missing talons, but it had to be for his plan to be successful. Sutata stood, packed away his dagger, and went to talk to Hanto, the Troll commander. Finding him alone, he whispered in a conspiratorial voice, "Hanto, I have thought of a plan that will benefit us all." Gazing at the irritating Troll with distrust, he demanded, "What plan, what are you raving about?" Lowering his voice even more, he informed Hanto, "I know what you and Zomba just discussed and I can help you."

Hanto sat alone for a long time after his conversation with Sutata had ended. Against his better judgment, but accepting the fact that he has not designed a plan of his own, he reluctantly went to talk to Zomba. The Troll Lord's mood lightened a tad at the approach of Hanto. Perhaps he had come up with a plan. "Lord, I have a plan for your consideration, but I must admit, it is not mine." Zomba quickly asked, "Whose is it?" Knowing Zomba could not abide the plan's author, he timidly responded, "It is Sutata's." Zomba's roar alarmed all his guards and most of the captives. "What, the vassal of Odyden would relate to me how to conduct my business?" Hanto attempted to calm the Troll Lord by telling him the plan may actually work. Comprehending other options were unavailable, Zomba angrily agreed to hear Sutata's plan.

Hanto took a couple of deep breaths, then began. "The

problem, as you well know, is our inability to move the captives northward with any amount of speed." Zomba simply grunted at the obvious. Hanto continued, "Sutata's plan puts him at the front of the loop of prisoners with a Human female at his side." Zomba sneered at his commander before sarcastically inquiring, "And that will speed the captives forward?" Perceiving that he was close to being dismissed out of hand by Zomba, Hanto gave it another try. "Zomba, the First-born Men care but little when we assault them, but show great concern when the females are involved." This Zomba knew was true, so he nodded in agreement. The Troll commander, now beginning to warm to the task, began informing Zomba of the details of Sutata's foul scheme. The lead female would have her hands bound behind her back, and a gag in her mouth, held in place by a woven cloth. "Why is that?" Asked Zomba, I really do not care if she screams." Hanto explained that it was to prevent her from biting. Zomba was confused by the statement, but allowed his commander to continue without interruption. "Sutata will be with the lead female of the slave loop. If travel slows or stops, he will know at once." Zomba acknowledged this and indicated that Hanto should go on. Easily bringing Sutata's vile plan back to mind, he told the Troll Lord," When the captives stop without being ordered to, a Troll with a bared sword would join each of the two Human males, for they would be the cause." Taking another deep breath, Hanto goes on, "Sutata, at the side of the lead female, would lift her smock, leaving it wadded about her head, her naked body available for all to view." The Troll Lord, now becoming engrossed with the plan, rolled his clawed for finger in a signal for Hanto to proceed. "Sutata will begin his exploration with the bound Woman's breast," he informed the suddenly attentive slave master. He further told him that Sutata had desired to suckle a hairless nipple of a Human female ever since the night they were first harvested.

Zomba realized that some thought had gone into a plan, but asked of Hanto. "How will sucking on a teat move the captives forward?" Having had the same discussion with Sutata, a ready response was forthcoming. "The Troll guards with the First-born males would tell them true, you will move forward at a brisk pace, or if you prefer, you may stand there and watch your female being violated by a Troll."

Beginning to the fathom the depth of this foul plan,

Zomba excitedly wanted to know, "And if the Humans still refuse to move forward? " Hanto, now almost certain the plan would be accepted, moved a bit closer to Zomba before telling him, "Sutata will introduce a well wetted fingertip to the depth of her vagina." Then with an evil grin adds. "I believe the female will be more than ready to move forward when the males create some slack in the rope."

The Troll Lord, having heard Hanto the commander out, stares at him in utter disappointment. "Troll, you well know the Evil One desires intact Elf and Human females." "You know also what a Troll's clawed finger a tender vagina will do; regardless how wet the finger be!" Hanto listened in stunned silence as Zomba informed him, "This plan is totally unacceptable, talk to me again when you have a workable solution."

Hanto attempted to tell him of Sutata's manicure, but with Zomba roaring for him to get out of his sight, Hanto retreated to the relative safety of his bedroll. Sitting quietly alone, the Troll commander went back over the details of the plan and could find no fault with it. He knew it would work, he just needed Zomba to hear him out. He also realized that this was not the right time to try.

Glento found out late in the afternoon of the next day that his guess had been right about his arrival time at the Algali Valley. For the last hour or so he had noticed the gradual sloping of the land. The Troll well remembered Odyden telling him to turn back if he had not found Wento, or his remains, before reaching the valley. After coming this far and enduring hardship, Glento was loathed to turn back.

Reasoning with himself, he decided that there was no definitive boundary or landmark designating the start of the valley. He would allow himself one more day to locate Wento and the priceless oil. Darkness came earlier in the valley, catching him in the open with no time to look for shelter. Glento clawed at the ground with huge hands, quickly excavating a shallow depression to fit the contours of his body. Spreading his bedroll, he stretched out, and with no daylight to distract him, soon fell into the typical dreamless sleep of the Troll Race.

Glento sat up with a start, awash with instant guilt, for the sun shining full on his face had awakened him. After permitting himself one more day to search for Wento, he deeply rued the lost time spent abed. Gaining his feet, he went in search of a suitable spot, before he returned to eat a small amount of his dwindling supply of dried meat. The Troll gathered up his meager belongings and began his hike into the depths of the Algali. He knew that by noon he would need to start his return in order to be clear of the valley by nightfall.

The faint odor of lingering smoke caught his attention just before noon. By following his nose, he discovered the scene of Wento's last stand. Peering at the melted metal from his weapons, he wondered where so great a heat had come from. Bending down to pick up a few shards of bone and claw to show Odyden, the Troll was amazed to see a container sitting beside the rock outcropping. Ignoring bone and talon, Glento delicately picked up the jar of lubricant and smiled smugly as he viewed the intact container of oil.

Glento realized he had been extremely lucky, for he had been within minutes of turning to the east and leaving the valley. Now, with the precious oil safely recovered, he should receive both praise and reward from the Dark Lord upon his return.

The Elf warrior Moluk was not pleased with Domigo's response. He felt the Human had more important things to do than indulge in sex. He also had no intention of making an issue of it for he foresaw the rising might of Man and wisely wished to remain an ally. Moluk discreetly motioned for Domigo to join him. "You must get the First-born together, at least the Men, and show them how to use arms so they can defend themselves." The First-born looked at Moluk, confusion written all over his face, "So when do you plan to instruct us?" Trying, without total success, to keep the irritation out of his voice, the Elf reminded him, "You traveled with me long. Did not you hear a word I said?" Admitting he had not been overly attentive, he pleaded with the warrior, "Show us what we need to know before the Trolls come for us."

The Elf knew that the Trolls, at least this group, were moving north, away from the Humans and would pose no threat. He did not inform Domigo of this detail. "Gather the Men, and Women if they wish. This afternoon and I will show them how to use the tools you have as weapons. Leave me now, I need to rest and tend to my arm, which sorely hurts."

Thinking over his strategy as Domigo walked away, the Elf realized he needed to be truthful with the Human. Calling him back, Moluk told him, "Domigo, there are some things I have forgotten to tell you." Domigo looked at him questioningly before asking, "Like what?" Deciding to relate all, he described what he had seen in the Trolls camp. "Do you mean," inquired the First-born, "that we are safe from the Trolls?" Moluk instantly glared at him. "I said the group of Trolls that were hunting you were now heading north, with captives, and would cause us no further trouble." Pausing to let this information sink in, he gravely added, "There could very well be other bands of Trolls searching for Humans.

The Elf warrior then told of large amounts of provisions and other supplies available for the taking. Most importantly of all, he told the Humans of the clothing made by the captive Elves. He explained to Domingo that if the First-born wished to venture north of the mild coastal plain anytime soon, they would need clothes to protect them from the cold. "What is this thing you call cold?" Asked Domigo. The Elf thought for a moment before he realized he did not know how to answer his question. "Just trust me on this Domingo. When you experience extreme cold for the first time, you will remember it forever." The Human, no more knowledgeable now than he was a minute ago, simply nodded his head in agreement.

Nearing the spot where he had left his horse, Moluk saw the First-born Alalyn sitting cross legged in the grass, his horse peacefully grazing, close enough for the Human to stroke its neck as he ate. Upon reaching his steed, the Elf removed his few belongings from the animal's broad back. "Alalyn," he said in a sharp tone of voice, then smiled when the First-born looked up. "Seeing that my horse has taken to you, could I get you to care for him while I rest?" Unable to keep the excitement he felt out of his voice, Alalyn nodded in assent.

Glancing around, Moluk noticed some First-born milling about. He yelled at them, asking if they would fetch him water and two mugs. Moluk walked off to find the shade of a tree, then wearily sat down, resting his back against its trunk. In a short time, a woman brought him a flask of freshly collected cool water and two wood mugs. The Elf withdrew two different dried herbal drugs from his tote, ignoring the voluptuous form of the naked Woman standing over him. Moluk put a pinch of one drug into a container, swirled the mug to stir it a bit, and then swallowed the concoction. He then placed a full handful of the other drug into the second mug, added water, then mixed it into a paste. The Elf slowly lifted his aching arm and looked with disbelief at the inflamed wound, already beginning to ooze pus. Grimacing in pain, he molded the herbal paste around the corrupt flesh, binding it in place with a woven cloth.

The First-born Woman, noting the pain on his face, sat down beside him and put a comforting arm around his shoulder. The Elf warrior peered at her intently, more in surprise than anything else, for he had not known the First-born were capable of acts of tenderness to members of other Races. Celena, a First-born Woman, felt the Elf's body begin to relax as the narcotic drug he had taken began to take effect. Moving slightly away from him, she gently lowered his head into her lap. Her shapely thighs would serve well as a pillow while the Elf warrior slept.

Sutata was a constant shadow of Hanto, following him whenever possible. "Have you finished telling Zomba the rest of the plan?" Receiving a negative response, he soon followed it with, "Have you told him yet?" Unwilling to deal with this any longer, he told Sutata to join him as they went to talk to Zomba. Sutata really did not wish to face the Troll Lord, whom he deeply feared, but he knew he had no choice. Being on a short break, they saw Zomba standing by himself, looking over his captives.

Zomba saw the two Trolls approaching and noted that one was the despised Sutata. The Troll Lord frowned, but before he could say anything, Hanto grasped Sutata's right hand and held it out for his inspection. Hanto saw the eyes of Zomba widen, for Trolls would not cede their talons willingly. When lost in battle, a missing claw was deemed a wound, although minor.

The Troll Lord now comprehended the depth of vileness that Sutata's plan entailed. He recognized the fact that he may have to give the molester credit, but it would wait until he viewed the captives moving forward at a decent pace.

Urging the obviously nervous Sutata to draw near, Zomba ordered him to the head of the slave loop. He was instructed to await Zomba's permission before touching the woman, and also warned fully of the consequences of claw wounds. Bellowing for all to hear, he ordered the guards to get the captives on their feet and moving, while secretly hoping the Humans would defy him. The proud First-born Men, while not conscious of it, were more than happy to oblige.

Traveling thru the mostly wooded lands south of the Free-Elves home, Dirthlyn pointed out to Dralon some of the landmarks he could remember from his youth. "Well," said Dralon, "it could not have been that long ago." Dirthlyn looked at him strangely and replied. "Aye, it was. I just told you I was but a youth," Dralon still did not understand, so he said nothing. "Dralon, I am an Elf warrior. Every twenty years or so, I am permitted to visit my homeland. I have been this way two or three times in the last fifty years." Dralon, now totally confused, simply nodded his head in understanding.

Within the day, the two wayfarers began to meet the native Elves, but none known to Dirthlyn. However, the ensuing day brought a joyful reunion, for the warrior embraced one of his own. Jefrael, his kin, talked excitedly for only a few more minutes before telling Dirthlyn that he wished to hurry ahead in order to have suitable quarters waiting when the two travelers arrived in the town of

Loraine. Gaining their assent, he hurriedly left for the Elfin town, pausing to look back once, before disappearing into the forest ahead. Dirthlyn felt that Jefrael was keeping something from him, but it would have to wait until tomorrow. He then told Dralon, "We still have a half day of travel to go. Why not set up camp early. Tomorrow we will arrive by noon, refreshed from our long rest?" Agreeing to this, they searched out the last camp site they would need for a while.

Just before the sun crested overhead, they found themselves on the outskirts of the Elfin town called Loraine. Staring at the lone figure moving towards them waving his arms, Dirthlyn sees it is Jefrael, his Elfin kin who had greeted him yesterday. Upon gaining the warrior's side, he blurted out. "Dirthlyn, there is great excitement but even more sorrow in town. Alfred returned first, bringing us joy, for the ordeal of culling our youth was done for another year." Inching even closer to Dirthlyn, he lowered his voice practically to a whisper before going on. "Not long ago Babaduk the Shaman also returned, bearing news so dire we could scarce believe it true!"

Unwilling to give his fellow Elves false hope, Dirthlyn told Jefrael. "Listen to Babaduk and dismay if you must, but he speaks the truth. Sometime in the future the Elves, as a Race, will cease to exist." Knowing the devastation, he has caused by the look on Jefraels's face, he gave him some advice. "Do not tell the others what I have told you. Let me talk to Babaduk first, then I will tell you, and truthfully, all which I am told." Jefrael, still too shocked to speak, nodded his agreement.

The First-born Maregon was a slow learner. Despite repeated kicks to his already battered rib cage, he had obviously forgotten he was supposed to get to his feet. Zomba the Troll Lord, stood in a position to see both the male Human captives, and the female at the head of the loop of slaves. He let an evil smile of anticipation cross his face. Strolling over to Maregon, he ordered him to get moving forward and was pleased at the blank look he received in return. "Human,"

he snarled, "since you do not wish to walk, perhaps you will enjoy the entertainment that the female at the head of the column is about to provide." As the First-born tuned his head to gaze forward, the drooling Sutata was ecstatic. He would now be permitted to molest the Human female, maybe even receive praise for doing so. Grabbing the bottom of the smock, he quickly lifted it clear of her body, leaving it in a crude ball encircling her head and totally exposing her vulnerable body.

Sutata looked back at the Troll Lord and was rewarded by a slight nod of his head. The tormentor moved to the right side of Sherlyna, the Human female captive. He grasped the wadded-up smock that covered her head with his taloned left hand. He used the claw-less fingers of his right hand to play with the hapless females' nipples. Sutata's fantasy of sucking on a hairless nipple was about to become true.

Zomba looked at Maregon to ask if he was ready to start moving, but instead drew his sword when he saw the look of pure hatred and rage on the face of the powerful New-born. Now, having gained a degree of comfort from the sword pointed at the Human's neck, he asked, "Are you ready to move forward?" The only response he got was an unwavering hate filled stare from the First-born. Growing uneasy under the gaze of Maregon, he turned toward Sutata once again and signaled for him to continue.

Licking his lips as fantasy evolved into reality the Troll pulled Sherlyna's head back viciously, thrusting her breasts forward to stand high. Cupping a hand beneath a breast he lowered his head and began greedily lapping her nipple with a ward encrusted tongue. Sherlyna struggled, twisting her torso to get her breast free of the Troll's foul tongue. She only managed to embed her nipple deeply between the guard's slobbering lips. Sutata was moaning with pleasure, sucking on the female's nipple was every bit as enjoyable as he had hoped. Now, if the First-born would just resist moving forward.

Moluk awoke from his sleep, still groggy from the effects of the narcotic drug he had ingested. Looking up, he was startled to see the face of Celena looking down at him with obvious concern. "How is your arm feeling now?" Moluk told her, "It is not as painful as before, but maybe it is because the drug is still working." Celena rose to leave, but noting the look of disappointment on the Elf's face, told him she would return promptly with food and drink. Sitting alone, Moluk realized he felt guilty about lying to Celena. The pain in his arm was nearly unbearable, and with the amount of the narcotic he had taken, he should be pain free. Moluk had suffered many grave wounds in his long life, but nothing compared to this. He was deathly frightened for his life.

The Elf warrior was unsure what to do next. There was a group of First-born still wandering about in the northwest with no inkling as to where the rest of the Humans were. He was supposed to gather volunteers and head north after two days of instructing the First-born in the use of arms, but that was before he viewed the Elf and Human captives. Should he trail the Trolls, trying to free the slaves, or head north to the Land of Horses as planned? More importantly, if he were to die, could the First-born even make it to the Land of Horses alive? All these thoughts and more swirled about his head as he waited in pain for food he did not want, but knew he needed, if he wished to keep what little strength he had left.

Just as Moluk was deciding on a course of action, Celena returned bearing food and drink. After eating a quiet meal together, Moluk thanked her for her kindness and asked if she would send Domigo to see him. Celena readily agreed to this, telling Moluk she would check on him later, to see if he required anything.

A short time later, Moluk saw the First-born nearing, and gestured for him to sit and eat, for Celena had left the uneaten food behind. Domingo declined the offer of food, but partook of the mead like beverage the First-born had learned to make.

"Domingo, if we are to leave to meet Dralon in the Land of Horses, you must organize the First-born." He then reminded the Human that all the weapons in the world would not defend them from the Trolls if they did not know how to handle them. Domingo agreed with Moluk, and told him so. "Good, then after this conversation has ended, gather the First-born willing to learn the use of weapons, and we will demonstrate how to use them." Domingo stood to leave, but was halted by Moluk. "Two more things, first, send a couple of Men to the Troll encampment. Aye, they are long gone. Bring back clothing and supplies enough for six, to be used on our northward trip." Domigo then blurted out, "And the second thing?" Moluk glanced in the direction of his horse before answering. "I have need of the First-born called Alalyn. If you can spare him for a day, send him to me. He can tell you later what I have asked him to do." Domigo informed the Elf that Alalyn would be sent to see him directly, then took his leave.

A minute later, Moluk, lifting his head from his cup of

mead, saw Alalyn standing before him. "Tell me Alalyn, how are you and my horse getting along?" The Human told him, truthfully, "I am in awe of the animal. As for his part, he tolerates me fairly well." The Elf warrior stared at him hard before responding, "Well said young Man. Would you like to learn to ride him?" Alalyn, now rendered speechless, could only nod his assent. Moluk told him to go back to the horse. He would meet him there momentarily. Opening his tote, the Elf removed his stash of dried narcotics and placed a pinch in his drink. After swirling his cup, he downed the mixture and went off to give a riding lesson.

Dirthlyn, with Dralon in tow, went to find Babaduk, leaving Jefrael standing alone and silent. Dralon too was silent, for he never envisioned a place such as this existed. Until now, the only structures he had seen were the communal lodge of the Elves and crude tents made of animal skins. Dralon was shocked by how many houses he could see, and wondered how many Elves lived here in Loraine.

The first Elf asked by Dirthlyn knew where Babaduk dwelled. Five minutes later, the two Elves were deep in conversation, with Dralon listening to every word. "Babaduk, are you telling us you know the cause of the malady that is destroying the Elder Races?" The Shaman replied, "I do, but there is absolutely nothing any of us can do about it." Dirthlyn wanted more of an answer. "And why is that, Babaduk?" The Shaman, with his new awareness of other thoughts, sensed the warrior would not cease his questioning until he learned the full truth. "Dirthlyn, hear me well, for I have no wish to ever repeat this." Seeing he had both the Elf's and Human's rapt attention, he began his tale.

Only a short while ago, the Gods discovered that Lord Odyden, the powerful of the Demi-Gods, had failed in his attempt to create his own version of Human life. He is now, as we speak, breeding Trolls that wish to feed on Human flesh and brains! He now seeks Elves and First-born, to use in his evil scheme. Elves he has captured already, the Humans still need to be caught.

Dirthlyn, scarcely able to believe what he is hearing, hurriedly asked, "But what is killing off the Elder-races?" Babaduk looked at Dirthlyn with a strange look on his face before telling him, "The Gods are." The warrior was now totally confused, "I was told the Gods created us, why would they wish our demise?" Babaduk did not answer this directly. Taking a few deep breaths, he continued his explanation. The Gods can think of no way to stop Odyden, other than by destroying him. This they are unwilling to do, for he is still a God. Knowing that Odyden needs Trolls for his diabolical plan to work, the Gods decided to lay waste to the Troll Race. The females would become barren, small wounds and minor diseases will quickly kill them. The Gods will show the Troll Race no mercy whatsoever.

Babaduk explained to them that the Gods had always planned on the demise of the Elder Races once Men appeared on the face of the earth. Now they were simply speeding up the event for the Trolls, and by inclusion, all the other Elder Races. In the case of the hearty Elves, this process could still last generations, for Babaduk planned on teaching them what to be aware of.

"Dirthlyn, and you Dralon, listen well. There is a good chance the three of us, along with the Gods, are the only ones who possess this information. I believe the Gods may have been able to keep the cause of the Trolls destruction from Odyden. I suggest you not share what I just told you with just anyone." Babaduk then began answering questions, as he knew he would, for the next two hours.

When done, the two warriors, one Elf, one Human, knew as much about the plans of the Gods as he did. Babaduk had wondered often about how much he would tell the First-born when they met. He now knew.

Domigo, beginning to act the leader, started to organize the First-born. Naldor, cool of head and well respected by the others, agreed to the leadership of the Humans until Dralon or Domigo returned. He then assigned three Men the task of gathering clothes and provisions for at least six, from the Troll's stash.

Within two hours, Alalyn, sitting high upon the back of Moluk's horse, approached Domigo, pride radiating from his handsome face. "Domigo, Moluk has asked me to ride north and locate the Troll's abandoned encampment, then into the west to find the missing First-born." Domigo protested, "But if you lead them back, my departure to the north will be delayed." Before he could argue further, Alalyn told him, "Moluk told me to hoist an ensign at the Troll's camp, as high as possible. He wants you to do the same here." Looking up at the mounted First-born, a blank expression on his face, he simply asked, "Why?" Alalyn hastily explained. "When I locate the lost First-born in the west, they will be able to find the Troll's camp by the high-flying banner." Domingo agreed this was a good idea since Alalyn, and more importantly the horse, would be able to return here. "The Humans will then pack clothes and provisions as they saw fit and bring them back to you." Domigo still seemed confused, "But why am I to hoist a flag here?" Recalling the words of the Elf warrior, he replied to Domingo, "The banner will aid the First-born, moving south with supplies, in finding our camp. With both ends of the trail marked, you can send for more provisions at your leisure." Domigo now thought this was a great plan.

Alalyn had turned his horse north when he remembered one last thing. "Moluk said that unless you knew of a better location, the ensign would well serve to mark the Realm of Man!" Moments later the First-born's form, astride the horse, was grew smaller as he went in search of the former Troll encampment.

Maregon launched himself at Zomba when he saw the Troll Lord turn his head to look at Sutata. With his hands bound behind his back, he intended to viciously smash his forehead into the Troll's leering face, but was stopped short by the rope binding him to the other captives. Sneering at the human trying to reach him and protected by his once again raised sword, he invited him to look forward, to where Sutata's vile plan continued to unfold.

The Troll sucking on Sherlyna's nipple knew he needed to act quickly if he wished to fulfill his dream of penetrating the female with his claw-less fingers. The First-born Men would not permit the female to be violated for long. He also knew, without a doubt, that Maregon would kill him if given even half a chance. Sutata moved his slobbering lips from her nipple and spat a glob of mucus into his cupped hand. Sherlyna relaxed a bit, being rid of the foul lips sucking on her nipples, only to let lose a muffled scream as she felt a slimy finger enter both her vagina and her ass. Her desperate squirming resulted in the Troll's huge, grossly lubricated fingers slipping deeper into her body.

Maregon had refused to look forward, but when he heard the prolonged wail from Sherlyna, he was forced to view the Troll's hand viciously pumping in and out of her body. Unwilling to let this continue, Maregon called out. "Zomba, order your vile Troll to stop. We will move forward." The Troll Lord stared at him blankly, as if he had not heard a single word, letting Sutata's foul attention to the female's body continue. Again, the First-born called out, "Troll, I will not beg you, nor anyone else, but if you leave the Woman alone, I promise to move the First-born forward."

Zomba let an evil smile of victory crease his face. He had gotten all he had wished for and more. The Troll Lord loosed a terrifying howl. Gaining Sutata's attention he ordered the ecstatic Troll away from the devastated female. Sutata slowly strolled back to Zomba, licking his fingers, as he went to receive his just reward.

The Elfin warrior Moluk was well pleased. His spirited horse had readily accepted the First-born Alalyn upon his back. Teaching him to stay there, at full gallop, a bit more challenging. Within an hour the Human had both a basic understanding of horsemanship, and a sore ass. Moluk spent the next full hour explaining how to care for the powerful steed. After giving Alalyn instructions, he had sent him off to find Domingo, while he went to join the First-born awaiting weapon training.

The Elf had previously assigned two Men the task of bringing one tool of each type to the gathering. Moluk stood silent for a few minutes, waiting for Domigo to arrive. Seeing him approach, the warrior grabbed an ax from the pile of tools and swung it in a vicious arc that just missed Domigo's throat. First-born," he yelled at the shocked Humans, while making eye contact with each, "That is how you separate the ugly head of a Troll from his gross body." Sensing the growing excitement of the First-born, he demonstrated the use of hatches, draw knives, and other sharp-edged tools, but especially long handled axes, in the art of removing Troll body parts.

The Elf studied the actions of Domigo, helping those who were timid or shy about using weapons, with almost a bit of pride. He had learned something after all from their numerous conversations concerning arms and defense. In an hour's time, Moluk could discern the swoosh of keen blades as they bit the air. As the First-born continued their training, Moluk became conscious of the fact that if Trolls wished to harvest more Humans, they needed to come in masse. If not, the result of the attack would be Troll carcasses befouling the warm breezes blowing gently across the Realm of Man.

Moluk was well satisfied and called for a break, informing the few Women who had attended that the instructions were over, and they were free to leave. The Elf waited for the females to depart, then asked the Men to gather about, for he had information to impart and a vital question to ask. "Humans hear me well. Dirthlyn, an Elf warrior such as myself, and Dralon, of the First-born, whom you well know, have gone north to capture horses such as the one I ride." Giving them a moment to absorb this, he went on, "Dralon needs volunteers. Upon the return of Alalyn, Domigo and I depart for the Land of Horses." The warrior looked each First-born in the eye before asking, "Who will travel north with us?" With no hesitation Erigon, Redali, and Trylon said they would go. Joslyn, suddenly fathoming the remaining Men would receive but little rest from the amorous First-born Women, and hoping to experience physical activities of a different type, begged to be included in the group. The Elf warrior had wanted a few more Men, but was secretly happy with the group he ended up with.

Needing to rest again and take more of his pain killing drug, Moluk informed the Humans they would meet early the next morning to make plans for their trek to the north. Leaving the Men talking amongst themselves, the hurting Elf retreated to his shady tree and his precious supply of narcotics. He was surprised and grateful to see Celena awaiting him with freshly drawn water and more food. Noting that she had cleaned both the containers he had used for drugs, he swiftly mixed, then drank, a pain killing cocktail. The Elf used the second container to blend the same dried herb, as before, into a thick paste. Moluk did not want Celena to see his arm, so using the pretense of needing a clean bowl, he requested her to rinse the dirty one in clean flowing water. The First-born gave him a questioning look, but left to do as he asked.

Moluk grimaced in acute pain as he quickly unwrapped his inflamed arm, the odor of corrupted flesh almost overwhelming him. The Elf recognized he needed help, and knew that hiding the extent of his injury from his Human allies was not the answer.

Celena returned bearing the washed bowl. Moving to

Moluk's side to hand it to him, she gasped in horror when she viewed his infected arm. The flesh was obviously rotting away. The First-born had seen nothing worse than a bruise or scrape. This foul wound was beyond her comprehension.

Moluk saw the look on her face and rued permitting her to view his arm. "Celena," he asked quietly," go fetch Domigo for me, for as you can see, I am in dire straits." Scant moments later, Domingo arrived. Although warned by Celena as to what he would see, he too drew in a sharp breath when he saw the Elf's forearm. "Moluk, what has happened to you? I thought you said the wound was but a minor cut." The Elf warrior looked at Domigo, agony radiating from his face. "I told you truthfully, it was a mere cut, but now it is killing me!" Then, in a whisper barely audible, "You must remove this foul appendage, or I will die!" Looking down in shock at Moluk, the First-born stammered, "What do you mean? Remove what?" The Elf, his eyes boring into Domingo's, harshly told him, "Human, steel yourself, for you must cut off my arm or I will soon perish."

The youthful First-born learned firsthand that friendship sometimes came at a terrible price.

Sutata sauntered up to Zomba the Troll Lord, confident of great praise, perhaps even a reward, for his successful plan to get the First-born moving forward at a brisk pace. The Troll Lord said pleasantly," I have decided to greatly reward you." The Troll was beside himself with joy, perhaps Zomba would let him privately molest the Woman. For his part, he would promise to do her no permanent damage. "Yes Troll," Zomba continued, his voice now low and full of menace, "as your just reward I have decided to let you live!" Dumbstruck, Sutata stammered out, "I do not understand!" The Troll Lord glared at him icily, before growling. "It is really quite simple Troll. I was planning on killing you for your insolence. I will now let you live. This is the greatest possible reward I could give you." Turning to walk away, Zomba looked back over his shoulder and lashed out at Sutata, "Now get these slaves up and moving before I change my mind!" Sutata did as ordered, but planed on making the Troll Lord pay dearly for this treatment, when he talked to Odyden the Master again.

In just a few minutes, for the first time since they left the Troll encampment, the captives were moving at a pace suitable to Zomba. He realized he owed much to Sutata, he also knew he would never thank him. It was enough, in his mind, that he let him live.

After two days of speedy travel, Zomba felt they were no longer being followed, if they ever were, but he needed to be sure of this. Summoning Hanto, he told him his plan and that he would be in charge until he returned. He planned on being gone at least twenty-four, but not more than forty-eight hours. Zomba then dismissed Hanto, telling him to send Sutata to him. When the still shaken Troll arrived, he described in vivid detail the punishment that would befall him should he touch the females without Hanto's permission,

Zomba walked to where he left his tote and threw a few provisions into it. He knew the task should be easy. He planned to hide in the immediate area and simply let the slave caravan move northward without him. Lying out of sight and quiet, the Troll Lord would need but a short time to determine if he was being followed by an Elfin warrior and his companions.

The Elfin warrior Moluk knew the infection in his

forearm was killing him. He asked Celena to gather wood for a small fire and for Domigo to fetch the keenest edged ax he could find, along with a short length of a large diameter log. Returning with his supplies, he saw Celena had come back and already stacked kindling into a loose pile. Moluk shouted out for Domigo to light the fire and then join him. When the fire was burning brightly, Domigo waved Celena to his side, and together they walked with dread to hear instructions they did not wish to follow. Upon reaching the stricken Elf, he gave them no time to feel sorry for themselves. "Celena" he ordered, "get the drugs from my tote, you have watched me mix them, and also a supply of cloth to wrap my wound." Celena moved away to do as requested. "Domigo my friend, bear up, for this will soon be over," Moluk said quietly to the First-born. Domigo did not say anything, but he totally disagreed. This ordeal seemed hours long already, and not about to end anytime soon.

Moluk had Domigo move the log next to him and he spread out his arm along its length. "Domigo, when Celena is ready, place the head of the ax into the fire for a few minutes. Be careful you do not burn the handle." The First-born stared incredulously at him before he nodded his assent. Moluk then continued, "When you strike my arm, leave the glowing head of the ax embedded in the log, then hold the stump of my arm against the heat of the blade until the bleeding stops. Have Celena help you, for I may struggle with the pain." Looking at the horrified face of Celena he added, "If I pass out, apply the paste to my wound and bind it." Domigo, realizing this would get no easier by delay, placed the head of the sharp broad ax into the fire.

Within minutes the metal ax head was emitting a soft orange glow. Domingo knew the time to act was upon him. The First-born pulled the ax from the fire and hurried to the Elf's side, anxious for the ordeal to be over. Moluk held up his good arm as Domingo neared. "Two things Domingo, first cut me just below the elbow, secondly, swing like you were attacking a Troll. You do not have the fortitude for a second swing." Domingo greatly resented this remark, as Moluk had hoped he would. Moving to the side of the log supporting the Elf's arm, the powerful First-born spread his legs, took measure of his target, and with a mighty stroke separated the rotting flesh of the Elf's lower arm from the rest of the limb.

The warrior had yet to utter a sound, but when Domigo, with the aid of Celena, held his bloody stump against the still glowing metal of the ax head, he moaned loudly, violently trying to remove the remainder of his arm from the searing heat. Suddenly the First-born felt the Elf's body go limp. Mercifully he had passed out. Domingo helped bandage Moluk's arm, noting with morbid satisfaction, that, per the Elf's request, he still retained his elbow.

Celena made sure the bowl with the pain killer was well mixed and within easy reach. She threw the remaining wood, along with the bloody log, onto the fire, shortly followed by Moluk's foul arm, with its attached hand. She stood watching the blaze, unable to tear her eyes away from the flames until the vile thing that once had been Moluk's arm, had been reduced to ashes. Celena walked away from the slowly dying fire to return to the side of the unconscious Elf. Celena looked carefully, but other than his steady breathing, she detected no motion. She went to collect the water she had brought with her, along with more cloth from Moluk's supply. Back at the Elf's side, she sat and wiped his fevered brow with a cool cloth, then placed his head upon her cushioning lap. Celena would now know the instant he regained consciousness and have the narcotic drink at his lips. Until then, she could only wait and watch over his still body.

Hanto, the Troll commander, stood roughly in the center of the loop of captives, yelling at the Elves and Humans to get on their feet and moving. Maregon and Samtoz, the two captive First-born Men, glared their defiance at the Troll, but knowing what would happen to the Woman if they resisted, rose to their feet and began moving forward as ordered. Hanto, now aware of Sutata's falling out with Zomba, wished to regain the Troll Lord's ear and confidence. He realized that now would be an excellent opportunity.

Before ordering Hanto to advance the slaves, Zomba had located a small outcropping of large rocks. Seeing a stand of pine trees nearby, the Troll used his sword to cut down three short, wide trees. Zomba pointed the ends of the trunks, buried the chips, and then returned to his stone lair. Zomba used his incredibly powerful clawed hands to loosen the soil in three locations in front of the rocks, forming a rough semi-circle. Inserting the pointed end of a pine into the earth at each location, the Troll Lord smiled. He had quickly rendered himself virtually invisible. Stretching out, Zomba made himself comfortable, for he knew nothing more was required of him save to remain both quiet and alert.

Hanto drove the slaves forward at a much faster pace than before. He was determined to impress Zomba with the progress he could get out of the captives. The two First-born Men had complained to him that the Elves and Women would be unable to maintain this pace. Hanto's response was the positioning of a female Elf, that Sutata could also molest, to the side of the lead captive, the First-born Woman Sherlyna. With the Humans now urging the Elves to keep moving, the forced march continued on its northern bearing.

It was only mid-morning and Zomba was already bored. The Troll Lord could never recall being prone on his bedroll in the middle of the day, not even for sex. He typically bent the She-Trolls over where found, and had his way with them. He wanted to move south, seeking out anyone attempting to follow him, but knew that if spotted by an Elfin warrior sitting high upon the back of a mighty steed, he had little chance of living. Nay, he thought, it was much more desirable to be bored than dead.

Celena felt the Elf stir before the moan formed on his lips. Lifting his head when his eyes opened, she raised the bowl of pain killer to his mouth and told him sternly, "Moluk, drink this." The Elfin warrior, after a tentative sip, eagerly drained the bowl. Peering up at the lovely features of Celena, the Elf wanted to tell her something important to him, but fell back into unconsciousness without uttering a word.

Domigo reappeared a short time later, "How is he doing?" She had no need to look at him. She heard the concern in his voice and knew that he had already gotten over Moluk's deliberate put down. "He awoke a few minutes ago and I gave him more pain killing drink. He quickly passed out again, but I believe his fever has abated somewhat." Domigo was well pleased with this news. He briefly thought of asking Celena if he could watch over the Elf for a while, giving her a well needed break, but sensed it would be a waste of breath, for she was not leaving his side. Instructing Celena to call out if she required help, Domigo left to give the other First-born the good news. He had only gone a few steps when he heard, "Domigo, come back, I need your help!" Quickly returning, he asked with grave concern, "What is it you need?" Handing him the empty container which had held the narcotic drug she requested, "Clean this, then bring both the water flask and Moluk's tote to my side." Domigo knowingly nodded his head in assent. Leaving her to do as asked, he knew his intuition had been correct. While he lived, Celena of the First-born would not long be separated from the Elf warrior with but one hand.

Alalyn galloped to the north atop the horse until he could slow the animal without being detected. Moluk had taught him much about riding, but naught about how to avoid a sore ass. The First-born knew he was searching for the abandoned Troll camp, so with the horse in a more comfortable lope, he concentrated on what he might find there instead of his aching butt.

The First-born was soon jolted from his daydream

when, in the distance, he could see an array of structures and realized it had to be the Troll's deserted camp. Disregarding his comfort, he urged the still fresh horse back into a full gallop and quickly closed the distance to the edge of the camp. Entering the compound, Alalyn slowed the steed to a lazy walk, taking in the empty animal skin tents. Alalyn decided to dismount and investigate three large piles covered with oiled hides. The first pile yielded the Elfin made clothing Moluk had told him of. Uncovering the next two rewarded him with a large supply of provisions, including coils of rope, which he was in need of. He also found large quantities of dried food, although most of it appeared to be flesh of some sort.

Alalyn had wandered deeper into the Troll's camp when he detected the odor of rotting flesh. Following his nose, the First-born soon found the Troll's stash of now badly decaying meat. He could not now spare the time, but if he located the missing First-born and sent them here, he intended to ask them to burn the putrid flesh. Alalyn planned to hoist an ensign high over the Troll's former camp. He would not let the lingering odor of the Ogre's rotting meat befoul the air of the northern limit of the new Realm of Man.

After tending to the horse, Alalyn secured a hatchet from the Troll's store and walked to a nearby stand of trees. The First-born chose three tall saplings, hewing the trunk close to the ground with just a single cut and then stripped them of their limbs. Carrying them back into camp, he located a spot of ground covered with various sized rocks and small boulders. Dropping the saplings, he returned to the hide covered mound containing the rope and picked out a coil of hemp with a small diameter, along with a long metal spike. He then visited the pile of clothing, picking out a square piece of cloth from an unfinished garment. Gathering up his supplies, the First-born returned to where he left the saplings and went to work. Alalyn lashed the three trees together, end to end, using a large overlap, not scrimping on the rope. Using the metal spike, he reamed a hole deep into the earth to support his flagpole. He was about to attach the square cloth to be used as a banner to the long mast, when he had a flash of inspiration. Alalyn quickly kindled a small fire, then placed a small limb into the center. Cutting the rope into appropriate lengths, he secured the ensign to the very top of the tall mast. The First-born went to the fire and withdrew the now blazing limb and kicked dirt on the burning end, smothering the fire. Using a previously unknown talent bestowed on him by the Gods, he drew a design on the piece of cloth, then stood back from his effort and allowed himself to smile.

Conscious of the fact he had spent enough time here, he grabbed the end of his makeshift flagpole and attempted, without success, to insert the end of the shaft into the hole he had reamed into the earth. After giving the matter some thought, he dug a shallow trench about five feet long, out from the center of the hole. Alalyn used the metal spike to loosen the soil in the trench. Then he removed the loose soil, deepening it as he neared the hole designed to hold the mast erect. This time when he raised the pole, it slid along the trench until its end wedged against the side of the hole. Alalyn needed every ounce of the strength given to the First-born as he struggled to keep the mast from toppling over. Lunging against the mast again, Alalyn felt the end of the shaft break away from the side of the hole, dropping solidly to the bottom with a satisfying thud. Stepping back a few paces, Alalyn looked up with pride at the flagpole standing tall above the grasses of the Southern Coastal Plain, even if it was somewhat tilted.

The First-born used small rocks, wedging them into the hole. He then tamped them to the bottom, holding the ersatz mast into place. He finished his task by filling the hole with gravel, tamping each layer into place. When done, he had the mast standing tall and true. He then gathered rocks and small boulders, which he piled high around the flagpole to secure it in place. When done, he had unknowingly created Mankind's first monument.

Alalyn knew he could delay no more, sore ass or not. Making a final trip to the mounds of provisions, he donned an Elf made tunic, mostly so he could hang a sword about his waist with a length of thick rope. Alalyn immediately felt better with a sword at his side. Not knowing how to use it bothered him little, for until an hour ago he had never used a hatchet. Reaching the horse, he gingerly gained its broad back and headed the powerful steed into the west, in search of the missing First-born. Glancing back over his shoulder, Alalyn looked with pride at the slightly fluttering ensign he had hoisted. Half the cloth depicted a mighty rearing horse, nostrils flared in excitement. The rest of the flag bore the image of crossed swords, the new emblem of the powerful First-born.

Moluk regained consciousness without movement, but when he opened his eyes, he saw the face of Celena staring intently down upon him with a strange mixture of relief and adoration that took him aback. "Moluk, how do you feel?" she quietly asked, while lifting the bowl of pain killer to his lips. The Elf warrior blinked his eyes several times, giving him time to collect his thoughts. "Celena, in truth, the sadness of losing a hand is less than the joy I feel from being relatively pain free." Hiding the excitement, she felt from this news, the First-born Woman smiled at him lovingly, then helped him regain his feet.

Moluk realized he was physically able to do little, but knowing plans still needed to be made for the northbound trek of the Horseman, he asked Celena to take him to Domigo.

Domigo, sitting with Erigon and Trylon, was startled to see the Elf warrior approaching, his intact arm draped over the shoulder of Celena. After asking Trylon to gather wood for a fire, Domigo left to meet the Elf. The First-born led the warrior back to where Erigon still sat and bid him to join them on the large log being used as a seat. Moluk sat at once, halting Celena as she attempted to join them.

"Celena", he said gently. "I need to make plans with the Men, the talk would but bore you," She looked at him with disappointment, but said nothing, so the Elf continued. "If you wish, go and prepare a place for us to spend the night. Take my tote and build a small fire to warm my body." Celena, now admitting to herself that she had wished to warm his body using her own since they had first met, said to him in a husky voice that the Elf had never heard before, "Moluk, I indeed intend to spend the night with you and you have my word that I will not let you grow cold." Moluk, unsure of where this was heading told her, "I look forward to the warmth."

Celena turned to leave but was stopped when Moluk gently took her hand in his and pulled her head down to his level. "Celena, I am now almost pain free due to the drink that you gave me, but its effects will wear off in about two more hours. Mix a new batch of narcotics like before, then and come and get me." Looking at her as a lover rather than a nurse for the first time, Moluk was mesmerized by the curves of her voluptuous naked body. Then in a whisper, he told her, "Coming to get me to take my medication will give me an excuse for leaving the Men."

Zomba lie abed all day long, his mood fouler with each passing hour, for he had yet to see or hear anything out of the ordinary. With full darkness nearing, the Troll Lord emerged from his rock hideaway, muscles stiff and cramped due to his inactivity. Using his superb night vision, the Troll scanned the landscape in all directions, including the direction the caravan had taken. Zomba, with the moon already ascending, now knew there were no Elfin warriors following him, and sensed there never had been. Angry at himself for unnecessary delays caused by phantom fighters, Zomba kicked the pine trees out of the ground, exposing his tote and bedroll lying between the rocks. Retrieving his meager possessions, the Troll Lord headed north. With a little effort he should be able to rejoin the other Trolls well before dawn.

Early in the afternoon, Hanto begrudgingly gave the order for a halt. The First-born were growing tired, the shorter legged Elves near exhaustion. The Troll commander howled to gain the captives attention. "Listen well slaves, a guard will come by shortly and give you all the water you wish to drink." A look of relief covered the faces of the timid Elves. The First-born simply stared with naked hatred at the Troll. Continuing on Hanto informed then, "I have more great news for you slaves. You may eat all you wish, but you will march six more hours before it is mealtime!" Maregon strained at the ropes binding his arms behind his back, the muscles in his chest standing out like heavy cords. Zomba was unwilling to free the two male First-born hands. Fearful of their strength, he forced them to kneel to eat their food, like an animal. Maregon dreamt of turning a Troll's heinous face into a mass of mush from repeated blows delivered by his mighty fists. For now, it would remain but a dream, for the bindings holding his hands refused to give.

Hanto realized none of the tired captives would move forward without proper encouragement. The commander called out for Sutata, and when he drew near, whispered in his ear before sending him to join the two lead females. Once again in his glory, Sutata hurried to the head of the slave caravan. He walked up to Kathwen, the Elf female, without saying a word. Spitting into his right hand, he picked her up by the waist with his left. He quickly flipped up her short tunic, exposing her surprisingly ample ass. The vile Troll used the tip of his well lubricated index finger to gain entrance to her vagina. Sutata began to forcefully insert more of his huge finger into her body, when he was rewarded by the sweet sound of her drawn out scream. The Troll commander swiftly took stock of the slaves. Elves were on their feet, staring mortified at the scene before them. The First-born, while also looking forward, were saving their energy and had made no effort to gain their feet. After all, it was just a finger in an Elf.

Hanto suddenly had a flash of inspiration, something even the gross Sutata would be proud of. "Humans," he bellowed," if you thought your precious female enjoyed having her breast licked by the Troll, wait until you see the pleasure her vagina receives from the wart covered tongue of Sutata!" The First-born Men jumped to their feet, soon followed by the females. Hanto shouted at Sutata, ordering him to release the Elfin Woman and get the captives moving. Sutata was bitterly disappointed, but did as he was told. Hanto was well pleased with himself.

This was turning out to be far easier that he had dared hope.

Zomba traveled hard until well after midnight,

thinking it strange he had not yet caught up with his Trolls, but thankful for the progress that was being made by Hanto. The Troll Lord was somewhat tired after his hard march and decided to rest for a while. Before the sun goes up, he would be heading north to rejoin the slave caravan. After a few hours of uneasy sleep, Zomba arose and headed out in search of his wayward Trolls and their captives.

Hanto drove the prisoners forward without mercy,

stopping only twice to disperse water and let the slaves relieve themselves. The sun had long set before Hanto allowed the captives to stop for the night. The Elves were totally spent. The First-born glared at the tired Trolls with open scorn. Seeing the First-born Maregon sneering at him, Hanto ran toward him, stopping a long sword length away. "Human, I have been kind enough to halt for food and rest, what is your problem?" Smiling pleasantly at the ugly Troll commander, Maregon responded, "I have no problem Troll. I was just thinking it was kind of you to give your short-legged kinfolk, who have but little endurance, a rest." The Troll commander said nothing, staring at his feet, apparently at a loss for words. Suddenly, the Ogre viciously lashed out with his huge clawed hand, turning one side of Maregon's face into bloody strips of hanging flesh. Instantly fathoming the consequences of his actions, he went in search of an Elf who was proficient with needle and thread.

Maregon endured the blow to his face without undue concern until he raised his hand to his face seeking the source of the blood quickly covering the tunic he wore. The First-born's hand found the strips of flesh that had been his cheek at the same time the first wave of pain washed over him. Maregon knew he was gravely hurt and needed to stop the flow of blood quickly. The mighty First-born stood in a daze. He had no idea what to do when the Elfin Woman Sherina hurried to his side. Maregon was indeed lucky, for the Elf had tended to grievous wounds before. "Lie on the ground, on your back, and be quick about it," she ordered. "And keep your hands away from your face!"

Working fast, in the light from a fire the Trolls had lit, she rinsed away what blood she could from his face then began smoothing the strips of face back together, binding them into place with delicate stitches as she went. Throughout the ordeal, the First-born said nothing, channeling his energy into thoughts of revenge rather than on the pain feeding on his face. Finished, Sherina studied her handiwork, adding a stitch here and there to areas that were still seeping blood. Satisfied that she had stopped all blood flow, she gently let water cascade over his ravished cheek, removing the last of the now drying blood. She made no attempt to dry his face. The still warm breezes and his own fevered brow would take care of that. Gathering up the few things she had brought with her, Sherina retreated back to her place among the slaves, wanting to get away before Hanto returned.

Maregon was still lying on the ground, bearing the pain of his wound without sound or movement, when he espied Hanto approaching. The First-born quickly closed his eyes feverously hoping the Troll would think him near death and order his hands unbound.

Waiting for Celena to depart, the Elf warrior inquired of Domigo. "What have you done to prepare us for our trip to the north?" The First-born responded, "I have sent Men to the deserted Troll encampment to bring back clothing and supplies." Moluk nodded his approval as Domigo continued. "Naldor, who is both even tempered and well respected by the First-born, has agreed to be leader of the New-born until our return." The Elf again nodded, then asked, "I am sure Alalyn told you of his assignment?" This time it was Domigo who dipped his head in acknowledgment. All was quiet for a moment, then Erigon spoke up. "Did not the plan call for you to leave two days after you arrived here?" The Elf warrior slowly shifted himself on the log to face Erigon. "Yes, it did, but it was mostly wishful thinking from the start." Seeing this meant little to the incredibly powerful First-Born, he attempted to explain further. "If Alalyn and the Men sent for supplies returned within two days it may have been a possibility. Now, with my wound needing a little time to heal, we will wait." Erigon, still not getting the information he wanted, harshly demanded, "For how long, Elf?" Domigo leapt to his feet and hurried to stand before Erigon, glaring down at him. "Erigon, if not for this warrior your sorry ass could very well be marching north with the other captives to an unknown fate!" Erigon, suddenly realizing the Elf had sacrificed his hand and part of his arm to aid the Humans, felt grossly ashamed of his actions. Rising from his log seat, the most powerful of the First-Born moved to humbly stand in front of the smallish Elf. "Moluk, I am truly sorry for my unthinking words." The Elf warrior saw the sincerity on the face of the First-Born and would hold no grudge. He then told him, "We will wait for the Men bringing supplies, for there are swords and knives for the taking in the Troll's hoard. They will surely bring back all they can carry." Erigon stared at the Elf with sudden understanding, "You mean I will carry a sword instead of a hatchet or draw knife?" The Elf looked at him with a sly smile before responding. "Aye Erigon, and with my teaching, your mighty arm will know how to wield it." Erigon could only smile at the thought.

The Men and Elf talked on, agreeing a few more days of time for Moluk's arm to improve would not make a great deal of difference in their overall plans. It would also give the First-Born a little time to learn how to use real weapons, not the tools they were now using. A short time later Redali and Joslyn showed up, disappointing the always horny First-Born Women they had been keeping entertained. Domigo bid them to pull up another log on the other side of the small fire, then updated them on the new plans. The two newcomers said they understood, and joined in the ongoing conversation taking place around the comforting campfire.

The First-Born Woman Celena had left the Elf warrior, returning to the place where she had cared for him. Not wishing to spend the night at the place where he had lost his hand, she quickly gathered up his few belongings and departed the sorrowful area. Celena knew there was a dense stand of pine trees nearby, the forest floor covered with a layer of fragrant needles. In a few minutes she disappeared from the view of Man, hidden away in her own private world. Celena cleared an area, making it safe for a campfire, then collected a large supply of firewood, stacking it neatly by the fire site. Next, she piled pine needles deeply, covering them with a surprisingly soft cloth from Moluk's tote. Realizing she had another chore left, she hurried off, returning shortly with food and extra water flasks. Celena was attempting to make the camp as comfortable as possible, hoping Moluk would stay here with her until departing for the north.

While setting up camp Celena had thought of nothing but the hours to come, her physical desire increasing by the minute. She had not been touched by a male or herself since the Elf warrior had appeared out of nowhere. The lustful First-Born Woman did not know if the tryst would bring her the satisfaction she sought, but she was determined to try.

Knowing it must be near time to rescue the Elf from the clutches of the boring Men, she quickly mixed a pain killing drink, then headed back to the council of Horsemen.

When Dralon the First-Born and Dirthlyn the Elf emerged from Babaduk's dwelling, Jefrael was awaiting them. "Dirthlyn, I have spoken with my cousin who informed me there is plenty of room available in the house if you would like to stay there." Dirthlyn conferred briefly with Dralon before telling Jefrael, "We would be pleased to enjoy the comforts of your cousin's house." The Elf, seemingly elated by their decision, told them he would lead them there. Following the guide Dralon was still in awe with the amount of structures he saw. He reckoned that if each building held but two Elves, there numbers would far exceed that of the First-Born. Jefrael led them down a long lane with Elfin dwellings on each side, stopping at the last cottage on the right. "Wait here a moment and I will see if my cousin is ready to receive us." Within a minute, Jefrael reopened the heavy wooden door at the front of the house and bid them enter. "My cousin is dressing but will join us momentarily." He showed them two rooms, each with a comfortable bed, although one bed was considerably larger. "Dirthlyn, do I really have to sleep on one of those?" Dralon inquired. "No, but I suggest you try it. As leader of the First-Born, you will not always be able to sleep under the open sky."

Dralon was standing silent, in thought, when he heard soft footsteps behind him. Turning his head toward the source, the First-Born took in breath with an audible gasp. Standing just behind him was the most stunningly beautiful woman he had ever seen. Dralon was still standing in the same place with his head turned, when Jefrael walked to his side and said, "Dralon, this is my cousin, Chandelle.

Waiting until Dralon turned to face her, the alluring Elfin Woman walked up to him, studying him in great detail. "I now know what our replacement males look like," she told the First-Born without malice. Moving even closer, she seductively asked. "Are the First-Born Women as pretty as you are handsome?" Dralon had no idea how to respond, so he said truthfully, "The First-Born Women, with their pretty faces and naked bodies, are a joy and bring me great pleasure, but I have never seen one as lovely as you." This time it was Chandelle who was at a loss for words. Jefrael came to their rescue when he asked, "Dralon, as my cousin's honored guest, which room have you decided to take?" The First-Born, still unable to tear his eyes away from the Elfin beauty, saw her glance to her left. Following her eyes, he pointed in the general direction she had looked and said, "I will take that room." Chandelle smiled wantonly to herself as she watched Man and Elf take their possessions to their appointed rooms.

Galloping hard despite the pain radiating from his saddle-sore ass, Alalyn was soon well west of the former Troll camp. He slowed his horse to a more comfortable gait and began his search for the missing First-Born.

Three hours later, with his horse growing tired and needing rest, Alalyn was growing concerned about the safety of the Humans. Perhaps Moluk had been wrong and there were still Troll hunters seeking out the First-Born.

Alalyn now had the horse at a walk, seeking a suitable resting spot with a water supply, when a figure in the far distance suddenly appeared and began waving their arms in the air. Alalyn cautiously turned his horse toward the stranger, relativity sure he was not dealing with a Troll and positive he could flee swiftly if need be. A few minutes later, Alalyn waved back at the naked form of a First-Born Man. Looking carefully, Alalyn could see more bodies emerging from the wooded tract behind the Man.

Aware that the First-Born had never seen a horse, Alalyn halted, letting the awe-struck Human come to him, instead of bearing down on him from atop the mighty animal. As the First-Born neared, Alalyn smiled, attempting to put him at ease before telling him, "Go ahead and rub his neck if you wish, my horse will not harm you," The First-Born moved closer and pensively reached his hand out to stroke the neck of the horse. Peering down, Alalyn recognized the face of the Human and asked him,

"What is your name?" Taking his eyes off the majestic beast to look at Alalyn he responded, "I am called by the others Davlyn, I am acting as leader, for we have lost contact with Domigo and Dralon."

Dismounting the tired horse, Alalyn inquired, "Is there fresh water nearby?" Davlyn told him there was a cool flowing stream within the wooded area where the First-Born had been hiding. "Davlyn", the horseman ordered, "take me there, for I have information and orders for you and the others." The naked First-Born spun and headed back toward the woods, Alalyn and his steed following close behind. Nearing the woods, Alalyn asked to be led to the stream. After allowing his horse to sate its thirst, Alalyn led him to an area with sweet grass and hobbled the animal.

While the horse drank, Alalyn had noticed numerous First-Born watching them from afar. This sight pleased him greatly, for he had no wish of returning to Moluk and informing the Elf warrior that he had been unable to locate the missing Humans. He now knew the First-Born had made a wise choice when they elected Davlyn as their leader. The morning after the Troll attack, Davlyn had silently led them to the wooded area. Moving a mere twenty-five yards into the dense stand of trees, they seemingly vanished from the lands of the southern Coastal Plain. If Davlyn had not chosen to show himself, Alalyn would still be wandering the plain, with no hope of ever locating the missing Humans.

Moments later, Alalyn saw the now dead fire pit that was being used by the First-Born and knew that he had arrived at the Human's haven. Davlyn saw him glance at the fire site and quickly explained it had only been used recently, after they were sure no Trolls were pursuing them. "Alalyn, we could hear things prowling in the night, to the west. The fire gave us comfort after dark." Alalyn nodded his understanding, then asked, "Do you wish any others to hear what I have to say?" Davlyn quickly looked about and saw that most of the First-Born had already assembled in a curious circle around them. Lifting his voice, he bid all who wished to come closer and hear the words of Alalyn. To a Man, all crowded as near as they could to the clothed horseman whose hip bore a sword.

"First-born", Alalyn began, "the Trolls have captured five of our kind, along with many

Elves. They are now fleeing to the north with their prisoners." A voice from the rear asked, "Why are they fleeing, we offer no resistance?" Alalyn sought out the questioner and responded, "The horse most of you saw belongs to a warrior of the Elfin Race, who sitting high upon its back, was slaying Trolls from a great distance away." Alalyn did not bother to explain about arrows, which they had never seen, but they seemed properly impressed anyway. Sensing them waiting, he continued, "Domigo, who most of you know, wishes you to travel east to the Troll's deserted encampment." Another voice rang out with the question Alalyn knew would come, "Are you quite sure the Trolls have departed?" This time Alalyn did not bother to seek out the person asking the question, simply telling all, "Aye, I have been to the Troll's camp and encountered naught but my shadow." Davlyn, paying sharp attention to the conversation inquired, "But how are we to find it? Are you going to lead us?" Alalyn stared hard at the capable Davlyn for a long moment before answering, "No, Davlyn, you will lead the First-Born. I have hoisted a tall ensign over the camp which can be seen at a great distance." Davlyn still did not seen to understand. Alalyn tried again," I will show you the direction to travel. Within half a day, at most, you will see the banner high in the sky. Follow it to camp." Now grasping what Alalyn wanted, he asked, "Will Domigo and the other First-Born be there to greet us?" Again, he is told no. "You will gather all the arms and provisions you can carry, then head due south. There you will rejoin the rest of the First-Born." Before Davlyn can ask, Alalyn informed him, "There is another flag, flying high in the south. You should spot it within a few hours of losing sight of yours." Glancing at the faces of the amassed First-Born, he saw they both understood and willingly accepted the plan. Suddenly recalling his own experience, he told Davlyn," If your Men wish to wear a sword about their waist, such as I wear, it is much more comfortable if you wear a tunic or smock." Then, against his better judgment, for he loved to watch the fluid movement of the nude First-born women, "You might suggest to the Women that they also collect clothing. We may not stay in the south forever."

Alalyn continued talking to Davlyn and a few other Men, the others having dispersed to talk amongst themselves, when he felt a large breast, topped by an erect nipple, nudging his arm. Rotating his head slightly, he took in the sensual form of the naked First-Born Shirlia, bearing food and drink. With a not so subtle look, she pointed to the northwest, telling him, "When your conversation was ended, come find me, for I can take care of all your needs!" Giving him a lusty smile, she turned and walked off in the direction she had indicated.

Alalyn was now at a loss. He was tired and hungry, plus his ass hurt. But perhaps part of that was his balls aching, for he had never gone this long without sex. Alalyn knew he had a difficult decision to make.

The Men holding council around the fire ceased their conversation when they saw a figure approaching. They feared something amiss, that anyone would interrupt their meeting, but relaxed when the naked form of Celena came into view. As she walked to stand at Moluk's side, the Men were delighted to see fully aroused nipples adorning the tips of her breast. Celena, ignoring the lusty stares of the Men, bent over to whisper into the Elf's ear. The First-Born, knowing she was already sexually stimulated, took in the view of her captivating ass.

The Elf heard her out, staring jealously at the Men ogling her obvious sexually aroused body. Nodding his head at Celena in a meaningless gesture, he stood and addressed the Horsemen, "My caretaker has informed me it is time for medication and rest." Giving them no time to pretest, he added, "I will rejoin you in the morning." Then walked off with his good arm over Celena's shoulder, his fingertips inadvertently brushing her stiff nipple with every step they took. Once some distance away from the leering Men, Celena took his hand in hers and guided it to fully cup her breast, or at least what he could fit in the palm of his hand. Moluk had been thinking about their last conversation since she had left, hoping he had not misunderstood its implication. Now, with the palm of his hand massaging her erect nipple, he had his answer.

Celena led him to the pine needle bed and bid him to sit. Leaving him for a moment, she returned bearing his bowl of pain killing drink. Handing it to him, she asked, "Are you in much pain Moluk?" Guessing the reason for her question he replied, "No Celena, and with the fresh drink I should be pain free for many hours." Then he watched as a passion filled smile of relief slowly formed on her face. "Moluk", she said quietly, "take your drink and make yourself comfortable while I light the fire, for I do not want you to chill when I take off your clothes." Then she added with a wanton smile, "After all, I did promise to keep you warm."

The Elf sat on the makeshift bed, and not being in much pain, sipped at his drink, enjoying the sight of the naked Woman lighting the fire. Celena was not sure how this tryst would work out, but glancing over her shoulder she saw him leering at her nude body, his hand under his short tunic. She quickly realized that with both of them horny, things would take care of themselves. With the fire now burning brightly, she went back to the bed of pine and sat down beside the Elf. Feeling no need to be coy, she reached her hand out and began running it up his thigh. Her one concern at the time was if the smallish Elf had a large enough penis to properly attend to her needs. As if sensing her thoughts, Moluk reached down with his intact arm, pulling his short tunic up to his waist, exposing a surprising large erect penis, capped with a swollen red head. Celena sighed lightly with relief and lust before moving between his knees and taking half of his cock into her warm mouth. Suddenly realizing she had absolutely no knowledge of Elfin sexual practices, she lifted her head from the cock of the disappointed Elf and asked, "Moluk I am sorry, I got carried away and never asked. Is this something that you enjoy?" The Elf warrior responded with gentle pressure on her head with his one good arm until the entire length of his now throbbing penis was embedded in her warm soft mouth. Happy with his unspoken answer, Celena made herself comfortable, stretching out on her belly while spreading the knees of the Elf wide. Lifting her head, but keeping the end of Moluk's cock between her lips, she pushed her fingers down around the base of his penis and felt the head of his cock swell in her mouth. She then slowly lowered her lips until they met her hand now massaging his balls. Celena moaned in satisfaction. She could feel her pussy becoming wet in preparation of being penetrated by a stiff penis. While waiting to become lubricated, she would enjoy sucking on the erect penis between her lips.

With her passion rising, she decided to give him a treat. Taking his penis deep into her mouth, she used the muscles in her throat to massage the bulbous head of his cock and was shocked and dismayed when he moaned loudly, as he spurted his load deep within her. It was now Celena's turn to moan, but it was in utter disappointment, for this was not even close to what she had in mind.

The Troll commander Hanto approached the still body of the First-born Maregon, fearful he had killed him when he destroyed half his face. He was also furious. The Elf assigned to help the Human was nowhere in sight. Peering down at the stricken form laying prone on the ground, he relaxed a bit. The Elf seamstress he had sent to aid Maregon had done a remarkable job of piecing his face back together. Other than the hundred or so stitches holding his cheek in place, he looked nearly normal. Hanto knew the First-born needed care, but he was unwilling to release any of the Humans to aid him. Calling to the nearest Troll, he told him to bring back the Elf who had saved the Human's life. Moments later, the guard and Elfin Woman returned. Hanto's eyes bored into the Elf's before telling her, "You need to attend to this Human as if your life depended on it, for if he dies, I will let Sutata have his way with you!" Walking away, Hanto ordered food and water, without limit, be given to the injured captive and his caretaker. He then retired to his bedroll in the center of the slave caravan, for he too was exhausted.

Maregon had laid quietly during the conversation and knew his hands would not be unbound. Opening his eyes, the first thing he saw was the cute face of the Elfin Woman. "Are you the one who saved me?" he whispered. When she nodded, he asked, "What is your name?" Without hesitation she responded, "My name is Sherina, one of the forsaken Elves." Maregon did not understand her statement nor troubled himself with asking. "Sherina, help me to sit up if you would, for I have a dire need for water." The Elf placed her arm under his back and eased him into a sitting position. Reaching for the water flask she had brought with her, she let him drink freely. "Maregon," she said kindly, "you also need to eat." The First-born shook his head, "I have no desire for food." Switching to her caregiver voice, she said, "By sun goes up, if not before, we will be forced to march again." Seeing she had gained his attention, she continued. "You will need your strength, for Hanto will show no mercy to laggards, even yourself." Maregon simply nodded in agreement and attempted to eat a bit of the proffered food.

The Troll Lord Zomba was at a total loss. He had been traveling fast since before sun goes up. It was now midday and still no sight of the Trolls and their captives. He knew they were ahead of him for the landscape showed signs of being tromp upon my many feet, but he could not fathom how they could still be so far ahead of him.

After a short rest, he did the only thing that was available to him and pushed on hurriedly to the north. Hours later, Zomba was becoming weary and frustrated. Where were his missing Trolls and slaves?

Zomba had told himself he would travel until dark, and now, with little light in the sky, he was rewarded for his determination. In the far distance he could see what appeared to be plumes of dust rising from the earth's surface. With a sigh of relief Zomba, sensed he had found his missing caravan. Tonight, with his mind at ease, the Troll would sleep well.

Zomba arose early, eager to get moving, for he knew the slaves were only a day's light march ahead. Moving at a pace his Trolls could not maintain, Zomba was at the area where he had seen the dust rising before noon. The Troll Lord slowed his pace when he encountered the patch of ground devoid of all vegetation. Stomping his clawed foot into the ground, he smiled as he watched the dust billow up around his foot. Zomba knew that if the caravan had not stopped exactly here, the location would lie just ahead.

He had barely moved forward when he found the spot they had rested for the night. He saw many places where the grass was flattened from the Troll's hard hide bedrolls and found uneaten oats that were scattered about. Zomba was about to hurry off, when he saw something that distressed him deeply. Peering closely at the dried reddish-brown pool staining the earth, Zomba knew it was blood. With his own blood starting to boil, the Troll Lord swore to himself that if Sutata had raped the First-born Woman Sherlyna, he would be blessed with a slow, painful death.

True to form, Hanto ordered the captives to their feet well before dawn. The First-born, with their leader gravely injured, aped the timid Elves, simply doing as told.

Maregon had spent a restless night with the Elf Sherina lying at his side. Just before the Trolls had awakened the camp, she had given him a priceless gift. When the Elfin Women had been allowed to forage for food while being held in the Troll slave camp, she had come across a narcotic bush, highly prized by the Trolls. Sherina had hid a few leaves in her clothing. "Maregon," she whispered in his ear," open your mouth." The First-born did not understand but did as he was told. Sherina placed a withered leaf on his tongue, warning him, "Do not eat or even chew on the leaf, simply let it soak in your mouth." Maregon did not answer, but grunted softly that he understood. Within five minutes, Maregon felt the pain in his face abating. He had never been more in debt to anyone in his short life as he now was to this Elf maiden.

Sutata noted the Elf standing at the side of the First-born and went to speak to Hanto, the Troll commander. "Hanto", he questioned, "should I return the Elf female to her place in the slave loop?" Hanto thought for a moment before replying, "No, you will leave her at his side." As he was walking away, he looked back over his shoulder and told Sutata, "Inform them both they may still have water for the asking." Sutata hid his sneer, thinking the commander was being overly soft. before realizing that Hanto's life could be on the line should the First-born die. Sutata relayed the commander's largesse to Elf and Man, then bellowed at the captives, ordering them to move forward. This time he had no need of threats.

Maregon spent the morning struggling to stay on his feet, barely able to keep up with the short-legged Elves. Sherina, when she found the Trolls would not stop to let them drink, used this as an excuse for the lost water flowing down the pieced together cheek of the First-born. The Elf caretaker was well pleased, for keeping the wound clean was the only way she had to prevent infection from the Troll's foul talons.

To the slave's great surprise and relief, Hanto called for a rest break well before noon. Then, to their shock, he told them they could rest for an hour or so. Hanto hated to stop the slave's progress, but so far, the injured First-born was still alive, and he intended to keep it that way. The Troll commander also knew he had been very lucky, for Zomba very well could have shown while the Human was close to death.

When the signal for a halt was given, the exhausted Elves plopped to the ground, raising their heads only when a Troll guard came past with a flask of water. The First-born, seeing their injured leader still afoot, remained standing, staring scornfully at the tired Trolls. Knowing Maregon's defiance was not helping him, Sherina urged him to sit quietly and rest. The two were now sitting side by side, the Elf Maiden stroking his hand, trying to get him to relax. Sherina shifted slightly, and Maregon, with a slight stirring of excitement, watched as she slipped her hand under her short tunic. A few seconds later, she withdrew her hand and sat as before, silently rubbing his large hand. "Maregon," she said in a voice none other would hear, "open your hand a bit." The First-born did as she requested, and she slipped another narcotic leaf into his palm. "Spit out the old leaf when you get the chance, the new one will last through the afternoon's march." Maregon had no idea how he would repay her kindness, for he owned nothing except the Elf made clothes on his back. Perhaps she would mention something she would like. He would do all he could to give it to her. The First-born raised his hand, as if wiping his lips, and swapped the old leaf for the new. Within minutes, the little pain he still had faded away, and so did he, his head cradled on the soft lap of Sherina.

Alalyn had made up his mind, sort of. Shirlia had offered food and drink, the warm wet recesses of her body, and a tasty dessert if he desired. The First-born hurried down the path the Woman had taken, and soon found her in a small clearing. She had spread bowls of dried fruit on a flat rock, along with a flask of water. She was on her hands and knees, trying without success to blow a smoldering fire into flame. Viewing the shapely ass, seemingly readily available, he quickly forgot thoughts of food or drink, for they were not going anywhere. Alalyn was removing his smock when he saw her look back over her shoulder and smile in approval when she saw his fully erect penis. Alalyn stood still for a minute, giving her time to move or change position. Instead, she gave him a lewd smile as she moved back away from the barely smoking fire, wiggling her ass enticingly as she moved. Putting her forearms on the ground, she lay her head on them, flexing the cheeks of her butt, now standing totally exposed and high in the air. She had done her part; the rest was up to him.

Alalyn, like the rest of the First-born, knew little of the ways of Women, but realized this one was ready to be fucked. Moving into position behind Shirlia, he wet his fingers well before dropping to his knees. Using his middle finger, he ran it slowly up and down the length of her vagina until her lips easily parted, leaving her pussy exposed to his probing fingers. Moving his fingertip in small circles, he gently found her opening and slightly penetrated her, hoping he had supplied enough lubricant. A moment later his concern ended when he encountered a wetness slicker than he thought possible. With little pressure, his finger disappeared into the depths of her silky-smooth vagina. Hearing her moan of approval, Alalyn added a second finger and continued his probing.

Shirlia, while enjoying herself immensely, was also growing in need by the second. During her last tryst, just before Alalyn had showed up, she had been in the exact same position, ass high in the air, totally exposed for a sex act. A young First-born had asked her for anal sex, explaining that he had never experienced it, promising to give her gorgeous ass his undivided attention. Having no plans for the immediate future, she agreed. Shirlia had been well pleased with the young Man at first. He had used a long tongue to lubricate her, then large fingers to spread the moisture deep to relax her sphincter muscle, making insertion of a large cock possible. Shirlia had been expecting at least oral attention to other parts of her now excited body, but the youth now had her well lubricated ass ready and in an indubitable position. He would not be denied. Recoating his swollen penis with saliva he carefully positioned himself behind Shirlia. Putting her forearms on the ground, she lay her head on them, while her ass cheeks nibbled at the head of the cock nestled at the entrance to her ass. Ready to attempt to enter her, he placed a large hand on each ass cheek, spreading her wide. Knowing she had agreed to have anal sex, Shirlia took the initiative. Relaxing her sphincter muscle completely she suddenly pushed back against his cock and felt the head smoothly enter her ass. The young Man gasped with pleasure, looking down between her cheeks, he could no longer see the head of his penis. Moving his hips forward in short thrusts, he was fascinated watching the length of his cock as it slowly disappeared up her ass. Giving one more firm push, the youth groaned with ecstasy, for his erection was now fully embedded within her hot body. Shirlia, feeling him totally within her, sighed with relief, for his cock, although rock hard, was not large enough to cause her any discomfort. The First-Born, letting his instincts take over, withdrew his penis, leaving only the head in, before smoothly pushing the full length of his cock back into her hot body. Shirlia felt him completely remove his cock from her ass but instantly knew why, when he cupped the twin globes of her firm ass and reinserted the red swollen head of his prick into her now wide-open ass. She recalled one of the First-Born Men telling her how they were totally mesmerized by watching their penis entering a Woman's orifice. The horny youth repeated this a few more times, only allowing her the head of his cock and an inch or so of thick shaft, before pushing himself deep into her body, until his balls nestled against her ass cheeks. Shirlia, with passion now rising, and believing this encounter will work out well, pulsated her muscles as she felt the now throbbing head of his penis bottom out in her ass. She was now completely relaxed and pushed back hard against the youth's belly, hoping to attain a bit more of his penis.

Suddenly to her utter surprise and dismay, she felt the swollen head of his cock, buried deep in her ass, swell even more as he ejaculated long and heavy spurts of hot youthful sperm deep into her upraised ass.

Withdrawing his softening penis from her still carnally inflamed body, he smugly said, "Well, I guess that load will take care of your needs for a while!" Trying hard not to show her physical frustration and mental scorn for the obnoxious youth, she asked him in a low husky voice, "You have not told me your name." In a boastful voice, filled with pride because of his prowess with Shirlia, he answered, "My name is Kenlyn. You may tell your friends about me if you wish, in case they are also in need of servicing."

Wishing him gone, she told him, "Kenlyn, I will be happy to tell the other Women all about my experience with you." Thinking of the future sex he would receive, Kenlyn left with a smug smile on his face. For her part, she could not wait to warn the rest of the First-Born Women about the short-lasting young First-Born.

Bringing her thoughts back to the present Shirlia wiggled her ass enticingly, pushing back hard against the two long fingers stroking smoothly in and out of her creamy pussy, wishing he would replace them with the typically large penis of the First-Born.

Hanto was now becoming concerned with the Troll Lord's absence. While happy with the progress he had made with the slaves, he had no idea of what to do if Zomba did not show up soon. This was why the slaves still rested instead of being driven northward. He was thinking of amassing the captives into a small area then have Trolls with drawn swords watch over them, allowing him to send two guards south in the hope of locating the missing Troll leader. While debating whether to do this Hanto heard the terrifying howl of a Troll in sight of prey. Zomba chad found them.

Hanto roared at his Trolls to get the captives on their feet, not wanting Zomba to think they were resting in the middle of the day. He then sent a guard to meet the Troll Lord, telling him they would stop and eagerly await his arrival. Hanto personally went to ensure Maregon was on his feet, sending the Elfin caretaker back to the vacant place in the slave loop. The Troll commander then walked about the caravan making, sure all water flasks and provisions were off the ground, as if they had been marching. All Hanto could do now was watch the approaching form of the Troll Lord.

As Zomba neared, he roared at two Elves toward the head of the slave loop, telling them to come to him. The timid Elves, fear on their faces, did as they were told, but Zomba simply stepped over the slack in the rope they had created, bellowing for Sutata. When the Troll came before him, Zomba ordered, "Fetch me the First-Born Woman you were allowed to molest. Pity on you if she is not intact." Sutata did not understand why the request was made, but left to do as told.

Zomba spent some time walking about the captives. He saw the exhausted look of the Elves and noted the look of scorn on the faces of the hated Humans. Zomba glanced up and saw Sutata and the First-Born Woman Sherlyna approaching. Staring at her swaying hips, and easy walk, he realized it was not her who had stained the earth with blood. Holding up a hand in a signal for them to stop, he told Sutata, "Send Hanto to me and waste no time doing it." The Troll rushed off and within a minute Hanto was hurrying toward him. The Troll Lord gave him time to stand at his side, growing uneasy, before he icily asked, "Whose blood stains the ground behind us?" Hanto knew his only option was the truth, so he told him, "The First-born who is always rebellious, pushed me past my limit with his taunts. I made a grave mistake and slapped his face." Zomba well knew what a forehand blow to the face would do to flesh, so he asked him with quiet concern, "Will he live?"

Hanto felt the wave of relief wash over his body as he responded, "Once his patchwork face has scabbed over, he will be fine." The Troll Lord, still not convinced that someone losing the amount of blood he had seen on the ground could be fine, grasped Hanto by his shoulder and had him lead him to Maregon.

The First-Born, noticing the approaching Trolls, put an

extra look of disdain on his face. Zomba moved to within a sword's length of Maregon, taking in his stitched-up face, before asking him, "When we march, will you be able to keep up with the Elves?" Maregon was silent for a long moment before scornfully telling the Troll Lord, "If your short-legged Trolls can keep pace with the Elves, I will cause you no delay!" Zomba gave Hanto a quick look, keenly aware of the reason the Troll had opened the Human's face, for the Troll Lord sorely wanted to open the other side.

Zomba told the nearest Troll he saw to bring Sutata to him, for although he detested the scheming Troll, he had been sent by the Evil Lord Odyden. When he arrived, Zomba informed them there was no Elf warrior or anything else following them. He ordered Hanto to cut the ropes binding the slaves. The two First-Born males would be freed from the slave loop, but their hands would remain bound behind their backs. The Elves would stay because they were told to, the Men would stay because the First-Born Women would each be tied to a Troll.

Zomba decided to give both slave and Troll a long rest, for come dawn, with Hanto driving them relentlessly north, they should encounter the foothills of the Great

Northern Mountains within a week.

Dralon had entered the room he had chosen and

noticed a second door in the side wall, but having never

been in a real house before thought nothing of it. He was

looking about to find a place to stow his weapons, when

the side door silently opened, revealing Chandrelle

standing naked in the threshold. "Dralon, would you mind

closing the other door?" It being a request rather than a

question, Dralon did as she wanted, barely able to tear his

eyes away from her remarkable body. She had two body

features that both fascinated and shocked him. Her breast,

while not overly large, played host to the biggest nipples he

had ever seen. Nearly an inch long without being fully

aroused, he fantasized about the size they would grow to

with his lips wrapped around them. But what really

shocked him was the complete lack of hair around her

vagina. Dralon stood silent and confused, glancing from

her semi-erect nipples to her hairless pussy. He had heard

newly conceived females were born without hair, then

when nearing sexual maturity, began growing delicate

pubic hairs, Dralon, seeing nothing but soft skin between

her thighs, had a sudden surge of guilt. Perhaps she was too young to engage in sex. This thought quickly exited his mind when he looked again at her breast and saw Chandrelle amorously rolling her swelling nipples between her fingertips.

"Chandelle, tell me something, why is there no hair on your vagina? Surly you are old enough to grow it." The Elf glared at him for a moment, trying to determine if he was serious or simply teasing her. Chandelle decided he had been toying with her and told him, "Dralon, as Elf males grow old their tongues become large and coated with abrasive bumps. I allow horny old male Elves to lick my pussy, keeping it totally hair free." She began to give him a lascivious smile when she realized he had been serious when inquiring about her obvious lack of pubic hair. Walking to stand in front of him, she reached out and placed the hand of the First-born over her vagina, moving his hand up and down, allowing him to experience the silky smoothness of her skin. Once Chandelle felt his hand on her naked flesh, she lost all interest in teasing him.

"Dralon, I use a paste made from herbs to dissolve the hair. I think you should lick my pussy and tell me if I have missed any." Dralon had no idea how to take this strange

Elfin beauty, but having desired her from first sight he, thought it was best to get undressed. While he was removing his clothing, the Elf slipped back into the room she had emerged from, returning without delay, bearing a small metal bowl covered with a tight-fitting lid. Placing the container on a small wooden table by the side of the bed, she sat down and took in the form of the powerful First-Born warrior.

"Dralon," she asked with a coy smile, "my Grandfather told me all First-Born are larger than us Elves, but I could not ask him if that included the size of their pricks." The First-Born was shocked when he heard this, and asked her sharply, "Who is your Grandfather to have such knowledge?" With no hesitation she told him, "His name is Babaduk, I believe the two of you have met."

Dralon had other questions for her, but she silenced him by putting a finger to her lips for her own question remained unanswered. Chandrelle wiggled a finger at him, signaling him to come to her. Dralon, not sure what to do, walked to the edge of the bed and stood between the spread thighs of the Elf, who sat still on its edge. Without a word, she cupped his swaying balls as she bent her neck to flick a wet tongue across the quickly swelling head of his penis. Switching her hand to grasp his shaft, she was both excited and slightly afraid of the sheer size of the still semi erect cock. Peering up into the face of the First-Born towering high above her, she told him, "Turn your palms toward me and cup my breasts. Again, doing as he was told, he gasped as the Elf leaned forward and took the head of his cock into her wet mouth, moving her tongue around in erotic circles. Dralon removed his hand from her tits and wet his fingertips before replacing them on her breasts. He began to gently pull on her huge nipples, while at the same time was able to enjoy the sensation of feeling his cock expand in her talented mouth. Chandelle had not moved her head more, simply relaxing her lips to let more of Dralon's now almost erect penis slip into her mouth. Afraid she would run out of room in her mouth before Dralon ran out of cock, she moved her head back to get a good look at the size of his penis. She was totally shocked at the size of the enormous shaft, topped by a bulbous head, which had been embedded in her throat.

Now, with her own passion running wild, she huskily asked Dralon, "Are you going to check my pussy for wayward hairs?" Dralon nodded eagerly so the Elf told him to join her on the bed and lie flat on his back. After waiting for him to get into position she spun on the bed and threw a thigh over him, straddling his chest with her legs. She then slowly inched forward on her knees, while reaching down with her hands to spread the lips of her vagina. When her pussy was near his chin, she looked down at the First-born and whispered, "Look Dralon, I have a special treat for you to nibble on!" As Dralon shifted his focus, Chandrelle pushed back the rest of the soft flesh surrounding her clitoris to show an astonished Dralon a fully aroused clit that was every bit as long and hard as the nipples adorning her breast. Having been given his instructions, Dralon lifted his head and greedily sucked the fiery protrusion into his mouth, his tongue now taking its own turn forming erotic circles about its tip. Chandelle moaned as Dralon raised his hands to her tits, her nipples hard against his palms. The First-born ran his fingertips down the sides of her breasts, captured her nipples, then gently pulled them to their full length, He then used his tongue to move lower and spread wide the lips of her wet vagina. The Elf moaned again as Dralon's tongue penetrated her pussy, for even his tongue was larger than any Elf she had ever known.

Chandelle's passion was peeking. Without a word she

suddenly reversed position, lying on her belly with her head above Dralon's throbbing erection and her open pussy straddling his face. Staring in awe at the swollen head of Dralon's massive cock, she was not sure how she had taken all of it into her mouth. But when she felt his tongue enter her again, with a moistened finger seeking the entrance to her ass, she lowered her head steadily until she had engulfed over eight inches of hard cock, the huge head lodged deep in her throat.

Man and Elf now began an erotic rhythm, Chandrelle lifting her head to run her lips up Dralon's penis, stopping at the top to suck on the now inflamed head, Dralon running his wet tongue up and down the length of her vagina. He would pause to insert his tongue into her pussy before moving his lips to her clit and drawing it fully into his mouth, while his lips caressed its tip. Chandrelle felt her climax nearing and was amazed the First-born had not yet ejaculated, for of all the Elf males she had given oral sex to, none had lasted more than a few minutes.

Dralon was struggling not to come. The First-born's sex tutor, Arena, had instructed him in sexual matters and made it clear that reaching climax together was very intense for both partners when they were at their sexual peak of desire. He also knew by the trembling of her hips, and now constant moaning, she was close to coming. He would now try his best to get her there. Removing his finger that had been teasing her ass, he slipped it deep into her vagina, coating his digit with her natural lubrication. Using the sides of both hands, he lifted her slightly from his face while he spread the checks of her ass, exposing the now vacant entry to her ass. Dralon extended his long tongue and began to flick it rapidly and with force at the swollen end of her clit, while at the same time seeking the portal to, then penetrating, her butt with his finger. Wiggling his finger, he slowly let it slide into her ass, her clitoris now being forcefully drawn into his mouth by the suction of his encircling lips. Chandrelle, on the cusp of orgasm, buried her lips in Dralon's pubic hair, the huge swollen head of his cock deep in her throat. As her climax washed over her, she violently thrashed her open pussy against Dralon's lips and tongue, unwilling to give up her grip on his massive penis until she felt the bulbous head swell and relax repeatedly, his climax merging with her own.

Both lie still for a while. Chandrelle enjoyed the reverse sensation of a once rock-hard cock slowly growing soft in her mouth. Disengaging herself from Dralon she stretched out beside him, resting her head on his chest, while a hand cupped his now flaccid penis and balls. Both were silent before Dralon asked, "What is in the bowl you placed on the table?" The still aroused Elf gave him a lust filled smile before telling him, "Dralon, rest for a bit until you can reach erection again and I will gladly show you why I brought it here." Once more he did not understand, but so far doing as told had worked out well. Shutting his mouth and eyes he relaxed and concentrated on the delightful sensations she was creating with her hand.

Glento, with the precious gallon of oil safely slung over his shoulder, was well pleased. A day after leaving the Algali Valley he had come across three Free Trolls, two of them alive. Holding up his empty hands to show them he meant no harm, he asked if he could come forward and talk. Glento walked up to them after they waved and nudged the dead body of the

Troll with his clawed foot. "Do you know what killed him?" The shorter Troll Bynego told him, "He suffered but a small cut to his knee from a fall on loose rocks two days ago." Glento nodded for him to continue. "Yesterday an infection began to eat away his leg, emitting an odor so foul it sickened us. Today, shortly before you showed, he begged us to kill him, for the pain was truly unbearable. But he died before we could draw our swords." Glento stared at Bynego, then at the taller Troll Jynego, before asking, "Would you have done as he requested?" Jynego responded at once, "Aye, why not? I was going to cut his head off." Glento said nothing to the two, but smiled to himself, Odyden could surely use a couple of young, strong Trolls for his slave stable.

Glento, glancing from the face of one Troll to the other, let excitement creep into his voice as he asked them, "Come with me, back to my master's fortress of stone in the mountains, where a great many of our kind already dwell!" Bynego, giving his fellow Troll time to think on it, demanded of Glento, "Who is your Lord?" The oil bearer eyed him warily as he told him, "His name is Lord Odyden, and he is the most powerful being on earth, in fact a God." The name brought instant recognition to Jynego and he blurted out, "He is widely known as the Evil One. It is said he has enslaved all who serve him." Glento quickly decided he needed to tell them the partial truth, since they indeed had heard of his foul master. Opening his hands palm up before them in a gesture of sincerity, he told the two, "Look at me, Trolls, I have never been abused by my Lord. If I simply obey him, food and drink are mine for the taking," Glento knew he had stretched the truth well past the breaking point but continued anyway. "My Master lets his loyal Trolls have their way with virgin She-Trolls, but this is not the best thing he does for us." Noting their now undivided attention, he lowered his voice to almost a whisper, before telling them. "Deep within Odyden's rock fortress we Trolls feed on the flesh of Humanoids, a pleasure so intense I cannot describe it." Both Trolls started to speak at the same time, wanting an answer to the same question, "Are you saying eating the meat of something called a humanoid is better than sex with a heated She-Troll?" Glento responded to this question with the truth, "You will find that inserting your bone into a She-Troll will pale to the enjoyment you will feel while gnawing on a Human one!" Sensing their growing excitement, he quickly went on. "Follow me to the mountain. Perhaps on the way we can recruit more Trolls, for you need to understand one thing of dire importance. The Human Race's intent is to dominate the earth. Lord

Odyden himself told me the cruel and powerful Humans are now in the South, breeding an army of Men. They plan to sweep north, slaughtering all Trolls before them." The tall Troll now wished to know, "What are the things called Humans that wish to kill us?" Glento told him true, "I have never seen one, but Odyden has told me they are foul, evil Beings, created by the Gods to eradicate all the Elder-races." The shorter Troll now joined in, "And your Lord can protect us from these Humans?" Glento, now knowing he had them enlisted to his cause, told them. "Odyden's only purpose in life is to destroy or enslave the Human Race. He has promised his faithful Trolls that they will feast on the warm flesh of the Humans. I know he will be generous and grateful for any help you can give him."

The two young Trolls walked off a way to talk privately. A few minutes later, they returned and Bynego asked, "When will this hoard of vicious Humans march out of the South-Lands?" Glento answered honestly, "I do not know." The two Trolls glanced at one another, both envisioning powerful beasts emerging from the tall grass of the Southern Coastal Plain, to slay all who stood before them. Noting the slight nod of Jynego's head, Bynego told him, "If your Lord can keep us safe, we will gladly follow you to his fortress of stone.

Aye, Glento thought, as he watched the Trolls gather their possessions, I have good reason to be pleased.

Moluk knew without asking that something was amiss. "Celena, what is wrong, I thought we came here to have sex?" Answering with disappointment in her voice she said, "We did, and you did. I was hoping for a little bit longer experience." Moluk gave her a blank look before asking, "Then why did you stop? I thought you were going to reposition yourself for an activity of your choice." Celena was unsure of what Moluk was trying to tell her. "You mean you are ready for more sex, right now?" Moluk had a flash of insight, recalling her saying she had no knowledge of the sexual practices of the Elves. "Celena," he said firmly, "look at me." Raising her head to gaze at him, she watched as he removed his tunic with one arm, exposing, to her utter surprise and delight, a penis that was still as hard as it was when between her lips. Moluk noted her lusty smile of relief and explained. "Elf males can ejaculate at will. If they are enjoying being sucked off, as I was a few minutes ago, they can come without losing desire or their erection."

Celena, not able to believe what she was hearing, asked him, "Moluk, when do you stop?" This time it was his turn to smile as he told her, "When our partner no longer desires sex!"

Moments later, after a passion filled kiss, Celena found herself on the bed of pine needles, flat on her back with spread knees high in the air, while the Elf wormed his tongue into her pussy. Celena still had a difficult time believing what she heard but decided to take the Elf's word. Realizing Moluk had already come once and should be in no great rush to have his cock attended to, she reached down and positioned her fingers to expose her fully erect clitoris. "Moluk," she hissed at the Elf between her thighs, "suck it, hard!" The Elf, still in awe of having sex with one of the mighty First-born, happily moved his lips up to encircle her aroused clit. Using a great deal of suction, he drew its hot length into his mouth, flicking hard at the tip with his tongue. With the Elf now busy lapping her gaping pussy and not likely to stop until told, the First-born Woman relaxed, playing with her erect nipples, her legs now resting on the Elf's solid shoulders, making it easy to arch her back and smear her open vagina against his face.

Celena was well pleased with the attention she was

receiving from the horny Elf's tongue. Long before now, some of her prior sex partners would have tried to insert a hard cock into her body, hoping she was ready to receive it. The Elf would gladly wait, licking her twitching pussy until she was ready.

D avlyn, leader of the First-born who had been hiding in the West, woke the Men who would travel with him to the abandoned Troll encampment well before day light. Two of the Men who had spent most of the night saying goodbye to the Women, looked at him groggily before rolling over and falling back asleep. Davlyn left them to their dreams, for he desired Men who could not wait to carry weapons. He had limited his group to six Men, the others would lag behind to protect the Women. Peering at the faces of the Men who had awakened to see him off, he picked two eager First-born from the group. "You Rolyn, and you Sanlon, do you wish to wear a sword as soon as possible?" Seeing their nods of assent, he informed them to get their gear together, for they were leaving at once. Telling the other First-born Men to follow when the Women and slackers had awakened, he led his naked group of First-born Men to the east.

Davlyn held the Men to a fast pace, the long-limbed Humans eating up the miles between them and the unseen Troll encampment somewhere in the distance. He was about to call for a rest when Rolyn yelled to him, pointing a finger at the horizon. Looking in the indicated direction, Davlyn was both surprised and relieved to see the ensign hoisted by Alalyn lightly fluttering in the breeze. Davlyn knew they could easily reach the Troll's camp before late afternoon, but the others who followed may very well encounter darkness before reaching the flag. He then thought of a simple solution to the problem. Calling Rolyn to his side, he told him, "You will stay here and await the others. Let them rest for the night, then rejoin us tomorrow." Rolyn readily agreed to this, and after a short rest and some water, the First-born headed east again, this time at an easy trot. The Men made good time. Even after stopping to rest when tired or thirsty, they still reached the abandoned Troll camp well before dark. They knew they had the time to discover the wealth left to them before darkness set in. But first Davlyn called the Men to his side. "Each of you gather a large armload of firewood. Meet me at the source of the stench that is befouling the air."

Dralon took the time to locate the hide covered mound of Elfin make clothing, selecting a piece of cloth from an unfinished garment. Following his nose, he soon found the stash of putrid meat. When the First-born returned with the wood, Davlyn tied the cloth over his nose and mouth. As he set about building a fire atop the reeking mass of rotting flesh, he was nearly sickened by the sight of squirming maggots, covering the meat like a grotesque living carpet. With the fire burning, he moved upwind, adding wood as fast as the fire would accept it. "Bring me more wood, larger this time," he gruffly told the Men watching him tend the fire. Shortly, the rancid odor of burning flesh forced all the First-born upwind, where they stood throwing ever larger logs onto the fire. Davlyn would not allow exploring, so the Men stood and watched the fire long after the sun set, until only a large pile of sterile ash remained.

With the task assigned to him by Alalyn complete, Davlyn told the disappointed group of Men they would wait until tomorrow to search the Troll's camp. He then went to find a sleeping spot, for he knew the curious First-born would be awaiting him come first light.

Celena, while thoroughly enjoying the Elfin tongue

lapping at her now sopping wet pussy, desired a change of position. Lifting her legs from his shoulders, she told him, "Moluk, lie on your back." He did as he was told and Celena was relieved to see his still erect penis. While not quite as large as the typical First-born cock, it stood hard and proud. Celena was going to lubricate his cock with her mouth, but when she reached down and touched herself, she simply swung her thigh over Moluk's hips, catching the swollen head of his penis between the lips of her vagina. Moving a hand between them, she grasped the Elf's shaft and gilded the head of his cock into the entrance of her vagina. Lowering her knees in little increments she felt the cock head slipping smoothly into her body.

Celena now just wanted to be fucked. Spreading her knees, she allowed her pubic hair to mingle with the Elf's as she began a firm, steady pumping action with her hips. Long minutes later, with her orgasm nearing, she had such an erotic thought that she almost came. Stopping her pumping hips, she leaned forward, leaving only the throbbing head of Moluk's cock in her pussy. She gave the Elf a long passionate kiss, her tongue entangled with his, until her entire body was shivering with need. Breaking the kiss, she breathlessly asked the Elf, "Can you come in my pussy and stay hard until I climax?" Moluk gave her a loving smile as he used his remaining hand to push her hips down, once again encasing his cock within her heated vagina. As Moluk's cock head bottomed out in her pussy, her hips instinctively began to pump, slowly rising so he could feel her wet lips stroking his shaft. She then plunged her hips down forcefully, embedding the head of his cock deep within her, to be milked by her vagina muscles. A half dozen strokes later, Celena felt the head of his cock swell and relax repeatedly as he squirted hot streams of sperm deep into her. Celena, rushing toward her own orgasm, could not believe what she is experiencing. With hips still pumping, she felt a hot slickness coating the lining of her pussy, a smoothness she had never felt before and thought impossible, with an erect penis penetrating her. With her own climax now upon her, she slammed her hips down, burying the swollen head of his cock deep within her vagina and continued to milk him with her pussy muscles. Feeling his penis still throbbing, she shuttered from an intense orgasm before collapsing on his chest.

Celena was amazed at the sensations created when the

Elf spurted his load into her pussy but then continued to fuck her with his fully erect penis. Lazily reaching her hand down to give the Elf's cock a thank you squeeze, she is shocked to find it still rock hard, slippery and still dripping their combined fluids.

With Moluk's hard cock in her hand, Celena had another erotic thought flash thru her mind, causing her to audibly gasp and nearly reach climax again. With her libido running wild, she had another sex act in mind, if her Elfin lover was willing to do it.

The Evil Lord Odyden, deep within his fortress of stone, was beside himself with rage. An hour before, one of his Pixies spies had returned. Learning from the Pixie that Zomba was now traveling north with Human captives, relief surged over him, for the First-born were essential to his plans. The helpless Pixie had no way of knowing, but its life was nearly over when Odyden asked his question, "How many First-born has the Troll Lord captured?" The Pixie told him, "I saw five my Lord, three females and two males." In an instant rage, Odyden roared at the wee, terrified Pixie, "Are you sure there were not more?" The

Pixie, trembling so badly that Odyden had a hard time understanding, told him, "My Lord, I followed Zomba and his charges for a full day. Unless Lord Zomba has more Trolls somewhere else holding captives, there are no others!" Allowing his rage rein, Zomba plucked the fluttering Pixie from the air, and serenaded by high pitched screams, tore off its wings. His rage still unabated, he inserted a pointed fingernail into each of the Pixie's eyes, giving his nail a twist for good measure. With an evil grin creasing his face, he gently placed the doomed Pixie on the floor and softly said, "You are now free to leave, but be careful on your way out, for there are Trolls about who wish to eat you."

Odyden's ire now switched to Zomba, who had explicit orders to capture twenty First-Born, ten of each sex. A few minutes later, after calming down, Odyden decided he would wait to hear the Troll Lord out before condemning him. Zomba had been totally loyal to him and he guessed the Troll would have good reason for returning with only five Humans.

Knowing his temper was accomplishing nothing, the Evil One thought back two days, when he had received information from another of his spies. This one had brought good tidings. Glento, the Troll sent in search of Wento and the missing oil, had been located well east of the Algali Valley, in company with two other Trolls. "Was one of them the slave Troll Wento?" he asked the Pixie. "No Sire, I know of Wento and he was not in the group." Odyden dreaded asking the next question, "Was Glento bearing anything other than his tote and bedroll?" The Pixie spy quickly answered, "He had a large jar strapped to his shoulder." Giving an audible sigh of relief, Odyden waved to signal the diminutive spy's dismissal.

Odyden was excited at the prospect of adding more Trolls to his slave stable. He intended to ask Glento how he talked the Free-Trolls into coming back with him to a formidable mountain fortress. He thought it would be a good idea to send him afield again, perhaps returning with even more Trolls for him to enslave. In the meantime, he would concentrate on the next step in his plan, creating a Troll mating cage, allowing him to harvest the sperm of the Troll Lord.

Odyden would tell Zomba that, as his reward, he could feast on the flesh of humanoids and have almost unlimited sex with the She-Trolls. With the She-Trolls now barren, they were in heat nearly constantly in a futile effort to conceive. Odyden would explain he had discovered that any cut or severe abrasion to the skin of a Troll lead to a quick, painful death, ergo the need for a cage to protect the She-Trolls from Zomba's claws and fangs. He would further massage the Troll's ego by telling him he cannot risk losing any more Troll slaves, and since there is material for only one custom sized cage, Zomba would need to service more than one heated She-Troll.

The Evil Lord's real plan was to tie a large hunk of warmed fresh meat, with a hole cut into it, between the upper thighs of a She-Troll. Odyden would position the Troll so the ersatz vagina was the only orifice available to Zomba. After the Troll Lord had sated his lust and departed, Odyden would retrieve the cut of meat and extract the foul substance that was the main ingredient of his diabolical plan.

Now calmed down and thinking rationally, Odyden was thankful the Troll Lord had not arrived while he was in a rage. He realized he very well may have killed him on the spot, his many years of dreams and schemes dying along with the Troll. Aye, he decided, he would welcome back the Troll Lord, for even the few First-Born captives he was retuning with were more than he had now. Odyden permitted himself a hint of a smile, for with any luck he would be able to start his heinous breeding program within a month.

T he breathing of Chandrelle, lying with her head on

Dralon's chest, had barely returned to normal when she felt his cock begin to swell in her hand. Before having sex with the

First-Born, she had not known if the Human would remain hard after coming, like the Elf males. But after experiencing Dralon's large penis, she was thankful for a short break.

As Dralon's cock grew, so did Chandrelle's passion. Without a word, she carefully removed the top from the bowl of oil sitting by the bed. Dipping her fingers into it she wet her palm and rolled back to Dralon's side. Lying on her side she reached down, seeking his now erect penis. Holding him firmly, she ran her hand up and down its length. Dralon gasped as he felt her hand move effortlessly on his cock. The sensation was like being encased in a juicy pussy with his penis being held in a firm grip.

"Dralon," she said softly, "dip you fingers in the oil and

play with my pussy." Not sure how much oil to use, he dipped his fingers repeatedly into the bowl, coating both his fingers and palm. Moving his hand toward her body, he was once again fascinated with her huge erect nipples. He rubbed the one further from him with his oily palm, figuring his lips could take care of the near one. Dralon ran his fingers slowly down Chandrelle's back, stopping at the twin globes of her ass before rolling her unto her back. Applying but little pressure, Dralon was amazed at how easily his middle finger slipped into her pussy. Chandrelle was wiggling her hips, urging more penetration, but he spread her lips by inching his finger upward to tease the tip of her erect clitoris. He gently captured the fully erect clit between his thumb and two fingers, pulling lightly to see how long he could make it grow. Hearing Chandrelle moan, he repositioned his hand, lying the length of his large middle finger between her lips and moving slowly from her clit to the entrance of her ass, but not entering her. Eying her flushed breast, begging for attention, he moved his head to suck her nipple into his mouth while finally allowing his finger to finally enter her pussy.

"Dralon," she whispered hoarsely, "Quit teasing me, put your fingers in me!" The ever-obedient First-born obliged her, inserting both his middle and index finger into her vagina before starting a pumping motion, slowly increasing the depth of penetration a half inch or so at a time.

A few minutes after Dralon's finger disappeared into her body, Chandrelle was ready. Rolling over and knelling with her head resting on her forearms and her feet hanging off the bed, she told Dralon to get up and stand behind her. Dralon got off the bed, but before he could position himself, she ordered, "Dip the head of your cock into the oil before you attempt to fuck me."

Dralon once again did as he was told. Moving behind her with the swollen head of his throbbing cock dripping oil, he gazed down at the spread vagina of the Elf and felt an unbridled surge of lust. Spreading the cheeks of her ass, he aligned his penis with entry to her vagina. The First-Born moved his hips forward in an unsuccessful attempt at penetration. Looking down between her ass cheeks, he could see that part of the flared head of cock was still visible outside her body. "Dralon, stop!" The First-Born instantly stopped pushing his hips forward, but made no effort to give up what he had gained. "Chandrelle, what is wrong? I thought this is what you wanted me to do," he said with deep disappointment, "It is Dralon, but please listen to me. I am Elf, not one of your full hipped First-Born Women. I do not know if a penis as proud as yours will fit in my vagina."

Dralon began to slowly withdraw his partially embedded cock head when he heard her yell. "No, do not take it out, leave your penis where it is." Rising from her forearms onto her hands, she told Dralon, "Get the oil and drip some on the shaft of your cock so it pools up around my pussy, and also oil all your fingers." Dralon did as told, replacing the bowl of oil on the table. "Now play with my breast" she said, "and let me push my pussy onto your cock." Dralon bent over to reach her tits and managed to slip the remainder of his swollen head into her oiled pussy. Chandrelle moaned softly in pleasure as the blood engorged head of Dralon's penis fully entered her pussy, and strong fingers found her huge hardened nipples. She then moaned loudly, for she realized that with the swollen head of a cock lodged in her pussy, the body would surely follow. As she relaxed her muscles, she pushed back hard against the enormous penis of the First-born. Chandrelle gasped as the first of what she knew was many inches of hard oiled shaft slid into her tight pussy. Resting for a moment, Chandrelle began moving her hips in a circular motion then gasped anew as the First-born instinctively pushed another inch of cock into her.

A few minutes later, Chandrelle was breathing hard, but it was as much from physical effort as desire. Peering down between her luscious ass cheeks, Dralon was dismayed to see that almost half his cock had yet to enter her pussy. Releasing her breasts, he moved his hands to her hips and pulled her toward him, trying to slip more penis into her vagina. Chandrelle moaned softly, and again told him to stop. "Dralon", she ordered, "get the oil!" The first-born excitedly stretched out his long arm and grabbed the container of oil. "Dralon, listen to me, pull your cock out, but leave the head in me." Feeling him comply, she told him, "Oil your penis shaft well and push it back in." Dralon dipped his fingers into the lubricant and coated his cock. Letting the shaft rest between well-oiled lips, he pushed his hips forward and watched with rising lust as over half the length of his cock disappeared into her dripping vagina.

Chandrelle was now thrilled with the sensations the huge penis was producing in her vagina. Knowing the oil was aiding his entry, she told him, "Pump your penis slowly and keep adding oil every time you withdraw." The First-born was well pleased with this request. He got to stare down between the twin globes of her ass and watch his huge cock disappeared into her wide-open pussy, before being re-oiled every time he pulled out. A dozen or so strokes later, he paused on the forward motion to let Chandrelle relax her muscles and ease a little more of his cock into her pussy. He could now see that nearly all of his massive cock was now buried within her body. He was determined to get the rest of it in. Pulling all of his penis except for the huge swollen head from her body, he slowly poured a thin stream of oil down the crack of Chandrelle's ass while steadily inserting his erection into her dripping vagina until he had no more to give. Feeling him totally inside her for the first time, Chandrelle let out a loud moan before telling him, "Put down the oil and fuck me!" The First-born returned the oil to the table, then covered her ass cheeks with his large hands. As he withdrew his cock, he squeezed her cheeks together firmly, keeping pressure on his penis during its entire erotic journey.

Human and Elf were now experiencing sensations neither had felt before. Dralon's huge penis was probing the depths of a vagina tighter then he thought possible.

Chandrelle, while stretched to her physical limit, had relaxed and was enjoying a fulfillment never felt before. Dralon was fucking her with long smooth strokes when she looked over her shoulder and said with a lewd smile, "If you wish, you can pull your cock all the way out of my pussy and watch it spread my vagina open as it slips back in." This time the First-born did not need instructions. Sliding his penis out of her, he pushed down on the shaft, enabling him to submerge his cock head into the bowl of oil. Dralon's hand spread her cheeks wide, exposing her now open vagina. Placing the dripping head of his swollen cock into her gaping orifice, both he and Chandrelle moaned as his penis slipped into her wet pussy with very little force on his part. Knowing this was her idea, he repeated it many times, each time allowing a little more of his throbbing cock to follow the swollen head into her well stretched vagina.

The First-born was now concerned. He was quickly nearing climax and knew he would need a substantial rest before being able to achieve another erection. "Chandrelle, I cannot stop, I am close to coming," he said hoarsely. "Then do it! I have climaxed two more times and I am too sensitive to continue much longer."

Dralon reached to her breasts, again playing with her enormous aroused nipples, as he pushed his cock deep into her pussy. This time he did not pull back, but pulsated the head of his cock, feeling her squeezing him in return. Mere seconds later, an intense orgasm racked his body, as her tight pussy muscles milked him dry. Dralon started to pull his still hard penis from her body, but Chandrelle was so sensitive that she jumped at the movement. "Dralon, let it shrink a bit before you pull it out. Then I think we will rest awhile." Dralon once again did as he was told and a few minutes later was on the bed with the wanton Elf, lying on his side with the head of his flaccid cock nestled between the warm and oily ass cheeks of Chandrelle. The mighty First-born's last thought before drifting off to sleep was that maybe beds were a good thing after all.

Davlyn's instinct had been correct. He was awakened well before dawn by the sound of Men milling about, waiting for him to rise. Sitting up on his bedroll, he shouted at the First-born. "It is too dark to see anything. I will meet you at the mound containing clothing at daybreak." Davlyn knew the night was hiding the disappointed looks on their faces.

At first light, Davlyn walked to the hide covered pile of clothing where he found the Men awaiting him. Reaching the mound, he told the First-born, "Alright, see what is under the hides." The Men quickly dug into the pile, finding tunics, leggings and sturdy leather jackets. At the bottom of the pile, almost missed, were boots also made of leather, half of which had a thick, double hide sole made for harsh terrains.

With the mound of clothing scattered about and nothing left to be discovered, the Men were more than ready to take on the stash of supplies and provisions. "Not so fast," Dralon yelled at the departing First-born, "we came to choose clothing to avoid having a sword hanging from our naked asses!" Knowing they could not wear swords unless they wore cloths, they returned to select their garments. All chose the simple woven tunics the Elves had made. Some elected to wear the single soled boots made of leather. One First-born went so far as to don leggings, covering him from neck to toe in clothing, drawing strange looks from his fellow companions. Surveying the now clad First-born, Davlyn wondered to himself if he looked as ridiculous as the others, with his powerful physique hidden under Elfin rags. Realizing by the look on their faces that the First-born would be denied no longer, he told them, "It is time to go find the weapons you so badly desire to carry."

The men were hurrying toward the other mound, when a First-born noticed movement on the horizon. Yelling to the others and pointing south, they could see three forms, which appeared to be human. Davlyn shouted to Rolyn, "Take the men and get swords. I will stay here and watch the strangers." As the First-born left, Davlyn shouted at his retreating form, "Bring back a sword for me!"

The First-born convened at the second mound and swiftly stripped it of its protective hides. Opening oiled skin tones and bags of promising size, the men discovered a store of long swords, and another of knives and daggers. The First-born had no clue as to which swords held the keenest blades, but the ones with the most shine quickly found a home on the hip of a First-born. One of the Men, holding a dagger, noticed scabbards in a bag with short lengths of rope attached to them. Emptying the bag, he soon found the lashings were the right length to strap a knife to his thigh or calf. Within minutes of arriving, all First-born were armed with sword and dagger. Checking to assure all Men were armed, Rolyn suddenly remembered Davlyn's request. Selecting two shining weapons, he waved for the Humans to follow him as he ran back to rejoin Davlyn and the approaching strangers.

The knock on the door came just after sun went up.

Instantly alert, Dralon noted the absence of his Elfin lover and her bowl of oil. The only evidence of her having been here was the oil stained cloth covering the bed. Throwing on his tunic, he opened the door to find Dirthlyn standing outside. The Elf warrior gave him a funny look before saying, "I trust you slept well?" Not wishing this conversation to go further, he simply nodded in agreement while stepping aside to let him enter the room.

"Dralon," the Elf told him somberly, "Babaduk has called for a council and your presence is requested. We are to meet at his house in one hour. I have been asked by Chandrelle to tell you breakfast will be ready by the time you refresh yourself. Dralon told him he understood, then asked, "Will you be back for me when it is time to meet with Babaduk?" The Elf warrior smiled as he said, "I too have been invited to breakfast. Now get ready, for I am hungry!"

Dirthlyn left him, and as he closed the door, he noticed Chandrelle standing in the side entryway. Waving him forward, she led him to her private quarters. Putting a hand on his back, she guiled him to a door on the far side of the large room. "Dralon, inside is a place where you may relieve yourself." And in this room," which she indicated with a pointed finger, "is a stone vat of warm water where you may bathe." Dralon was at sea with all of this and it showed on his face. "Dralon, I do not have time to hold your hand. Go in that door to relieve yourself, then go through this door and take a bath," Chandrelle said tersely. "We Elves do it daily, and if you wish to sleep with me, you will too!" Dralon nodded as he headed toward the first door, then stopped when she said, "There is clean clothing on my bed. They may be a bit small, but they are far better than the rags you are wearing!" The proud First-born gave but a quick icy glance at her, but it was enough to cause the few remaining hairs on her body to stand on end. Realizing she had overstepped her bounds, she told his retreating back, "Dralon, when you are done, meet me for breakfast. Please!"

The First-born took his time. The stone vat of water,

while a pleasure to soak in, did no better job of cleaning him as would a swift running stream. Drying his hair and body with a cloth he found hanging from a peg in the door, he entered Chandrelle's bed chambers to don the clothing lying on the bed. Once dressed in the garments that fit him surprisingly well, he had to admit that they were much more comfortable than the crude slave-made ones. Perhaps, because of his foul mood, Dralon's mind returned to his warrior mode. He checked his bow and arrows, strapped his sword to his hip, and went in search of food.

Dralon did not travel far after exiting his room for he could hear Chandrelle's voice. Moving down the hall, he found them in a room with a large table seemingly covered with food. Babaduk, seeing him standing in the hall, stood and bid him enter. Dralon glanced around the table and saw Dirthlyn, Jefrael, Alfred and two older Elves he did not know. As if reading his thoughts, Babaduk said, "Dralon, the two Elves unknown to you are town Elders, Narlyn and Biluk, whom I invited to this meeting." Retaking his seat, Babaduk told Dralon, "Now sit and enjoy your breakfast." Dralon looked at the short Elfin chairs and feeling a bit foolish, unstrapped the sword from his hip, lying it at his feet as he sat down. Dralon, now no longer miffed at

Chandrelle, was thankful she had seated him at her side.

Dralon was peering at the various dishes of food, attempting to find something he would consider fit for breakfast. He had also noticed that the Elves did not eat with their fingers. "Dralon," Chandrelle said sweetly, "Let me fix you a plate of foods I am sure you have never tasted before." Setting a clay plate before him, she picked up a fork and, without making him uncomfortable, showed him how to use it. Urged on by Chandrelle, the First-born tasted the food and was shocked by the wide variation of flavors. Bacon, eggs and cheese were among his favorites. But his biggest enjoyment came when Chandrelle handed him a large chunk of warm bread, covered with a thick coat of sweet butter. Ignoring the talk around him, the First-born did not talk or lift his chin until his plate was empty. Raising his head to look at Chandrelle, he asked," Do Elves eat like this all the time?" Shifting in her chair, she placed a roasted apple, dripping with honey, on his empty plate, a hand on his thigh as she began to explain. "Babaduk came to my door an hour or so ago, asking if he could hold his meeting here. I of course agreed, and he said food would be provided for all." Dralon nodded, then asked, "What were you planning on feeding us before you knew guests were coming?" Squeezing his thigh, she told him, "Bread with eggs, cheese and some fresh fruit." Discreetly running her hand up his leg to gently brush the head of his penis, she told him, "With someone your size, I hoped it was enough." Turning to face the table she said, "Eat your apple, it is the only one left, and I want to clear the table." While Dralon finished eating, Chandrelle and Jefrael quickly emptied the table.

Noting the First-born was done eating, Babaduk pushed back his chair and stood, preparing to address the small group he had gathered. He had no need to ask for their full attention.

Moluk, with his penis being massaged by Celena, could scarcely believe his good fortune. Ever since feeling well enough to appreciate the beauty of the First-born Woman, he had dreamed of possessing her. He now had a Human lover with a seemingly endless sexual appetite. She had asked him if he wanted to engage in one more sex act. He answered yes, and was now keeping himself hard by thinking of what sex act she had in mind. Celena was still aroused by the thought of the Elf using her body for his own pleasure, provided he could shoot a load of hot lubricating sperm, as he began to penetrate her with his amazing Elfin cock.

After all she had been through with the Elf, she now felt relaxed and in a playful mood. Sitting up suddenly, she replaced the hand on his cock with her mouth, running her tongue in lazy circles around the head of his penis. When the saliva started dripping off his coated cock she rolled onto her belly, stretching out, with her head lying across her forearms. The First-born Woman said not a word, but started flexing the sphincter muscles of her ass, causing her comely ass cheeks to wiggle invitingly.

The Elf got to his knees and peered down at Celena's face, but her eyes were now closed. Switching his gaze to her body, he noticed her ass twitching every few seconds, as if she was winking at him. Moluk, still on his knees, moved to the side of the prone Woman and, lifting a leg, straddled Celena's upper thighs, letting the head of his penis nestle between her butt cheeks. Moluk felt her whole-body shiver. He hoped that it was in anticipation of being fucked in the ass.

When Celena felt the Elf's cock touch her ass cheeks, she lifted her head. The First-born glanced back at the Elf and gave him a lascivious wink while she continued to move her rear in a libidinous manner. She had experienced anal sex only once before. The First-born's penis had been large, the lubricant minimal. By the time she had relaxed enough to enjoy being fucked anally, he had come in her ass and quickly lost both his erection and interest in helping her to climax.

Watching Celena's wanton actions, Moluk guessed what she wanted. All doubt was removed when she reached back with both hands to spread the cheeks of her ass. She had hoped he was lubricated enough to gain entry, then relaxed when she felt the head of his cock easily worming its way into her anus. The Elf was enjoying himself by watching the head of his penis disappear up her ass when he heard her whisper, "Moluk, lubricate my ass." He abruptly realized what she desired. The Elf removed his cock from her ass, leaving the tip resting against the tight opening. Grabbing his penis with his hand, he pumped the skin covering the shaft a dozen times before directing a large spurt of cum at her hand opened orifice. The Elf quickly smeared the silky-smooth sperm around the entry to her ass, coating the swollen head of his cock in the process. As he eased the head of his penis past her sphincter, he allowed his cock to shoot another stream of hot lubrication into her ass. The Elf shot four more spurts of cum up her ass, slipping in deeper each time he came, until he felt his balls resting against Celena's butt.

With a loud moan, Celena released her hold on her ass cheeks, totally encasing Moluk's throbbing erection within the sperm slickened walls of her quivering anus. Celena lie motionless other than raising her hips to meet the Elf's inward thrust, barely able to believe anal intercourse could be so enjoyable when well lubricated. She was in no hurry at all for the encounter to end, but every small movement of the hard Elfin cock in her incredibly creamy ass was making her body tremble. Breaking her silence, she said, "Moluk, stop moving for a while. Push your cock all the way in, then just let it soak in my body."

Moluk changed position, stretching out his body atop hers, the head of his penis hidden far up her ass. The lovers managed to remain still for a few minutes, both enjoying the sensations when Moluk inadvertently moved a bit, causing his penis to withdraw slightly from her ass. Celena instinctively raised her hips, recapturing the swollen head of his penis with her ass muscles and pulled his cock back within her. Unable to stop himself, the Elf flexed his penis, causing his cock to throb, as it began spurting streams of hot sperm deep into her already creamy ass. Celena, now unable to stop herself, massaged his erection with her ass mussels, milking his penis, as a monumental orgasm wracked her body.

The now almost totally spent Elf was lying on Celena's back, his still hard cock buried in her ass. Hearing her moan, he reversed his initial actions, shooting a load into her butt before he began to move. He pulled his cock out a little at a time, until he was on his knees. He finished with one last spurt that he spread up and down the length of her ass crack with the now deflating head of his cock.

Moluk rolled off the First-born's back, onto his side, hoping Celena was finally sated, for even Elves had their limits. For her part, Celena was satisfied, but in the back of her mind she wished that the First-born Trylon was here. It was said the dark skinned male processed the largest penis of all the New-born, ergo no Woman could endure anal sex with him. In her present creamy condition, she would have been more than happy to try.

Babaduk's eyes circled the table, taking in the faces of the Elves and their Human ally. Sensing their eagerness, the Shaman began. "Some of you know part of what I have to tell you, none of you all, so listen, and well."

"The Gods have discovered that the Demi-God Odyden is planning on using Trolls to help him dominate the Human Race. To thwart him, they have placed a doom on all the Elder Races. She-Trolls have already become totally barren. The last Trolls have already been conceived. Pixies. Fairies, Gnomes, Dwarfs, and all other Elder Races, will be greatly affected." Dirthlyn started to say something but Babaduk raised a finger to his lips for silence and continued. "Elfin Women, due to the extreme hardiness of our race, will still bare an occasional child, but miscarriages will be the rule until they too became barren." Seeing the stricken look on the faces of the Elves, Babaduk sought to give them hope. "Hear this Elves, all is not lost to us or even our offspring, but this is what we must do. Listen carefully, lest the Elfin Race quickly disappear from the face of the earth!"

"At all cost, avoid any wound that breaks the skin, for it will lead to a sure and painful death. Childhood maladies are also deadly, but there is nothing we can do to prevent them." Babaduk had now come to the most important part of his dissertation.

He told them that sex between Humans and Elves was not only possible, but desirable, missing the furtive glance Chandrelle gave to Dralon. Children from such a union, due to the blood of the mighty First-born, would be immune from both the Elfin wasting disease and the curse of the Gods. The creator of the First-born would not permit the Curse of the Elders to effect the offspring of the Humans. Having relations with a diseased Elf was another matter altogether. Staring coldly at Dralon, he warned him, "Humans must be extremely careful of having sex with young Elves, for if they are infected, their child will also be diseased. "At this time, he allowed Dralon a question. "So the Human will become infected with the wasting disease?" Babaduk took his time before answering. "Not necessarily. Dralon, listen to me. Humans can become infected only if they have contact with the body fluids of an openly infected Elf. But remember what I told you. The child from this union will surely carry the deadly infection."

Biluk, one of the town Elders, asked another question.

"Babaduk, if one of the First-born becomes diseased, do we send them to a containment center?" The Shaman said nothing for a long moment, simply closing his eyes and letting his mind pick up the thoughts of Dralon. Deciding on a response, Babaduk opened his eyes and told Biluk, "At the very first sign of infection, they must be destroyed." Biluk protested at once. "But they could live many years, even decades, with the Elves in a guarded compound." Babaduk looked at the Elder, who was actually younger than himself, with patience, as he explained. "The First-born are totally unlike us obedient Elves. Telling them to stay within an enclave would be meaningless to them. The only way of stopping them from leaving is to kill them."

It was now the turn of the other Elder, Narlyn, who protested. "Babaduk, all the warriors are at the enclaves. If the infected Humans are not there with them, who do you propose slay them, surely not us?" In the ensuing silence, Dralon rose to tower over the Elves. Looking down intently at each Elf, he told them, "The First-born will deal with any diseased Human. There is a good probability that they will violently resist being put to death." Although Babaduk had known what Dralon was thinking, he still lowered his head in thanks, grateful the Elves would have no hand in the slaying of the mighty Humans.

The Shaman gave all a few moments to fathom what he had said before he continued. "The Evil Lord Odyden has constructed a vast underground fortress in the heart of the Great Northern Mountains. There he has amassed a small army of violent slave Trolls, for reasons unknown to me." Babaduk sensed the total lack of understanding on the part of Dralon and bid him to ask his question. "Why should the First-born be interested in where this Odyden and his Trolls are?" Babaduk gave him a warm fatherly smile before answering. His response made Dralon's blood run cold. "Because the Evil Lord's only avowed purpose in life is to kill or enslave the entire Human Race!"

Glento and his two newfound companions had made

remarkable progress on their journey back to Odyden's mountain. With a strong Troll on each side of him, Glento felt no need for caution and had pressed on as fast as possible, reaching the foothills leading to the mountains much sooner than he thought possible.

The Trolls were moving along a raised stone pathway, built long ago by Dwarfs living in the mountain, when they heard the terrifying roar of hunting Sno-cats. All three Trolls froze at once, hoping the cats were not hunting them. Glento relaxed a little when the cats roared again, for they were not drawing nearer. The Troll was considering staying put until the Sno-cats had moved on when he heard Trolls shouting in the distance. Glento drew his sword as he took off at a run, yelling for Bynego and Jynego to follow. As he ran forward, Glento heard the roars turn into growls and snarling. The felines had come within striking distance of their prey.

Rounding a sharp bend in the path, Glento saw the scene of attack just below him. Two adult and three younger cats had five Trolls trapped against a rock outcropping jutting out from the stone path. The lead cat had crouched down, preparing to spring, but the Trolls quickly formed a tight circle, all swords pointed at the snarling feline. In a daring but foolish move, one of the young cats charged the Trolls and was rewarded by a sword tip in its shoulder and a lost ear from another sword stroke that nearly opened the cat's neck. Roaring in pain and rage the Sno-cat retreated to rejoin the others.

Watching the action from above, Glento was amazed the Sno-cats had not sensed the threat looming above them. The Troll knew the adult cats could leap and reach the stone path, but would meet blade before they could land. Silently waving the other two Trolls to join him, Glento led them to the edge of the path. Whispering, he told them to watch for an attack from below, but otherwise make no sound or motion. Retreating a short way back along the path, Glento found an area where the rocks were loose. Choosing a boulder about twice the size of his head, he managed to pry it out, using his powerful taloned hands. Glento slipped the container of oil from his shoulder and placed it in the hole, confident it would remain safe. The Troll then snatched up the boulder and hurried back to the others, slowing to silently approach the edge of the path. Peering down, he saw the Sno-cats had spread out into a wide semi-circle. When they charge each cat will target an individual Troll. Managing to heft the rock high over his head without grunting, Glento picked the nearest crouching adult cat and hurled the stone downward with all his might, hoping to crush the Sno-cat's head. He missed, but the rock hit the cat just forward of its haunches, shattering the spinal cord. Screaming in pain, the huge feline launched itself at the nearest Troll, then roared with primal rage at its sudden immobility. The targeted Troll, taking full advantage of the situation, darted out from the group of Ogres and delivered a blow to the head of the Sno-cat, burying the blade deep into the cat's brain. With meaningless roars, the rest of the cats quickly left in search of easier prey.

Gazing down at the relieved and grateful faces of the Trolls below, Glento yelled to them. "Trolls, it is much safer here. Climb up and join us." A few minutes later, five Trolls and their belongings had managed to climb a rock outcropping and join them on the stone path. Glento quickly asked the assembled group, "Where are you heading?" A tall, lanky Troll named Arnego stepped forward and told him, "Nowhere in particular, but something strange is happening to us Trolls. We were seeking strength in numbers"

A suddenly excited Glento smiled to himself as he began telling them of the benefits to be had by serving the kind and generous Lord Odyden. Thirty minutes later, the glib Glento had recruited five more clueless Trolls for the Evil Lord's stable of slaves. Ordering the Ogres to gather up their gear, Glento went to retrieve his precious oil, then led them northward, again thinking to himself, aye, I have good reason to be pleased.

Rolyn and the other newly armed Men ran back to rejoin Davlyn who was intently watching the three approaching strangers that were definitely First-born. Strapping on the weapon Rolyn handed over, Davlyn signaled for him to join him, as he moved forward to meet the Humans. Drawing nearer, Davlyn recognized one of the Men as Kydon. When he stopped in front of him, Davlyn asked, "Why are you here?" Looking at the clothed and armed First-born he said, "Moluk, an Elf warrior and ally, told our leader Domigo that there were supplies and weapons here. I see he was correct." Davlyn nodded in agreement, then told him, "I am leaving to find Domigo now. Alalyn told me he is south of here, his location marked by a high flying banner." Kydon gave him more information. "He is but a hard day of travel from here. Shortly after you lose sight of this flag you will see another ensign standing tall in the south. You will find Domigo there."

Having found out all he needed to know, Davlyn told Kydon, "I am taking two Men and leaving. Follow when you have eaten and rested." As he turned to go, Kydon held up a hand to stop him. "Davlyn, wait, there is something I need to tell you. Domigo is planning on traveling north, with a group of Men and the Elf, to the Land of the Horses. He ordered us to bring him clothing, weapons, and dried food for the trip." Davlyn said he understood, telling him Rolyn would show him where to find the supplies he needed. "No," Kydon said, "you do not understand. You must take what supplies and arms you can carry south. Domigo well may be waiting on them so he can leave."

Realizing the wisdom of this request, Davlyn led the group back to the abandoned Troll camp. The naked First-born could rest and eat, his Men would gather supplies to take to Domigo. One hour later, Davlyn told Rolyn he was to wait here until the rest of the First-born arrived from the west, and remain until he heard from Domigo or himself. Burdened with all the provisions that they could carry, Davlyn and his companions set off to the south, in search of the main body of First-born.

Shirlia was sleeping peacefully, curled on her side beside the warm body of Alalyn, his flaccid penis tucked warmly between her buns, when she was rudely awakened by Itona. "Shirlia, you must get up! We are leaving for the east as soon as we can gather." Looking over her shoulder at the First-born Woman, she told her that she was awake, then turned her head back, disappointed there would be no morning sex.

The day before had been everything she had hoped for. Alalyn had removed his fingers from her pussy, but not before inserting a third and slipping a wet index finger into her well lubed ass. Unlike the quick triggered Kenlyn, when she moaned and wiggled her butt enticingly, he pushed his finger into her body even more deeply while he reached between her spread thighs to play with her erect clitoris with the thumb and forefinger of his other hand.

Alalyn had not stopped using his fingers until she was nearing climax. In a smooth motion, which surprised her, the First-born swapped his fingers for the head of his swollen cock without missing a stroke. Taking his time, while listening to the drawn out moan of pleasure from Shirlia, he slowly buried the length of his penis into her throbbing vagina. Feeling her beginning to climax, he reached under her to gently pull on her nipples, his cock pulsating against the contractions of her pussy.

Alalyn slowly eased his rock hard penis out of Shirlia's pussy and moved to stand before her. Looking up at the glistening phallus above her, she rose to her hands and knees, the dripping head of Alalyn's penis staring at her. Giving him a lewd smile, she opened her mouth wide as she engulfed half of his cock between her wet lips, then slowly eased the rest of his shaft into her throat until her lips were mingled with his pubic hair. Alalyn gasped as she ran her lips up his cock, to greedily suck on the head, before traveling downward again. A dozen slow strokes later, she felt his penis head swell in her throat, threatening to choke her. Pulling her head back, she encircled the head of his cock with her lips, then flicked her tongue rapidly across its tip. Alalyn moaned, arching his back as he reached orgasm. Shirlia, her fingers gently massaging his balls, did not remove her lips until she felt his cock begin to soften in her mouth.

The totally spent First-born touched Shirlia's face gently before lying down on his side. The First-born Woman curled up next to him, her ass cheeks keeping his deflated penis warm. In the morning she had planned to awaken him and his cock with her lips. Now, she knew there no time. Sitting up, Shirlia shook Alalyn's shoulder, "Wake up, we are moving to the east." Are you coming with us?" Alalyn looked at her guiltily, knowing he should already be heading back to meet Domigo. Shaking his head in regret he said, "No, I am traveling with Domigo and others north, to capture horses." Shirlia silently watched Alalyn dress and strap on his weapon before asking softly, "Will I see you again?" Seeing her dismay, he told her, "Of course, our leaders will want to reunite all of the First-born in one place." Shirlia nodded sadly before asking," Will this happen soon?" Answering truthfully, the First-born told her, "This I do not know." Not knowing what to say, Alalyn walked to Shirlia and gave her a long passion filled kiss, then silently turned away to retrieve his horse. Five minutes later, she saw him wave to her from a distance, heading southeast to rejoin Domigo and the future Horsemen.

The Troll Lord Zomba held to his plan, permitting the slaves a long rest, although in truth he wished the slaves were being driven north by his commander Hanto. Zomba was dreading the upcoming reunion with the Evil Lord. Not only would he need to explain his lack of captives to Odyden, but also his missing slave Trolls. Right now he wanted nothing more than for the vis-a-vis to be over, his fate known.

Holding true to form, Hanto had the captives awakened, fed and watered well before sunrise. Using the first rays of daylight, Zomba toured the camp, ensuring the First-born's hands were secured behind their backs and the females were bound to a Troll. While standing behind the powerful and proud Maregon to inspect the bindings holding his hands, the First-born suddenly turned to face him. In a soft voice filled with contempt, he asked the mighty Troll Lord, "What is the reason for the long delay? Did your short legged Ogres require yet another rest?" This time Maregon's sarcasm was ignored, as Zomba walked to Hanto's side and ordered the commander to get the slaves moving. Maregon heard the Trolls shouting, and knowing a First-born Woman would be molested if he resisted, moved forward with the rest of the captives.

Hanto, under orders from the Troll Lord, held the slaves to a steady but undemanding pace. Zomba did not think it wise to deliver a bunch of starved, exhausted captives to Lord Odyden. Calling for Hanto, he asked him. "How is our food supply for the slaves holding up?" Since he was in charge of supplies, Hanto responded quickly. "We have food for two more weeks, maybe three if I ration it." The

Troll Lord shook his head, "No, I want you to increase rations by half now, then double them when we reach the mountains. Hanto protested instantly, "But we very well could run out of food!" Again Zomba shook his head, "I think we will have enough, but if we run low, I have a plan." With the conversation over, Zomba dismissed his commander, telling him to relay his orders to the guards responsible for feeding the captives. Late that afternoon, with the camp set up for the night, both Elf and Human were startled when the guards gave them almost enough food to satisfy their hunger.

For almost a week Zomba's plan served him well. Benefiting from the relatively easy pace and sufficient food, the captives were regaining their strength, the color returning to their gaunt faces, even the sewn together one of Maregon.

The trouble struck in the cold predawn, two day's travel into the lower mountains. The long drawn out scream of agony woke the whole camp. A Troll guard, seeing it was an Elf female, signaled for the nearest Elves to help her. Zomba approached and silently watched the Elves, fearing the problem was one of his own making. The Troll Lord heard the screams change to moans and sobs before dying out, affording him momentary hope. Telling the Troll next to him to fetch and light a torch, Zomba went to examine the Elf. Moving the light near to her face, the Troll Lord saw it was the female Elf who had found the vast supply of ripe berries when they were in the south. Bending down, he ran his hand lightly over her body, then her extremities. The Troll Lord let out a grunt of disgust, for he had allowed the Elf to freeze.

The Elf had spent the night lying on her side, atop her bedroll, unsuccessfully attempting to keep warm. After hours of shivering, her exhausted body finally gave up and she had fallen into a troubled asleep, only to be quickly awakened by the terrible pain in the foot and hand making contact with her rock bed. The initial terrified scream had come when she touched her fingers and realized that they were as hard and unyielding as the stone slab she lie on.

Zomba stood looking down upon the Elf, confusion on his face. Seeing his commander a few paces away, he bellowed at him. "Hanto, get all captives to their feet and have them wiggle their fingers. Let me know if any of them has a problem doing either." Ten minutes later, Hanto returned and told him none of the captives were showing signs of distress, other than being cold. Zomba knew something was not right. Nineteen Elves and five Humans survived the night, none the worst but for shivering, while body parts of a lone Elf froze solid.

Suddenly aware that a cold gray dawn had arrived, Zomba realized his thoughts would have to wait. With summer gone and the possibility of snowfall in the mountains at any time, Zomba needed to formulate a plan to keep his charges from freezing to death on Odyden's doorstep.

Exhausted from his epic love making session with Celena, Moluk slept until the sun woke him. The Elf was surprised by the amount of pain the stump of his arm was causing him. Lightly shaking Celena by her shoulder, he awakened her and asked her to mix his pain killing drug. The Woman gained her feet and disappeared into the dense pines, but returned shortly to brew Moluk's narcotic drink. "Moluk", she said sternly, "We need to change your bandage." Moluk nodded in agreement and Celena went to get the necessary supplies. When she came back and unwrapped the wound, both were dismayed to see a redness not there the day before, but neither mentioned it to the other. "Celena, put extra paste on my arm, then rewrap it. I must meet with the Horsemen. Celena did as the Elf asked, then told him, "When you are finished with the First-born, I will be here waiting for you." Moluk smiled at her, his pain quickly waning, as he went to meet the Humans who would sojourn to the Land of Horses with him.

Returning to the site of last night's fire, Moluk noted most of the First-born were already there, including Domigo, leader in Dralon's absence, and Erigon, most powerful of the Humans. Also there was the red haired Redali, along with the dark skinned Trylon. Looking up at the approaching figure, Moluk saw it was Joslyn, joining the group with a sheepish look on his face, knowing he was late. These Men, along with Alalyn, would make up the party venturing north to rendezvous with Dralon and the Elfin warrior Dirthlyn.

The Elf stopped at the side of Domigo and asked him," Has Alalyn returned from the west yet?" The First-born shook his head no while informing him, "I have sent Men north. The First-born bringing us supplies from the Troll's camp will appreciate the help." Moluk agreed that was a good idea, then told Domigo. "Have one of your Men go south to the sea. The reeds I require to make arrows lie south of here. Have him bring back all he can carry." Domigo waved over the nearest First-born, by the name of Fragon, and gave him the orders. The Elf suddenly remembered that he needed feathers from waterfowl. He told Fragon he needed one long feather for each reed. The First-born surprised them when he said he knew of a small saltwater inlet, not far to the south, teeming with both reeds and waterfowl. Promising to be back by early afternoon, he turned and left.

Domigo asked Moluk to join him on the log seat, then told him, "Fragon may return with hundreds of reeds. We cannot take the time to make that many arrows." Moluk answered calmly, "I know that. I plan to teach Naldor and you how to make arrows. He will teach the First-born and you shall teach the Horsemen." Domigo continued to protest, "The First-born have no bows and yours is too small for them!" Moluk nodded, "I know this also, I will explain how to make a bow to Naldor and leave mine here for him to copy on a larger scale. Besides, the Sons of Man can practice with it while they are growing up." Grinning at Moluk, the First-born said, "Let me guess, we will make our own bow and arrows as we travel north." Smiling back, he told Domigo, "You are right."

Knowing they had many matters to discuss, Domigo stood and called for the others to join them. The Men and Elf spent the morning going over plans for the trip. At midday two Women brought the assembled group food and drink, which remained mostly untouched as they continued their conversation.

An hour or so later an excited First-born rushed up to the group. "Domigo," he blurted out, "the sentry you posted to the north has returned. I am to tell you numerous armed Men are approaching from the north and a mounted rider is converging from the northwest!" The Elf warrior smiled at Domigo. The last Horseman and the horse had returned.

Two hours later, Alalyn was sitting with Domigo and the others, minus Moluk, who had gone to check on the condition of his horse. "Alalyn, I know you found the missing First-born," said Domigo, "for some of the Men are already here. But did the Trolls capture any?" Alalyn happily told him, "No, the First-born were capably led by Davlyn, who hid them in a dense stand of trees. I would have never found them if he had not shown himself." Domigo then asked, "And you sent them to the Trolls abandoned camp?" Alalyn nodded and said, "I told them of the flag marking the encampment and of the supplies there. I told Davlyn to gather what arms and provisions they could carry and head due south, looking out for another high flying ensign." The Elf warrior stood to slap Alalyn on the shoulder with his remaining hand. "Well done young Man, I could have done no better myself." An embarrassed Alalyn was mumbling his thanks when he saw Davlyn and his group of First-born hurrying toward them.

Domigo stood and walked to Alalyn's side, awaiting the approaching Humans. The Elf sat quietly, hoping the Men had transported back more than the weapons they proudly bore. The rest of the Horsemen, seeing the arms they carried, rushed to form a semi-circle around Domigo and Alalyn. Davlyn and his group closed to within a few paces of the assembled Horsemen, the two factions of First-born Men staring intently at one another. Alalyn broke the awkward silence by waving Davlyn forward. "Domigo, this is the leader of the western First-born, Davlyn." Stepping up to Davlyn, Domigo quietly asked, "Did you bring back anything other than arms from the Troll camp?" Davlyn gave him a hard look before responding, "I left what food and clothing we could carry at your main camp, before bringing the weapons here. I assumed you and your Men would want first choice." Domigo gave him a grateful nod, wishing to himself that this First-born was going north with the Horsemen.

Moluk slowly gained his feet, the pain in his arm once again seemingly growing by the minute. Joining Domigo, he told him, "Let your Men pick weapons, then sent them to don clothing to hang them on. We will accomplish little ere they are armed." Domigo thought about it for a moment before yelling at his Men, "Go to our camp and pick your clothes, then come back to choose your arms." The Elf warrior gave him a quick nod of admiration. He had ensured the Horsemen would return in a timely matter to finalize their plans.

Davlyn walked to Domigo's side and told him, "There is a vast amount of supplies at the Troll's camp. All the First-born, including the Women, could not transport half of what is there in a single trip." Domigo eyed him coldly before demanding, "What are you trying to tell me?" Davlyn quickly responded, "We should relocate the First-born to the Troll's abandoned camp. There are many tents set up and the Elves have built a few crude structures we could enlarge. We could use this camp when we are gathering seafood from the sea."

Domigo asked Davlyn to join him as he walked back to camp but said nothing, obviously deep in thought. Long minutes later, he broke his silence. "Davlyn, I can find no fault with your plan, in fact I like it. The western First-born smiled to himself, for he had no desire to live forever on the nearly treeless grasses of the Southern Coastal Plain. Making up his mind, he told Davlyn, "We will head north as soon as I can gather the First-born, for there is nothing keeping us here."

A few minutes later, the two Men reached camp. Domigo moved off to select clothing from the large pile lying in the grass. Pulling a tunic over his head and putting on a pair of thin soled footwear, he returned to Davlyn, wondering if the other First-born felt as foolish as he did wear clothing. Domigo started to say something, but stopped and watched Davlyn, wondering why he was untying the straps holding his weapons. Davlyn reached out, attempting to give Domigo his sword and dagger, but the First-born declined. "These are you weapons. I will not take them from you." Davlyn gave him a warm smile as he told him, "No, one of my Men have my arms. I chose these for you, before the weapons were picked over. As leader, you will not carry a rusted blade." Hearing this, he gratefully accepted the arms, once again looking the part of a leader. "Davlyn, have your Men select their weapons, then bring the rest of them back here. I will gather the First-born to tell them of our change of plans.

Glento could scarcely believe his continuing run of good luck. He and his group of Trolls had found four more Ogres wandering aimlessly. This time, he simply ordered the Trolls to join him. And just this morning, following the sound of distressed bleating, they found a mountain goat with a severed hamstring, probably inflicted by a Sno-cat. Beating the cat to the goat, he had enjoyed the taste of warm flesh, still dripping blood, for the first time since leaving Odyden's fortress.

Days ago, when they had entered the mountains proper, the nights had turned sharply colder, but the hairy Trolls, with leathery feet and hands, barely noticed. What Glento had noticed was a faint glow high in the mountains from the ventilation shaft of Odyden's vast underground workshops. He had no intention of pointing out the light to the Trolls with him. The less they knew, the better.

Just before dark, Glento found a cave large enough to house his Trolls for the night. The oil-bearer had spent a quiet night in the cave until just before daybreak, when a trace of a scream echoed thru the mountains, its source apparently below them. Glento sat up, instantly wide awake, as he heard another scream, definitely coming from lower on the mountain side. Fumbling in the dark to light a torch, he saw all the Ogres were awake. "Bynego, you come with me," he shouted. And in a quiet voice, "Jynego, stay here and keep your eye on the rest of the Trolls. I will howl if I need assistance, for that was not the scream of a Troll in distress."

Glento extinguished his torch, not wanting to announce his approach, as he and Bynego began their dark decent down the mountain side. As they inched their way down the slope the Trolls could hear the scream change to moans before giving way to silence. Glento could now hear excited voices, clearly Trolls, talking amongst themselves. Suddenly, a torch illuminated the scene just fifty feet below. Glento was astonished to see a huge Ogre bending over a prone figure, rubbing his hands over the body. When the Troll stood to speak to his companions, all doubt was erased from his mind. He was staring at Zomba, Lord of the Trolls and Odyden's chief henchman.

Glento remained silent, studying the many bodies he could see in the torch's light. He readily identified the Elves, but saw figures on the fringe of light which were unknown to him. Towering over all Elves and taller than all the Trolls save Zomba, Glento guessed he was getting his first glimpse at the proud and powerful Human Race.

The oil-bearer realized he now had a problem. If Bynego found out Zomba and his Trolls were Odyden's slaves, he and the others would quickly desert him. Thinking for a minute, he came up with an idea. "Bynego, stay hidden here. I will meet with the Trolls. If they mean to do us harm, I will signal you by raising my left hand high over my head and you can go back to warn the others." Glento was already heading downward when he heard the Troll agree to the plan.

By now dawn was breaking in the Great Northern Mountains, and Glento managed to get within speaking distance of the camp without being spotted. Seeing Zomba still talking to another Troll, he softly called out his name. The Troll Lord instantly turned toward the sound, sword already in hand. "Who is there?" he demanded. From the shadow of a large boulder, the Troll's voice answered. "I am called Glento, loyal servant of the Lord Odyden." Zomba lowered the tip of his sword as he ordered, "Show yourself." The Troll Lord watched as the Ogre emerged from the shadows, hands held palm up before him. Zomba recognized Glento and re-sheaved his sword before asking him, "What are you doing here, are you alone?" The oil-bearer quickly told him of the mission Odyden had sent him on before saying, "Zomba, I have a problem." The Troll Lord, with problems enough of his own, eyed him coldly as he asked, "And what might your problem be?" Glento quickly began, "I have a goodly number of Trolls traveling with me. I intend to take them back to Odyden's fortress." Zomba, with his eyes lighting up, interrupted, "Did you just say many Trolls?" Glento nodded, "Aye, My Lord, at least ten, maybe a dozen. I never really bothered to counted heads." A huge grin creased Zomba's ugly mien as he said, "Then your problem is over. You and the Trolls will travel with me back to Odyden's lair." Glento shook his head. "No, you do understand. They believe they are going to serve a kind and generous Master!" For the first time in months Zomba laughed long and hard. "You told them that and the fools believed you?" This is the reason they are traveling with you?" Glento thought for a moment before saying, "That and the fact that I told them the Gods had created the Human Race to slaughter the Trolls. I told them Odyden could offer them protection from the savage Humans." Upon hearing this, the Troll Lord swiftly devised his own plan.

Bellowing for Hanto to join them, Zomba signaled with a finger to his lips for Glento to remain silent. When his commander joined them, he was told, "All of us Trolls are mercenaries. We are being paid by Lord Odyden for capturing Elves and Humans." The Ogre gave Zomba a blank look, having not the foggiest idea of what he was talking about. Lowering his voice, he told the commander, "Glento has many Free Trolls with him. We will tell them they will share in the reward for bringing the slaves to Odyden." Hanto protested at once, "What reward? Why was I promised nothing?" Zomba looked at him in disbelief. "There is no reward, you fool. But if the Trolls Glento has gathered know they will be enslaved; they will resist joining us." Zomba continued, forming his plan as he spoke. "The Trolls do not know Glento is one of us. He will tell them we are Free Trolls who have captured a few Humans and many of their Elfin allies. He will tell them that if they help us herd the captives to Odyden, we will cut them in for a small share of the reward."

"But what if one of our guards lets it slip that we are Odyden's slaves?" Asked Hanto. Zomba was silent for a minute before telling the commander, "When you tell our guards my plan, promise them I will personally cut out the tongue of any Troll who utters the word slave." The Troll Lord then finalized his scheme. "We will keep the First-born at the head of the group, with us. Glento's Trolls can stay at the rear, guarding the docile Elves." Zomba placed a huge clawed finger on Hanto's chest. "Under no circumstance are the new Trolls to come into contact with the Humans, for I fear the First-born sense we are but Odyden's vassals."

Satisfied with his plan, he told Hanto to talk to the guards and for Glento to go fetch his trove of Trolls. They had not gone three paces when Zomba called them back. "I want all conversation with the new Trolls limited to the three of us" Both nodded they understood, and went back to their assigned task. Half an hour later, the Troll Lord allowed himself a slight smile, for with Glento's charges, he would now be in command of more Trolls than he left with. His elation was quick lived when he suddenly remembered he still had to figure out a way to keep his captives from freezing to death.

Dralon had a hard time believing what he had just heard from Babaduk. "Why would the Gods that that created us want to kill or enslave us?" Admonishing Dralon, he said, "You were not listening well. I said the most powerful of the Demi-Gods is attempting to enslave the Human Race. He wanted to birth his own version of Mankind, but having failed in that endeavor, now wishes to destroy the First-born."

Dralon finally realized their plight and asked Babaduk, "What can we do to defend ourselves against Odyden?" He did not like the response he received. "At this time there is little you Humans can do save stay alive and multiply. We Elves have our own grave problem. As your allies, Odyden will also seek our destruction." Dralon protested loudly, "There has to be something we can do to help ourselves!" Babaduk gave a slight nod as he said, "I think there are a couple of things we can do that might help."

Taking a couple of slow deep breaths, he began. "Dralon, I will send Alfred south to the Land of Men and have him bring back half of all the Men, Women and children. We will teach them the skills they need to prosper." Dralon had a better idea, "We should bring back all First-born and concentrate our power in Loraine." Babaduk fairly roared at him, "No! If Odyden's Trolls were to overwhelm us here, the Human Race would cease to exist. I will not take the chance of that happening!" Dralon instantly understood the wisdom of the Shaman's words and had nothing more to say on the subject. Babaduk's voice regained its normal tone as he continued. "I have spoken with the Elders; henceforth at least half of all Elfin males will be trained as warriors. The rest will be taught needed trades, mostly the forging of iron, for we will soon have dire need of weapons." With Babaduk silent for a moment, Dralon dared to interrupt. "I assume the First-born Men will be trained as warriors. Can our Women be taught your trades?" The Shaman gave him a quick nod, "Aye Dralon, and they will."

An hour later, plans were being made for Alfred's departure. He told the group not to expect a quick trip. "Why is that, surely you know the way." Turning to face the Elder who had questioned him, he said. "The way is not the problem; the approaching winter is." The entire group was now listening intently to hear what else the guide had to say. "You must also realize that when I reach the First-born, they will have to gather and dry enough food for the return trip. There will be little to forage as we travel north." "A moment later Babaduk asked, "Can you foresee any other difficulties, what about water?" Alfred responded, "Water will not be a problem for the First-born, keeping them warm will be. From what I have been told, the Humans are still running around naked on the Southern Coastal Plain."

Babaduk suddenly realized he had failed to ask Dralon an important question. "How many First-born are in the south?" Dralon told him truthfully, "I am not sure, but counting the children, we must number at least one hundred." As Babaduk listened to Dralon's answer, an idea began to form. "Alfred, how much would an ox-cart slow you down?" The old Elf surprised him when he said, "Very little, for it seems the alternative to the cart is my companions being burdened by the weight of woolen clothing. Babaduk looked at each member of the group as he asked, "Are you in agreement that we send an ox-cart of clothing south to the Humans?" As the Elves nodded their consent, Dralon asked to speak. Raising his voice slightly, he asked, "Babaduk, could you also have sent two or three Elfin maidens south with the Men? They could ride on the cart and alter the size of the clothes as they moved south." Babaduk stared at the First-born for a moment, reading his thoughts. Having learned what he wanted to know, he looked back at the Elves. "Dralon has come up with a good idea. Narlyn, when the meeting ends, find three comely maidens who are handy with needle and thread. Ask them if they will travel south and aid the Humans in any way, they may see fit." The Elder said he would have little problem finding volunteers.

Domigo shouted at the four First-born nearest to him, "Go tell all the Humans to gather here. I have something important to tell them." He waited fifteen minutes, then began, knowing any stragglers would hear soon enough. "The Men I sent north to secure supplies have returned. Alalyn has located the missing First-born in the west. Some of them are with us now." A voice from the crowd rang out, "Where are the rest?" Hiding his annoyance at the interruption, he said, "The rest of the Humans are north of us, waiting at the abandoned Troll encampment." Before the question could be asked, he told them, "Aye, it is safe there. The Trolls are long gone."

Domigo remained silent for a few minutes, letting the excited chatter die down. "First-born, make yourselves ready and say your goodbyes to the Horsemen, for tomorrow Davlyn will lead you north to our new home. The travel is but short and there are things awaiting your arrival that may well please you." Again he let the murmurs quiet before finishing. "Naldor will be in overall charge, but Davlyn will still head up the Western First-born and be second in command. These two will remain in charge until Dralon or I come back or send word otherwise." One of Men then asked, "If Naldor is in charge, why is Davlyn leading us north?" Not wanting this meeting to drag on Domigo told him tersely, "Moluk wishes to teach a few things to Naldor and a couple other Men. They will follow you north the day after tomorrow, when the Horsemen depart.

Domigo strode to Naldor's side and told him to pick two Men to stay behind. "When you have chosen, come find me. I will be with Moluk." Turning away from the group, he went in search of the Elfin warrior. Ten minutes after locating the Elf, Naldor and his two companions joined them. Domigo wasted no time. "Naldor, listen to me. Moluk has just the rest of this day and tomorrow to teach you how to make a bow and arrows." Naldor was quick to point out, "We will never have time to learn to shoot!" Trying to reassure him, Domigo said, "I have spoken to Moluk about this. He will demonstrate how to shoot. He assured me proficiency will come with practice."

"One more thing. Naldor. The warrior told me he can teach you more about swordsmanship in an hour than you will figure out on your own in a year. Take advantage of his generous offer." Domigo's tone of voice ensured Naldor that this was not a request. The Elf , who was standing next to Domigo asked, "Has Fragon returned with the reeds and feathers I requested?" The First-born smiled as he pointed to a small mound a short distance away. "There appears to be hundreds of reeds and a large bag of feathers waiting for you." An hour later, with Moluk's expert instructions, the Men were making functioning arrows. While not iron tipped like the Elf's, they would be deadly against unprotected flesh. The Elfin warrior then explained the needed materials and the techniques used in bow making. By the time he finished, the Elf was confident that each Human would soon possess a deadly longbow.

Showing them how to use it proved more of a problem. Attempting to use Naldor to demonstrate its use proved futile. The bow was simply too small for the First-born to use. Moluk solved this problem when he had his bow lashed to a short forked tree limb, the other end bound tightly to the stump of his arm. Ignoring the pain radiating from his arm, he pointed to a stubby tree growing out of the tall grass, about twenty yards off. The First-born were amazed when the Elf loosed half a dozen arrows in a matter of seconds, five finding their mark. Moluk lowered his bow as he turned to face the awe-struck Humans, a smile forming on his face. He now knew the First-born would surely become archers to fear.

When Narlyn left the meeting to find three Elfin Women who would go south with Alfred, Babaduk called Dralon to his side. Chandrelle followed without being asked. "I have an idea and want your opinion." Dralon simply nodded for him to continue. "We should send some Elfin Men south, not youths, but grown Men with skills." Intrigued, Dralon asked, "What skills?" Babaduk told him, "A carpenter, farmer, and iron smith would be an excellent start." "How long will they stay?" Dralon wanted to know. Giving him a hint of a smile, he said, "Dralon, they are Elves, they will remain until told otherwise."

The First-born was silent for a moment, formulating his next question, when Babaduk spoke up. "I will send Gabreal, a warrior who is here on leave, south with Alfred to Mankind's birthplace. It will make little sense to build a stronghold in the south without having the means to defend it." Dralon started to tell him the Elf warrior Moluk was with the First-born, but Babaduk held up his hand to stop him. "Dralon, listen to me. Moluk is among our most feared warriors, but even I cannot tell if he is dead or alive." Already knowing that Dralon agreed, he said. "I will send Gabreal south. With two warriors among the group, I will worry but little." With this one sided conversation over, Babaduk turned to another subject.

The Shaman stared at Dralon as he told the mighty First-born warrior, "I know why you want the Elfin Women sent to the south. You are hoping for more carnal relationships between Elf and Man, such as you and my Granddaughter share." Dralon began to stammer out a denial, but a blushing Chandrelle quickly hushed him. "Dralon, speak naught but the truth, for my Grandfather can read minds!" It was now the First-born's turn to stare at Babaduk. "This is true?" The Shaman broke eye contact as he bowed his head slightly and answered with a simple, "Aye, it is true."

Dralon took in a long slow breath, giving himself time to gather his thoughts, before he told Babaduk. "Then you know I was hoping to speed up the inbreeding of our two Races by sending the Women south?" Babaduk nodded his head as he told him, "Your idea is noble. You wish to prolong the Elfin Race by infusing it with the potent blood of the mighty First-born." Astonished by what he had just heard, Dralon felt truly grateful the Elfin Shaman was his ally.

Babaduk, with a slight frown on his face, ended the brief silence by asking Dralon, "Since you are having sex with my granddaughter, would you care to guess her age?" Suddenly nervous as he recalled her baby soft skin and wrinkle free face, Dralon said, "I never asked her, but surely she must be in her late teens." Chandrelle again blushed, and Babaduk gave him a fatherly smile as he laughingly told Dralon, "My granddaughter is nearly seventy years old!" Dralon shook his head in disbelief. If true, the Shaman had to be well over a hundred years old. Reading his mind, the Elf answered his question. "I sired my first child late in life. I have seen all of two hundred and fifty years go by." Walking to the proud and powerful First-born warrior, the Shaman placed both of his hands on his shoulders and spoke to him in a soft voice. "Dralon, this is our gift to you and the other First-born for aiding us without being asked. The children from the union of Man and Elf will possess the wisdom and longevity of my Race, and the pride and physical might of yours. Your offspring will be leaders of Elf and Men into the untold future."

Chandrelle, already having heard more than she had wished for, mumbled a hasty goodbye and hurried out the door. The two Men talked on for a while until Babaduk said he needed to leave to recruit tradesmen. As he left, he thought about telling the Elfin Men of the ever lusty First-born Women dwelling in the south. He quickly changed his mind when he realized he only needed three or four volunteers.

The chill in his private quarters woke Odyden well before dawn. Moving to the stone fireplace, with its natural flue to the surface of the mountain, the Evil Lord threw firewood on the still glowing embers. He could have used his power to cause stone to glow and emit heat as he did in the rest of his fortress, but he enjoyed viewing the dancing flames. Odyden was standing in front of the fire warming his body, when he heard his name being called from behind the massive wood door of his quarters. Knowing all the Trolls knew not to disturb him here unless it was important, he bid the guard enter. As the door swung open, Odyden paid but little attention to the Troll, focusing instead on the obvious exhausted Pixie cradled in his clawed hand. Switching his gaze to the Troll he demanded, "Can the spy talk?" The guard nodded, "Aye, My Lord, but the voice is weak." With a move that stunned the Troll, Odyden plucked a pillow from his bed and moved a small table next to the fire. Laying the pillow on the table, he ordered the guard to place the Pixie spy on it. When the Troll complied, the Evil One grasped his throat with a hand that felt like cold iron. Letting his reptile-like eyes glow yellow, he told the terrified Ogre, "Say one word about what you just saw, and the young Trolls will feed on your living flesh!"

Ignoring the mortified guard scurrying out the door, Odyden picked up a chair and went to the table holding the diminutive spy. Sitting down, he bent his head near the Pixie and asked in his most unthreatening voice, "Can you speak?" In a faint voice, the spy replied, "Aye, My Lord, I have things to tell you." Attempting to hide his eagerness, he asked the Pixie to proceed.

After taking a few shallow breaths the spy began. "I was in the lower mountains and foothills searching for Zomba as you ordered. I saw nothing, and being nearly exhausted was returning to rest when I spotted them." Odyden instantly demanded, "Where are they?" The Pixie took another breath and continued. "Zomba and his group are well into the mountains, perhaps two days hard travel below here." Odyden then asked, "Were they moving at a good pace?" The spy responded, "It was before dawn. The scene was lit by torch, but it appeared one of the captives was hurt or maybe frostbitten." Apprehension crept into his voice as he asked, "Was it one of the First-born?" He relaxed a bit when the Pixie said, "No, it was a smallish figure, surely an Elf." Leaning in even closer, the Evil Lord asked quietly, "Did you hear anything that was being said?" The wee spy took another shallow breath before telling him, "No, there were more Trolls hiding in the mountains above, I would have been seen in the torchlight had I flown closer." Unable to stop himself, Odyden roared at the Pixie, "What Trolls? Why would Zomba have part of his party hiding in the mountains?" The now trembling spy told Odyden, "I do not think the Trolls were members of Zomba's group. They seemed to be hiding from him."

Odyden was totally befuddled. Who does the Troll Lord have his guards hiding from? And more disturbing, if the Trolls were not his slaves, what were they doing on his doorstep? His dilemma was solved when he again heard his name being called. Cracking open the door, he saw one of his Trolls holding an iron cage, used to keep the Pixies and Fairies from being eaten by the Ogres when they were within the fortress. "This spy has news for me?" demanded Odyden. The Troll, terrified at being in the presence of the Master, mumbled, "The Pixie claims to have arrived at Zomba's camp just as the other spy left." Extending his arm, he opened the door a bit more and took the cage from the guard, closing it silently without another word.

Odyden hurried to the table by the fire, placing the cage

next to the pillow nestling the other Pixie spy. Livid with excitement, Odyden hissed at the caged spy, "Tell me, what you have learned of Zomba." The wee Pixie retreated, shaking with fear, to the far side of the cage. Odyden, in an ominous voice so soft the Pixie could barely hear said, "Tell me what you know about Zomba, now, or I will feed you to the Trolls!" Remembering tales of Odyden's treatment of his underlings, the Pixie began his report posthaste.

"I was in the mountains proper, looking for signs of Zomba and his captives. Just before daybreak, I saw a faint light reflected off the mountainside. As I arrived at its source, I noticed Galien, the Pixie on the pillow, departing the area. The spy had stopped only for a second, to take a deep breath, but Odyden instantly urged him to go on. Fearing for his life, the spy quickly continued. "I hid in the rocks and watched as many armed Trolls emerged from a cave. They joined with Zomba's group, although they were kept somewhat separated." "Was there any sign of conflict?" "No, My Lord, I saw no weapons drawn, nor did I hear voices raised in anger." Odyden was still confused, but no longer worried about hostile Trolls on his mountain. Eying the spy again, he demanded, "Are you positive it was Zomba leading the Trolls?" "Yes Master", the spy replied, "I have seen the Troll Lord numerous times, and it was he I saw. I also recognized Hanto, Sutata and Glento. At the mention of the last name, Odyden stopped breathing for a second. With a roar of growing excitement, he howled at the Pixie, "Did you say Glento is with Zomba? Are you sure?" A huge smile formed on the Demi-God's face as the spy assured him Glento was indeed in the company of the Troll Lord.

Standing with Hanto and Sutata, the Troll Lord asked his commander, "How is the slave's food supply holding out?" Hanto informed him, "We have provisions for three more days at the current allotment." A well pleased Zomba then said, "Let them eat their fill, for I plan to be on this wretched mountain only one more night!" With full daylight now upon them the captives were amazed when the guards placed large bowls of food before them and did not snatch it away when they had grabbed two handfuls.

The bane of the Trolls, the mighty First-born Maregon, did not know where they were going, but he guessed they had to be close, for the snowcapped crest of the mountain now loomed over them. He also guessed, correctly, that

Zomba was not giving them extra food out of kindness. He was attempting to keep them from freezing to death.

With the morning feed over, Zomba walked about the camp, checking to see that all was in order. Glento's Trolls were at the rear with the Elves, separated beyond talking distance from the First-born, who were in the lead. Glento had told his Trolls to keep the Elves well away from the Humans, ensuring his Trolls would not come into contact with Zomba's. With each of the First-born Women tied to a Troll, Hanto ordered them to begin the arduous ascent up the face of the frozen mountain. The way was hard, but not overly so, for it was the sole path leading to Odyden's fortress.

Suddenly, just before midday, a dense cloud, carried on down currents from the top of the mountain enveloped them. Instantly, Man, Elves and most of Glento's Trolls began to gag. A stench of indescribable vileness had descended on the group, threatening to steal their breath. Zomba, relatively unaffected by the disgusting odor, glanced around at his charges. Distressed, he saw many Elves and two of the First-born Women on their knees or bending over, disgorging their generous morning meal. He is distraught, not because of their plight, but because he knew he must take the time to feed them again, now, for with every yard they climbed the temperature fell.

As this thought ended, a sudden blast of icy air dissipated the foul cloud as quickly as it had come. Zomba watched as the captives sucked in lungsful of clean, cold air, slowly regaining their feet or standing erect. Zomba ordered Hanto to feed and water the slaves, telling him he would be back after talking to one of Glento's Trolls, who was waving at him. Stopping within speaking distance of the Troll, he tersely asked, "What is it you want?" Looking brazenly at Zomba, the Troll said," Tell me that foul stench did not come from the fortress where we are going!" Zomba thought this was a fine idea, so he told him, "No, the odor is from the mountain venting noxious gas, as it is wanted to do from time to time." Giving the Troll no time for further questions, Zomba spun on his heels and walked away, knowing well the odor came from Odyden burning the refuse of his fortress. But the Troll Lord knew the vile sickening stench came mostly from burning the feces excreted by his feeders, after they had ravenously devoured the flesh of humanoids created in his workshops. Zomba feverously hoped Odyden would not decide to burn another foul load before he arrived.

Odyden stood and walked to the fireplace, staring at the flickering flames to calm himself. After a few minutes, he returned to his seat at the table and asked the Pixie in an almost friendly voice, "Were you able to hear any of Zomba's conversation?" The Pixie responded, "No, Zomba and Hanto were standing between the two groups of Trolls, in the open, talking to one another." "So you did not hear any talk?" "I did, My Lord," answered the spy. "I heard a Troll tell another that an Elf had frozen during the night. He was joking that a Sno-Cat would be enjoying a cold treat when they moved on." "And that is all you heard?" demanded Odyden angrily. The Pixie spy, sensing approaching death, could only shake his head as he echoed Odyden's words, "And that is all I heard, "My Lord."

In a gesture which surprised him, Odyden opened the cage and bid the Pixie to join the other on the warm pillow. The Evil Lord had come to realize that, with his declining slave base, he needed to preserve the ones he had. He also knew he was pushing the limit as he personally went to get them food.

Odyden returned shortly with the food and both Pixies seemed to be in much better condition. As they ate, he inquired, "Can either of you return to Zomba after a brief rest?" The Pixie Galien, although bone weary, wanted nothing more than to be out of Odyden's presence. "Lord, send me," he implored, "with an hour or so more rest, I can fly to Zomba's location in minutes." Odyden's eyes glowed as he demanded, "How far away, exactly, is the Troll Lord?" The other spy, Daliwyn, spoke up. "If the group moved on after I left, they should be no more than half a mile away by now." Switching his gaze to Daliwyn, he asked, "Are you strong enough to leave now?" To Galien's utter dismay, he said he was. Odyden walked away, returning a minute later with a gold ring hanging from a length of sturdy twine. As he tied the ring around the Pixie's neck, he told him, "Show this ring to Zomba. He will know I sent you. Ask him his needs and promise him I will fulfill them. Placing Daliwyn back into the iron cage, he hurried to his door and called for a guard. A Troll appeared within seconds and was told to take the spy to the stairway leading to the surface and release him. Odyden quickly forgot about the other Pixie, for he now had much to do.

Chandrelle had not gone far when she saw her Grandfather leave. Knowing she needed to talk, she hurried back to Dralon. The First-born stared at Chandrelle in disbelief, unable to believe what he had just been told. "Chandrelle, are you really seventy years old?" She shook her head, "No, I am only sixty eight," then added coyly, "in the prime of my childbearing years." The First-born, not knowing how to take this statement, said nothing, to the Elf's dismay.

Dralon went to his chair at the table to retrieve his sword. Strapping it on he walked back to Chandrelle, telling her, "I came north to capture horses for the First-born following me." She gave him a questioning look as she said, "I know that Dralon, what is wrong?" Dralon placed his hands on her shoulders, holding her at arm's length, and told her honestly. "I feel like I am being caught up in a plan and I have no idea what the plot is. Also, since I have been here no one has even told me the location of the horses, let alone how to capture them." Now caught up in his rhetoric, he added. "One more thing, I need to get away so I can think things out without having my thoughts read!" Chandrelle allowed herself a faint smile of relief, most of Dralon's unease was not caused by her.

The awkward silence following his outburst was interrupted by a knock on the door. If he had not seen Babaduk leave, he would have sworn he was still there, reading his mind, for at the door stood Dirthlyn telling him to make ready for the trip to the Land of the Horses. Dralon told Chandrelle he had much to discuss with the others before leaving, then seeing the disappointment on her face, promised to return by sunset. Hearing this, Chandrelle cheered at once. And knowing that this would be their last night together for a while, she told him she would have a cooked meal awaiting his return. Giving her a quick smile as he closed the door, he left to make travel plans with the Elf.

The news that the Horsemen were leaving for the north saddened the First-born, especially the Women. Having the personality that made them natural leaders also made them popular sex partners for the always lusty females. Ten or so of the Women decided a going away gathering was in order. Two of the females left for a saltwater inlet to the south where clams and oysters were plentiful. Some gathered fruit and vegetables while two went to fetch bowls of the fermented berry drink they had learned to make. The rest busied themselves collecting wood for a fire. They could see no good reason to grope about in the dark, seeking out a new sex partner.

By early afternoon the ambitious Women had everything set. Itona, who had come up with this idea, sent Chenena to tell the Horsemen that there was food and drink waiting for them when they had finished playing with their swords. Sitting with Marena, drinking the potent fruit juice, she realized she had a problem. "Marena," she said, "how many Horsemen are there?"

"There are seven, plus Moluk, but Dralon is in the north and the Elf will stay with Celena." Itona took a sip of her drink before telling Marena, "Then we have a problem. If we do not ask more Men to join us, some of us Women will remain as horny as we are now." Agreeing with her Marena got to her feet. "I will go find six or so Men who want to have sex." Giving Itona a slightly drunken grin, she went on her way.

Three hours later, with a blazing fire holding the darkness at bay, the First-born were engaged in a drunken orgy. Itona was well pleased, for with the Men Marena had invited, there were now more Men than Women, but still a greater amount of female orifices then penises to fill them. By prearrangement, the Women were bringing their partners to near climax, only to abruptly stop and seek out another Man.

A few rotations of partners later, with the Men fully aroused and frustrated, a booming voice rang out, slightly slurred by drink. "Women! What is wrong with you? I have the biggest cock here. You should be fighting over it!" The boast by Tylon, the dark skinned Horseman, was met by giggles from the Women. Arerena, her lips buried deep in Domigo's pubic hair, took exception to Tylon's claim as she reluctantly raised her lips from his massive cock. Arerena, who had experienced sex with the black First-born, called out drunkenly, "Tylon, compared to Domigo's penis, yours is but a pimple!" This time the roar of laughter that followed included that of the Men. Standing to pull Domigo to his feet, she led him to the side of Tylon, commencing Mankind's first big dick contest.

The drunken Women quickly formed a semi-circle around the two Men. A couple of the females who had prior sex with one or the other Men, were touching themselves. Most just stared at the two huge erections with open desire. "So Arerena", asked Dybora, pointing at Tylon's erection, "If that is but a pimple, what do you consider a cock?" Another round of laughter rang out in the night air. When things quieted down again, Itona said she had an idea.

Selecting two of the Women fingering their vaginas, she told them that once blindfolded they would be judges to determine which First-born had the largest penis. Leading the Women nearer the fire where the light was better, she bid them to kneel. She then told Karena to open her mouth, wide. Telling the group not to call out names, she pointed to Tylon. "Go first, you will be number one." Tylon hurried to stand before Karena, his balls beginning to ache from his prolonged erection. As he reached down with his hand to guide his cock into her lips, he heard Itona call out. "No hands!" Removing his hand from his penis, he bent over a little at a time, finally easing the swollen head of his cock between her open lips. Karena wet the head of his cock with her tongue, then moved her head forward, making six inches of fully erect penis disappear between her lips. She reached up to caress Tylon's balls but heard Itona again yell, "No hands!" Moving her head back a bit, she remoistened his shaft with her tongue before moving her head forward again to ease another inch of cock down her throat.

Five minutes later, with the huge black cock of Tylon threatening to erupt, Itona knew Karena could not quite swallow all of his penis. "Number one", she called out, "stop, it is number two's turn." The dark skinned First-born, with a look of extreme disappointment, slowly withdrew his throbbing penis from between Karena's clinging lips.

Dralon, fully aroused from watching the sex show, hurried toward Karena but Itona stopped him before saying, "Use Dreana's mouth, Karena's jaws are sorely in need of a rest." Domigo changed direction, moving to stand in front of his designated Woman. He quickly realized the problem Tylon had faced. With his massive erection up around his belly button, there was no way to insert his penis into her mouth without using his hands. The First-born solved this problem by following Tylon's example, spreading his legs a little at a time until the head of his cock greeted her lips. Dreana wet the huge cock head between her lips, then was shocked to find that it would barely fit into her wide open mouth. A few minutes later, with aching jaws, she admitted defeat. "Itona, there is no way I can swallow this penis." Telling her to relax, she said, "Number two, since you are not close to climax, see if the results are different with Karena." Hearing Dreana say she had failed, Karena was determined to lodge the First-born's cock deep in her throat. Wetting her lips well, she opened wide when Domigo's penis touched her lips and managed to take half the length of his cock into her mouth. Moving her head in a short bobbing motion, most of Domigo's now throbbing penis slowly disappeared behind her full lips. Karena slowly moved her head back but kept the massive head of Domigo's cock locked between her lips. Taking a deep breath she inched her lips down his penis until he moaned, her chin resting on his balls. Three strokes of her head later, Itona saw Domigo's back stiffen and his legs began to tremble. "Stop", she yelled at Karena, sorely disappointing both Domigo and Karena.

By now most of the Men were standing behind the Women, playing with their hardened nipples, their erections trying to worm their way into their rectum or vagina. Sensing the orgy would soon continue, Itona knew she needed to end this contest quickly. She told the two judges to lie on their back and to spread both their legs and pussies. Pointing at the two males, she said, "Use your tongue to ensure your partner is well lubricated, the contest is nearly over." Bending eagerly to the task, the Men soon had both Women moaning, their spread vaginas dripping wet. To the Women's dismay Itona shouted out, "Karena, Dreana, get on your knees and rest your head on your forearms. The First-born Men are both tall and hard, they need you asses high in the air!"

Tylon knelt behind Dreana and eased the grossly swollen head of his cock into her wet pussy without undue effort. Domigo, on the other hand, was struggling to insert his massive cock into Karena's wide open vagina without causing her discomfort. A minute later, the dark skinned Horseman is fucking his ecstatic partner with long smooth strokes, while Domigo is still trying to ease the last inch or so of his erection into Karena. Suddenly, Itona called out again, "Switch partners!" Tylon, now determined to release his load, hurried to Karena's upturned ass. Kneeling behind her, he pushed down gently on her back with his left hand while aligning his penis and her vagina with his right. Two huge black hands, in stark contrast to the creamy white flesh of her ass, spread her cheeks wide as he inserted the blood engorged head of his swollen cock into her pussy. Half a dozen thrusts later, Tylon let out a moan, his balls resting against Karena's belly.

Hearing the sharp intake of breath from Dreana, Itona switched her gaze in time to see the last of Domigo's cock head disappearing into the Woman's vagina. The First-born, used to the ample size of Arerena's pussy, was growing frustrated. Leaning forward he put his hands over her shoulders, attempting to pull her back onto his erection, but she shouted over her shoulder, "Slow down, you are hurting me!" Domigo eased the head of his cock out of Dreana, not wishing to cause her further discomfort.

Walking over to Itona, he saw Tylon withdraw his overly long penis from Karena's pussy, then lie on his back. Lifting a knee, Karena straddled his body and lewdly wiggled her hips, capturing the engorged head of his cock with her vagina. With a long moan she lowered her hips until Tylon's huge erection was totally buried in her body.

Domigo reached Itona's side, telling her tersely," Next time, partner me with a Woman, not a girl!" Giving Itona no time to respond, he headed off, waving for Arerena to join him. After a few frustrating yards, he suddenly stopped and yelled at the assembled group, "Horsemen, hear me and well! We meet at dawn tomorrow. If you are not there, I will replace you with someone who is!" To

Domigo's displeasure, the Horsemen, busy watching Karena's ass as her clutching pussy milked Tylon of his load, did not bother to respond. Turning his back, he walked away, knowing it was time for the main orgy to begin.

The Pixie Daliwyn had wished every bit as much as his fellow spy Galien to get away from Lord Odyden. But he also knew the time away from the Evil Lord would be of limited duration, for Zomba was but a short flight away.

Only minutes later, the other Pixie, Galien, spotted Zomba and his captives, the Elves, hard pressed to climb the frozen rock making up the mountain path. The Pixie had noticed that when he had left, snow was beginning to fall at the top of the mountain. Now, hovering in the grey afternoon, fifty feet above Zomba, the first large snowflakes began to descend.

Zomba let loose a terrifying roar that echoed throughout the mountains, cursing the weather. He knew from bitter experience the tremendous amount of snow these sudden storms could drop. He realized that snow above the knees of the short legged Elves would make travel virtually impossible. As his echo died away, Zomba thought he heard a faint voice calling out his name, but saw no one nearby. The second time he heard his name called he glanced up and saw a Pixie hovering directly over his head. The Troll pretended he still heard nothing, planning to swat the Pixie to the ground. Luckily for both, he saw the gold ring hanging from the Pixie's neck just before his huge hand made contact. Holding his hand frozen in the air, he ordered the Pixie to alight on it. "I know by your ring that the Master sent you, for I wear the same. What does he want from me?" The wee spy, even more uncomfortable with the Troll, who was prone to eat his species, than he was with Odyden, quickly answered. "My Lord said for you to tell me what you need, and he will see it done." Zomba thought about his response for a long time. Being this close to the fortress he wanted to deliver his captives without aid. He also realized that without help they would possibly die in the quickly developing blizzard. Swallowing his pride, he drew his hand near his face. quietly telling the Pixie, "Tell Lord Odyden I need a way to keep the captives warm and that our food is nearly gone." After ensuring the spy understood, the Troll Lord flicked his wrist and sent the diminutive Pixie back into the air, hoping he would make it through the blizzard. If not, the body heat of the Elves would serve to keep the rest of his party alive.

Leaving Chandrelle's house Dralon saw Jefrael waiting for him and Dirthlyn. "Come with me, I will take you to Marduk, who has captured horses before." Jefrael took them to one of the communal houses scattered about the Elfin town. This one was used mainly as a place for the Men to drink ale and converse. Entering, Jefrael introduced Marduk, who appeared to have indulged in a few drinks already. Bidding them to sit, Marduk walked off, returning a minute later with four metal mugs of ale, although he had left a full mug in front of him. After passing out the drinks and taking a long pull on his, he began.

"I have good news for you. Babaduk has devised a tranquilizing dart that will drop a horse to its knees within seconds without causing any permanent harm." The Elfin warrior Dirthlyn interrupted. "I attach the dart to an arrow?" Knowing he had not explained much of anything yet, he told Dirthlyn, "The dart fits inside a hollow reed. Your expelled breath will propel the dart a great distance."

Before more questions could be asked, he continued. "Babaduk has left two reeds here with a generous supply of untreated arrows. He urges you and Dralon to practice using them." Going to a table in the corner of the hall he returned with two lengths of smooth reed and two leather pouches which he gave to Dralon and Dirthlyn. The First-born quickly opened their bags and dumped the contents onto the table, revealing about a hundred darts which appeared to be the sharp thorns from local vines. He knew from personal experience that only leather clothing would keep them from piercing the skin.

Dralon glanced at Dirthlyn and knew he had the same thought. Both warriors could not wait to try their new weapon, knowing well they could be used on objects other than horses. Marduk downed the rest of his drink, then picked up the full one sitting in front of him before concluding. "The Elders have ordered the warrior Franlyn to return from the Elfin enclave. He helped Moluk break his horse to saddle and should be able to help you." Dralon, anxious to get away, asked Marduk, "When will Franlyn get here?" Finishing off his mug of ale, Marduk burped deeply before telling him, "We expect him today, tomorrow at the latest."

Dralon said nothing for a long while. He had enjoyed Chandrelle's food, bed, and body, but now it was time to accomplish what he had come for. "Dirthlyn," he said as he stood, "what needs to be done to make ready for our trip?" The Elf swiftly replied, "You need to do nothing except pack your personal gear. We are taking a cart pulled by a donkey with us. The cart is already loaded with all the supplies and provisions we require." Dralon smiled with relief as he sat down, accepting another mug of ale from the fresh round Marduk had provided. The First-born, after draining half his mug, asked no one in particular, "So when, exactly, are we leaving?" Before anyone could give an answer, Biluk the Elder entered without bothering to knock on the door. "Dirthlyn," he spouted out, "I have received word that Franlyn is nearing the outskirts of town. He should be here in an hour or so.!" Dirthlyn stood and thanked the Elder for the information. Turning to face the others, he told them, "Make ready, for when the sun rises tomorrow, we leave to capture horses." Dralon finished his drink, then nodded to Dirthlyn in sincere appreciation.

Odyden stormed out of his quarters, ordering the Troll stationed outside his door to gather all of his slaves except the ones assigned to the workshops. Mere minutes later, with his eerie eyes glowing brightly, he addressed his underlings. "The time has come! Our guests will be arriving shortly. I want the First-born Men housed with the Elfin Women. Quarter the First-born Women with the Male Elves." Odyden glanced about, but seeing naught but rapt attention, he continued. "I want them kept warm and well fed, in fact do anything within reason to keep them comfortable." He paused for a moment, permitting his terrifying eyes to seek out each Troll, before telling them, "If you harm any of my slaves without my permission, I will personally teach you to wish for death!" Odyden dismissed the Trolls with a wave of his hand, telling them to go and do as he bid.

The Evil One now hurried to check his mating cage. Ordering the guard at the door to step aside he entered the small room holding the metal cage. Using the dim light from glowing rocks, Odyden checked his contraption and found all to be in order. Closing the door as he left, he called the guard to him. "In the chamber there is a wood box with a lid. I want three large pieces of fresh meat in it at all times. If they are still there after twenty-four hours, you will replace them with fresh cuts". The Troll, afraid of speaking, but also afraid of the consequences he faced for silence, asked, "I am but one of many who may stand watch before this door. Do you wish me to tell the other guards your orders?" Odyden lashed out with a backhand blow to the Ogre's face with enough force to drop him to his knees. With his eyes blazing with rage, Odyden seized the guard's neck in a death grip. Lifting him off his feet with little effort, the Master drew the Troll's face to within inches of his own. Making no attempt to hide his ire Odyden hissed at the guard, "Say but one word of what I just told you and you die. Slowly, and in great discomfort!" The Troll, bound in the vise-like grip of Odyden, managed a slight nod of his head. As his eyes began to lose their glow, the Master lowered him to the floor and relaxed his hand.

As soon as the Troll felt his feet hit stone, he dropped to one knee, bowing his head. "My Lord," he said with a trembling voice, "tell me your wish and it will be done." Odyden exhaled slowly, his violent temper again under control. "Stand up Troll", he said calmly. "Tell your shift commander I ordered you to take the morning watch every day." Seeing the Troll nod in understanding, Odyden finished his instructions. "You will start your task at daybreak tomorrow and continue until I tell you to stop. Tell the procurer of meat that you are acting under my orders. If he is overly concerned about where the meat is going you can tell him that I said there are many things in my fortress that crave living flesh. You can add that I assume he does not wish to be one of them!" Walking the guard to the door, he told him, "Go locate the procurer and your commander. Tell them what I ordered." As he was closing the door, Odyden whispered in a soft voice that terrified the guard, "If you wish to live, do not cause me disappointment." Scurrying away, the door closed silently behind him.

With the rising of the morning sun, Davlyn had the few First-born who were awake go rouse the others from their slumber. Having heard of Domigo's threat to replace any tardy Horsemen he ran toward the site of last night's gathering. As he came within sight of the still smothering fire he feared for the worst. Naked bodies were lying in a rough circle around the fire, wooden bowls and cups scattered about, some still full. One Woman was using her lips in a futile attempt at arousing her last sex partner.

Davlyn stopped at the side of the nearest First-born male he came to and kicked him hard in the ass. "Get up!" he ordered. "You were told yesterday we were heading north in the morning." When the Man gained his feet he was told, "Wake the others and get them back to camp or I will leave you here." Wading into the circle of naked flesh, Davlyn used his foot to roll over any face down Male, pleased when he found no horsemen.

Seeing the First-born beginning to stir, Davlyn roared at them. "Get dressed, gather up your belongings and get back to camp, now!" Frustrated that the First-born would not be traveling north as early as planned, he left in a foul mood, slowing making his way back to their camp.

When he arrived, he saw Domigo and the Horsemen watching from a distance. Davlyn quickly trotted over to tell him, "There will be a bit of delay before we leave. Some of the First-born have overslept." Domigo gave him a hard look before saying, "When you are ready to depart, we will see you off. The First-born had all of last night for saying their goodbyes." Moving close to Davlyn's side he told him," You are doing fine, there is nothing I can do to help." Giving him a pat on the back he sent Davlyn off to rejoin his group.

By the time he took the short walk back to the First-born, he was feeling better about things. This group, which included almost all the Western First-born, had their belongings with them and were waiting to leave. Less than ten minutes later, the first of the stragglers, with sheepish looks on their faces, began to arrive. A long twenty minutes later, a red-eyed First-born approached Davlyn and told him, "I am the last, nothing remains at the site save last night's embers." Davlyn, tired of yelling, simply told the First-born, "Get your belongings together, we are leaving soon." It seemed to him that he had said the same thing a hundred times in the last half hour.

By mid-morning the First-born were finally assembled and ready to leave. The Horsemen paid a quick visit to say goodbye to friends and lovers, but as promised, soon left to resume preparations for their own trip. Davlyn chose two of his Men to take the lead, telling them to keep the high flying ensign at their backs. He would bring up the rear, encouraging any lagers to keep up the pace. Still irritated at the First-born for ensuring a night in the open, he gruffly ordered his men to get the group moving. Ten minutes later, at the end of the long line of First-born, Davlyn is finally moving north toward his new home.

The Pixie spy Daliwyn was in dire straits. The ever increasing snowfall had slowed his fluttering wings to the point he was losing altitude. Using all the strength left in his tiny body, he fought to stay aloft, but sensed he would not make it back to the stairwell of Odyden's fortress. A sudden gust of wind, racing down the face of the mountain, ended his futile attempt of staying aloft. The force of the wind slammed Daliwyn to the surface, breaking both of his wings and numerous ribs. Lying in the snow, the Pixie knew his days were over. Trying to get enough air into his lungs to breathe was agony, calling out for help impossible. Unable to do anything but moan softly, Daliwyn watched as the snow quickly covered his body, creating his own funeral blanket.

Odyden, having taken care of his most pressing needs, was resting in his quarters, calmly talking to the

Pixie Galien, attempting to gather any information he had missed. As he began to ask the spy another question, he heard a knock on his door and excitedly hurried to open it, disappointed to see only his guard standing there. "What is it?" he gruffly asked the Troll. Lowering his head to avoid looking into the master's eyes, he replied, "The guard you posted at the stairwell has returned with a Pixie, but he thinks he is dead." Not willing to have the Pixie mangled by the hands of the Trolls if still alive, Odyden ordered the Troll to take him to the tiny spy. They did not have to travel far. The Troll, sensing the importance of the spy, was not far from Odyden's quarters. Reaching out, Odyden gently lifted the still figure from the Troll's taloned hand, fearing the Pixie was indeed dead.

Dismissing the guards, he rushed back to the warmth of his chambers, placing the Pixie on the pillow he had used before. Touching the spy's wee chest with his finger, Odyden felt naught save cold flesh. Dejected, the Master sat down, pondering his next move. "My Lord", he heard Galien say," Is Daliwyn's body frozen?" Annoyed that his thoughts were interrupted, he growled, "No, the snow kept his body from freezing." The Pixie pleaded, "Master, listen to me. Is there any blood staining Daliwyn's body?"

Suddenly attentive, Odyden studied the tiny form carefully before he said, "No, why do you ask?" Galien explained that Pixies went into a deep coma resembling death when gravely injured, but seldom died without the spilling of blood. Odyden glared at the Pixie as he demanded, "Are you telling me that you think he is still alive?" The Pixie answered honestly. "I do not know. Until his body warms there is no way to tell." The Evil Lord, having little hope of the Pixie's survival, told Galien. "Tend to him the best you can, I will return in a while." Closing and locking the door behind him, Odyden went in search of the guard who had found Daliwyn.

His look was short. The Troll was in the guard house, blood dripping from his chin, thanks to the chunk of raw meat he was gnawing on. It was the watch commander's reward for a job well done. Entering the room, Odyden asked the Troll who he did not recognize, "What is your name?" The guard, startled to see the Master standing before him, mumbled, "I am called Treno, My Lord." "Well, Treno," Odyden said pleasantly, tell me something. How do you think the Pixie, who has a broken wing, perhaps two, manage to fly back to the stairway?" The guard shook his head. "He did not make it to the stairs, My Lord. I was stationed some distance away from the stairs as ordered, when a violent downdraft threw me to the ground." "Odyden interrupted, "Get on with it Troll, I have many other things to do!" Treno quickly continued. "As I struggled to get up, I saw something strange that looked like a snowball, mixed in with the flakes. I searched for many minutes before I happened to step on a lump in the snow. I dug the Pixie out from beneath my feet and returned to the fortress. The rest you know." Surprising himself, Odyden told the guard, "Well done", then added, "I may have a task for you shortly." The Evil Lord heard the Troll respond, "Anything, My Lord", as he turned and left for his quarters.

Odyden was still unlocking his door when he heard Galien call out excitedly, "Master, Daliwyn is alive!" Odyden rushed to the Pixie's side, seeing for himself the slight movement of the spy's chest. "Can he speak?" Odyden demanded of Galien. "I do not know Master; I saw him move slightly just before you arrived." Odyden went to a table in the far corner of his quarters, then returned with a small piece of wet cloth which he held under the nose of the Pixie. Two shallow breaths later, Daliwyn coughed in pain but opened his eyes. "Can you hear me?" asked

Odyden. The spy mouthed a yes as he nodded his head, but the Master heard no sound. As he turned toward the fire to throw away the cloth, he clearly heard a voice say, "My Lord." Odyden turned and glared at Galien, but the Pixie shook his head, pointing at Daliwyn.

Odyden felt a wave of relief wash over him as he rushed to the pillow holding the injured Pixie. "Did you make it to Zomba's location?" he asked with hope. "Yes, My Lord, I spoke with Zomba as you ordered." Trying to keep his excitement from showing, he gruffly asked, "Would you be so kind as to tell me what he said?" Daliwyn took a few painful shallow breaths before telling him, "Zomba said he needs a way to keep his captives warm and that he has run out of food." Odyden stared at the Pixie, noticing his eyes were beginning to close. "That is all he said to you?" As Daliwyn drifted back into unconsciousness he replied, "Aye, My Lord, that is all he said."

It was now Odyden's turn to take a couple of deep breaths. He knew the hungry captives, once too tired to stand, would quickly succumb as the raging blizzard drained the heat from their bodies.

Remembering his promise to Chandrelle and knowing this would be their last night together for a while, Dralon slowly walked to her house, his libido on the rise. As he entered, Chandrelle called out to him, telling him that she needed a bit more time to prepare their meal, then she would join him. Dralon walked down the hall and looked into the eating area. The Elfin Woman was standing in front of a table of food, her back to him. His lust grew when he saw she only had a cloth wrapped around her waist; her hair still wet from her bath. Leaving his clothing in a heap on the floor Dralon silently approached Chandrelle from behind. He thought she did not know he was there, but as he began to reach around her the wrap covering her suddenly fell to her feet. Knowing the Elf was not going to make him wait until later for sex, he cupped her breasts in his hands. Dralon became fully erect as he felt her nipples quickly harden to incredible size between his fingertips.

Chandrelle had wanted sex since she awoke this morning. She had bathed, but not dressed, hoping the First-born would take advantage of her nearly naked body. She was now getting her wish. As Dralon played with her breasts, she felt the head of his cock rubbing against her lower back, inches too high to permit any attempt at anal penetration.

Lying in bed last night after having sex, she had teased him into telling her of his sexual experiences with the lusty First-born Women. He told her Arerena had taught most of the Men how to give pleasure to a female, using fingers, tongue, or penis. "And the First-born Women use just their vaginas?" Asked Chandrelle. "Of course not," answered Dralon, "they also use their hands, mouth and ass." She was silent for a long moment, then rolled onto her side, placing her lips next to Dralon's ear. After reaching to cup his balls in her hand she hoarsely asked, "Are you telling me your females can take your cock up their ass?" The First-born, tired and wanting sleep, told her. "Of course, they can," neglecting to tell her most could not.

Chandrelle remained awake long after Dralon had fallen asleep, deep in thought. The First-born had not asked her for anal sex, but had readily told her he had enjoyed the act with the Human females. Chandrelle had fell asleep determined to provide him with any pleasure the First-born Women could offer.

The Evil Demi-God Odyden now had to make the most difficult decision of his life. If he did not act, the captives would soon perish on the frozen mountain side. If he attempted to alter nature to save them, the ire of the Gods could very well destroy him. Odyden also knew he had but little time to dwell on his problem.

Opening the door of his quarters, he told the guard outside to send Treno to him. Odyden barely had time to begin pacing the floor before the guard knocked on the door, telling him Treno was waiting outside. The Master opened the door and bid the Troll to enter and take a seat.

Odyden wasted no time. "Treno, I want you to pick two Trolls that you trust. The three of you and myself are going to save the captives trapped in the blizzard." Not knowing what to say, the Troll remained silent, waiting for Odyden to continue. "Tell the Trolls you pick to pack up all the dried food they can carry. You will gather as many bedrolls as you can handle." Treno said he understood, then asked, "When are you planning on leaving, My Lord?" Odyden told him they would meet in an hour at the stairwell to the surface. "I will be waiting Master. I will leave now to pick the Trolls and tell them your orders." Odyden held up his hand, stopping Treno. "No, you will give them orders yourself. You are now my newest commander." Treno bowed his head, not wanting the Master to see the elation on his face, as he quickly left to choose the two hearty Trolls that he had in mind.

Odyden knew Zomba was not far below the fortress. A guard stationed at the top of the stairwell had reported a primal roar that could only have come from the Lord of the Trolls. Summoning the watch commander, he ordered three coils of heavy rope be brought to the stairs.

While he waited, Odyden thought again of using his occult power to simply stop the snow, but was too fearful. The Gods had created Trolls, Elves and Mankind, but The One had formed the world and the gods. No, this close to his goal he would not attempt to alter nature and risk arousing the ire of the One.

Going to a locked storeroom, Odyden filled an oiled leather bag, then tied it to his waist. When he returned to the stairs three guards were waiting with the rope. The Evil Lord ordered the end of one rope to be tied around a solid rock pillar. After checking the knot, he personally tied the three lengths of rope together. He started to tell the Trolls what he needed them to do, but decided to wait for the others. A full twenty minutes before the hour was up, Treno and two other Trolls appeared, all heavily laden with sacks strapped to their backs. "Treno, you and the others can remove your sacks. You will need your strength for later." Odyden signaled for the group of Trolls to draw near, "I am going down the mountain first with the rope. I expect all of your hands to hold it." Treno, trying to be of help asked, "Do you wish me to tie the line around your waist?" The Evil Lord spun and stared at him, giving him a look that caused his blood to run cold. "I will not suffer being bound by any mortal, least of all a Troll!" Treno lowered his head, his joy of being named a commander already dissipated.

Odyden, regaining his composure, said. "Do not concern yourselves with me. Once I grasp the rope I will not let go.' Continuing his instructions, he told them, "Allow about three feet of slack in the rope, when it becomes taut, feed out another three feet." Treno interrupted, "But how do we know when to stop?" Odyden took a deep breath, assuring himself he had their undivided attention. "When you feel three sharp tugs on the rope you will know I have reached the captives." Treno, again trying to curry Odyden's favor, blurted out, "Then we follow you down." Odyden once again glared at him. "No, Troll, shut up and let me finish. When you feel my signal, uncoil the remaining rope. I will drop it down the mountain. If anyone slips, they may be able to grab it and save their life." Taking the time to look at each Troll, he told them, "You will wait until you see fire on the frozen mountain. You will then descend using the rope and join me. Do not forget your supplies." Before they could ask, he told them, "Make no mistake, you will see the fire!" He then told them, in a statement that surprised even himself, "You may as well stay here at the bottom of the stairway. The blizzard will greet you soon enough."

After asking them if they had any questions Odyden grasped the end of the rope then ascended the stairs. Standing at the top, with the snow swirling around him, Odyden considered melting a path with his gaze but quickly realized he could create an avalanche that would sweep the captives away. Yelling at the Trolls to give him slack in the line, Odyden began his descent down the mountain.

Davlyn's short trip to the abandoned Troll camp proved almost uneventful, save a few of the First-born, who needed copious amounts of water to ward off the effects of the prior night's drinking. Davlyn permitted them to stop well before dark, for many of them had slept little, if at all, the night before. After dark, with the camp settled in for the night and a small fire burning, Davlyn went to talk to the two Men he had placed at the head of the column of First-born. Knowing what he wanted before he asked, Bilyn told him, "We saw the ensign two hours before we stopped for the night." Davlyn then asked, "Can we reach the camp by noon?" Bilyn told him, "If we leave at sunrise, we will be there well before then." Smiling at this news, he told them to get some sleep, for he intended to wake up the camp well before the sun rose.

The First-born returned to his bedroll by the fire and promptly fell asleep, only to be awakened a short time later by the howling of animals. Davlyn sat up, but the sentries were already putting more wood on the fire. Sensing the animals posed no threat to his group, he quickly fell back asleep.

Davlyn was already awake when a sentry came to arouse

him a full hour before sunup. As he left the camp site to relieve himself, he told the sentry to get the others on their feet. The first-born, who had engaged in the orgy the night before last and caused the delay yesterday morning, were among the first to be ready. As the sun yielded enough light for the First-born to see the ground before them, Davlyn ordered Bilyn and Stevlyn to again take the lead. By the time the sun had fully cleared the horizon, last night's camp was well behind them. The ensign they were heading to was clearly visible in the morning sky.

Odyden cursed himself as he moved down the face of the mountain. He was spending more time waiting for slack in the rope than traveling. Still, within fifteen minutes, he could make out figures below him; some of the Elves cemented in place by snow up to their waist. Odyden thought about calling out to Zomba, but realized announcing his arrival would serve no useful purpose. A dozen or so waits for more slack in the line, and Odyden stood on the flat outcropping of rock harboring the snowbound group.

The Evil One stood motionless in the swirling snow,

getting his first look at the Human Race. He quickly realized that the Gods had indeed created the New Race in their own image. The ever defiant First-born Maregon, sensing he was being stared at, quickly found and locked eyes with the tall, gaunt figure who had seemingly appeared out of nowhere. Lord Odyden, incensed that a mere Human would dare stare at him, decided to teach the First-born what true fear felt like. Closing his eyes for a moment, he reopened them to envelope Maregon in an eerie glow. Instead of withering under his gaze, the First-born continued to stare at him, now with a look of total indifference. Seething with rage, Odyden shifted his glowing eyes to the tallest figure on the rock. The Troll Lord Zomba had glimpsed the luminous eyes on the far edge of the rock a moment before and was already heading toward him. Dropping to one knee, Zomba quietly said, "My Lord, this is not how I wished to greet you, but I am truly glad you are here." Looking over the kneeling Troll at the freezing captives, Odyden told him, "Get to your feet, we have much to do!" Zomba quickly gained his feet, then asked, "What is your plan, My Lord?" Returning his eyes to normal, Odyden explained what he wanted done. "Leave as few Trolls as you feel necessary to guard the captives. Have the rest of your party remove the snow from this forsaken rock." Zomba lowered his head, not understanding exactly what Odyden wanted. Losing patience with the puzzled Troll, Odyden hissed at him, "Have your Trolls throw the snow lying on this slab of rock down the mountain. Surely you can do that!" Zomba gladly left Odyden's side to relay the Lord's orders to the guards. An hour later, after using feet, hands, and finally their stiff hide bedrolls, the Trolls had cleared the rock of snow. With this task now complete, Zomba was forced to return to Odyden's side for further instructions.

The Evil Lord, with his temper now under control, told him calmly, "Herd everyone to the far edge of this rock, away from here. Have them turn their backs to me and not turn around until told to." Odyden did not explain what he was going to do and Zomba had no intention of asking. Rejoining his Trolls, he soon had the entire group standing near the far edge of the slab, their backs to Odyden. The Troll Lord failed to see the single guard edging his way back toward Odyden, keeping to the face of the cliff, hidden by the heavy snowfall. The Master moved away from the face of the mountain, untying the leather bag bound to his waist. Before placing the bag on the rock, he removed three small egg shaped canisters and carefully removed the oiled parchment covering them. Odyden then returned to within fifty feet of the face of the cliff. Taking a deep breath, he threw the first canister slightly to his right, at the point where the slab of rock mated with the mountain. The incendiary orb exploded into a huge ball of fire, totally engulfing Odyden's body. Ignoring the searing flames, the Master threw another egg straight ahead, the third exploded to his left. He had taken only one step backward, out of the flames, when he heard a body screaming in agony. Looking to his left, he saw a Troll covered in flames, the exposed flesh of his body already frying in the intense heat. Zomba, hearing the screams and knowing no one was in the area except for his Master, ran to his aid. The fireball had died out, leaving the blazing figure highlighted on the rock. Zomba was almost upon him when Odyden seized his arm in an iron grip, stopping him cold. Zomba looked at the Master in shock, "My Lord, I thought it was you burning!"

Odyden, still holding on to the arm of the Troll, did not respond. The burning Troll had stopped screaming. He had fallen to his knees and was now moaning woefully. "My Lord," pleaded Zomba, "he has served me well, let me try to save him, or end his misery!" The Master shook his head no as he told the Troll, "Go bring the whole group forward to watch this Troll suffer. I want them to know that there are dire consequences to pay for not obeying my orders." A few minutes later, with all gathered around, the moans of the Troll ceased. Odyden figured he was dead or in deep shock. Either way he did not care.

The Evil One suddenly realized he had made a mistake, but it turned out for the better. He had never tugged on the rope to signal the Trolls above to drop the rest of the line. If any of the rope had been burnt by the fire, it would now end up far down the mountainside. Giving the line three sharp tugs, Odyden was rewarded by a hundred feet or more rope lying on the rock. The Master dug out the end of the rope and went to the smoldering body of the Troll. Waving for Zomba to join him, he ordered him to tie the rope around the Troll's ankles. "My Lord," Zomba said with a slight hint of sarcasm, "I do not think this Troll is going to run away." Snarling, Odyden told him, "Shut up Troll, just do as you are told." The Troll Lord dutifully did as it was told, going as far as double checking his knot. As he stood up, the stricken Troll emitted a low moan. "Lord, he is still alive! Should I try to help him?" Odyden shook his head. "No, call two guards and have this carcass thrown down the mountain. If he is fortunate, the fall will kill him before the cats begin feeding."

Having given his orders, Odyden walked back to the face of the cliff and looked up, hoping he would see Treno and his companions descending the mountain.

Chandrelle looked back over her shoulder and gave Dralon a lusty smile before climbing onto the table and positioning herself on her hands and knees. She slid a bowl of oil from the center of the table to the edge, by her knee. "Dralon," she whispered, "Dip your finger in the oil then play with my butt." Thinking this a fine idea, the First-born curled up his right index finger before dipping into the oil. Moving his hand to her ass, he let the oil drip off his finger down the crack of her butt, creating a small reservoir of oil by the middle finger of his left hand held against the entrance of her ass. A moment later her sphincter muscle relaxed and Dralon's finger entered her body. Turning his hand as he gently pumped it, he soon had his finger buried in her butt up to the second knuckle.

The First-born removed his finger, ignoring

Chandrelle's protest. Dipping all his fingers into the oil, he moved to her side, running his right hand up and down the crack of her ass, while his left moved between her thighs to spread the lips of her vagina. The Elfin Woman moaned in pleasure as his fingertips found and caressed her fully erect clitoris, while the middle finger of his other hand smoothly penetrated her relaxed and lubricated ass.

Enjoying the throaty moans coming from Chandrelle, Dralon alternated between inserting his fingers into her pussy and playing with her aroused clit, while slowly easing the full length of his finger into her butt. The Elf again looked back over her shoulder at Dralon, her face flush with desire. "Put another finger in my ass!" The First-born continued to play with her pussy with one hand as he slowly removed his finger from her ass. Dipping into the oil again, Dralon returned his hand to her ass. Being as gentle as possible, he slowly eased the tips of two fingers into her ass, then was delighted when he heard her hoarsely say. "Dralon, push your fingers all the way up my ass!" The First-born began a pumping motion, slipping more of his fingers into her with every forward thrust. A few minutes later, with three fingers now smoothly slipping in and out of her butt, Chandrelle reached back to grasp Dralon's erection, shocked anew at its size. Releasing his cock, she crossed her forearms, lying her head on them, ergo raising the height of her ass.

Chandrelle, now beginning to tremble with desire, cried out, "Dralon, take your fingers out and stick your cock in my ass." Dralon started to protest, but she cut him short. "Dralon, shut up and stick your cock up my ass!" Sensing her urgency, he withdrew his fingers from her body and reached for the oil. Pushing down on the shaft of his penis, he totally submerged the swollen head of his cock in the oil. Dralon moved into position behind her, the blood engorged head of his penis poised to penetrate her body. Telling her to relax, he used both hands to spread her ass cheeks, then pushed his hips forward in short but powerful strokes. He heard Chandrelle gasp loudly as her sphincter relaxed and the head of his cock entered her well-oiled ass.

The First-born did not move for a minute or two, simply gazing down, totally aroused by the sight of his huge cock partially embedded in the Elf's comely ass. He was jolted from his fantasy when he heard her whisper, "Do not stop now. I can take more of your cock up my ass." Dralon quickly reached for the oil, pouring it onto her lower back. As the lubricant began running down the crack of her butt, he squeezed the cheeks of her ass together, once again trapping the oil in a small pool.

Dralon eased his cock into her a little at a time, pulling back after each forward motion to coat the shaft of his penis with oil. Chandrelle was now taking a deep breath every time Dralon withdrew, moaning loudly as she felt his cock penetrating virgin areas of her body. A few strokes later, Dralon echoed her moans, his throbbing penis now totally buried in her ass, his balls massaging her aroused clit.

"Dralon," Chandrelle called out breathlessly, "Are you all the way in me?" On the verge of coming, he grunted and flexed his cock, the huge head of his penis swelling even more. "Dralon, pull out just a little and play with my nipples, but do not move your cock. Reaching forward to cup her breasts, his penis withdrew from her body an inch or so.

Chandrelle, on the verge of her own orgasm, was determined to make Dralon come with her. Using her ass muscles, she clenched down on the cock buried deep in her body, feeling it twitch and swell in return. With the First-born playing with her breasts and helping to support her upper body, Chandrelle moved a hand to her open pussy to lubricate her fingertips. When her fingers found and gently squeezed her fully erect clit, her orgasm began. Now too sensitive to touch herself, she reached further back and cupped Dralon's balls in her hand. Moaning loudly between sharp intakes of breath, the Elf used her ass muscles to coax Dralon's now spurting penis back into the depths of her body, as an intense orgasm racked both of their bodies. Dralon knew better than to swiftly withdraw his still hard cock from her sensitive body, letting it grow flaccid, before carrying her to her bath, then to her bed for a short rest. The food would still be here when they returned.

Gazing up the mountain, Odyden's keen eyesight quickly located Treno and his laden Trolls descending the mountain with little difficulty. Calling Zomba to his side, he ordered him to move the Trolls and captives toward the face of the mountain, as near as the hot rock would permit. When the Troll Lord returned at the head of his charges, Odyden told him to have the guards place their stiff hide bedrolls edge to edge on the hot rock slab. With the hides in place, Odyden waved for Zomba to join him. "Move the captives on to the warm hides. Have them lie down so they can warm their bodies. I will not have the cold take another." As he moved off, Odyden yelled back to Zomba, "Tell the others I plan to fire up the other end of this forsaken rock. I believe they will know what to do this time."

Five minutes later, with a new fire burning brightly, Odyden went to check on Treno's progress. Looking up he was pleased to see the three Trolls had descended to a point just above the make-shift camp. "Treno, hold up until I tell you to come down," Odyden shouted, his booming voice cutting through the storm. The Master ordered Zomba to make a path of hides to the face of the cliff, giving the Trolls a place to stand without burning their feet. After waiting impatiently for the walk to be built, the Evil Lord shouted to the Trolls just above him. "You can come down now, but do not dally. Join me at once." Ten minutes later, three Trolls, laden with food and bedrolls, stood at Odyden's side. The Master waited perhaps twenty minutes before ordering the Troll Lord to have the captives moved to the middle of the stone slab.

"Zomba," Odyden ordered, "give my esteemed guests all the food they wish, for ere the sun sets tomorrow, they will be enjoying all the amenities that my warm fortress can provide."

Elf and First-born alike, their hunger returning along with their body heat, ate greedily. Even the rebellious Maregon accepted the food from the guards without comment. Odyden stood silently, taking in the scene before him with satisfaction, before moving to Zomba's side. "The captives are both warm and well fed," he informed the Troll Lord." I am going to return to the keep." Zomba protested at once. "My Lord, the snow falls still. This rock will soon again become a slab of ice!" Odyden handed the Troll the bag of incendiary orbs he was carrying, telling him, "When the center of the slab begins to cool, throw one of these at each end." Zomba smiled, then nodded in understanding, so the Master continued. "When the captives are done eating and relieving themselves, have them lie close together at the center of the rock. Have your guards cover them with the extra hides to keep the snow off of them."

As Odyden turned to move off, Zomba blurted out, "My Lord, when will you return?" Odyden spun, staring at the troll, but quickly relaxed. He had planned on sending a Troll down the rope in the morning with instructions. He realized he should have told Zomba this before walking away. "Zomba, listen to me. The snow will stop falling shortly. At first light, send the First-born up the rope. I have observed them. They will have little problem reaching my fortress. I will have armed guards waiting to greet them." Zomba then asked, "Should I feed them first?" Odyden shook his head. "No, inform them food, drink and warm comfortable quarters await them." Sighing deeply, the Evil Lord continued his instructions. "Half an hour after the last of the Humans depart, start sending up your Trolls who are strong enough to take an Elf with them. Then send up the rest of them." With a confused look on his face, Zomba asked, "What am I to do with the remaining Elves?" Odyden tersely answered, "Nothing Zomba, simply keep them warm and safe. I will send down fresh Trolls to escort the rest of the Elves to the fortress." The humbled Troll bowed his head in silent agreement, thankful his Master had taken over responsibility for the captives.

As Odyden turned toward the rope, he put his hand on Zomba's shoulder. "You will be the last one to ascend the rope. Then, with a forced smile that briefly crossed his face, he asked, "When you arrive, would you like a young She-Troll, or the flesh and brains of a humanoid first? I promise to have both available upon your arrival." Zomba answered without hesitation. "Lord, my loins ache sorely, the She-Troll first, so that I may enjoy the Human treat without discomfort." Speaking over his shoulder as he walked away, he told the Troll, "Keep your charges safe one more night. Your reward awaits you."

Zomba watched his Master move off to climb the rope with little difficulty, disappearing shortly into the still falling snow. The Troll Lord retreated to his bedroll and sat down wearily, thankful that his ordeal was almost over,

Alfred woke well before dawn, anxious to begin the trip to the Land of the First-born. After eating a quick breakfast, he went to the stable and was surprised to see his traveling companions, along with Babaduk, waiting for him. As he approached the group, the Shaman gave him a warm smile as he said, "How nice of you to join us." Alfred ignored the old Elf's comment, asking. "Is all in order for our trip?" Babaduk told him, "You have a cart full of food, supplies, and clothing, seven Elves, a warrior, and an ox in its prime. If you cannot think of anything else you may need, you are ready to go." Alfred looked to the warrior

Gabreal. "Do you think we have everything we require?" The warrior, having already checked the wagon and its contents, gave Alfred a nod in agreement.

With the party set to depart, Babaduk walked with them to the outskirts of the Elfin city. As goodbyes were being exchanged, Dralon showed up to add his own. The two watched the departing Elves until they disappeared into the forest, before turning back to meet the group going to capture horses. They walked in silence for a while before Dralon told the Shaman, "I am sorry for being late. I had to say goodbye to Chandrelle." Babaduk, having already grown tired of Dralon's thoughts of his early morning "goodbye", told him. "Do not worry about it, an hour or so will make no difference. The horses are not going anywhere."

A few minutes later, rounding a sharp bend in the path leading back to Loraine, Dralon got his first close look at Trolls when two of them rushed out of the woods behind him. The First-born drew his sword without thinking as he spun to face the Trolls. Using his long arms to full advantage, he swung his weapon upward in a vicious arc, opening the chest of the nearest Troll, the tip of his sword coming to rest against the throat of the other. Ignoring the gruesome gurgling sounds coming from the dying Troll, Dralon increased the pressure on his sword, but did not open the neck of his other adversary. The young Troll lowered his arms, dropping his sword as he turned his hands palm up, thankful to still be alive.

Dralon lowered his sword to the Troll's belly, telling him to move back from the oozing body of the nearly dead Troll. Waving for Babaduk to join him, he asked their captive, "Why did you attack us? Getting no response, Dralon probed the Troll's bellybutton with the tip of his sword. The Ogre bent over, relieving the pressure on his naval, and soon began to speak. "We were trying to capture Elves", he told Dralon. "Why?" The First-born demanded with a slight wiggle of his sword. The Troll took a deep breath, then began telling his amazing story.

"Weeks ago, we were to the east, looking for other Trolls that would let us join them to ensure our safety. We found a group, but they made as felt uneasy, so we decided to follow them for a while. They traveled to the Great Northern Mountains, where they met a large party of Elves and Trolls." Dralon interrupted, "Did the Trolls know each other?" The captive shook his head. "No, the group we were following seemed leery of the others. We were surprised when they joined them." Dralon, feeling no threat from the Troll, lowered the point of his sword to the ground, bending to rest both hands on the hilt, his eyes now level with the shorter Troll. "You still have not told me why you wished to capture Elves," Dralon told him in an icy tone. The Troll, remembering what he had heard of the vicious new Human Race, was quick to answer. "We were able to sneak close enough to the Trolls to hear their conversations. They said the leader of the group who had captured the Elves, was taking them to Lord Odyden's fortress." Dralon's huge right hand flashed out, seizing the Troll's neck in a death grip. "Why?" Gasping for breath, the Ogre said, "We heard the Trolls saying Lord Odyden was paying a bounty for any Elf brought to him." The First-born eased the pressure on the Troll's throat, then asked, "Why did you not join the others and share in the reward?" The Troll, fearful for his life, answered honestly. "We heard the Trolls we were following say they were only going to get a small reward, since the Elves were close to being delivered to Odyden. We decided to travel to the east and hopefully harvest our own Elves." Lowering his head in shame, he said softly, "You know the sad result of our efforts." After signaling Babaduk to his side, he asked him, "Is the Troll telling us the truth?" The Shaman put a hand on Dralon's arm, backing him a few feet away from the Troll. "Yes, what he said is true, but he omitted the fact that he also saw First-born among the prisoners." Dralon bent down and withdrew the dagger strapped to his calf, curtly brushing the Shaman aside. Taking two long strides, the First-born held the gleaming blade under the nose of the Troll. "How many First-born are being held captive?" When the Troll told him he did not know what he was talking about, Dralon increased the pressure on the knife. Before skin was breached, Babaduk shouted, "Dralon, stop! He does not know what you are talking about." The First-born asked the Elf what he meant; the Shaman explained.

"Our would-be assassin heard some of the Trolls say that the new Human Race coming out of the south were a hideous, brutal race, desiring nothing from life save the slaughter of Trolls. He has no idea who the First-born are."

Dralon lowered his dagger as he rephrased his question. "How many captives, who look like me, are the Trolls holding?" This time the Troll gave a ready response. "I saw five. Two were male. If there were more, I did not see them." Dralon glanced at the Elf, who said, "The Troll is telling the truth. He is now wondering why you have not killed him, since you surely must be a member of the New Race. Keeping one hand on the hilt of his sword, Dralon sheathed his knife. Standing fully erect to tower over the Troll, he asked him, "What is your name?" The terrified Ogre told him, "I am called Datato." "Well, Datato," Dralon said calmly, "promise me something that will cause you neither pain nor discomfort, and you are free to go." Hardly able to believe his good fortune, he asked the First-born, "What must I do?" Dralon quietly told him. "Tell all of your kind that the Human Race wish them no harm. We simply want to be left alone. The Evil Lord Odyden is using enslaved Trolls in his plan to destroy the First-born. Fear Odyden, not us Humans, for he is truly your real enemy."

As the Troll stood, rooted in place with a confused look on his face, Babaduk walked up to him. After making a show of staring the troll in the eye he told him. "You are thankful for still being alive, and wondering if the First-born is telling you the truth." The Ogre stared at him in amazement. "How did you know what I was thinking?" The Shaman gave him an icy smirk, before informing him, "The First-born are a mighty race that can also read minds. My companion was kind enough to teach me. Lie to them at your own peril. Now I suggest you go and do as you were bid, for the First-born is close to changing his mind!" Babaduk looked in amusement as the grateful Troll picked up his sword and scurried away to the west. Returning to the First-born, he told him, "The Troll believed everything we told him and will do as you asked." Dralon laughed at the old Elf. "You did not have to tell me that. After all, it was I who taught you how to read minds. An hour later, with all in order, Dralon and his party finally departed on the quest he had traveled north for.

Using the rope to help him climb, the Evil One was

halfway to his fortress when he had a thought that physically sickened him. In his haste to save the captives, he had totally forgotten about the gallon of precious oil. Without the hard-earned lubricant, the captives were useless to him. Quickly descending to the now warm slab of rock, Odyden bellowed out Glento's name. The Troll, disturbed from his slumber, rushed to kneel before Odyden. "My Lord, what do you desire of me?" Glaring at the Troll with blazing eyes, he demanded, "The oil! Where is it?" A wave of relief washed over Glento as he told Odyden, "Safely stashed, my Lord, and under the watch of a trusted guard." Letting out a sigh of pure joy, Odyden said softly," Bring it to me." A few minutes later, the dejected Troll watched Odyden ascend the rope once again, the oil strapped securely to his back. Not one word of praise, promise, or reward had been uttered by the Master. The Troll could only hope that tomorrow would bring better tidings.

Zomba, lying on his bedroll, heard Odyden yell for Glento, but feigned sleep, not wanting to face the Master. The Troll Lord had been uneasy since Odyden told him he would be the last one up the rope. He thought Glento, and knew Sutata, would attempt to talk to the Master before he arrived at the fortress. As he watched Odyden ascend the rope, he heard the Master call for Treno to follow him.

Zomba now gave deep thought to the idea of throwing Sutata off the mountain during the long night. Glento, thankful to still be alive after a terrifying late-night visit from the Lord of the Trolls, would do as he was told. Zomba, weary of this whole ordeal, closed his eyes for moment, then swiftly fell into a deep, dreamless sleep.

The pain in Moluk's arm was increasing at a rate that frightened the one-armed Elf warrior. He sorely needed to return to Celena for another pain killing narcotic drink, but the sun was beginning to set, and he still had to show Naldor and his companions the correct way to handle their swords. After an hour of instruction, the Elf traded their iron swords for ones made of wood. Stepping back a few feet, Moluk glared at the First-born. "You three must instruct the rest of the Humans in swordsmanship." Then in a slightly taunting tone, he said, "Let us find out if three Humans can mark the body of a one-armed Elf!" Five minutes later, with ugly red welts marking the spot of missing limbs or pierced organs, Moluk called for a halt. "Well done Men. With a bit more practice, I will not be able to best the three of you." Naldor gave a quick glance at his companions. He knew that if not for fear of hitting the Elf's stump, his arms, legs, aye even his neck, would be marked by sword. Naldor broke the brief silence. "Thank you for instructing us Moluk. We will indeed practice."

Unable to bear the pain any longer, the Elf wished the First-born good luck with their new home to the north, telling them with false hope that they would meet again. The First-born watched in silence as the stricken warrior, who had done so much for them, clenched his stump to his chest and slowly disappeared into the encroaching darkness.

The Evil One, traveling easily up the rope, soon gained the sanctuary of his rock lair. Telling the guards waiting at the stairwell that he needed no assistance, Odyden hurried to his private quarters. Flush with pleasure, he carefully untied the treasured oil from his body before permitting himself a moment of rest.

Scant minutes later, with growing excitement, Odyden opened the door to his chambers and bid the ever-present guard outside to enter. The guard had barely cleared the threshold when Odyden told him, "Go find the watch commander and send him to me." When the guard left, Odyden walked to the far corner of his quarters to a sturdy table holding his supplies of drugs and potions. Selecting a hollow wood tube, the Master poured an ounce of clear liquid into it, sealing it with a cork. Hearing approaching footsteps, Odyden hurried to his door, opening it before the Trolls had a chance to knock. Waving them in, he wasted no time. "Commander, an hour before daybreak have ten fully armed guards stationed at the top of the stairwell. Shortly after daybreak, the first of our new guests, the Humans, will ascend the rope." The Troll commander, hoping to gain favor, told the Master, "I will have my guards bind their hands when they arrive." Odyden gave him an icy look, but keeping his temper under control said calmly, "No, Troll, warn your guards to keep a long sword length away from the First-born, especially the two males. They are extremely powerful and show no fear." The Troll commander lowered his head as he said he understood. Odyden then continued. "You have already been instructed as to where to take the captives and how I expect them to be treated. Leave a couple of guards to wait for the Elves who are able to climb the rope. They will cause you no problem. Simply tell them what you wish them to do." Pointing a finger at the Troll commander, Odyden asked if he had any questions. "No, My Lord," he responded, "all will be ready." Odyden dismissed them and asked that Treno be sent to him.

While he waited, he went over his plans again in his mind, but could find no fault with them. Finally, decades of dreams and schemes were coming to a head. Totally absorbed in his thoughts, the knock on the door startled him, for he usually knew when someone was nearing his chambers. Odyden called out for the Ogre to enter, knowing it was Treno, his newest commander. The Evil Lord gave him a smile without warmth as he said, "I have a task for you, not difficult, but of vital importance." Handing the Troll the wood tube of fluid, he told him what needed to be done. "At first-light, when the She-Trolls awaken, choose a young one and pour the liquid from the tube into her morning drink. Wait five minutes, then bring the She-Troll to me. She will obey you without question." The commander gave him an odd look. "You want me to bring a She-Troll here?" The Master shook his head, "No, Treno, outside my door will be quite close enough." Odyden was silent for a moment before telling him, "You can tell anyone who may ask, that the Troll feels ill, and you are bringing her to me for help." Treno dared venture an opinion, telling the Master that he thought this was a fine idea. The Master, now totally satisfied with his plan, told Treno he could leave, but not before warning him that he did not deal with disappointment well. Odyden locked his door, then undressed before lying on his bed to rest, for he knew this night would not bring sleep.

Naldor and his two comrades woke well before dawn, anxious to be on their way. Following the main group of First-born was a simple matter of staying on the trampled grass. Before noon, Maxlon, who was in the lead, stopped and pointed out the ensign fluttering in the morning sky. Knowing they would reach their destination before sunset, Naldor called for a rest. As they sat quietly, Maxlon told Naldor, "Yesterday, when Moluk challenged us to fight with sticks, I held back for fear of hurting him." The second First-born, Salon, quickly added, "I did the same!" Naldor looked coldly at both the First-born before him. "I know that, but hear me and well. Give the Elf warrior two hands and a honed iron sword and we would be hard pressed to still be alive!" He taught us much. Practice what you have learned." The three First-born finished their mid-day meal in silence, each lost in their own thoughts.

Lord Odyden arose from a sleepless night well before dawn, his mind racing with possibilities of the things that could go wrong. Donning his clothes in haste, he hurried to the chambers that would hold the prisoners. He relaxed a bit when he found the temperature of the cells were perfect. Not hot enough to cause great discomfort, but warm enough that clothing would be uncomfortable. Looking around the cell, he saw that fresh sweet hay had been spread along one wall, topped by woolen mats, to be used as beds. In the far corner, wood buckets were provided for their waste. A large wood tub with constantly flowing water would give them the means to keep their bodies clean. The Evil Lord had been serious when he said the captives were to be comfortable. His Trolls could only dream of such luxuries. With all seemingly in order, Odyden headed off to see his commander.

As Odyden entered the guardhouse he saw the Troll commander Arnego, who he had spoken with yesterday. He also noted that Treno was present. Locking his gaze on Arnego, he asked, "Is already on your end?" The Troll quickly stood up and responded, "Aye, My Lord, ten armed guards will join me within minutes." Odyden did not bother to answer, instead glancing at Treno, who gave him a discreet nod in return. Reminding them that all would be fine if they followed his orders, he turned to leave, telling them he would join them later. The Master walked to the stairway leading to the surface and noticed extra guards already milling about. Knowing that he had done all he could, Odyden returned to his chambers to await the arrival of the She-Troll.

Barely fifteen minutes after the sun rose, the powerful First-born Maregon stood at the top of the steps, surrounded by ten swords held by leery Trolls. Urging the Human away from the stairs with their weapons, the Trolls watched in fascination as four more figures that resembled their Lord appear from below. Arnego, recalling what Odyden had said, and seeing for himself the mighty First-born Men, concentrated on the females, driving them downward with gentle sword pokes to their asses. The Ogres moved the captives deep into the underground fortress, the natural light from the sun giving way to small rocks which emitted an eerie light. Arnego stopped them in front of a long line of thick iron bars embedded deep into solid rock. Maregon saw the two thick doors granting access to the cells and knew these would be their new accommodations. Arnego, using his sword, directed the Women to the door on the right. One of the Trolls, trying to imitate him, attempted the same thing on Maregon. The First-born, feeling a sword-tip touch his back from the fully extended arm of the Troll, froze. Knowing the guard had not moved forward, Maregon spun with speed that shocked the Trolls. Delivering a blow from his huge right hand, he crushed one side of the Troll's face. The injured Ogre dropped to his knees, screaming in pain, his sword forgotten. Before any Troll could react, Maregon held a sword for the first time, daring any Troll to step forward and try to poke him again.

Arnego knew this must end at once. He was already fearful of Odyden's reaction. Telling the nearest guard to hold his sword, he entered the cell holding the Women. Grabbing the one closest to him by the hair, he put his dagger to her throat. "First-born", he yelled, "listen to me. Put the sword down and enter the cell or I will open her neck!" Knowing he had no choice, Maregon dropped the sword and did as he was told. But he promised himself that the next time he held a sword, it would taste the blood of Trolls.

An hour later the Trolls showed up with a large group of Elves. Maregon figured a mistake had been made when the guards herded the Elfin Women into his cell and housed the males with the First-born Women. Later in the day, the last of the Elves arrived, but the same process was repeated. Maregon could not fathom what is happening, but realized he could do nothing about it. For now, he was pleased to be warm and well fed.

Odyden heard the shuffling feet of the drugged She-Troll well before she and Treno reached his door. The Lord opened the door to his quarters slightly and slipped outside, locking the door behind him. "Treno", he said softly, "did you have any problems with the other Trolls?" Treno shook his head, "No, Lord. No one paid any attention to us." Smiling to himself, Odyden said, "Good, now you can return to your duties".

The Evil One watched the Troll depart before taking the She-Troll by the arm. With no need to speak, he led her in silence to the room containing the iron mating cage. Taking her inside, he closed the door and talked to the terrified Troll standing guard outside. "We have talked before and so far, you are doing well. Now listen to me and well." Seeing he had the Troll's rapt attention, he continued. "I will be inside this room for an hour or so. If any Troll appears, kill him without warning. You will pay no mind to his rank or status." Leaving the Troll with morbid thoughts of having to kill a friend who came looking for him, Odyden slipped into the room, locking the heavy door behind him.

Going to the meat locker, he removed a large slab of flesh, noting with satisfaction its freshness. Taking his time, the Master carefully shaped the bloody hunk of meat, preparing it so it would be capable of capturing Zomba's foul offering. Moving to the She-Troll, he ordered her to spread her feet, then securely tied the ersatz vagina between her upper thighs. He then guided her into the mating cage, adjusting the straps to hold her in the correct position to receive Zomba's carnal attention. As he left, he told the She-Troll, "Relax until you feel your body being moved, then wiggle your hips, moan, and scream until the movement stops. I will free you shortly thereafter." Exiting the room, the Evil Lord told the Ogre at the door, "You may return to the guard house now. I will inform you when to return to your station."

Odyden hurried off to the stairwell, happy that things were going so smoothly. Elation washed over him when he learned from Treno that the First-born were already enjoying the comforts of their new home. Odyden's good fortune continued as he watched most of the slave Elves appear at the top of the stairs without the aid of Trolls. The Master stood back from the stairway, a smug look on his face, as he viewed his well-oiled plan unfold before his eyes. The Evil One remained silent as four of his guards were sent to escort the Elves to their new quarters. A short time later more captives appeared, with the assistance of Zomba's Trolls, from below.

Odyden was heading back to the stairs to send a guard down to count the captives left on the mountain when Sutata appeared and rushed to his side. "My Lord," he said breathlessly, "I need to talk to you about Zomba's total indifference to your orders!" The Evil Lord's fine mood dissipated in a heartbeat as he lashed out at Sutata. "Troll, I have more important things to do than listen to your whining. Get out of my sight before I put you in charge of the Ogres mining the treasures in the waste from the workshops!" Sutata, seeing his eyes begin to glow, scurried off, suddenly thankful to be out of his presence.

The Master forced himself to relax as numerous Trolls who were unknown to him ascended the rope, followed by Glento and Hanto. Odyden yelled for Hanto to join him and was surprised when Glento passed him with just a respectful nod of his head. When his commander reached his side he demanded, "What is happening on the rock below?" The Troll noted the slightly glowing eyes of the Master and responded at once. "Lord Zomba stands alone on the

Rock below, but I am to tell you he forgot to send up the unused supplies." Odyden grabbed

Hanto by the throat, "Are you telling me the Lord of the Trolls sent all who were on the rock to my fortress and now stands guard over orts?" Hanto nodded as he said, "But besides the leftover food, many hide bedrolls remain." The Evil Lord took a deep breath, then calmly said, "Hanto, send one of your Ogres down the rope. Tell him I am inpatient for Zomba's return and that the supplies can wait." Hanto gave the Lord what passed for a smile as he told him. "Zomba waits below, rope in hand. Three sharp tugs on the line will have him here in short order." Odyden glared down at his minion, "Troll, what you are waiting for? Go yank on the rope!" Hanto rushed to do the master's bidding, giving the rope three sharp tugs. Mere seconds later, Odyden and Hanto heard a terrifying roar ring throughout the mountain chain. The Troll Lord was finally coming home.

Davlyn's group, with Heathlyn and Bilyn leading the First-born, easily reached the abandoned Troll camp before noon. They were warmly welcomed by the Humans already there. Umiki, having heard there were real weapons here, dropped the draw knife he had received from the Elfin compound and dug into the first hide covered mound he came across. A moment later, he raised his head, yelling for Davlyn. "There is nothing here but clothing! Where are the swords?" Striding to Umiki side, Davlyn told him," You can keep searching if you wish, but it might be quicker to simply ask one of the First-born who are already here." Taking the advice, Umiki was shown the mound holding the arms. Sorting through the swords he was disappointed. Most of the blades were rusty, or their edges show signs of hard use. Mumbling to himself, he failed to sense Davlyn standing behind him. "Umiki," he said softly, "I suggest you choose a sword before all are gone. There are many more First-born than swords." Davlyn walked off to rejoin his group, glancing over his shoulder to see Umiki selecting a sword.

Davlyn took his time walking back to the main group, stopping often to speak to the First-born who were now being called the Westerners. Reaching the main group he had led north, he watched in dismay as they tore into the supplies left by the Trolls. "Stop!" he roared at them. "You will not act like the brutes that abandoned these provisions." The First-born quickly halted their scavenging, looking sheepishly at Davlyn. As he regained his composure, he called for Heathlyn and Bilyn to join him. "I want you to take half a dozen Men and clear everything out of four tents. The weapons and iron implements will go into one. The food and clothing into two more. We will put the odds and ends the Trolls left into the last. We can sort everything out in due time." The two First-born, knowing better than to argue with an irate Davlyn, left to do as he ordered.

As he watched the two depart with a group of First-born, he noticed that Umiki had rejoined the group. Walking to his side, Davlyn told him, "I have a task for you." Umiki cocked his brow. "And what might that be?" Ignoring his slight indolence, Davlyn told him, "I want you to organize the First-born into work parties. When Heathlyn and Bilyn are ready, have your workers transport the mounds of supplies to the proper tent." Umiki gave the leader of the western First-born a genuine smile. He had been miffed since not being chosen a Horse-Man. Now he would be able to demonstrate his leadership abilities. Davlyn told him he trusted him to do a fine job, then went off by himself to think. He had talked Domigo into letting him move the First-born north. Now he had to figure out how to turn it into a homeland.

The Evil Lord looked on, almost in awe, as the huge form of the Troll Lord appeared on the stairway. Descending the steps, he met Zomba halfway and handed him a large mug of wine from his private stash. He had laced it with a drug which would dull the Troll's senses. "Well done", the Lord said cheerfully, "a drink to your success." The Troll greedily emptied his cup, then stood before Odyden, an expectant looks on his hideous face. "Yes Troll," Odyden said as he took the empty mug, "the She-Troll awaits your attention."

Odyden led him to the top of the stairs, where a waiting guard handed the Troll another mug of wine. After giving Zomba time to finish his drink, he gave the Troll a curt nod as he said, "Follow me." Odyden then took him to the locked door holding the drugged She-Troll. "Zomba, listen to me, your sex partner is in an iron cage to protect her from harm." The Troll looked at him in dismay, disappointment etched on his face. "Relax Troll, Odyden said sincerely, "The only part that you are interested in is readily accessible." The Ogre gave Odyden a drug induced leer as he pleaded, "My Lord, open the door!" Smiling to himself, Odyden unlocked the door, telling the Troll, "No one will dare interrupt your pleasure, for I will personally stand watch outside the door."

A scant ten minutes later, which seemed like an hour of roars and moans, the Troll Lord exited the room. Odyden quickly closed the door, then told the Troll Lord to go to the guard house, where the fresh body of a humanoid would serve as his reward. In a rare act of generosity, the Evil Master had supplied an extra head for dessert.

Reentering the room and locking it behind him, Odyden quickly freed the She-Troll from the cage. Telling her once again to spread her legs, he carefully untied the slab of meat from between her thighs, fearful of anointing the stone floor with Zomba's foul ejaculation. Hurrying to a small table in the corner of the room, Odyden carefully drained Zomba's sperm into a vial, before tossing the meat back into the locker. With his precious liquid in hand,

Odyden led the She-Troll out of the room, telling her to stay put as he rushed off to the guard house. Standing in the open doorway, the Master was disgusted as he viewed Zomba tearing open the humanoid's torso, greedily stuffing its dripping organs into his gaping mouth.

Odyden made eye contact with Treno, then pointed to the guard assigned to the mating cage, signaling them to join him outside. "Treno, the She-Troll is waiting outside the mating room. You may have your way with her if you cause her no harm, then return her to the others. If anyone asks, tell them I gave her drugs and she will be back to normal shortly." Scarcely believing his good fortune, Treno rushed off before the Master could change his mind. Odyden then addressed the Troll in charge of guarding the mating cage. "Get rid of all meat in the box, then clean it out. I will tell you when to refill it." As the Troll nodded, Odyden finished, "When you are done your task you are free to do as you wish until I send for you."

The Evil One watched the Troll leave before glancing back inside the guard house. The Troll Lord was moaning in ecstasy as his huge rough tongue scoped brain matter from the cracked skull he held between clawed hands. Shaking his head in disgust, Odyden returned to his room.

He had better things to do than be nauseated by the sight of Zomba eating brains.

Maregon spent hours going over every inch of his cell, looking for a way to escape. He found nothing save solid rock and iron bars. Walking to Keenlyn, the other First-born male, he asked, "Why do you think we are sequestered with the female Elves?" Keenlyn shook his head, "I have no idea, but I sorely miss the First-born Women". Maregon remained quiet, so Keenlyn asked, "Did you have sex with the Elf that was caring for you?" This time it was Maregon who shook his head. "No, Sherina tried once when we were sleeping on our sides, but even with saliva I could not achieve penetration." Keenlyn thought for a moment before saying, "There are almost two dozen young females caged with us. Surely a few will be able to accommodate our penises." Maregon grunted, not even bothering to respond. Keenlyn let his imagination run wild for a while before he blurted out, "Why not let the Elves have a sit on a penis contest. It's not like we have anything better to do!" Maregon dismissed him with a laugh, "Let me know when they start squatting!"

O dyden stood in the corner of his quarters, carefully mixing the concoction that would lead to the First-born's downfall. Along with the oil and Troll sperm, Odyden mixed in a muscle relaxant. Taking a minute to think, the Evil One smiled to himself as he added a few drops of a liquid that would instantly numb any flesh it touched. Dipping his finger into the oil, Odyden rubbed the mixture into the skin of his inner wrist, assuring himself there was still some sensation. Now he needed the captives to use it.

Going to the door, Odyden told the ever-present guard to fetch Sarella, an Elf female his Trolls had captured many years ago. When she arrived, Odyden told her tersely, "I have an important task for you." Lowering her head, she said, "Yes, My Lord", having experienced his vile temper firsthand. The Master handed her two clay jars with lids as he told her to pay attention. "I want you to take these two containers of oil to the cells holding the new prisoners. Act like you are sneaking the oil to them. Sarella said she understood, so Odyden continued. "Tell the female Elves that the oil you stole was the master's personal lubricant and that it will greatly enhance any sexual act. Tell them to keep it hidden, and that you will try to return in two days to see if they require more." The Elf said she would do as told but begged a question. "What is it you want to know?" Odyden demanded with impatience. The Elf told him, "They will probably wonder why I am doing this, what would you have me tell them?" Odyden thought for long minute before saying, "Tell them it is revenge for me raping you when you were captured by my Trolls." The Elf shook her head, "My Lord, you are mistaken, you never had me." Odyden gave a sigh, still in awe at the brutal honesty of the Elfin Race. Shut up Sarella, the captives have no way of knowing that. Besides, tell them they are your kin, you are simply showing them kindness."

Odyden summoned the guard from outside his door. "Go to the watch commander and tell him I want the Trolls guarding the prisoners to disappear from their posts for the next fifteen minutes. Tell him I said he need not wonder why." The Master let the guard out, then paced the floor for a few minutes before telling Sarella, "It is time, go follow your instructions."

Carrying the jars with care, Sarella headed off to the

area of the fortress holding the captives. As she neared the cells, she realized Odyden's orders were indeed being followed. There was nary a Troll in sight. Knowing her time was limited, she hurried to the cell containing the Elfin Women. Amazed to see an Elf on the other side of the cell, half a dozen Women rushed to the bars. "Who are you?" asked Debrea. "Do not ask questions, I have no time to answer them", Sarella said in a hushed voice, "just listen to me." The Women grew quiet, eager to hear what the Elf had to say. "The jar I am holding contains Lord Odyden's personal sex lubricant. It is said to ease penetration and greatly enhances sex. If what I heard about the size of the First-born penises is true, you will need it." Some of the female faces turned red, others gasped, either in fear or anticipation. Sarella knew not which.

Handing the jars to the Elves, she asked that they give one to the captives in the other cell. Debrea readily agreed, but asked, "Why are you showing us this kindness?" "You are my kindred, but I also seek revenge. If the Master had used this oil when he raped me, I still might be able to bear children." She then made them a promise to return in two days, before disappearing back into the bowels of the fortress.

Michelle, the boldest of the Elfin Women, asked Debrea, "Do you think the Men will try to rape us?" Debrea shook her head, "No, if the First-born want to fuck us, there will be no "trying" on their part. We may be better off offering it to them." The youngest Elf among them, who had just joined the conversation, asked innocently, "What is it we are going to offer them?" Debrea, her voice rising over the giggles of the Women, told her bluntly, "Your vagina for starters!" Gasping in horror, the virgin Elf fled to the far corner of the sleeping area, as far away as possible from the vile First-born Men.

Maregon and Keenlyn stood silently at the back of the cell, trying to figure out what was occurring. They watched as something was passed between the bars, amazed there was no guards in sight. Their confusion only increased when they heard the Elves laughing. They were about to ask what was going on, when Michelle walked over and took matters in hand. Reaching under Keenlyn's short tunic she fingered his cock, shocked that it was already beginning to swell in her hand.

Odyden, hidden in a secret passageway behind the cells, was almost beside himself with joy. The captives had just arrived, but with nothing to do and with comfortable quarters, they were quickly finding a way to avoid boredom. The Evil Lord knew from breeding Trolls that their sperm could survive three days. He had no doubt Zomba would request a She-Troll before then. His one great concern, if he was successful in creating a Troll hybrid, was the length of time it would take before they could reproduce. The Troll Race was extremely fast growing, reaching sexual maturity within six years, sometimes even earlier. Mix in the genes from Elves and Humans and he had no idea how long it might take. Odyden feverously hoped he would not have to wait a decade or more to find out if his monsters could breed with one another, creating his new Race. For now, everything was going better than planned. He had thought about taking one of the First-born Women as a sex slave, but with only three breeders he could ill afford it. He had watched the Human Females discard their clothing in the heat, becoming aroused at the sight of their ripe naked bodies. Knowing he could always change his mind at a later date, Odyden stripped his own clothes from his body, as he bent his eye to the peek hole.

Michelle reached up to grab a handful of Keenlyn's long dark hair, bending his head to meet her eyes. With her face beginning to flush with desire, she told him, "Some of the Elves may want to have sex with you, but are afraid of being forced into it." As she wantonly stroked his nearly erect penis, she coyly asked, "Do you have any idea how I can ease their fear?" The First-born gave her a lusty smile, hardly believing his fantasy is about to come true. "Michelle", he said with a grin on his face, "I have an idea. I will get naked and lie on my back. You and the other willing Elves can help yourself to my cock!" The Elf, now fully aware of the size of his erect penis, asked a bit fearfully. "You will not force me down upon it?" Keenlyn bent his head and gave her a gentle kiss, "No My Lady, you can have as little or as much of it as you desire." Michelle asked him to go lie down in the straw covered sleeping area, saving her knees from the stone floor. Walking over to Maregon as he moved to the sleeping area, he asked the other First-born, "What are you waiting for, they are ready to squat!"

Michelle rejoined the other Elves, who had been watching intently. The first question she heard was, "Is his cock as big as Sarella said?" Giving the Women a wide-eyed grin, she said, "Let me put it this way ladies, I hope the jar of lubricant is full!" Michelle stripped and was oiling her vagina when she looked over and saw Maregon on his back next to Keenlyn. Both were sporting full erections. Grabbing Debrea by the shoulder with one hand, she whispered in her ear, "Why not join me", while her other hand was busy sneaking an oiled finger into her pussy. Debrea had three of Michelle's fingers in her vagina before she let out a soft moan and told Michelle, "I think I am ready to make a cock disappear!" A minute later she too was naked, both Elves using their fingers to lubricate the vagina of the other. They were amazed at how easily their fingers penetrated the other's body.

The two First-born Men watched the Women with growing arousal, sorely wanting to touch themselves. The two comely Elves held each other's hand as they approached the Humans. Even though their pussies were slicker than they had ever been, when they saw the throbbing blood engorged penises of the First-born, they both had second thoughts. Keenlyn saw the unease on their faces and smiled easily. "Remember what I told you. You may stop at any time. We will not force you to do anything." This was enough reassurance for Michelle. Quickly straddling Keenlyn, she grasped the shaft of his cock, rubbing the swollen penis between the oiled lips of her vagina until the head of his cock penetrated her body. Leaning forward to give the First-born a kiss, she lowered her hips and was shocked when half of Keenlyn's massive cock disappeared into her willing body without discomfort. Michelle raised and lowered her hips a few times before looking at Debrea. "What are you waiting for," she said with a gasp, "Their cocks feel much smaller than they appear!" Debrea quickly made up her mind and left the sleeping area, but only long enough to dip her fingers into the oil again. Returning, she oiled Maregon's penis before asking him a question. "If I bend over, will you stop if I ask you to?" The First-born, already on his knees, promised to go slow and willingly stop if she asked. Debrea dropped to her hands and knees, looking over her shoulder at the other Women. Some were flush with desire and touching themselves, but most stood with a shocked look on their face. At this point she but little cared who was staring. With her ass high in the air and her pussy spread, she was only thinking of the huge cock about to enter her body. Knelling behind her, Maregon pushed down on the Elf's back, raising her ass as high as possible. Using his right hand, he rubbed the head of his cock up and down the length of her oiled pussy lips, then moaned as the head of his penis slipped into her vagina. Placing his hands on her ass cheeks, he spread her as wide as he could without causing her discomfort. "Debrea", he said softly, "Are you sure you still want me to do this to you?" In response, the Elf moaned as she pushed her hips backward, then gasped in pleasure as most of Maregon's huge cock was swallowed by her pussy. As if on signal, both stopped all movement, the First-born enjoying the sight of his cock deeply implanted in her vagina, the Elf relishing sensations she had never felt before. As he bent forward so his hands could find the Elf's erect nipples, his penis slid deeper into her. Maregon took in a sharp breath when his fingertips made contact with the largest nipples he had ever caressed. After moving his hand to the Elf's mouth, she generously coated his fingers with saliva, which he used to lubricate her breasts.

A few minutes later, with his balls beginning to ache, Maregon bent over even further to whisper in her ear and felt most of his cock enter her body. "Debrea, are you feeling any discomfort?" Letting loose a loud moan, she told him, "The only thing I can feel right now is the largest cock I have ever had in me. Put it all the way in!" But the only thing he heard was her moans and heavy breathing as she used her pussy to massage the head of his fully inserted penis. Maregon had just begun to fuck the Elf in earnest, when he heard Keenlyn yelling at him. "Maregon, stop, look around you!" Diverting his attention from Debrea's trembling ass, the First-born was shocked to see half a dozen naked Elves ogling them, most of them fingering their well-oiled vaginas. Looking at Keenlyn, he asked honestly. "What am I supposed to do? This was your idea, remember?" His cell-mate smiled at him as he said, "Unless you wish Debrea as your only sex partner, I suggest you pull your cock out of her and give these other lovely Elves a chance."

Seeing Keenlyn push Michelle off his erection, Maregon slowly withdrew his penis from Debrea's clinging pussy. Ignoring the horny Elf's protest, he aped Keenlyn, lying on his back, his huge erection reaching skyward.

In the hidden passageway Odyden managed to watch

two of the waiting Elves gasp and moan as they impaled

themselves on the First-born's penises before moisturizing his palm again. With his passion sated for the moment, the Evil One headed back to his quarters, but part way there he heard Zomba call out to him. Odyden stopped at once, hoping there was not a big problem that needed his immediate attention. Meekly walking up to the Lord, he softly asked, "My Lord, would a She-Troll after the evening meal be too much to ask?" Turning his back to hide the smile on his face, he pondered the question. Odyden let the Troll fret for a while before turning back to face him. "You are not giving me much time Zomba, but I am going to make it happen. In fact, come to my chambers after you eat, and we will have a drink before you go visiting." Hurrying back to his quarters, Odyden barely heard the Troll Lord profusely thanking him.

Reaching his quarters, he told the ever-present guard to bring the Elf slave Sarella to him. Ten minutes later, he tersely told her, "Follow me." Odyden took her to an area near the cells holding the captives and told her to stay there. Disappearing down the hidden passageway behind the cells the Master was relieved to see that both containers of oil were still in the possession of the female Elves. He also noted with hatred that the First-born were still availing themselves to the Elfin Women. Rejoining Sarella, he told her, "Wait five minutes, then go to the female Elves. Tell them to keep both jars of oil because there are only three First-born Women, and you will bring them their own supply." Odyden then told her to be waiting outside his chambers in three hours. When he knew she understood his orders, the Master went to the tunnel holding the cells and summoned the guards. He walked them around a corner, out of sight of the cells, as he explained in detail what he expected from them. After giving the Elf time to deliver her message he curtly dismissed the guards, watching as they went back to their posts.

Unwilling to wait until he got back to his quarters, he told the first Troll he saw to send Treno to his chambers. A long hour later, Odyden relaxed for a while, having done everything necessary to ensure Zomba's tryst was successful. Fifteen minutes later, Odyden was pacing the floor, worried about Zomba's absence. Before his unease could grow into anxiety, he heard the heavy footsteps of the Troll-Lord approaching his chambers. Opening the door before there was a knock, Odyden waved for the Troll to enter. Nodding at the Ogre in passing, the Master walked to a table, filled two metal cups with wine and handed one to Zomba. "To your successful hunt", he said with a forced smile. The Troll quickly drained his cup as expected so Odyden took it from him, turning his back to Zomba as he refilled it.

Ten minutes later, the Master was disgusted by the sound of Zomba rutting with the She-Troll. An hour later, Odyden was done with his obnoxious task, having sent Sarella to the cell holding the Elfin Men and First-born Women with the newly mixed lubricant. Knowing the Humans would have no difficulty accepting the smaller Elfin penises, Odyden omitted the numbing agent. Although tired, the Master was extremely pleased with the day's events. The Elfin Women were almost fighting each other over the chance to impale themselves on the impressive erections of the First-born. The First-born Women now had their own supply of oil, and he had Zomba's excess sperm in cold storage. Yes, Odyden thought, a good day indeed.

Deciding to check on his breeders one more time, Odyden went to the hidden passageway behind the cells. Bending his eye to the peek hole, he was not surprised that the two First-born Men were alone in the sleeping area, eyes shut, either resting or asleep, the sex over for the time being. As he looked around the rest of the cell, he quickly realized he had made a mistake. Half a dozen naked and still horny Elf females were bent over, their asses pressed against the cell bars, being serviced by the male Elves in the other cell. Bolting upright, the Master hurried back to his chambers, intending to have the bars between the walls sealed up in the morning. But lying in bed with the day's events racing through his mind, he opted to keep things as they were. After thinking matters over, he knew there was no way the two First-born males could keep all the Elfin Women satisfied. Letting his mind wander for a moment, the answer to his problem came in a flash. He wanted to breed flesh eaters that resembled the Humans they would feed on. With the Elves now allied with the First-born, Odyden realized that carnivorous beings, which would be welcomed into both camps, would be a very desirable thing. The Evil One soon fell asleep, a sinister smile etched on his face.

Awakening from the best rest he had experienced in a long time, Odyden allowed himself a leisurely breakfast before going to spy on his captives. To his delight, the First-born males and all the Elves females save one, were now totally naked in their overly warm cell. In the other cell the now naked First-born Women were shamelessly teasing the Elves. Their libidos were at a fever pitch after learning the Elves could maintain a full erection after coming.

Odyden felt his penis growing in his hand as he watched the women lubricate their vaginas with the oil Sarella had provided. Kathwen was more than ready to be touched by some of the young Elves, hoping to erase from her mind the memory of Sutata's foul violation of her body. Looking about and seeing at least eight Elves with ready erections, she quickly decided she would lube her ass as well. Reaching her hand out to the nearest Elf, she enticed him to stand before her. Kathwen looked at the confused Elf with a look of total innocence on her face before dropping to her hands and knees, taking most of the Elf's erect cock into her moist mouth. She had barely begun to suck more of his penis into her mouth, when the First-born felt the expectant erection of another Elf probing between her pussy lips, trying to gain entry. A moment later she felt her ass cheeks being gently spread by the Elf, then was shocked as a cock, which felt as large as a First-born's, easily penetrated her oiled vagina. Moaning softly, she relaxed her muscles, letting the swollen penis slip deep into her body, while her wet lips traveled up and down the length of cock in her mouth.

Odyden shook his head in amazement, stroking his rock-hard cock as he watched the First-born Nacelle urge an Elf onto his back. Lifting her leg, she straddled the Elf, using her hand to guide the inflated cock into her well-oiled pussy. Nacelle let loose a little gasp as she lowered her hips, delighted the young Elf could nearly fill her well used vagina. As soon as her pubic hairs mingled with his, she stretched out her legs behind her, lying on top of the Elf. She then began to clench and relax her vagina muscles, causing her butt cheeks to wiggle enticingly.

Odyden watched as an aggressive Elf dipped his fingers into the oil, lubricating his fully erect penis. Elbowing two of the gawking Elves aside, he moved to straddle the two sets of prone legs. Kneeling down Furlyn, slipped an oiled fingertip into the First-born's ass, smiling to himself when he felt her push backward, trying to swallow more of his digit. Furlyn quickly obliged by easing his finger all the way into her ass. The Elf pumped his finger in and out of her ass a dozen or more times before he added a second. Moments later, a lewd smile formed on his face as a third finger elicited a moan of pleasure from the libidinous First-born. Removing his hand, the smiling Elf replaced his fingers with his fully erect cock, inserting all of it into her willing ass in one long, smooth motion. Knowing other Elves were waiting for their turn at her body openings, Nacelle withdrew her mouth from the cock in it. She turned her head to give Furlyn a lusty smile. "Do not concern yourself with my satisfaction. Come in my ass as soon as you want."

In his secret lair Odyden could watch no longer. Breathing heavily, he milked a huge load from his throbbing penis. As the Master returned to his chambers, he knew he had made two mistakes. He now realized that decades ago he should have had Sarella as a sex partner, willing or not. He also had learned Elfin Women could accommodate a large penis. So much for his theory of "shallow containers." Erasing these two minor thoughts from his mind, Odyden enjoyed a satisfying sleep for the second night in a row.

Awaking the next morning Odyden opted to forego breakfast. Instead he hurried to the captives he could not resist spying on. To his disappointment, all was quiet in the slave's quarters. Odyden was ready to leave when he saw Maregon roll onto his back, exposing his erect penis. Seeing Aprelle staring at him, the First-born called out to her, asking if she would care to join him.

The Evil Lord permitted himself a slight smile. The sex would begin shortly. He knew the female Elves were bending over and pushing their butts against the bars separating the cell. The Elfin males had ready access to their bodies, but Odyden really did not care. Even the two First-born males had their limits. He also noted one Elfin Woman remained clothed. As he exited the hidden passage, he thought of taking the obvious shy Elf for his sex slave, if she had not yet been fucked by one of superbly endowed Humans.

Zomba, being Lord of the Trolls, was the only one in the fortress, besides Odyden, with private quarters. The room was small, hewed from the bowels of the mountain, but it had a sturdy door which no one, save Odyden, would dare enter without invitation. Lying on a pile of hides from Snow-cats and wolves he had killed, the Ogre sensed something was amiss. His Evil Master was being too kind to him. He had killed many of the Lord's slave Trolls and had returned with but few of the Humans Odyden had requested. Yet the Lord was graciously giving him virtually anything he asked for. Zomba did not know what was happening, but greedily took advantage of the situation. With these thoughts in mind, Zomba rose from the pile of skins to go search for Odyden. He desired both the flesh of a humanoid and the body of a She-Troll. With a bit of luck he might be offered a drink or two of the strange tasting wine that he had come to love.

The Evil Lord, who was trying to orchestrate the downfall of Mankind, was well pleased. The days have quickly evolved into weeks. Odyden was elated because the disgusting ordeal of rendering Zomba's foul emissions into a sex lotion were finally over. If the Women were not pregnant, after more than two months of using his special oil, his plan was doomed.

Safely entombed in his hideaway, Odyden had carefully studied the forms of the Elfin Women. To his immense satisfaction he knew the slightly swollen bellies of numerous females were maturing his Zombas-To-Be; a totally new Race, created and controlled by him alone. The proud and haughty Humans would accept him as their Master, or they would be decimated by a vast hoard of his marauding flesh eaters. Odyden was returning to his chambers, planning to celebrate his success with a glass of wine, when he happened upon his favorite commander, Treno. Forgetting himself in his excitement, he blurted out to the Troll, "I have done it! In a short time my Zomba's-To-Be will emerge!" As the words flowed from his lips, he realized he had made a grave mistake. No one had ever been told of his plans for the captives. Luckily the Troll stared at him with a blank look on his face as he asked, "Zomba's-To-Be?" Lord Odyden let his eyes begin to glow as he asked, "What did you just say?" Not wishing to face the master's ire, Treno was quick to tell him, "I thought you said Zomba's-To-Be, my Lord." With sudden inspiration, the Master let his eyes return to normal before saying to Treno in bewilderment, "No commander, I said my Zombies will soon emerge." The Troll seemed to readily accept Odyden's explanation and the Lord, bursting with pride, knew he had to share his excitement with someone.

"Treno, I am going to share some information with you, but if you utter a word to anyone, I will feed you alive to my flesh eaters!" Given no choice in the matter, the Ogre simple nodded to the Evil One. Telling the Troll to come with him, the Master returned to his quarters, bidding the Troll to sit. After pouring a large cup of wine for each of them, Odyden began telling Treno the amazing details of his vile plan.

"The Elves and Humans in the cells are the breeding stock of a new Race I am creating." Unwilling to tell the Troll the full truth, he said, "Using my occult powers, I have instilled in the new Zombie Race total contempt for the Elves and First-born." Stopping for a second to catch Treno's eye, Odyden said softly in a voice that made Treno's blood run cold, "I also imparted in them the desire for the living flesh of Elf and Man, especially their brains!" Pausing for a moment to refill their cups, Odyden concluded by telling the Troll, "The Elves and their new ally the First-born, will bend their knee before me as their Lord and Master. If not, my Zombies will sate their appetite on their still living bodies!" Hefting his cup of wine Odyden stood tall, letting his eerie eyes glow full. Staring down at the Troll, he uttered a toast filled with determination. "To the downfall of the haughty First-born and the wretched Elves!" In total awe of Lord Odyden, the Troll could only nod his head in agreement, thankful he and his kind were not the recipient of the Evil One's attention.

The Troll Treno, finally dismissed by the Master, silently closed the door as he exited Odyden's quarters, awe etched on his face. He wondered if he could trust anyone with the truly strange story he was dying to repeat.

www.ingramcontent.com/pod-product-compliance
Lightning Source LLC
Chambersburg PA
CBHW071300140726